THE MAN WHO LOVED TOO MUCH

Book 1: *Archipelago*

by John Rachel

Published by
Literary Vagabond Books
Los Angeles • Osaka
literaryvagabond.com

The Man Who Loved Too Much,
Book 1: Archipelago
Copyright © 2014
by John Rachel

Trade Book ISBN #978-0-692-31005-2

Cover Art by Archimedes Delusio III

Table of Contents

Chapter One: *THE EARLY YEARS* .... *1986 - 1995*

Balloons
The Boy In The Bubble
Let the Light of God Shine on the Children
The Secret Life of Penguins
Mom and Apple Pie
Mr. Rogers and His Dancing Puppets

Chapter Two: *WING WALKING INTO ADULTHOOD* .... *1996 - 2001*

Puberty Never Strikes Twice
Stranger in a Strange Land
The Bunker
The Devil Wears A Jockstrap
Scholastics

Chapter Three: *INTRODUCTION TO REAL LIFE 101* .... *2001 - 2002*

Perspective
Skin Deep
Date Rape
She Walked Into The Room
The Invisible Man
Father Knows Best

Chapter Four: *DANCING ON BROKEN GLASS* *2002*

Welcome Home!
Shadow Boxing
Girls in White Dresses with Blue Satin Sashes
Summer of Discontent
The Greatest Gift of All

Chapter Five: *LOVE IS A TRAMPOLINE* .... *2002 - 2003*

Yet Another Surprise Party
No Pain No Gain
Does Anybody Really Know What Time It Is?
Cream Colored Ponies and Crisp Apple Strudels
Just the Two of Us

Chapter Six: *LEAPING OFF THE MÖBIUS STRIP* *2003*

Welcome To The Motel California
The Great Escape
Surrogate Bride
Friends Are Forever

Acknowledgements

Special appreciation goes out to Justin Beardsell for helping me bridge enormous generation gaps and connecting me with contemporary youth culture. Also to Ryan Paul Burke and Max Coldham Brewer for bringing me up to speed on currently popular traditional and designer recreational drugs.

As has become my heartfelt custom, I want to thank my best friend and wife, Masumi Nishida, for her encouragement and faith in me, and her magnificent ongoing role as my teacher and guide in discovering the wonders of Japan and Japanese culture, despite my resistance to achieving even a rudimentary grasp of the Japanese language.

For their inestimable, seminal contributions to my literary and intellectual development, and my tentative, fleeting grasp on reality, I also wish to express my appreciation and awe shucks to: Tom Robbins, Kurt Vonnegut, John Irving, Stanislaw Lem, Studs Terkel, E. L. Doctorow, Jerzy Kosinski, Ken Kesey, Sinclair Lewis, Ralph Ellison, Bertrand Russell, Ludwig Wittgenstein, Ralph Nader, Noam Chomsky, Naomi Klein, Chris Hedges, Howard Zinn, Bill Moyers, Malcolm X, Martin Luther King, Buddha, Jesus of Nazareth, the Dalai Lama, Nelson Mandela, Mahatma Gandhi, George Carlin, Cornell West, Thomas Kuhn, Aldous Huxley, Neil Postman, and Jared Diamond.

Inspiration … Masumi Nishida, Rebecca Jones, Randy Calligan, Julia Isabel, Nic Pendrake, Gerald Everett Jones, and Lance Collins.

Perspiration … Gary Cambra, Alexa Wiley, Megan Stonic, Sabrina Nagel, Chelsea Nouvelle, Kamaria Wilson, Chad and Rachel Hamar, Kate Mann, Shannon McAllister, Keary Kase, my adopted mother and father (may they rest in peace), my natural mother (may she be reincarnated as a sane human being for another go at it).

Conversation … Travis Rood, Mickey Finn, Mansur and Neelofar Langoo, Sigismund and Ursula Hadelich, Ron Ruiz, Gilly Atkins, Oliver Lamm, Russell Swider, Gary Clark, Judy Rachel, Kristi Cobb, and Alex Malherbe.

Very special recognition is in order for the original and very tasteful cover art by my graphic artist, Archimedes Delusio III. It is a vast understatement for me to say how impressed I am with what you do, Archie, lacking optic nerves in both of your eyes. And let me also add, you sure do make a mean tofu loukaniko! Yum yum! You're going to make me fat.

Lastly, for their belief in me and their unwavering enthusiasm, thanks and butterfly kisses go out to my unapologetic publisher Literary Vagabond Books, specifically the svelte and droll head of that organization, Sybil Fairbanks, and my new editor there, Cassandra Nutterknoll. Both of you are studies in and witness to the irrepressible power of the human imagination.

Chapter One

THE EARLY YEARS
1986 – 1995

Balloons

It was an especially cold Thanksgiving on Woodward Avenue in Detroit. Today was the annual Thanksgiving Day Parade and the crowd alternated between shivering and cheering. People shuffled and stomped, attempting to keep their feet from freezing. Gusts of steamy cold blew from their dripping noses and through clenched teeth.

Suddenly Billy started screaming. "My balloon!! My Balloon!!"

"Harold, do something. His balloon!"

"Goddammit, Irene. Do I look like I have wings? It's too late."

Up up it went. The string had slipped from Billy's grasp and the balloon was off to wherever balloons go. The stratosphere? Balloon heaven?

"You stupid little fuck. I told you to let me tie it to your wrist. But you're so goddamn smart. See what happens when you don't listen."

Billy's face instantly melted into a chastened mask of humiliation and defeat, as he started to cry like his puppy had been crushed under a bus.

"Nice work, Harold. Give the kid a complex. Let's find a vendor and get him another one."

"Over my dead body! He'll learn something from this. Next time something is so goddamn important to him as that there balloon …" Harold jerked his thumb skyward at the latex dot which was all but invisible by now. "… maybe he'll take better care of it."

"Jesus Christ, he's only three. How could I have married such a heartless man? Come here, sweetheart." She reached down and picked up the heartbroken and tremulously sobbing young boy, face streaked and blotchy, mittens wet with the fresh tears of tragedy.

Another parade float approached and would soon be right in front of them.

She pointed. "Look, Billy. Look at the dinosaur."

Sure enough, big as a moving van, bloated with helium, tethered to the 8-wheel steel flatbed of a float frame covered with artificial turf, and looking about as realistic as cardboard and crayons, was a Tyrannosaurus Rex. Its mouth was agape in what was supposed to be a scary, imminent man-devouring chomp. Several repairs were visible on the rubber underside, patches which were poorly matched in color to the skin of the faux beast. To underscore the implausibility of the threat, eight baton twirlers circled around the float, dancing, kicking their bare legs high, tossing and twirling gleaming chrome batons in the clear November air.

"Grrr!! Grrr!! Careful he doesn't eat you up." She tickled his cheek with her wool-gloved finger and tried to elicit a smile.

Billy had already stopped crying and just looked confused. He seemed more interested in the baton twirlers than the gas bag monster.

Next came a landlocked riverboat float, bearing the Flint Banjo Club players. This was their historic parade debut and they enthusiastically picked and twanged their way through various Dixieland and bluegrass favorites to a crowd which almost seemed to notice. Two mounted policemen followed, their horses snorting and blowing foggy jets from their wet nostrils.

"Harold, I need to powder my nose. Can you take him?" Giving her husband no real choice in the matter, she abruptly reached over and pushed the boy up against his father's chest.

"Mommy, I have to—"

"Just sit tight, Billy. Mommy will be right back."

"But, Mom … "

His father took Billy, obviously under protest, and slung him up on his shoulders. The boy completely caught off guard by the sudden and heavy-handed move, grabbed on desperately to keep from falling, wrapping his arms tightly around his father's neck.

"Easy! Easy! You don't have to choke me to death."

Billy knew better than to try to talk to him and just settled in an uncomfortable slump against his father's head. Before she had left, he was trying to tell his mom that he had to pee. But she was off to find a ladies room and it would have to wait until she got back.

He had to go. Really bad.

To make matters worse, his father was bouncing him. Whether this was to entertain Billy or just to try to stay warm was a moot point. The pressure of the full kidneys built quickly and all Billy could do was concentrate on holding it in. He couldn't even look at the parade floats. He closed his eyes and bit on his lower lip. The critical pressure in his groin quickly intensified. He clamped his legs together as hard as he could against the urgent and painful need for release.

"What the fuck are you doing up there? This ain't no wrestling match. Back off with the leg lock."

His dad reached up under Billy's arms and shook him to drive home his point. That was all it took for the dam to burst. Billy let out a tiny whimpering cry. Then silence. He tried to stop it but his urethral valve was open and it wasn't about to be turned off until the job was done.

At first Billy's father only noticed a slight increase in the temperature around and below the collar of his coat. Then he felt the wetness and sensed the faint odor of the boy's young discharge.

"Is that what I think it is? You little shit!"

Billy was swallowed whole by shame and fear. He fought desperately to keep from crying and covered his face with both hands as his father roughly lifted him off and held him out in front of him to confirm his worst suspicions. Billy was still going. Pee dripped from the bottom of his wet trousers, past his shoes, onto the pavement.

Billy's father was fast to act. Still holding Billy at arms length, he turned around and headed away from the street, towards the public restrooms, just as Billy's mom was making her way back to join them.

At first she was puzzled at the way Harold was carrying the boy, then terrified by the look on her husband's face. Obviously something had gone very wrong.

"I asked for a son and you gave me this piece of trash."

She tried to grab for Billy, both to rescue him from his father's rage and offer him whatever comfort might be needed. But Harold was too quick. He muscled past her and walked over to a large wire trash basket, already nearly full of newspapers, crumpled lunch bags and food wrappings.

He dropped Billy in head first and stormed away.

"Billy! Billy!"

She was there within seconds.

"Are you all right? My poor little boy! My poor little boy!" She fought back her tears and tried to hide her anger, though the back of her eyes were angry hot embers and an ache for her abused little boy filled her chest with sulfurous pangs. As she reached down and uprighted Billy, she saw his wet pants and realized what had happened. She immediately drew him into the kind of hug that only a mother can provide a frightened child, covering his cheeks and head with kisses.

"It's alright. It's alright, my sweet handsome young man."

The cushioning of the paper refuse already stuffed in the wastebasket had broken Billy's plunge. He wasn't hurt. No bruises. No scratches. Surprisingly, he wasn't crying. He just blinked and stared off in the direction his father had taken.

Then he turned and whispered. "Can we watch the parade?"

"We probably should get you some new pants. Looks like you ran through the lawn sprinklers while I was gone."

To take advantage of the masses of people attending the event, several stores were open for business, though it was a national holiday. His mom carried Billy into two clothing shops and they found some jeans he really liked. The new pants were a little big on him but at least they were warm and dry.

By the time they returned to the parade route, things were reaching a climactic conclusion. This, of course, was the arrival of none other than Santa Claus himself, on a motorized sled drawn by unmoving reindeer figures, deer-in-the-headlights gazes epoxied into their eyes, with the biggest reindeer celebrity of them all, red-nosed Rudolph himself, in the lead.

Billy's eyes widened as the Santa float approached. Within minutes, there he was right in front of them, the man with the giant belly, rosy cheeks, red and white fur-trimmed suit, and a huge white beard which flowed down on his chest like angel hair. Santa laughed his deep, sonorous 'ho ho ho' and waved like a prom queen to the excited children and conspiratorial adults who were bonded together in a special covenant to perpetuate and promote the Santa myth, just as their parents had done before them.

When Santa had passed and only the top of his waving arm could be seen over the high back of his red and gold sled, Billy finally lowered his own tiny hand and let it hang at his side.

Lost in thought, Billy watched his own fidgeting hands, then looked up at his mom.

"Mommy. Can Santa bring me a new dad?"

Billy didn't get his Christmas wish. Harold was there to stay.

Irene realized that as a companion and father, her husband lacked everything. On the other hand, he was a good provider, something Irene's generation and someone from her working class background valued a great deal. She couldn't remember the Harold who had courted her, the young man she had fallen in love with. The Harold she ended up with was certainly not what she had bargained for. But he did provide a decent house to live in and kept food on the table. She had cast her lot with him and that was that. She would stand by him and stick it out till the bitter end.

That's what you did.

Billy was an only child. Small favors from a busy God. Of course, it probably had more to do with the fact that Harold and Irene never had sex anymore, and hadn't from the time they found out she was pregnant with Billy, than with intervention at a divine level.

The good news was that, lacking any other children and anything other than a token presence by her mate, Irene could lavish all of her attention on her beautiful young boy, carving out a protective cocoon, and creating a world in their home within which Billy could grow up and, if her maternal fantasies were fully realized, blossom into a sensitive, loving person.

That's exactly what she did.

However he turned out, Irene was determined that Billy would be a much more fully functioning human being than his father, which admittedly wasn't setting the bar very high. In point of fact, she looked far beyond the Neanderthal benchmark set by her husband, and had rather ambitious and idealized notions of how she wanted her son to turn out.

Billy seemed to have a good head start from the get-go. He came out of the womb with his eyes open and was too busy gawking at a nurse to cry when the obstetrician whacked him on the butt. He just stretched his arms and gave a what's-the-big-deal yawn as they cut the umbilical cord and de-slimed him. The doctor said it was just a gas bubble coming out of his empty little tummy, but Irene swears to this day that Billy smiled at her the instant he laid his eyes on her. Closer observation would have noted it was the instant he laid eyes on her breasts. Whatever the key aspect of his enchantment, it was obvious he loved his mom.

As a baby, he rarely fussed and was delightfully easy to take care of. Irene could never remember Billy having a tantrum, and even his "terrible twos" were more tender than trying. On the whole, Billy was remote and pensive, never demanding, seeming to always either be daydreaming or completely and curiously fixated on some activity of the moment. Irene surely couldn't complain. Billy was a better companion in these pre-school years than her husband was in these middle years or, for that matter, most of their marriage.

During these early years, she got the greatest satisfaction in coddling and cuddling her boy, watching him grow day by day, becoming a "little person". He was a very quick learner, and by the time he was four was reading at the level of a 2ⁿᵈ or 3ʳᵈ grader. Billy also could add and subtract, was already starting to learn to multiply and divide, and could even count up beyond a thousand. He had a good sense of humor and caught most adults off guard with quirky come-backs when they patronizingly talked to him as they typically would a 4-year old.

Billy became fascinated with playing cards and loved to watch when his mom had friends over in the afternoon to play Euchre, their favorite card game. One day he asked if he could play.

Betty Buskirk, a matronly blimp of an ex-nurse from across the street was utterly charmed. "Isn't that cute? Let the little tyke play, Irene. Has he got any money?"

They all clucked and smiled.

But by the end of two weeks, the smiles became a little bit forced, as he methodically cleaned them all out of their precious pennies. Billy just kept on winning and grinning.

"Is it my deal, mom?"

Despite the commonly heard mantra that winning isn't everything, that it's playing the game that's the fun, the joys of their daily Euchre games started to dwindle along with their reserves of pocket change. The chuckling waned and conversations became thin. Gradually, as their losses mounted, the damage this "high-stakes gambling" might be doing to the development of this precocious boy became the new urgent concern and replaced their long-vanished delight in letting Billy participate in grown-up fun.

Farrah the anorexic cat woman: "I'm wondering, Irene, if this is good for him."

Billy: "Trump."

Carol who had lost both of her ovaries and her uterus to cancer: "This could make him an addict, a compulsive gambler. It's how it starts, you know."

Billy: "King takes it."

Lucia in the middle of her third divorce: "Doesn't he have a cartoon show to watch?"

Billy: "My hand."

Irene: "He's just having fun. Don't be such sore losers."

Even at four, Billy could take a hint. He sensed in his precocious little mind that his card-playing days with mom and her friends had now come to an end. He gathered his coins and put them in a little leather pouch he had found in his father's toolbox.

"Thanks so much for letting me play. Aunt Lucia, Aunt Carol, Auntie Farrah and Aunt Betty. I think I'm going to go now. I really want to ride my bike."

His mom looked at him puzzled.

"Billy, you don't have a bike."

Holding up the pouch. "I will soon, mom. Maybe later we could go to the bike shop to have a look."

He beat a quick retreat to his room.

"Your son is a goddamn hustler, Irene."

"I'm so proud of him."

So proud that her eyes twinkled when she watched him play in the back yard.

So proud that she gleefully dressed him like little Charlie McCarthy every Sunday for mass.

So proud that she more often than not let Billy get away with just about anything and everything.

For example … when Billy was five.

It was the big day. The crossing of a threshold from which there was no return. A passage through the portal which held all of the possibilities of the future. A life-altering migration towards independence. The laying of a basic foundation for the self-reliance that would buttress the entirety of his adult life. One small step for a child, one big leap for Billy Green.

Today was the first day of kindergarten.

At breakfast, even Harold acknowledged there was something very special about today.

"So the big boy is going to school, eh? Good luck, Billy. Try not to shit your pants."

As Irene watched him conquer the tall steps of the school bus, she tried her best to hide her maternal anxiety and only let her excitement show.

The entire time he was at school, she was distracted and did everything she could to keep herself busy. By noon the house had never been so clean. She kept reassuring herself that he was alright and nothing could possibly go wrong. After all, this was as normal as the sunrise. Kids all over the world went to school everyday. What could she possibly have to worry about?

It was approaching one o'clock. School would be letting out. She rushed out to the school bus stop a half-hour early, then paced like a caged snow leopard.

Finally, the bus arrived and Billy was the last of eight kids to step out.

He ambled down the three tall steps and the pneumatic door closed behind him.

"How did it go Billy?"

"Fine."

"Tell me about it."

"It was fine."

"Aren't you excited? Your first day at school!"

"I'm fine."

That was it. That's all he had to say about it.

Next morning, Billy didn't get right up when his mother called. Harold had left an hour earlier and she was busy fixing eggs and cereal for Billy's breakfast. But when it was ready, no Billy.

She called again. "Come on, Billy. Time to eat. You don't want to be late."

After a few minutes, still no Billy. So she went and peeked his room. There he was in bed, still in his pajamas, the clothes she had laid out for him on the chair untouched.

He heard her tiptoe in.

"Can't go to school today, mom. Don't feel so good."

"Oh Billy, are you alright? Do you have a fever?" She checked his forehead and face with the back of her hand. "You don't have a fever, hon."

"Can't go to school today. I'll be okay."

"Alright. Just rest. I'll check on you in a while. Let me know if you need anything."

"Breakfast."

"I'll bring it up to you. Eggs and cereal. Your favorite."

And so it went every day for the rest of the kindergarten year. Breakfast in bed. Hooky from school.

After a few weeks, they skipped the ritualistic feigning of illness and maternal concern. Irene was clueless as to why Billy refused to go back. Still, she never pressed the matter. Truthfully, she was pretty darn glad to have him at home. At least she didn't have to worry about what potential evil or harm lurked out there, ready to inflict itself on her precious boy. And frankly, she really loved his company. The house had seemed abysmally empty the five hours he was in school that first day.

Billy never told his mom what had happened. He was a little embarrassed about the whole thing and just decided it was best to keep it to himself.

That one single day that Billy attended kindergarten had turned out to be a colossal disaster. The bus ride there was fun but as soon as he stepped off the bus, a miniature replica of the Incredible Hulk, who called himself The Fist, walked right up to Billy and punched him squarely in the face. Blood started gushing from his nose and Billy just lay face down in the spreading crimson puddle crying, until a teacher finally came over and rescued him. It happened to be the very same teacher who was assigned to teach Billy's kindergarten class — Mrs. Stephens — who took him sympathetically under her wing. While her teaching assistant rounded up the rest of the wide-eyed students and gave them crayons and paper to draw, Mrs. Stephens took Billy to a small room right off the classroom where they kept supplies, books and toys. Without missing a beat, she grabbed a towel and a couple blankets.

"Here, just lie down and you'll be alright. What's your name?"

"Billy Green."

"Well, Billy Green. I don't know how this happened but let me clean you up a little bit and then we'll take you down to see the school nurse. Okay?"

She wetted the towel and carefully and gently cleaned his face. The bleeding had stopped and fortunately none had splattered on his clothing.

"Just rest here for now. I'm going to call the school nurse. But if you feel like it, you can come out and join us. We're drawing pictures of our favorite animals. Sound like fun?"

Actually it didn't sound like fun. And Billy had no desire to go out there and be laughed at by all the other kids. He just stayed put and closed his eyes, imagining he was someplace else. Anywhere else would do.

Fifteen minutes went by. He heard the door open. He expected either Mrs. Stephens or a woman dressed in white with a stethoscope dangling from her neck. It turned out to be neither. It was one of his new fellow kindergarteners.

"Hi. I'm Veronica. I'm a nurse."

"No you're not."

"Well, let's make-believe then. Me and my friends play doctor-nurse all the time. Want to?"

"I guess. I'm not doing anything right now. How do you play?"

"First, I need to examine you. Take off your pants."

"Take off my pants? Are you sure?"

"That's how we play. Now take them off."

Billy timidly did as he was instructed, then lay back down. Veronica reached over and tugged at his underpants.

"These too. Take them off. Come on."

Billy very slowly slid his J. C. Penney undies down to his knees. Veronica started giggling. Then she reached over and held Billy's penis delicately between her thumb and index finger.

"I don't have one of these. Wanna see?"

Billy had never given the matter any thought. Ever before. Not even once. But for some reason, right now, he *did* want to see. He really *really* wanted to see. It seemed as urgent as life and death.

"Okay."

First Veronica reached under her little play dress and removed her panties. Then very slowly and with a mixture of shyness and double-double-dare-me teasing, started to lift her dress.

"What's going on in here!!" Mrs. Stephens stood aghast at the spectacle of a boy with his pants down, willy hanging out, and a little female playmate doing a striptease right before her eyes, in the sanctity of her kindergarten school.

"He made me do it. He dared me, after he showed me his … you know." Veronica started crying but it was really a stretch to believe these were real tears.

Billy was mortified, embarrassed, ashamed, angry and wishing he was invisible all at once. Now he really had a good reason for imagining he were anywhere else, in the hope he might magically be transported there.

Veronica ran out of the storeroom, leaving her little girl panties on the floor, while Billy scrambled to get decent.

Mrs. Stephens seemed confused. She looked to be in her early twenties. This had to be her first teaching job. She seemed to be weighing her options — what she should do next.

"Please get dressed. Curiosity is natural. I just wished this hadn't happened here. First day of school. Hopefully, young man, you will not in the future be making a regular habit of this. Understood?"

"Yes, ma'am."

"Now, why don't you come and join class and try not to cause any trouble. The nurse is not in today. You feel okay?"

"I'm fine. Thank you. You're very pretty, you know."

She wasn't. But she'd take what she could get, even if it was from a difficult 5-year old boy. She took Billy's hand and led him to his seat. He sat down and proceeded to draw his favorite animal.

It was a naked little girl.

That was Billy's first day of kindergarten.

By the time he got home, the dull pain in his face and the events in the store room weighed heavily on him. He couldn't tell his mom what had happened to see what she thought. Definitely not an option.

What should he do? It was a tough call.

Of course, he wanted to see what the little girl had under her skirt. But by the same token, he didn't need his nose bashed in again. Billy felt confident that the ease with which the bully had used his face as a punching bag that first day had set a dangerous and easily repeated precedent. Moreover, considering how Veronica turned on him and lied, prospects of seeing "hers" were probably pretty remote.

That night after dinner, Billy went to his room and made a decision. No way was he going back to that school. He would do whatever he needed to do to avoid it. But he wasn't going back. No way José!

His mom went right along. She ended up being a complicit co-conspirator to a 5-year-old skipping the entire first year of his formal education.

She knew, of course, that something had happened that first day. Frankly, it didn't matter to her what it was. She didn't have to know. What had occurred had upset Billy tremendously. A good mother trusts her child. Especially one as special and wonderful as her little Billy.

He was her beautiful blind spot.

As it turned out, Billy's kindergarten year was hardly wasted. He continued studying on his own, assisted by the tutoring of his mom. Natural curiosity and a gift for applying himself — which was way beyond his five years — meant that he never needed to be coaxed or bribed to study, or to pick up a book, or to play instructive games. Irene made regular trips to Northland, a suburban mall on the north side of Detroit, to buy every educational game, book, puzzle, toy, science kit, map, and learning aid she could afford on her limited allowance from Harold. Billy plowed through them like he was studying for the bar exam.

The upshot of all this home schooling was that by the time Billy was ready for the first grade, he probably could have taught it.

When Billy turned six, Irene was now faced with the tough decision as to where he would be attending first grade. The inner city schools in Detroit were glorified prison camps and babysitting services. The working class suburban public schools weren't much better. While she and Harold were far from devout Catholics, it looked like a good parochial school might be the best route. Catholic schools were by all accounts tough, no-nonsense institutions, staffed by serious educators. So while they did perform a lot of religious indoctrination, they had excellent reputations academically, from elementary grades through high school.

Harold's job at the Chrysler truck assembly plant in Warren had settled them, at least for the foreseeable future, in Troy, a nearby suburb on the north side of Detroit. There they were buying a modest two-bedroom tract house on a land contract. In terms of choice of parochial schools in the area, there wasn't any — unless Billy were each and every day to commute quite a distance. Just one Catholic school a little over three miles up the road, in the adjacent community of Madison Heights, was all there was. As far as Irene was concerned, there wasn't much more to think about. The decision had been made.

Starting in September, Billy would be attending St. Jerome Catholic Elementary School.

"I don't give a rat's ass where you send him. Just as long as he gets educated so he don't end up a bum like me." Harold slugged down the rest of his beer. "I need a chaser for that. More suds here, woman."

Irene had, of course, already made up her own mind to send Billy to Catholic school. But since it involved a substantial outlay of money for tuition, books and other school supplies, she thought she had better bring Harold on board. As she had in the past when confronted with difficult family decisions, she would fabricate the illusion that Harold himself actually played some important role in the decision making process. Usually after five or six beers, he was pretty pliable. After seven or eight, he could be convinced he wrote the Magna Carta.

Obviously, this time around that wouldn't be necessary.

The more Irene learned about Billy's new elementary school, the more excited she became.

St. Jerome's was the jewel of the Archdiocese of Detroit, unique even among schools nationwide. It was headed up by a Father Bartholomew McAllister, a priest already in his late seventies but still energetically devoting his all to the parish, concentrating particularly on shaping its school and instructional program to conform to the strict principles he originally learned in his preparation for Jesuit priesthood at College of the Holy Cross in Worcester, Massachusetts.

Father Bartholomew was "old school" in the purest sense. While most other Catholic schools across America, from the 1970s forward, had bent to the social, economic and utilitarian pressures to modernize and streamline their educational environment, it was his stated objective to keep St. Jerome's running the way Catholic schools ran in the good old days. He believed that abandoning the foundation laid by Paul and the Byzantine Popes, meaning surrendering to the contemporary rush to modernize the Church, did not necessarily make it more relevant, only more user-friendly, and regrettably more compatible with some of the very things which Catholicism in principle should oppose — rampant materialism, easy sex, instant gratification, despiritualization, idolatry, falseness, frivolousness, and the heretical notion that God was a lifestyle choice. In his view, the Church started to wander from its spiritual center somewhere around 1600. If he could have had his way and could somehow justify it, he would have built catacombs in the subterranean strata under St. Jerome Catholic Church.

Much of his fanaticism sprung from his involvement in the Priestly Fraternity of St. Peter, the extremely conservative clerical society of apostolic life founded at the Abbey of Hauterive, Switzerland in 1988. He joined them a year after its inception. This fanatical coterie of ultra-orthodox priests promoted such legacy practices as performing the Tridentine Mass which was in Latin, using the Roman Missal in church services, and administering the sacraments in accordance with the Roman Rite. Basically their agenda was a call to ignore all of the reforms instituted by the Second Ecumenical Council of the Vatican — which had met for over three years and concluded its work in 1965 — and just keep things the way they had been for centuries.

Though in the back corridors of church high command he was viewed as a bit extreme, the Archdiocese gave him their full support. They were especially gratified to have his unique and precious school as a noble example of Catholic pedagogy at its traditional best, even if it was an anachronism. It was a chronic drain on their coffers, since they had to subsidize the school in ways that others didn't require, but it was worth it, as a sort of living historical monument and as public relations ammunition against accusations that the Catholic Church was selling out to populism and modernity in order to survive. Even the Pope had given his nod of recognition and approval. An effusive letter of praise from His Eminence was framed and hung on the wall of Father Bartholomew's office.

Father Bartholomew's most conspicuous nod to traditional orthodoxy was the presence of eleven nuns who were all of the Dominican Sisters of St. Mary. They were housed in a convent which sat between the rectory and the school itself. This was viewed as both bold and improvident because nuns had long ago been almost totally phased out as teachers in America and Canada, as their numbers had dwindled and it became impossible to fully staff schools with them. One by one lay teachers were hired to replace them, these aging women of God who after giving their whole lives to the church and to the instruction of its youth, retired or passed away. When a parish school got down to only a few of the sanctified ladies, it became impractical to house them. Those last few remaining nuns, usually older but not yet retirement age, were quietly reassigned to do overseas missionary work or perform as support staff in hospitals and other Catholic service facilities. The convents then were either torn down, or more often than not, turned into administrative offices or community outreach centers.

Similarly anachronistic but consistent with his conservatism, Father Bartholomew also required that all students wear uniforms, in order to avoid the risk of immodesty and nip in the bud the prospect of turning the school into a runway competition for the latest fad clothing. He also reinstituted the tradition of requiring daily attendance at mass, something which proved less than popular, to put it mildly. Even the nuns were on occasion heard grumbling about it.

His only concession to the stark realities of contemporary life was a high fence around the entire school grounds, topped with razor-sharp barbwire, and a security guard posted at the entrance. People often speculated as to whether this was to keep the kids in or child molesters out. But these were not the safest of times in the greater Detroit metropolitan area, and though located in the suburban white north, the school wasn't situated in the best of neighborhoods.

Billy's arrival his first day of 1st grade at St. Jerome's, and in fact his steady attendance over the next two years there, were entirely uneventful. No bullies. No show-me-yours, I'll-show-you-mine.

This time around, from the very start, he loved school. At least he loved the schooling aspects of it. Studying at home with his mom as his own personal tutor was comfortable. But at school they had all of these *great things* — workbooks, teaching aids, world maps, textbooks, artist brushes and drawing paper, clay and sculpting wax, alphabet and arithmetic games, videos, story books, and on and on. His school was a Toys 'R Us to make you smart.

Yes, they definitely had all this great stuff.

Best of all they had the nuns!

Granted, sometimes they were cranky and mean. However, most of the time — whether they meant to be or not — they were incredibly funny. They took everything so seriously and they tried so hard.

They would pace back and forth at the front of class, pointing at this or that with their long pointers, writing frantically on the blackboard, or reciting from their teachers texts — brows furrowed and voices rising in pitch as they tried to pound some apparently amazing, crucial, earthshattering fact or idea into the impregnable, distracted, television-saturated minds of the young bodies lazily propped up at their desks.

Yes, how they tried! They sure deserved a lot of credit.

Billy truly respected the ladies in black. They took their jobs very seriously.

But more to the point, he was incredibly fascinated by them.

He had never seen or imagined anything like them.

He spent hours wondering about them. Why did they choose to become nuns? It sure didn't look like much fun. They had to wear those weird habits, holy gowns which pinched their faces into tight inexpressive masks. All their physical movement and freedom was imprisoned in casements of bulky black bed sheets. Their feet were bound in ugly orthopedic clodhoppers, probably left over from an Amish turn-of-the-century barn sale.

He wondered what they did in the convent at night. Did they watch TV? Play cards? Maybe they played Euchre! Did they sit around in their underwear? Or did they still have those infernal habits on? Did they gossip? Tell secrets? Eat junk food? Paint their toenails? Brush their hair? Did they even have hair?

It was baffling, mysterious, magical — the pure stuff of boy wonderment and fantasy — to think about what went on behind those locked doors and drawn drapes in the dim evening candlelight of the convent. Oh! To be a fly on the wall!

At first he was extremely shy around them. Their medieval gowns, accessorized with rosaries and crucifixes and other ecumenical whatnot, their mystifying choice to never marry or have children, the special bond they shared among themselves which so thoroughly insulated them from the rest of society, plus the mystery and magic which Billy had actively conjured in his own imagination, all conspired to make them almost totally unapproachable. But very slowly as time went on, some of this mystique gave way to familiarity, and he started feeling a little more at ease.

This was toward the end of 3rd grade.

By now, his obsession with them had built to unbearable levels, and though his courage was nearly sufficient for him to begin to actively engage them, his mind was still fuzzy as to how to approach it. His initial terror had evolved into a mild and amenable shyness. It was now a tactical issue. He wanted to get inside their world. He just needed to find a way.

Finally, one day he did.

On an impulse — abandoning all of the forethought and fastidious mulling that until then had absorbed so many days and nights and taxed his immature mind — Billy plunged through the imaginary glass wall, and signed on to a game that would establish the ground rules for his next couple years at St. Jerome's.

Every day in 3rd grade, one full hour of instruction was devoted to religion.

Typically, Sister Grace — his 3rd grade home room teacher — would pound away at the commandments and church rules which the students were expected to memorize, and then throughout their lives adhere to with unerring obedience. Or she would read selections from the official Catechism of the Catholic Church, which was as interesting as listening to transcripts from probate court hearings.

But one day, as a special treat intended to inspire their highly impressionable young minds, and to give them an appreciation of the glorious history of the Catholic Church, Billy's class got to watch three short videos. One was on the extraordinary life of St. Francis of Assisi, another on St. Dominic, and finally one on Blessed Mary, Mother of Jesus — aka the Virgin Mary.

Each video in storybook fashion presented the biographical details of the holy celebrity, citing the powerful spiritual lessons epitomized by the beautiful and exemplary lives they lived.

The first video romped through the high points of the life of St. Francis — the fasting and visions, the alms to the poor and abandonment of worldly things, his pilgrimage to Rome and preaching a life of repentance, and his founding of the Order of Franciscan Friars. There were dramatic sequences of St. Francis shedding his clothes and giving them to a beggars, his kindnesses to lepers, and his surreal visions at the Church of San Damiano in his hometown of Assisi, of a bloody and dying Christ speaking parliamentary English to him from the crucifix. It was a top notch production. The special effects were great.

According to the second video, the mother of St. Dominic just before giving birth to him had a dream in which a dog came leaping out of her womb carrying the torch in its mouth that would "set the world on fire". This bizarre imagery was apparently a prophecy of his creation a few decades later of the Dominican Order of Priests. The narrator also explained that early in his twenties, he had set up a monastic community for women near Carcassonne, France. This became the foundation for the Order of Dominican Sisterhood, to which Sister Grace and the other nuns at the school belonged. St. Dominic also advocated the theological precedent of praying directly to the Blessed Virgin Mary. Mary, as the Mother of God, was the most famous Mary on the planet and understandably the iconic patron for most nuns, whatever their order. But order of the nuns at St. Jerome's combined the punching power of both Dominic and Mary — hence the name, the Dominican Sisters of Mary. The video, with solemn choir music swelling in the background, used an actor who looked a lot like George Clooney, in compelling scenes of St. Dominic proselytizing for the austere life of humility and self-denial. It portrayed his passion for tracking down heretics and other enemies of the church, eradicating heretical beliefs, and vanquishing pagan rituals. It brushed off — in fact didn't bring up at all — the Inquisition, a dark side of Dominic's fanaticism which historically had cast the Church in a very sinister light.

The final video was the showstopper.

Virgin Mary, as the sacred vessel who brought Jesus into the world, was the rock star of Catholicism. The eager faces of Billy's classmates lit up, as familiar scenes unfolded before them. Her early chaste years of marriage with Joseph. Their long trek in escaping from the terrifying edicts of Herod. The birth of the Christ child in a manger in Bethlehem. Mary watching her Son being tried and condemned to die. Her praying and looking up at the dying Jesus on the crucifix, blood trickling down his face and body from the crown of thorns on His head and the sword gash in His ribcage. Then finally her in the tomb with a ghostly pale and very dead Jesus draped across her lap. It was a moving and macabre journey — gory and glorious. By the conclusion, most of the young girls in Billy's class were crying. It was a slobbering sob fest.

But never accuse the Catholic Church of wasting an opportunity for some no-holds-barred exploitation. These kids had now been rendered defenseless, whimpering receptacles of piteous longing, most definitely ripe for the picking! Time to go to work on them.

In a jolting leap to the present day, at the very end of each video, a Cardinal Józef Szoka — young by Cardinal standards but clearly chosen for his paternalistic charisma and videogenic good looks — gave a short but highly persuasive talk on the virtues of priesthood or committing one's life to being a nun. A phone number and mailing address were provided, but more ingratiatingly, the children were encouraged to come forth and talk to their own priests and nuns about any calling they were now experiencing, toward committing their lives to the Lord Jesus Christ. While maybe not perceived as such by the kids, it was clear that these videos were in the final analysis cleverly-wrought recruiting tools, each an unapologetic sales pitch for a lifetime of servitude to the Church.

After the closing choral music and production credits for the final video — the one on the life of the Virgin Mary — faded to black, the classroom lights were switched back on. Sister Grace had an uncharacteristic glint in her eyes.

"Okay! Lois? What would you like to be when you grow up?"

"Why, Sister Grace, I think I want to be a nun."

"That's wonderful, Lois. Peter? Peter Hill? How about you? What would you like to be?"

"I really want to be a priest. Do you think I could?"

"I don't see why not. Just be a good boy and you can enter the seminary to become a priest. Mary Lou? How about you? What do you want to be when you grow up?"

"I want to be a nun. That would be so great."

"Wonderful. Wonderful. And Billy Green? What about you?"

"I really think I want to be a nun."

There was some giggling and whispering about what an idiot Billy was.

"Now Billy, don't you mean a priest?"

"No, Sister Grace. I want to be a nun."

Now the class was laughing and getting boisterous.

"Class, calm down. Billy, listen to me. You are a boy. You can't be a nun. Nuns are girls."

"But I want to be a nun. I really want to be a nun."

A boy in the back started it and soon the whole class was chanting.

He wants to be a nun.

He wants to be a nun.

He wants to be a nun.

Billy, buoyed and emboldened by the reaction of the other kids — and certainly enjoying the limelight — started insistently repeating his own stated intention, and didn't stop.

"I want to be a nun. I want to be a nun. I want to be a nun … "

Sister Grace's mood instantly turned foul. She had lost control of the class. Billy was being an upstart and setting a horrible example to the rest of the kids. She knew what she had to do. She had to shut him up. Immediately!

She marched over to Billy's desk and grabbed him by the back of his neck. She gripped him hard, sinking her fingernails deep, then shouted at the top of her lungs.

"Billy, you can't be a nun!!"

Despite the pain of her surprisingly strong grip, Billy forged ahead.

"I want to be a nun. I want to be a nun. I want to be a nun … "

Desperate now, she took her other hand and clamped it over his mouth. Billy could still be heard but it was muffled.

"I want to be a nun. I want to be a nun. I want to be a nun."

Suddenly he stopped and with a single big wet slobbering sweep of his tongue licked the inside of her palm. She pulled her hand away and looked at it in disgust.

"Ugh!"

Sister Grace was livid. She grabbed his ear with her dry hand and twisting it violently made him stand up. This really hurt. Billy now stopped insisting on nunhood but instead gave voice to his pain.

"Ow! Ow! Ow! You're hurting me."

"You are coming with me. And if you give me any more grief, I'll rip your ear off!"

She took Billy to the administrative area and deposited him in the office of Mother Superior.

"This is Billy Green. He is a troublemaker and a sinner and I think you should talk to him. Thank you very much, blessed Mother. May God be with you. You'll need it with this child of the Devil."

After discussions with Billy and protracted negotiations with Sister Grace, Billy was reinstated in her class. But a pattern had been established. He continued to toy with Sister Grace and she continued to march him down to the office for the apparently ineffective counseling of Mother Superior.

None of the subsequent incidents were as overtly confrontational as the I-want-to-be-a-nun skirmish. Billy adopted a lower profile — polite and demure at least on the surface — but kept up a steady barrage of needling and subtle harassment. He would demonstrate implausible levels of enthusiasm for bland and monotonous subject matter. He would raise his hand to get permission to go to the bathroom. Then when it was granted would just sit there looking pained, like any minute he would explode. One of his favorites was when called on to provide an answer on the blackboard to write it backwards.

It was low-level guerrilla warfare, which invariably kept his fellow students laughing but on the downside fostered his bad reputation among the nuns. He was a frequent and hot topic of conversation in the convent after school hours.

This adversarial relationship, which Billy thrived on as much as Sister Grace resented, was finally terminated by the routine predetermined order of events of an elementary school. June arrived and Billy moved on to the next grade, perhaps no wiser as to what made these nuns tick, but with a reputation among his peers for knowing how to push their holy buttons.

His new teacher nun wielded some notoriety herself. Everyone knew about Sister Bernadette. The kids about to enter the 4th grade approached it with fear and trembling. The kids who had made it through a year with her, left with a enormous sigh of relief and pride, as if they were one of the surviving troops in the World War II storming of the beach at Normandy.

She was a cranky old woman — estimates ran in the 80s and 90s — who even if just waiting around to soon die, wouldn't be exiting the battle grounds of parochial education without inflicting as much pain and guilt as possible on the 9-year olds who would quake and cower in her classroom over her remaining years. Her store of patience in the warehouse of her pedagogical assets had long ago been permanently depleted. Her love of children and for teaching them — if she had ever had any — was a forgotten memory buried under decades of unconcealed animus, going in both directions. After more than fifty years in the classroom, all of their faces looked the same, she expected the worst, and usually getting it, responded accordingly.

Nobody messed with her.

She had heard about this Billy Green and she was ready for him.

Of course he knew about her.

The stage was set for an epic battle.

For the first few weeks, during which Billy tried to size up his new adversary and gauge if there was any maneuvering room to initiate his finely-tuned bag of tricks, he and the formidable Sister Bernadette seemed to be honoring some manner of understood but unspoken detente. They kept their wary eyes on one another. The peaceful calm of a tightly run prison camp prevailed.

Then Billy gradually, in almost imperceptible increments, notched up his campaign of subdued sedition. He started with bits of guarded irony. Little flecks of patronizing flattery, which the other students saw for what they were but were on the surface innocent enough that the good nun really couldn't call his bluff.

"Sister Bernadette, you're the best teacher I ever had."

"It's *I've ever had … I've.* But thank you, Billy."

"I just wish I could be in the 4th grade next year too. And the year after."

"If you don't study harder, Billy, you might be."

Nobody was fooled. It was obvious Billy was at it again.

Still there were no signs of open conflict. No blood spilled. No body bags. So far so good. Billy decided to ratchet things up a bit more.

It was a big mistake.

Sister Bernadette was uncanny. She missed her calling when she became a nun. She should have worked for the CIA. Everything Billy tried, no matter how innocuous, stealthy or cleverly covert, ended up having the lid blown off by this preternatural robocop nun. Passing notes that said *At 10:15 everybody start whispering.* Coming to class early and drawing funny pictures on the blackboard — usually involving a nun in some humiliating pose or embarrassing activity.

Dusting Sister Bernadette's chair with a fine layer of white chalk. Gluing all of the pages of her catechism book together so that it was a fused clump of fireplace kindling. Dropping a pencil and bending down so that he could look up Janet LaFleur's skirt — an exercise he found increasingly captivating for reasons he didn't understand. Busted every time!

"Billy, you can do that after you and Janet get married, not before."

Reichführer Bernadette was all over him and it always ended the same way, with him standing in the hall all alone, no books, no games, no nothing, for at least an hour. Later in life he would maintain that all he did for the entire fourth year of his schooling was stare at a polished linoleum hallway and metal student lockers.

With failures mounting, he decided to ease off for a while and bide his time. Sister Bernadette was out of his league. At least for now.

His self-discipline and patience was finally rewarded toward the end of the school year. Time was running out. But Billy had been ready to spring, like a tree monkey or Australian dingo, given the right opportunity.

It was video day again. Today's featured short movie was on Bernadette Soubirous, better known as St. Bernadette of Lourdes.

This clearly had very special meaning for Sister Bernadette. She had originally been inspired to join a religious order and take her vows of celibacy, upon learning as a young girl about the miraculous story of St. Bernadette. Even before she became a novice, there was no doubt in her mind who her namesake would be for her ordination.

The story of Bernadette was indeed amazing and magical. The video captured it well.

She was born in 1844 to a poor family in Lourdes, a small town in southern France. When she turned 14, she started having visions of "a small young lady". The apparition was later given the official imprimatur of the Church and dubbed The Lady of Lourdes. Lady of Lourdes told Bernadette, *"Please go to the priests and tell them that a chapel is to be built here. Let processions come hither."* Her local priest and many of the townspeople were initially skeptical, until the small young lady appeared again and instructed Bernadette to dig in the ground at her feet until she found a spring, then drink the water from the spring. Others drank the water and claimed that as a result they had been cured of their illnesses. When these inexplicable cures were verified, chapels and churches were built at the site and over the years thousands of people made a pilgrimage to Lourdes to seek miracle cures from their maladies. There was a generous amount of footage in the video of people in the recent past making such visits, splashing the holy water on themselves and praying at the grotto.

Another powerful moment in the video dramatized one of the miracles visited upon the young Bernadette herself. It showed her clutching a candle until it burned all the way down into the hand she was using to hold it. The flames licked at her flesh and should have seared her and caused excruciating pain. But Bernadette just sat in calm contemplation, displaying no signs of discomfort or injury. Billy's classmates at first groaned in empathetic agony, then beamed with awe and delight as the miracle unfolded before their eyes. It was an intense few moments.

Predictably, there was the signature infotainment advertisement tagged on at the end, yet another shameless pitch by Cardinal Józef Szoka for turning one's life over lock-stock-and-barrel to the Holy Catholic Church.

After the video finished, the deep acidic lines of ill-temper in the face of Sister Bernadette seemed a little softer, the normally hard furrow of her brow a little more relaxed, the guttural tone of her voice a little lighter and more melodious.

It was a kinder, gentler Sister Bernadette than the children had ever seen.

"Class. Is there anything you'd like to say? Are there any questions? Margie? Yes?"

"Sister Bernadette, do you have to go to Lourdes? Or can you just pray directly to St. Bernadette for her help and blessings?"

"It's best to go there. But you certainly can pray to her. I myself say a special prayer every day to St. Bernadette. She's my patron saint and very special to me. Who else now? Carlos? Did you have a question?"

"I just wanted to say that I really liked the movie. St. Bernadette is the best saint of all. Someday I hope I can go there myself and pray for my sick grandmother."

"I hope you get that opportunity as well, Carlos. Yes, it is a wonderful story, isn't it. Billy? You have a question?"

Billy took a deep breath, then spoke in a clear voice.

"Yes, Sister … I do. My father is a fat pig and a drunken asshole. Do you think if we took him to Lourdes he could be cured?"

All of the saint-in-training feel-good vibes instantly vacated the room. The other students tensed as soon as they heard the "bad word", one which they used regularly on their own time but would never let drop in school. All eyes turned to the front of the class, like the viewing gallery at an execution.

Sister Bernadette became rigid from head to toe, and her face returned to its shrunken-head wrathfulness — the bitter cup they had had to swallow every day of class now for almost nine months.

From this normal rest state of routine virulence, she then quickly plunged into the deep caverns of stored ire.

It was an awesome, if terrifying, thing to watch.

She seemed to be spontaneously combusting from the inside out. Her face was red with rage and she was panting. Each sharp breath seemed to deepen the crimson tone of her skin. Her eyes bulged and became wrath-of-God guns of malignant fury. Slowly she raised her trembling hand and pointed her finger at Billy, ready to deliver a lethal blow of denunciation and rebuke.

But before anything resembling the expected torrent of vilification came out of her twitching, contorted mouth, her eyes suddenly rolled back in her head. Sister Bernadette suddenly keeled over and collapsed on the floor.

The boys sat in paralyzed silence. The girls simultaneously inhaled a gasp of shock and disbelief. Three goody-goody girls then quickly jumped up from their desks. Alicia Parks ran out of the classroom presumably to get some help. Margie Keeler and Sue Majzarski knelt down next to the recumbent body of the nun, and made disconnected, confused and frantic gestures in an obviously futile effort to do something-anything.

Margie started crying, then snapped her head around, pointed at Billy, and screamed a vituperative volley.

"You've killed her! You've killed Sister Bernadette, Billy Green!"

Moments later, Mother Superior came running into class, then an ambulance arrived. Two paramedics carted the unconscious nun away on a gurney, rushed her into their vehicle to be taken sirens-blaring to the emergency room of a local hospital. That much information was easily available.

Killed her?

Billy was certain he hadn't.

Billy reasoned that they wouldn't be taking her to emergency if she were dead. They'd take her to a funeral home. Or wherever they take dead people. So she must still be alive.

This was later confirmed by Billy's mom after repeated telephone calls to Mother Superior at the convent's main number and to the St. Jerome rectory business line.

Sister Bernadette was indeed alive, conscious, and responding well to the excellent care she was getting. There would be no homicide charges.

It was also relayed in very discrete hushed tones to Billy's mom, that the good sister couldn't remember anything — at least at this point — about why she was in the hospital and what had triggered her collapse.

Billy felt very relieved.

Billy also felt bad. But not that bad. The cranky old witch had it coming. Someone had to put the ornery old witch in her place and deep down he harbored not a little pride that he was the one to do it.

Of course, his public face painted a different picture.

"I don't know what happened, mom. I just asked her a simple question."

"Billy, Mother Superior wasn't there and still hasn't gotten the whole story. But she gets the impression that what you said was more the equivalent of dropping a bowling ball on her head."

Taken at face value, despite the foul language, his question did have some merit, and at some level was certainly heartfelt. After all, Billy's father fit the description and Billy for as long as he could remember had wished something could be done about it. If a little Lourdes holy water could do the trick, why not?

But in the sacrosanct environment of a Catholic elementary school, especially with the remark coming from a student who was already a known troublemaker with a solid aptitude for pushing the wrong buttons, what happened was regarded as a gross effrontery, a harsh bit of misconduct which had to be punished. He had *almost* killed the poor nun, after all. That was the version of the story that had gotten some traction anyway.

It turned out that, according to the doctors, she hadn't had a heart attack or anything serious. She had probably hyperventilated, fainted, or collapsed from overexcitement. Her attending physician recommended some bed rest, while they further monitored her. She would be unavailable for the last few days of the current school year, but would no doubt be back on the job after summer vacation, striking terror into the hearts of a brand new batch of 4th graders.

Despite feverish circulation of rumors that Billy had tried to kill a nun — mainly among the school kids themselves who were ecstatic over the idea of such a sensational event happening in *their school* — the situation was pretty straightforward and unlikely to result in any highly serious repercussions.

Nobody could really pin anything on him. Billy had said something off-color. She blew a gasket. Considering she was old-going-on-ancient, her gaskets were probably already worn pretty thin. She was a sturdy old antique, hadn't come close to dying, but had most probably experienced some manner of fainting attack. It would be a long stretch to charge him with attempted murder or accuse him of anything other than a spontaneous act of mischief. Boys will be boys.

But Billy would not get off scot-free. His assigned judge and jury, Mother Superior, called him into her office with the job of meting out some order of appropriate punishment. Despite his tenable innocence, Billy feared the worst. He hoped he would get off with life and not have to face the electric chair. Paranoia running deep, he was willing to plea-bargain.

"What do you have to say for yourself, young man?"

"I'm sorry. Is Sister Bernadette alright?"

"She will be fine. She's getting some rest. Young man, I know exactly what you said and I don't approve of your language. But I met your father."

"You met my father?"

"Your parents came in yesterday. Your mother loves you very much, Billy. You shouldn't embarrass her. She was very upset."

"And my father?"

"Generally men don't drink beer in my office when they come to talk to me. That and put their feet up on my desk. Have a nice summer. Next year, *please* try to behave yourself."

The Secret Life of Penguins

Word continued to spread. Billy was a local legend. The kids loved both his real and imagined antics. The false rumor of his attempted if unsuccessful murder continued to be viral in his school. He was a 10-year old anti-hero.

The nuns also talked and commiserated among themselves.

Judgment was passed. The verdict was in.

The nuns didn't like this little smart aleck at all.

Except for one.

That was his new 5th grade teacher Sister Mary Felicia.

As the new school year began, Billy conscientiously heeded Mother Superior's suggestion. He actually behaved himself.

It wasn't nearly as much fun, but he wanted to avoid at all costs the possibility of his parents being called in again. Not for his own sake. But for the sake of anyone who might end up having to meet his father.

No one deserved that.

Not hardened gang leaders and drug pushers.

Not bank robbers and child molesters.

Not even Nazi war criminals.

Certainly not these innocent if ridiculous women of the cloth.

It was a matter of conscience, a moral choice for the ethical treatment of penguins.

He was at last beginning to understand them. He understood they meant well. It really blew his mind that they had sacrificed the chance to get married and have children in order to serve God. At the same time, the whole proposition of dressing up the way they did and wasting their lives trying to teach someone like himself seemed silly and masochistic — not that he knew the word masochistic. He decided that whatever was going on, he could respect it even if he couldn't relate to it.

This meant that even if he didn't feel their pain, he didn't want to feed it. Subjecting them to his father would be like throwing gasoline on the fires of their self-inflicted suffering.

He wanted no part of it.

Maybe he was getting soft in his old age. Gosh, he was 10! Where did all those years go?

The immediate upshot was that he wasn't at all tempted to run Sister Mary Felicia through the usual Billy Green gauntlet of amusing stunts and games.

Plus, there was something very different about her. He actually found it easy to behave himself with her.

Right off, she was very young, especially compared to all of the other nuns who appeared in his pre-pubescent eyes to be well beyond the century mark. Her youth was a surprise bonus.

But that wasn't the whole story. It wasn't just her age. While that set her apart, it didn't account for the enormous, growing fascination he was feeling.

Though he couldn't quite put it into words, he eventually sensed what made her so unique. And why he didn't need to be a 'bad boy' in her class to enjoy it. Why he never got bored or restless. Why his mind didn't wander and a need to be funny rush in to fill the vacuum of airless pedagogy his prior teacher nuns dully exuded into the classroom.

What Billy started to notice was that there was always a *certain something* in the way Sister Mary said and explained things — some little twist, some quirky nuance, some tongue-in-cheek, subtle hint of an inside joke — that he had never encountered before. It was as refreshing as it was a strange new experience.

He was intrigued.

He wanted to know more.

One day after the final bell had rung and it was time to go home, Billy remained in his seat after the other kids had cleared the room.

"Yes, Billy. Do you have something on your mind?"

"Sister Mary, I was wondering … are you sure there's a God?"

"Why do you ask?"

"Well …" Billy gestured with both hands and head in a sweep that took in the school and church grounds. "… there's all this here. Isn't it kind of pointless if there isn't a God?"

"All of this doesn't need God to exist. It only needs a church. The Catholic

Church."

"So do you believe in God?"

"You're a very smart little boy. Maybe too smart. Look at me Billy. I am wearing a habit, this is my crucifix, and here at my waist is the rosary given to me the day I took my vows, consecrating my life as a bride of Our Lord and Savior Jesus Christ. What do you think?"

"All of that doesn't need a God. It just needs a church. Just like you said."

Sister Mary Felicia smiled. It wasn't the contrived, patronizing, or manipulative smile of the other nuns. It was the sweet smile of a young lady enjoying herself because she had stumbled on a 10-year old boy with a bright, inquisitive, combative mind. The smile of a young lady who maybe had met her match.

"It's very difficult to explain. There are things and we can't imagine how they got here — planets, stars, animals, ourselves. So we say God created the world. There are mysteries which we can never solve. So we say God knows all and works in mysterious ways. There are times when we feel isolated, unclaimed, unloved. So we say God protects and loves us — we who live out the mysteries of Heaven and Earth, who wander through the world he has created."

"Sister. When I go home and look at my father, I find it hard to believe there is a God."

"Billy. I want you to know that you are always welcome to talk to me. Perhaps … perhaps as we eventually get to know one another better, I can answer your questions more freely."

"I would like that, Sister Mary."

Billy left feeling like he had a friend.

And talk again they did.

The months rolled by and they talked and talked. There was no particular order or agenda. But nothing was off-limits. They would discuss whatever Billy wished to talk about.

Usually, he just remained in his seat after the last school period bell. Sister Mary would continue sitting at the table at the front of her classroom, making a few final class notes.

"Yes, Billy?"

"I've been reading about the Crusades."

"So what do you think?"

"I think they really sucked!"

She couldn't help but let out a giggle.

"The Popes said they were going to war to convert the pagans. But that wasn't it at all."

"That's very true. They wanted to reclaim some of the holy sites that had been taken over by the Muslims. Places like Jerusalem, Bethlehem and Gethsemane. The Holy Lands."

"Then they were no different than the Romans. The Popes just wanted land, more power. I don't think it had anything to do with God or religion. They killed thousands of innocent people. They chopped off heads. They hung their naked bodies like slaughtered cattle. They even ate some of them. The people they killed weren't all pagans. Most were Muslims and Jews, people that believed in God. Christians were Jews before they became Christians."

"Awful things happen, Billy. Even in the name of God."

"But there were over twenty crusades. Millions died. Many of them women and children. Most of the warriors went into it blindly, just wanting to serve God and the Church. Thousands of soldiers were slaughtered. Sacrificed for nothing."

"They gave their lives for what they believed in. Only God can judge right and wrong."

"How did God feel about the Children's Crusades? 30,000 children out of France and 50,000 out of Germany. A lot of them were sold as slaves in the lands they were trying to liberate, all in the name of the Church. Many starved to death along the way. 3,000 drowned when their ships sank. They were my age. Not just boys. Little girls too. I read all about it."

"Sometimes, you have to look at the whole picture. Over many centuries. Over many lives. It's about the greater good. The total good far outweighing the total bad."

"It's kind of hard to think about anything but the blood and the suffering and the deaths."

"Most of the nuns here have never thought about any of this. But I have. I know all about it. It's horrible. It makes me feel ashamed, Billy. At the same time I also know the Church does some wonderful and amazing things."

"But it does really terrible things."

"The Church saved me, Billy."

"You're only one person."

"That's not enough for you?"

His mini-rant came to an abrupt halt.

He was embarrassed and trapped by what must have appeared as callousness. He didn't want to have to answer her. No, in truth it wasn't enough. One person versus millions?

At the same time, he was sure glad that she was there with him. However the Church had saved her and made this new exciting friendship possible, he was grateful. Maybe he couldn't put it into words but the feeling was certainly there. How incredibly important this renegade nun had become to him! Thank God for this quirky woman dressed like a penguin who was taking the time to talk to him, be with him, and actually let him be himself, say what was on his mind.

"I'm really glad you're here."

"And I'm glad you're here too, Billy. God bless you."

One time they went to a city park not far from the school. As now was the established routine, Billy had remained after the last bell. But it was such a beautiful day, Sister Mary suggested they go for a walk and enjoy the new spring air and listen to songs of the birds which had been silent over the winter months.

They ended up playing on the swings, then sitting under a maple tree which was showing the first few buds of the new season.

"Sister Mary, I don't get the whole Pope thing. He just seems like an regular man to me. And some of the things he says sound pretty stupid."

"Yet we are supposed to believe he speaks directly with God and we should listen to every word he says as if it was spoken by God Himself. Right? Is that what bothers you?"

"Not only that. But some of the Popes were horrible men. They were serious sinners."

"My goodness! What've I been teaching you?" She laughed at her own joke.

"This is just some stuff I found out on my own. I don't think you want to hear this."

"Like Pope John XII? The Catholic Church's own 10th Century Hugh Hefner?"

Billy looked confused. "Who's that?"

"The Playboy Magazine guy."

"My dad used to drool over that magazine. Right in front of my mom. Probably still does."

"Horrible Popes. Hmm? I could probably name a few more."

"Do you know about Pope Clement VI? He had mistresses and prostitutes."

"Billy! What do you know about these things?"

"Only what I read about, Sister Mary. But it's pretty easy now to find out about this stuff. It's on television. In magazines. My dad rents these movies, too. I'm not supposed to know. But I do. I read that Pope John XIII had a daughter and he raped her."

"I think it was John XII that was the rapist. He did that to a lot of very young girls including his sisters. It gets confusing because he was John XIII's father. But John XIII killed most of his relatives, including his mom. And he had 45,000 prostitutes working for him in Rome. He made an enormous fortune that way. Finally, some jealous husband killed him after he found out that John XIII had slept with his wife."

"See, Sister Mary. Thirteen is a very unlucky number. Even for the Catholic Church!"

"The point is, Billy — and you have to promise you will never tell anyone I said this …"

"I promise."

"The point is that I too think they are just men. They do the same stupid things men do all of the time everywhere. They succumb to temptation. They sin. I especially don't believe they are any different than any of the rest of us in terms of talking directly to God."

"Do you talk to God?"

"We don't seem to be on speaking terms. He must be very busy. I don't hear from Him."

"I take that as a 'no'."

"You may take that as a 'no'. I do not talk to God personally. But neither does the Pope. And in terms of their infallibility, I seriously doubt it."

"What's infalli … I don't know that word."

"Infallibility. It means they can't make mistakes, at least in terms of Church doctrine. It's all tied together. They get the word directly from God. God does not lie or play games. Therefore what the Pope says is absolutely true. That's infallibility. Like I told you, Billy. You never heard me say this. But I don't

28

believe it for a minute. The Popes have made countless bad calls and they still do. They may be even more fallible than the rest of us, since they believe they're actually talking to God on high. That would make anyone crazy."

"Sister Mary. When I grow up, could you stop being a nun so I can marry you?"

"Are you proposing to me, Billy Green? Let me think about it. How old are you?"

"Ten."

"Okay. So I have a few years. I'll let you know. Promise. That is, assuming you don't meet some beautiful girl who steals your heart and breaks mine."

They both started giggling. Sister Mary was laughing so hard she pulled a handkerchief from the long sleeve of her habit and wiped her eyes. Or maybe she was actually crying.

"Like the adults always say on TV, I can't believe we're having this conversation."

"I can't either, Billy. I can't either."

Finally one day, Sister Mary came around to answering the very first question Billy had asked her. The one that had initiated their special friendship. The one about whether she believed in God. It certainly took quite a bit of doing. But Sister Mary Felicia in the end finally admitted she was an atheist.

This was a secret she had promised herself she never could or would divulge. It was too shocking and totally against everything which she symbolized as a nun. Obviously, if anyone in the ranks of the Church itself found out, that would be the end of her sacred vocation. She would be immediately booted out and would probably face excommunication by Papal edict. It had taken many months of after-school chats for her to finally feel comfortable enough to open up to Billy and for him to finally find out what she really believed and exactly what made her tick.

What a story!

She had started her preparation to become a nun right out of high school. The bitter truth was, Loyola Marymount University in Los Angeles, CA — where she received her degree — and the Dominican Nuns of Corpus Christi Monastery — the novitiate where she eventually took her vows — were battered-woman shelters for her. She had nowhere else to turn.

Sister Mary Felicia back then was Anna Marie Fontana. And her father beat and raped her from the time she reached puberty. She had to have three abortions by the time she finished high school. No matter how much she pleaded with her counselors at school, no one listened. No one would believe her. Her father was a rich entrepreneur, a magnate in the garment import business, the highly regarded CEO and Chairman of the Board for three different privately-held corporations, supplying chain stores and malls across America with fad teenwear manufactured in China, India, Italy, Greece and Turkey. More importantly, he was a generous benefactor for the elite private school that Anna attended in their hometown of Greensboro, North Carolina. There was even a building named for him on campus — the Fontana Home Economics Building.

Anna couldn't even look to her mother for protection. Her mom had to have known what was going on. But she turned the blind eye of an alcoholic society woman, who could not risk the possibility of a scandal tarnishing the queenly status and high-society prestige she enjoyed in her country club circle.

Finally Anna found asylum. From the day she began college at Loyola Marymount till the present, the comforting arms of the Catholic Church became Anna's surrogate mother and a safe refuge from her father's carnal rampages.

Anna's parents on the surface were extremely proud. They milked the fact among their upper crust friends, many of whom were Catholic, that their daughter had chosen to walk a sacred path of spiritual dedication.

Under the sugar-coating and saccharine smiles, it was another story. Her mother was just plain glad to get rid of her, deeply relieved she would no longer be in the house, having long feared it was just a matter of time before the lid blew on her husband's incestuous behavior. Her father was really pissed that the tight, clean little cunt he had come to relish was no longer his for the taking. He'd probably have to go back to tracking down underage teen prostitutes.

To Anna's immense relief, her parents never attempted to visit her during her preparation for nunhood, or her two years as a novice. Now they had no idea where she was or what she was doing. Sister Mary requested that her location be kept secret.

"Now you know things about me that no one else in the world knows, Billy."

Billy then likewise opened up and finally shared all the gory details of living with his own bloated, belching, farting, beer gulping, whale carcass of a father. Sister Mary always listened with concern and a compassionate glint in her eyes. This time as Billy talked about his dad, she deferred to his painful candor with a knowing and sympathetic silence.

"So now, Sister Mary, you also know all about me. But there's still one thing I'm very curious about. I think it's the very first question I ever asked you."

"About whether I think there's a God? That one?"

"Yes, Sister. That's the one."

"Billy. If there were a God, things wouldn't be this way for us, now would they?"

"Sister Mary, you are cooler than Madonna. Way cooler."

Billy's year with Sister Mary as his teacher finally ended, but after he had moved on to the 6th grade he still regularly went back and visited her. At least once a week. Often more. Their conversations ranged from the philosophical to the bizarre to the silly.

"What if there is life on other planets? But the aliens are nothing like us."

"Have you looked around? There seem to be some right in this school. And I don't just mean the students."

She was as unflappable as he was persistent in his pursuit of an intimate knowledge and thorough understanding of all things nun — and all things Sister Mary.

"Sister, what do you wear under your habit?"

"A neoprene wetsuit. You can't be too careful. There is always the possibility of a tsunami wiping out all of North America."

They met on the spontaneous playground of their imaginations.

"Hey Sister Mary, do you ever want to climb Mount Everest?"

"Why Billy, I already have."

"Wow! Was it hard?"

"The tough part was swimming from here to India, then walking 4000 miles in a two-piece bathing suit to get to Nepal. After that, Everest was a snap."

"I know what you mean. Holding my breath all the way to the moon was pretty tough. Then I get there and find out there's no air up there. I thought I was going to blow a holy gasket getting back."

Often their discussions still got very heavy. One day — this was the final month of his 6th grade, after which he would no longer be attending St. Jerome's, though he didn't know that at the time — they talked for over two hours about all of the innocent people who had recently died in the bombing of Iraq by the U. S. under the leadership of President George H. W. Bush, then about the millions of innocent people who had died in the two World Wars many years prior. Somehow that segued into reiterating how unconditionally they both hated their respective fathers. Perhaps they held their fathers responsible, each in his own distinctly cruel way, for selfishly wreaking so much havoc on the lives of others, just like the men who waged wars and slaughtered so many defenseless civilians. They sat and cried for the longest time.

It never failed to astonish Billy how close they had become, how easy it was to talk to Sister Mary, how open they had become with one another. After all, he was just going on twelve. And she was … well, he had never asked her. But she was a lot older. At least twenty. Twenty five? Wow!

Billy had over the last couple years developed an innocent but deep affection for this strange and wonderful woman of God. It was his first schoolboy crush. Except it went way beyond a crush, which is usually as meteoric in its onset as it is in its plunge to the dull ennui of fling burnout. Billy felt feelings he had never felt before. Not mother love. Not pet love. Not bicycle love or superhero love. Not a love anyone else had probably ever felt before.

What Billy felt was nun love. For one very special nun.

Though it was well beyond the grasp of his socially immature mind, if he were a little older and if she didn't dress so funny, he might ask her out for a date, whatever that was. And do whatever you did on dates. Sounded like a good idea.

It didn't escape notice that Sister Mary was spending a lot of time with Billy. She was in due course called in by Father Bartholomew McAllister himself, to explain and account for her actions.

"Now it's my understanding that the boy's not even in your class now."

"I had him in my class last year."

"Isn't this kind of unusual then, Sister?"

"He's a very unusual boy."

"That's what I hear."

"None of the other sisters like him. I don't know why. But they seem to think he's trouble. He likes to ask a lot of questions. He's very bright … and … and challenging. No one else seems to understand Billy."

"And you do? You've decided to take him under your wing."

"I have, your blessed Grace. He's very special and I try to give him … I give him … he's my little friend and as I have watched him grow and blossom academically, I have shared with him all that I can as a teacher, to foster the development of his beautiful mind."

"Just be careful, Sister Mary. Make sure that it is just his soul you nurture. To walk the path of our Savior and to understand and honor the divine laws of the Holy See, that is your main function here, you know."

"I understand, your Grace. You would be proud."

It was a sad day when Billy had to leave St. Jerome's. He wanted to continue on to the Jr. High School there, but times were getting tough in the auto industry. His father had been laid off sporadically over the past couple years, and in contract negotiations, at the behest of the Big 3 corporate chiefs the union had succumbed to sob stories of market loss to the Japanese and agreed to significant wage cuts. Moreover, the cost of school tuition and supplies at St. Jerome's had gone up almost every year he had attended. The simple fact was, Harold and Irene just couldn't afford for Billy to keep going to a private parochial school. Next year it was off to Troy Jr.-Sr. High.

Billy would miss St. Jerome's. He had excelled academically even as his notoriety had built to critical mass among the less-than-amused nuns. Billy felt it had been a sporting good time but unfortunately now it would end.

Most of all, he would miss Sister Mary Felicia and all the special attention she had given him over the past three years. He would dearly miss their rare and extraordinary friendship.

He finally told her the last time they had met, just a few days ago, that he wouldn't be coming back. Today was the final day of school and time to say good-bye.

He waited outside her classroom and when he was sure all of her students were gone, entered. She was sitting at the table in the front of the class staring at her hands, which appeared to be folded in prayer. It was obvious that she was expecting him.

"So young man … summer vacation and then off to the big public school."

"Yes. That's it. I just wanted to thank you. You're my best friend … ever."

"Would you come with me, Billy? Just for a minute."

Sister Mary stood up and they walked out of her classroom down two doors to a small combination office and library, used for parent-teacher conferences and special meetings. All of the walls were lined with shelves of books and there were no windows. She closed and locked the door, then switched on a small desk lamp. It shined brightly on the desk but lit the rest of the room with only a soft subtle ambient glow.

Sister Mary Felicia turned, then put her hands squarely on Billy's shoulders and … kissed him.

He stood there, arms at his side, rigidly upright, at a loss what to do next.

His first impulse was to pull away. But a little voice in his head told him to just go with it. So their lips remained pressed together. Then he started to feel, very slowly at first, the soft, luxuriant caress of her tongue against his lips. He allowed them to part a bit and now she gently explored his tongue with hers. Then he felt the delicate wet pleasure of her mouth drawing on his with a beautiful caressing motion that he wished could go on forever.

Something else completely unprecedented happened in that moment.

A warm firm urge built in his pants. He was not old enough for a solid erection but what he did feel was a gentle hardening which spread a pleasurable longing from between his legs through his entire body, a longing which begged for something more, a nebulous urge he could not even begin to grasp. It was a warm, agreeable, anxious but unsatisfied craving, a promise of secret delicacies.

It felt really good.

Finally, Sister Mary pulled away. Her eyes were still closed. She opened them and smiled. A single tiny tear ran down her left cheek.

"Good-bye, Billy."

And that was Billy Green's first kiss.

Mom and Apple Pie

Billy's mom couldn't believe how fast her little boy was growing up. It only seemed like yesterday that she had brought him home from the hospital and lay him down in his bassinet for his first night at home.

She loved him as only a mother could love a child and then some. Billy was the most important thing in her life. Whereas so much of her tedious, lackluster days as a housewife and as the spouse of an ignorant, indifferent man gave her no satisfaction or joy, her son gave her hope and the promise of making a difference in the world. Maybe reaping some small rewards during her time here on Earth. While she was not fanatically religious, she did attend mass every Sunday, so there was also the expectation that being a good mother would be viewed favorably by God and she might achieve good standing in the afterlife as well.

So while Harold plodded absentmindedly and mechanically down the flat narrow path of his empty routine life, almost completely oblivious to her and Billy, Irene devoted her days and her life to safeguarding and nurturing her one and only child.

Even as a toddler, she constantly talked to him, read him stories, taught him songs, danced little awkward dances with him, and bought him toys, books, games, and little mister clothes.

Now that Billy had become a teenager — only a few months ago he had turned thirteen — the challenges were entirely different, but she was there, up to the task. Within the limits of her imagination and the family budget, Billy had all that she could provide.

Not that Harold understood or approved.

"What is all this crap? Do I look like a fucking millionaire?"

"Harold, don't be a curmudgeon. He's our son. You want the best for him, don't you?"

"I didn't have any of this and I turned out just fine. You're spoiling him rotten. He's going to grow up thinking the world owes him a favor."

"Yes, Harold. You turned out to be a real gem."

"Fuck you, Irene."

To his credit, Billy was quite the opposite of his father's scurrilous depiction.

He always let his mom know how much he appreciated her attention and generosity. He never displayed one iota of that sense of entitlement that seems to plague children from toddling to late adolescence, often right on into adulthood. The linguistic transition from 'mommy mommy' and 'daddy daddy' to 'gimme gimme' never happened. Billy never asked for *anything*, which only increased the pleasure his mother got from giving to him.

Irene always tried her best to be a devoted wife and homemaker, but lacking even the barest appreciation or even acknowledgement by her husband for all the time she spent keeping the house tidy, his clothes neat and clean, preparing the meals, paying the bills, bringing him his beers in the evening as he lay slumped in the La-Z-Boy in front of the TV — lacking any sign other than an occasional grunt that he was aware she even existed — each and every morning she knelt down and said a prayer of thanks that she had a son like Billy.

Of course, during the weekdays while Billy was at school, she had the house to herself. Then, maybe around 3 or 4 o'clock Billy would come home and they would talk, go over his schoolwork, sometimes go to the park or the zoo, go bowling or ice skating. Or she would take him to a department store and they would shop.

It was quite remarkable that Billy and his mom spent so much time together, considering that most boys his age were typically hanging out with their friends, playing pickup games of baseball or basketball, skateboarding or riding their bikes around town.

In the evenings and on weekends, they worked around Harold, like you would a big box of old discarded clothes that was on its way to the Salvation Army. Usually ornery and mute, he would flop down, sitting for hours in a pose of dull complacence, a blob of blank isolation, glazed eyes locked on the TV screen, sucking on a Pabst Blue Ribbon beer, more often than not cramming handfuls of barbecue potato chips or Cheetos into his mouth. Except for the gruff recurrent *"Irene, need some more suds here"*, usually the only sounds that issued from him were the sputtering butt-flapping honks of him flatulating.

Sunday evening was special and the occasion of Irene's big, entirely futile, attempt to get them to resemble and act like a real family. She always prepared what was by their standards a great dinner, usually consisting of a tossed salad, meatloaf, mashed potatoes with lots of butter and gravy, and then dessert. The meal always opened and closed with two of Billy's favorites. For starters, Irene prepared deep fried chicken wings with spicy barbecue sauce on the side. Then to close out the meal in grand style, she baked her own custom deep-dish apple pie. The upper crust was sprinkled with brown sugar and raisins, and as a bonus treat she dished out huge slices of the magnificent pie with scoops of caramel-vanilla ice cream melting on top.

There was always plenty for second helpings.

"More pie, Harold?"

He patted the mucilaginous bloated belly of a man-pregnant-with-child, hovering above his belt like a massive lard-filled beach ball.

"I'm on a diet, Irene. You know that. I'm gonna look like Brad Pitt any day now."

His horse laugh sputtered raucously, then mutated into a deep lung-purging cough, replete with oyster-sized gobs of mucous, which he unceremoniously wiped on the table cloth.

"Can I have some more, mom? You make the best apple pie in the world."

Harold sneered and then gave Billy a sharp but painless slap on the head.

"You've really turned into a brown-nosing little shit, you know that?"

"Mom makes good apple pie, dad."

"But she fucks like Grandma Moses."

Billy sat silently. He couldn't let his father get to him. Nor could he let the vile man get the last word. He didn't quite understand what his father had just said. But he knew it was cruel and meant to hurt his mom.

"You know what Sister Mary Felicia used to tell me at school?"

Billy held up in front of him the last forkful of apple pie from his plate.

"Always count your blessings."

Billy's father stood straight up from his chair, and with one burly shove upended the table, strewing the dishes and silverware across the room and sending Billy sprawling. Then he went into the living room, grabbed the remote and tuned in to the tail end of a baseball game. The Tigers were playing the White Sox at Comiskey Park.

Irene was leaning against the kitchen counter with her face in her hands, quietly crying.

Billy started picking up the broken dishes.

Sunday evening dinner was always very special.

Tonight was no exception.

The apple pie was excellent.

Mr. Rogers and His Dancing Puppets

There was one thing Irene couldn't provide for Billy.

That was a real father.

A father that loved his son.

A father that took joy in his son.

A father that was proud to be a father.

A father that took time to do father-son things.

A father who Billy could look up to as someone special.

Mr. Rogers had lived in the neighborhood for as long as anyone could remember. He was in his early fifties and had worked as a union electrician on commercial buildings his entire life. He was a model neighbor, kept his house in tip top shape, and was often seen working on his yard during the spring and summer months, keeping his perfect lawn trimmed and free of weeds, planting and tending to the copious flowers and several fruit trees in his yard. Anyone on a stroll by his property was greeted with a charming smile and a tip of his Detroit Tigers baseball cap, or a friendly wave. He was an avid bowler and could be seen returning every Friday night, dressed in his yellow electrician's union league shirt, a bowling bag in one hand and his bowling shoes swinging in the other.

In some ways, he was a very typical man, blending in and not particularly distinctive in appearance, working class bland in his styleless clothes and bargain haircut. He was of average height and build, had grayish eyes, gray-flecked brown hair, thinning enough to hint at the onset of male-pattern baldness, and was certainly cordial, but not overly gregarious.

There was one thing, however, that set Mr. Rogers uniquely apart from just about anyone in the suburb of Troy and probably all of Detroit itself, something which made him a popular, if not legendary figure among all of the children who knew about it. Mr. Rogers was a master puppet maker, and on his basement walls hung a fairytale cast of perfectly crafted characters from all of the stories the children had grown up hearing. Of course, there was Pinocchio and Howdy Doody, superstars of puppetry who were actually puppets. But also looking down from their respective places on the long wall above Mr. Rogers' workbench were Mickey and Minnie Mouse; the Lion, Tinman and Scarecrow from Wizard of Oz; Hansel and Gretel; the Three Little Pigs; Aladdin; Daffy Duck; the Three Musketeers; Snow White and her Seven Dwarfs; Robin Hood; Santa Claus; even Superman, Batman, the Marlboro Man, and Winston Churchill. It was a dazzling display, and frankly most all the kids found it almost disconcerting to stand there as the audience for such an eclectic array of realistic-looking fairy tale, cartoon, iconic, and comic book characters.

Only on rare occasions did Mr. Rogers invite anyone into the sacred chamber of his woodworking shop. But when he did, it was a very special occasion indeed. The by-invitation-only, hand-picked children, at most three or four at a time, would be treated to a show they would talk about for months.

Mr. Rogers, applying his vast knowledge of everything electrical, had put together a complex motor-driven robotic array, which he could manipulate with a set of levers and switches giving him total control of the puppets. He could have them perform intricate synchronous movements, could entirely by himself make them gesture, dance, and even do acrobatics more convincingly and with greater precision than any team of the best puppeteers could manage.

Mr. Rogers and his dancing puppets. That's what the kids would talk about for hours on end.

Billy had actually seen one of Mr. Rogers' shows once, but that was several years ago and his memory of the occasion, while still precious, had blurred with time. He was maybe six at the time, so it had been almost seven years ago.

Because of a teacher conference, school let out early today, and Billy was on his way home. He took the long way, taking a lazy stroll through the park with its adjoining baseball diamond, where eight or nine of his schoolmates had met to scrub together an impromptu game. As he approached the yard of the Rogers house, he was surprised to see Mr. Rogers standing near the front edge of his lawn, looking at a curbside tree which had fallen on bad times and appeared to be nearly dead.

"Hello, Mr. Rogers. You're home from work early today."

"And it looks like you're home early from school, young man. Or are you playing hooky?"

"I burned the school down. The heat was too intense to roast marshmallows. So here I am."

"A little joker, you are. Looks like this tree has had it. Time to bring out the chain saw."

"Looks like it."

"I could use some lemonade. You want to join me? Do you like lemonade?"

They went to the screened porch. Billy sat down. Mr. Rogers went inside, then returned with two glasses of the icy drink in hand.

"Yessiree. Lemonade sure hits the spot."

"Thanks, Mr. Rogers."

They sipped in silence. Mr. Rogers emptied his glass first.

"So, have you ever seen what I have in my workroom down in my basement, uh … I don't think I know your name."

"Billy. Billy Green. My mom is Irene and we live in that blue house at the end of the street. You can see it from here."

"You don't have a father?"

"Oh right. Sometimes I forget. His name is Harold. But you probably have never seen him. He works a lot and when he's at home doesn't come out much. Our yard is a mess. Not like yours. You really take nice care of your place. You must really like gardening, Mr. Rogers."

"I do I do. But getting back to—"

"Your puppets? Oh yes, I saw them a long time ago. Maybe I was six or seven. Don't you remember me?"

"Of course. Yes, I do." Looking up and down Billy's still-growing body. "You've changed a lot. You're becoming a young man."

"Do you still make them dance?"

"Yes, I still make them dance. Many other things, too. I've taught them lots of new tricks. Say, I'm just guessing, but I'll bet you'd like to see for yourself. Come on. Just bring your lemonade and follow me. I haven't been down there for a couple weeks. It'll be fun."

Mr. Rogers led Billy through the kitchen and down the steep stairs to the basement. He unlocked a door at the bottom and turned on the lights. Billy's eyes widened as he took in the sights. It was more spectacular than he remembered.

Mr. Rogers went to the far end of the room, flipped a couple switches and simultaneously the cast of twelve or so puppets which were slumped in a line the length of the workbench, sprung to attention. An array of small powerful stage lamps, pointing from a rack hung on the ceiling, also came to life and flooded the puppets with light.

Mr. Rogers then started playing with the levers and pushing the buttons on a control box, and the puppets responded accordingly. Soon they were leapfrogging back and forth, performing somersaults, and stacking themselves in a cheerleader pyramid. The brief show climaxed with the collapse of the pyramid and the puppets rolling back to an upright position, all at attention, saluting.

Billy was awe-struck.

Mr. Rogers quietly laughed — apparently he still got quite a bang out of seeing the show, though he himself had created it — then pulled up a stool and sat next to Billy. Mr. Rogers put his arm around him and beamed a friendly, paternal smile.

"You liked that, eh? Pretty good, if I do say so myself. More lemonade, Billy?"

"No thanks, Mr. Rogers. That was amazing! Really amazing!"

That sat in silence for a few minutes, Billy studying the puppets, Mr. Rogers with his hand still on Billy's shoulder.

"You know the legend of King Arthur and his knights, don't you, Billy?"

"The Knights of the Roundtable? Sure I do. We had them a little in school. But I've read a lot about them."

"The Knights loved King Arthur. They were very loyal to their king."

"They fought and died for him."

Mr. Rogers got up and moved several of the puppets out of the way. Then he flipped a few switches dimming all of the stage spots but two, which continued illuminating the very center section of the bench.

"I have a very special show that no one else has ever seen, Billy. Would you like to see it?"

"Wow! I sure would."

From a cabinet off to the side of the workbench, Mr. Rogers took out two incredibly lifelike figures. One puppet already sitting on a throne, and another standing upright. It was King Arthur and a very handsome knight, both dressed elegantly in their dress armor.

He then stood on a stool and pulled down some custom pulleys and wiring that had been tucked up in the rigging on the ceiling. These he attached to King Arthur and the Knight, then sat back down on his stool.

"I think you're really going to enjoy this, Billy."

When he flipped a few more switches, the two figures came to life and medieval music started playing over the speakers — formal processional music with recorders and a pianette.

The knight circled with courtly grace, stopping periodically to bow to the king. The king formally bowed back and smiled from his throne — actually smiled! Billy had no idea puppets could do that.

The knight then came over at the feet of King Arthur, genuflected and bent forward in a very deep reverential bow. This brought his face directly into the lap of the king. He remained there for a minute or two as King Arthur with two smooth opposing circular motions, ran his hands over the knight's head and shoulders.

Billy was mesmerized and wondered if King Arthur was bestowing some special blessing on a knight for displaying such humility and loyalty.

When the knight brought himself back upright, Billy saw something but wasn't quite sure what he was looking at. There was now some sort of shaft protruding from King Arthur's lap, a long slender pipe-like shape, the color of flesh.

"The knights loved to show their king how much they admired him and always wanted him to be proud and happy."

Billy was confused.

"But what … what was that … uh …?

He turned to Mr. Rogers and his face flushed with shock.

Billy had never seen an erect penis before, not even a picture of one. Mr. Rogers was slowly and smoothly stroking what appeared to be a long sausage which was sticking out of the front of his pants. He turned to face Billy, reaching with his free hand for the back of Billy's neck.

"Show me, Billy. Just like the knight. Show me how much you love me and my puppets. Come here, now. Put this in your mouth."

Mr. Rogers started to pull Billy's head down into his lap.

"Come on, Billy. Just lick this like it's a delicious lollipop."

Billy swung his arm and broke the grip Mr. Rogers had on the back of his neck, but before he could turn to run, the stronger man's arms instantly sprang back attempting to reassert control. Billy ducked and with his face sickeningly close to Mr. Rogers' pulsing erect penis, shoved at the man's chest as hard as he could. Mr. Rogers went over backwards and Billy heard him groan in pain as he hit the floor. Mr. Rogers then yelled, "You little cocksucker! Come back here!"

Billy was up the stairs, through the kitchen and out the door, faster than he had ever run in his life. He didn't stop to look back until he got out to the street. He still kept running as fast as he could, though there was no sign of Mr. Rogers at the swinging screen door of the porch.

When Billy got home, his mom was in the kitchen. He was still a little out of breath.

"Billy! You're sweating up a storm. How about some lemonade?"

"Not really in the mood for lemonade, mom. I think I'll just lay down for a while and read."

"Suit yourself. I'm off to the supermarket. Homemade pepperoni pizza for dinner tonight!"

Billy spent the rest of the afternoon in his room. Reading was out of the question. He barely noticed the new Xitizen Cain CD that he had playing in repeat-mode on his stereo system.

He couldn't sort it all out. He knew that adults did a lot of things kids didn't do. Things he didn't yet know about. His parents were total prudes when it came to anything about sex. So he really knew very little about it. His mom read a Catholic publication called *Listen, My Son* which was supposed to give him some fundamental insights into the miracle of creation. While it had an abundance of vague and high-sounding language about God's glory and wisdom in creating the special love that is shared by a man and a woman — a special love which Billy sensed would litter the planet with more snotty-nosed Catholic kids — it completely lacked any nuts-and-bolts details about what actually took place. Everything Billy knew about sex he got from the other misinformed kids around him. That usually entailed a lot of snickering and very little useful information.

Nevertheless, what little he did know didn't jibe with what had just happened. The memory of Mr. Rogers' swollen blue-veined member almost made Billy puke. His gut told him there was something very wrong about the whole thing.

Then again, he was just a boy. Maybe this is one of those grown-up secrets which adults finally share with you when you're old enough. Mr. Rogers — at least until today — seemed like a very nice man.

Billy heard his mother call up the stairs. "Billy, time for dinner."

Apparently, the pizza would have to wait for another evening. When Billy came down and took his seat at the table, he discovered his father had nixed the idea and demanded his own preferred grease-soaked fare of pork sausage and fried potatoes with gravy.

Billy didn't have much of an appetite and just pushed the food around on his plate.

"I have a question."

Billy's father didn't seem to hear and just kept on noisily chomping on his sausage and fried potatoes, his mouth wide open for all to see the masticating mulch. But his mom perked up instantly.

"Of course, Billy. You can ask us anything. Is this for school?"

"No, not really. Just something that came up. So ... I was wondering ... well ... uh ... "

"For fucks sake, spit it out or shut up." Harold downed almost a whole glass of beer in one huge gulp, wiping his foamy lips and chin on the back of his shirt sleeve. "More suds here while you're up, Irene."

Billy's mom got up and headed to the fridge.

"Well, I was wondering if a boy should ever let a man, you know, an older person, put his, uh ... thing ... his pee pee thing, like, you know, his penis ... uh ... in the boy's mouth."

Billy's father was in the midst of fork-lifting a huge helping of fatty pork into his cavernous tongue hangar. At first he choked, then gagged, then splooged the entire mouthful of unchewed mushy contents onto his plate and the area of the tablecloth immediately in front of him. He threw his hands into the sky and rolled his head back as if to beseech the Lord for His assistance. Then in one continuous motion he suddenly dropped his chin back on his chest and belched like a walrus. Finally lowering his hands back to the table, he turned and stared at Billy as if he were looking at a disemboweled sheep.

"You want to know if you should ever let a man stick his dick in your mouth? Like sucking his cock? Christ, you're one for the books. Where the fuck did you come up with that?"

"I can't say. It's—"

"You can suck my dick if you want to. Since your mother is too high-falutin. Too prissy and pure to slick lick a little happiness into your father's miserable fucking life. I think you and I can do some business. We'll keep it in the family."

Billy had never ever seen his mother really angry. She was always supremely patient and pathetically submissive. But tonight would make up for hundreds of missed opportunities.

"Harold, you will not talk to our son like that! You are never to use that language again, in my presence or in front of Billy!"

"I say whatever I please, exactly how I feel like saying it." Shaking his head. "Whiny bitch."

He went back to stuffing his face.

Irene started screaming at the top of her lungs.

"No you won't! Never again! Did you hear me, Harold? Never again."

"Whaddya gonna do about it, you feeble-minded cunt? Pee your panties?"

For the first time Billy could remember, his mother made a decision and stood her ground.

She rushed upstairs, hurriedly threw handfuls of hers and Billy's clothes into a suitcase, adding some toiletries, their tooth brushes, and a couple of magazines, then jammed it shut. She grabbed Billy and led him out the door.

"What the fuck! Goddammit Irene! Just where do you think you're going?"

She didn't answer him. She didn't look back. She kept right on going.

Too lazy to bother coming after them or too indifferent to care, Harold just stood in the doorway until they were two houses down the street, then turned and went back in the house, locking the door behind him.

It was a warm night and when they weren't under a streetlight, Billy could see stars.

"Where are we going, mom?"

"I don't know yet, Billy. Don't worry. I'll find us a place to stay."

They stopped at a 7-11 fairly close by. She bought Billy two hot dogs, a bag of Frito's, and a slurpy, then used the coin phone to call a lady she knew from church. They had become pretty close friends and the woman had both an older son in college and a girl two years older than Billy who went to the same school.

"You remember Mrs. Maddox? Suzanna Maddox? She's coming to pick us up."

Mrs. Maddox pulled up in the rescue vehicle, a 1993 Oldsmobile Bravada SUV.

She turned out to be a very kind and accommodating host. Not only did she carry Irene's bag into the house but seemed genuinely pleased to be able to help out in a time of need.

Mr. Maddox was an aerospace engineer at a military tank plant in the nearby town of Warren. He was on travel the majority of time Billy and his mom were there, but the few times he was around, he greeted them with a cordial smile and friendly small talk. Overall he seemed fine with having them as guests.

They ended up staying almost a full week. Irene slept comfortably on a rollaway in the den. Billy was given the vacated room of Daniel, the college boy.

In the next room was Jackie. He had noticed her at school. Who couldn't? She spent more time being counseled and reprimanded for her appearance than the rest of the student body combined. Ratted bleached and dyed hair, ablaze in bold shades of shocking pink and hazardous-material-warning yellow. Thick punked out makeup. Torn, fashionably tattered clothing, all black. Miniskirts over patterned tights or skin-clinging leather jeans. Spiky Barbarella boots. Shiny metal chains dangling everywhere. Walking the halls of Troy Jr.-Sr. High School, she looked like the schizophrenic step-sister of Wendy O. Williams.

Billy spotted her frequently over the short time he stayed with the Maddox's. But it was brief glimpses more like seeing a shooting star than a harvest moon. Usually Jackie was in a hurry, going somewhere, coming from somewhere. Without fail, on the rare occasions she spent any time at home, immediately after arriving she slammed and locked her bedroom door. On would come her stereo and their shared wall would vibrate with the pounding, riot-grrrrl screaming of Bikini Kill or the mad fuzz-bomb guitars of Seven-Year Bitch.

He instantly became a fan. Both of the music and of the girl.

The girl particularly fascinated him. He obsessed over getting to know her. Seeing what made her tick. He finally decided he'd even settle for talking to her just once, merely to say that he had. It was a groupie thing. He was the groupie.

He thought long and hard, then initiated a carefully calculated strategy of charm, which he was positive would kindle an irresistible curiosity in her and get her to open up to him.

It consisted of his smiling cheerfully at her on every possible occasion — passing on the stairs to their rooms, trading places with her to brush his teeth at the bathroom sink, at the kitchen table in the morning where every day she sat carving her omelet into a swastika. He even grinned invitingly at her in the hallway at school on the rare occasions she whipped past him.

Each and every time, his sunny overture received the same inauspicious response. She sneered, laughed, then scowled at him like he was a disease.

So much for making a new friend.

In sharp contrast to the arctic climate surrounding the mutant teenager in the family, the atmosphere of the rest of the Maddox household was thoroughly summery and upbeat. Whether this was normal or temporarily conjured up to lift the sagging spirits of their house guests, wasn't clear. In any case, both Billy and his mom were quite comfortable. They thoroughly enjoyed being there.

Of course, no matter how much they wished it could, this arrangement couldn't last forever. After only a couple days, guilt started to descend on Irene, both about imposing on the hospitality and kindness of the Maddox's, and for abandoning her Harold. She couldn't imagine how he was functioning. He wasn't marginally capable of cooking, doing laundry, setting out his clothes — none of the day-to-day things which keep a person going. His ability in the kitchen appeared to be limited to opening a bottle of beer, and he still relied on Irene to do that. What was going on with him? How was he holding up?

On the fourth day, Irene called him.

"Harold?"

From the instant he heard her voice, he unleashed a tirade of non-stop threats and obscenities.

She immediately hung up on him.

Next day it was the same thing.

On the following evening — their sixth at the Maddox's — Harold and Irene had "the talk".

When she opened the call with her usual "Harold?", instead of yelling, she heard silence. Irene went on to explain how she wanted to come home but there were some changes that had to be made. That she wasn't asking for a lot but what she was asking for was important. Eventually Harold himself started talking. They were on the phone for two hours.

Irene kept insisting that she would come back home under one condition. The condition was non-negotiable. It was that Harold would never ever use foul language in front of either her or Billy again.

It didn't seem like a lot to ask. But for a man who worked in an auto factory, where rarely anything was said which did not include a burst of expletives, for a man who had been in the company of the surly, sordid, and vulgar his entire life, it was like asking him to become a ballet dancer.

"I'll try."

"Trying's not good enough. You have to promise."

"But Irene ... "

"If you want me back, you have to promise."

For the first and only time in their relationship, he relented.

Harold promised to clean up his mouth. Irene promised to come home the next day.

All was forgiven.

Returning home was strange. The contrast to the light and lively Maddox household was sharp and disheartening. Aside from the absence of Harold's usual barrage of expletives and crass sexual references, nothing had changed. They probably never would.

But true to his word, with monumental effort Harold sanitized his otherwise ungrammatical and coarse utterances, of any and all of his usual stock-and-trade profanities. In time he actually started to make light of the whole thing by turning it into a game, rendering the Herculean task a bit more bearable. He'd find both common and off-the-wall substitutions for the foul language he usually used.

"Dagnabbit!"

"Golldang!"

"Gosh darn!"

"Fudge it!!"

"Kiss my ash!"

"That son-of-a-barn."

The substitutions were so completely out of character for him, Harold felt awkward and ridiculous. But on the flip side, the effort brought out an antic side of him, a slight easing of the withdrawal pains he suffered not being able to cuss around the house any longer. It actually ended up providing some unexpected entertainment for the three of them.

It was the first time Billy could remember seeing the slightest hint of a sense of humor in his father. It was very slight but still suggested that under the elephant-thick skin of bitterness which had calloused Harold's heart and cocooned him in an impregnable shell of misery, there was the faint but flickering light of a man who could still feel something, maybe even occasionally smile again.

Sometimes he'd slip up.

"Fuck — I mean fungus — my balls itch."

"Can it, Harold!"

"You could show a little sympathy here. They feel like they've been soaking in taco sauce."

"Harold!!"

Such occasional relapses notwithstanding, the tiny but detectable change in the atmosphere of the Green household was refreshing, even if it offered little hope for any major overhaul of the relationships Irene and Billy had with Harold.

Truly gratifying was that Irene had stood her ground and asserted herself, even if it was only this one time. Whether she would ever again summon the courage to hold Harold in check, and challenge his tyranny of the household, remained to be seen. But this was a good start and at the very least, Irene had discovered that deep inside her somewhere, she had a reserve of strength which she had never known existed.

Something else good came out of all of this.

Really good.

It happened during Billy's stay at the Maddox's. This was on the very last evening before they would end their six-day retreat and return to the bland hell of their own household.

It was a little after 11 pm and Billy was just getting ready to going to sleep. He heard a soft knock at his door but before he could get out of bed to answer, she slipped in and quietly closed the door behind him.

"Alright! A boy in his skivvies. Such a beautiful thing."

It was shocking to see her without her punk paraphernalia and Halloween makeup. She was a very pretty girl. Somehow the pink and yellow hair now just added a playfulness to the lovely features of her face. She was barefoot and only wearing pale blue boxer shorts and a simple white t-shirt, through which Billy could see the tips of her nipples, adding yet another layer to her appeal.

"Jackie … "

"Call me Ripper."

She came over and sat down on the bed next to him. Slowly and delicately she removed his underpants. She reached over and switched off the reading lamp next to the bed stand.

Soon Billy was breathing hard and feeling sensations he had never felt before. He writhed. He pitched. He panted. He groaned. The world exploded.

It was over in less than two minutes.

His breathing calmed and his body relaxed.

"Is your name really Ripper?"

"Are you retarded?"

"I don't get it. Your parents call you Jackie. How many names do you have?"

"There is only one name. I am officially Jackie the Ripper. Don't you forget it! Family calls me Jackie. Friends call me Ripper. See, my fucking loser parents named me Agatha. Agatha! Can you believe it? What would *you* do, toilet breath, if you were named Agatha?"

"Does my breath really smell like a toilet?"

"My god! You are so clueless." She leaned over and licked his cheek and kissed the end of his nose. He detected what he would later in life recognize as the scent of his own semen. "I only said that because I like you so much. I better go before Fred and Wilma find me up here with you. Be a good boy."

"If I was named Agatha I would … "

But she was gone. And tomorrow he would be gone too.

Billy had learned a lot in five or so minutes. For example, the whole thing with Mr. Rogers kind of gelled into some vague understanding of what the man was after. The thought of himself doing that to a man made his stomach queasy.

But having it done to him, even by a seriously demented girl like Ripper, really made sense. It truly rocked! His whole body still tingled with the aftershocks, and he felt — at least right now — a relief, a release, the long-awaited satisfying fulfillment of a warm pleasant longing that had been building in him all this time. Literally for over a year. From all the way back, when sensations he had never felt before spread from his partially erect penis throughout his whole body, as Sister Mary put her hands on his shoulders and leaned her lovely breasts against him — that unforgettable moment when she gave him his first kiss.

This too was another first. A really great first! The first of a lifetime of what would turn out to be thousands of repetitions of a very specific sexual act — one he most definitely would never tire of. Each occurrence perhaps might appear mechanically almost identical to all the others but each would be, in its own way, beautifully unique and without parallel. Each one would carve into his erotic psyche its own distinct and spectacular memory. As had tonight's ...

At age 13 — Billy's first blowjob.

Chapter Two

WING WALKING INTO ADULTHOOD
1996 – 2001

Puberty Never Strikes Twice

Puberty never strikes twice.

If it did, most people would pack it in early, and that would be the end of the human race.

As it was, suicide rates among teens was astronomically high — and this was for the first and only onset of the hormonal reconstruction of little people into big people. Across America, suicide was the third leading cause of death among adolescents, behind accidental injuries and homicide. It was the fourth leading cause of death for children as young as 10. Boys were four times as likely to take their own lives as girls. On the other hand, girls were twice as likely as boys to attempt suicide. So it appeared that the boys just pulled it off better. Besides mental disorders, it was stressful lives and poor communication with parents which were said to be the main factors that drove teens to self-destruct. Between 1970 and 1994, the rate of teen suicide more than doubled.

Life was tough all over. Obviously, a lot of kids took it pretty hard.

Billy had a better toehold than most kids on the treacherous climb. Not that he had a good reason to. Very little preparation had come his way from the adults around him, certainly not from the nuns in elementary school, nor the teachers and counselors in junior and senior high school, and most definitely not from his parents, who he surmised were still trying to figure out the connection between the awkward humping of the early days of their marriage and Billy's appearance on the scene. Billy was sure that his father couldn't spell either 'conflict' or 'resolution'. And his mother — bless her well-intentioned heart — was so downtrodden and overwhelmed by her marriage to a Neanderthal, all of life's wisdom she had accumulated over the years could be summed up in one word:

Help!

Billy was both smart and perceptive. A lot of what he figured out came from watching others — mostly his classmates. With a little empirical surveillance and a lot of patient persistence, he pieced together a pretty adequate roadmap through the minefields of adolescence. It was a process of trial and error, and since he preferred others do the trials and suffer the errors, this amounted to observing the ill-considered wrong turns and misdirected forays of the kids around him.

It always amazed him how anxious they were to share their misadventures and mishaps with anyone who would listen. They would often try to top one another, to see who had done the stupidest things, or who had put themselves in the most embarrassing situations.

"So like my mom comes home early. Like she was supposed to be with my grandmother at like the old folks home. So I'm like completely naked and Donnie here and I are like doing it. Doing _it_! Like what was I supposed to like say? So I say, 'Hi mom. How's grandma?' She like goes bananas! But Donnie here is like so cool. He just says, 'Could we maybe have a little privacy here?' So then, I like really flipped out and started like laughing so hard! Donnie's like really pissed because he wants to like finish. Okay? Then like my mother comes back into the room and like dumps a bucket of ice water on the both of us. Like I thought I was going to like die laughing."

"I finally tell my mom and dad I'm gay. They have no idea what I'm talking about. I mean, we're talking about two people who never watch TV or go to the movies. Both of them sit around all the time reading these religious books. They're these fucked up Christian Scientists, you know? Last year when I almost died from food poisoning they wouldn't take me to the doctor. So I snuck out of my room — I actually climbed out on the roof — so I could go to emergency at Northside General. Anyway, when I brought this guy home and we sat there together — I mean really close together — they still couldn't figure it out. Mom. Dad. Get a fucking clue!"

"The bitch found my diaphragm. 'Hey, mom, what are you doing going through my room anyway,' I say. She says she wants to know what I'm doing with this. Duh! Gee mom, try and guess! So I tell her no way am I gonna get pregnant. So you know what she says? She looks at me and says, 'You're right. I should have used one of those and then I wouldn't be stuck with such a little slut for a daughter!' She called me a slut! And told me I was an accident. Like they never wanted me in the first place. I feel like running away. Or killing them. I hate them! I hate them more than they could ever know!"

"Big fucking deal! I failed trig. But see, my folks have been talking to the neighbors. Which means they find out about the party I had when they were gone. The scumbag narcs told them about the drinking and the police coming. So they decide I'm a teenage alcoholic. Now they want to send me to some mind fuck clinic place in Grand Rapids, wherever the fuck that is, to like dry out. It's run by a bunch ass-lickers from MADD. Ever heard of that? It's mothers against drunk drivers. There's a long-ass waiting list. So until they can get me in there, I'm grounded. I'm in fucking prison, man! I'm so fucking horny. Man, how am I gonna get laid, if I can't even leave my own house?"

Other times, they just wanted to show how wild and crazy and cutting-edge they were. Or how much they knew about sex and drugs and partying.

"So Steve keeps pushing me to try it. Like it seems really ickey to me. But I love the guy, so I do it. He promised not in my mouth. He'd let me know. But he was so turned on, he forgot. I mean, he went crazy! It wasn't so bad. A little slimy. But I really liked doing it. Now he goes down on me. And, let me tell you, _that_ is *so amazing! Listen, girls, like you really gotta try it 'coz you don't have to worry about getting pregnant. And it's really really intense! I mean, <u>really</u> intense!"*

"Dude, we were like really blown away. This was the best shit I've ever smoked. Then I'm talking to this chick and we're feeling real good and I can tell she's diggin' on me. We end up in this closet. It was one of those big walk-in deals. Like I could've lived in there, with the little bit of shit I own. So we're getting down and you won't believe this but right before I came, she stops me. Like I'm so fucking high and I'm ready to explode and she stops me! 'Hey, what gives?'. Like she says, 'You're gonna dig this.' Then she pulls out a straw and a tiny razor blade. She leans over and cuts a hole in my sack. I mean, can you believe this? Then she sticks the straw in and blows up my balls the size of a softball. She says, 'Okay, go for it.' I'm telling you, I'm not making any of this up. As I'm coming, she let's the air out and whoa! <u>Totally</u> fucking unbelievable!! I thought I'd blown a hole in the ceiling!"

"Like we were pretty wasted. And I knew the guys were up to something. They kept wanting us to drink more and more. Like I had to push it away or I would've crashed and burned before we even got started. So we're in this hotel, you know the No Tell Motel by Hazel Park Race Track. What a dump! But we only needed it for a couple hours. There were two queen-sized beds and a shower. What else do you need? (Giggles) Anyway, they turn off all the lights and close the drapes real tight. I'm so drunk the whole room is spinning. It's so dark I can't see anything. Then Jimmie is on top of me. At least I thought it was Jimmie. But something seemed different. And then right as we're getting down to it I realize, this isn't Jimmie. It's Mark! They had traded places. So I start laughing and says, 'Hey Carolyn, just to let you know. Mark is really hot! Hope you're enjoying Jimmie over there.' She was moaning so loud I don't think she heard me. So I guess she was pretty happy with Jimmie after all."

Billy never had any stories to tell. He just listened. Listened and learned. Here's what he learned:

Nothing is sacred.
God is calling in sick.
Everybody is dispensable.
People are in pain.
People will do anything to make the pain go away.
For guys sex is a hammer.
For girls sex is a sponge.
It takes more energy to cry than to laugh.
People create their own heaven.
People create their own hell.
Everybody is both beautiful and ugly.
Everybody is insecure.
Life is a race to the top.

There are no winners.
It is impossible to tell the truth.
People lie to themselves then lie to others.
Freedom is an illusion.
Life is a train to nowhere.
People want to get off the train.
It takes two to tango.
Sex destroys love.
Love destroys sex.
Love makes the world go round.
The world stopped spinning a long time ago.

Billy was no longer the center of attention, as he had been in elementary school. He had withdrawn into his own quiet space.

But everyone knew him. He was the *smart kid*. The one who got good grades. Girls thought he was cute and he had a lot of female acquaintances. Guys ignored him except to sit next to him in class so they could cheat on their tests.

Billy just watched. He hoped what he was seeing was not previews of coming attractions.

So far life had been a bad movie. Lousy actors. No character development. A wandering and pointless plot. A lot of bad camera angles.

It had some promising moments which would then get lost in flatline tedium.

There has to be something better than this.

He watched and waited.

The smart kid.

Stranger in a Strange Land

What could Billy really say about his high school years? What could he actually even remember? He would later look back on them and be reminded of a television which had been detached from the cable feed — visualize a random blur of snow and a wall of hiss.

He could remember a vast and varied cast of characters but nothing of what had happened. Just the day-to-day humdrum of a fish in a bowl with other fish.

He remembered John Fulton, perhaps the most egotistical shit who had ever walked the Earth. Captain of the varsity football, basketball and baseball teams, Class President, Prom King, and President of the Debating Club, this self-absorbed Adonis strutted around the school like he had the deed to the place. Usually Missy Cordakis, his little prize princess, would be right there with him, on his pumped-up arm. Missy was a superstar in her own right. Prom Queen. Head cheerleader. Lead roles in all of the school's musicals and dramas — *Annie Get Your Gun, My Fair Lady, Sound of Music, Grease, The Miracle Worker, Elizabeth The Queen, Romeo and Juliet*. President of both the Glee Club and the National Honor Society. The yearbook's Senior Class Female Most Likely To Succeed. However, senior year their promenade through Camelot came to a screeching halt. John got Missy knocked up and they both quit school. He got a job to support his shotgun bride and their soon-on-the-scene baby daughter. Billy heard years later that they had eventually settled in the ultra-right wing community of Howell, 30 minutes west of Detroit, and now had five kids. Rumor had it, that John Fulton had become a pot-bellied alcoholic, by day selling used cars, and in the evenings reliving his glory days of high school over rounds of boilermakers in the local taverns.

He remembered Bertholdt Buehl, who preferred to be called just Bert. Bert spent the entirety of his high school career perfecting the art of bomb making. His bombs were puny harmless affairs which periodically were heard popping off in some corner of the school or the school grounds. One day, Bert took Billy into his confidence and explained — though Billy hadn't solicited an explanation — that the explosive part of the bomb was the easy part. He was trying to perfect different possible ways of triggering the devices. He had already done detonations from a pay phone, another time using a modified TV remote, and now was adapting the radio controller for a little battery-powered toy jeep. Once he had put the finishing touches on these and other remote detonation devices, he would up the destructive power of his bombs. It wasn't clear what he planned on blowing up, but whenever Billy would later in life read about some terrorist incident, he wondered if Herr Buehl might somehow be involved.

He remembered Marlene Goetz, probably the last person in the United States of America to get polio since the introduction of the Salk Vaccine in the 1950s. Either the vaccine she got was faulty or for some reason did not take. She was rendered paralyzed from the waist down. Marlene preferred not to use one of the compact motorized wheel chairs which had become a common sight. Billy had heard that actually her parents couldn't afford one. Instead she dragged her limp atrophied legs, strapped into bulky metal braces, from one end of school to the other on forearm crutches. Marlene made Billy uncomfortable. Not surprising. Handicappers made all the kids uncomfortable. But Marlene went out of her way — no small feat considering her limited mobility — to run into Billy. She was always too friendly, fizzy and full of foamy optimism. Billy avoided her when he could, which made him feel incredibly guilty, especially when he later found out that just before completing college, Marlene was killed in an automobile accident. Fate has a cruel sense of irony.

He remembered Dennis Culpepper, who held the school track record for the longest time running the mile — 37 minutes 51 seconds. It was not an official timing. His proud and very obese parents brought their own stopwatch and stayed to the very end. The mile was the last event of the track meet and everyone else had gone home. The huge towers of floodlights had been turned off and Dennis completed his run in the dark. He collapsed at the finish line and his mom and dad cheered like he had just won five gold medals in the Olympics. Dennis also probably also held the school record for calorie intake, though no one had actually calculated the total. He typically bought three complete meals everyday at lunch, then went around and gathered any unfinished desserts from the abandoned lunch trays around him.

He remembered Roxanne Whittier, who in 9th grade Billy thought was the sexiest girl on the planet and who was for two years running the object of all of his youthful erotic fantasies. Roxanne didn't have to try. She was just plain beautiful, and hid in the soft folds of her dress, the promise of lustful adventures which would unlock all of the mysteries of love and sex and the things that go on between a boy and girl — exploits about which Billy had not the slightest clue. Roxanne was, unfortunately, way out of his league — Billy wasn't in the same solar system. Even in the 9th grade, she was always seen in the company of older guys. Guys long out of high school. Guys with cars and money and cool clothes, expensive watches and swagger. Billy never heard what happened to Roxie.

He remembered Freddie Roper, aka Dog. Freddie pretty much kept to himself when he could. But when anyone approached him, his bizarre MO was to become a dog. Sometimes he would just bark and pant a bit, other times slip into a full-blown canine persona, down on all fours nipping at the person's ankles. This obviously made him the subject of a lot of ridicule, and the convenient target of the jocks and bullies at school. But he persisted. Apparently, this was how he related to the rest of the human race and he was going to stick with it. Freddie's favorite good times were at high school assemblies, when the entire student body filed into the gymnasium and sat on bleachers which were rolled out from the sidelines to accommodate the thousand plus students. Freddie would slip away unnoticed, then prowl underneath the bleachers. He would sniff around down there and try to look up the skirts of the girls. To open their legs and improve the viewing angle, he would lick their ankles or give a gentle bite to their calves. During a typical assembly, little screams and expressions of panic could periodically be heard from all areas of the bleachers, though more frequently from the freshman section. Freddie liked the young girls. Billy later heard, but had no way of confirming it, that Dog had taken a position as a dean at a private girls academy in Illinois. Bow wow!

Billy remembered Darlene Thomas — aka Bottle Lenses — the straight-A nymphomaniac who wore eyeglasses typically associated with cataract victims. She was a mousy oversexed girl who had provided an awe-inspiring number of his male classmates with their first fuck.

Billy remembered Tom Barc, the most terrifying bully in the Detroit metropolitan area, who if you tried to talk to, would instantly beat the shit out of you. Tom was most certainly headed for a life of serious crime but never reached his full potential. His father, apparently an equally charming individual, killed Tom just after he turned seventeen.

Billy remembered Cathy Louise Baker. You always had to address her by her full name. Even the teachers when they called on her, would say the whole thing. *"Cathy Louise Baker, what do you have for Question #3?"* She ended up being the class Valedictorian, then forgoing college, became a secretary at Chrysler Corporation — the Dodge assembly plant.

Billy remembered Tim Thacker. He was the first person — and it turned out only person — Billy had ever seen masturbate in public. It happened in Mrs. MacIntosh's social studies class, 9th grade. He didn't seem to think anyone would notice. As if a panting guy rubbing his crotch with his eyes rolled up in his head culminating in a huge wet spot spreading down his pant leg is something you might miss. From that day on he was called Thacker the Whacker.

Billy remembered Theresa Karpinski, maybe the strongest woman in the world. She was a stunning beauty and phenomenal athlete — basketball, soccer, gymnastics, track and field. After high school, she moved to Montreal and joined *Cirque du Soleil*, performing high-wire daredevilry and aerial ballet.

Billy remembered Michael Dobrowicz — aka Juicer — who managed to survive five serious car crashes before even reaching his senior year. Three were high-speed head-ons, and police stated unequivocally all five should have been fatal. All were alcohol-related and reflected Juicer's ongoing love affair with beer. When he turned eighteen, facing some serious criminal charges from his most recent demolition of the family station wagon, he escaped the long and short arm of the law by moving to a commune in New Mexico. He disappeared there in a cloud of hashish smoke.

Billy remembered Sally and Sandy Flasher. Identical twins. He couldn't tell them apart and no one else could either. They graduated with the exact same grade point average — 3.42 — and SAT score — 1847. Though kind of scrawny and unattractive in high school, they apparently filled out and fleshed up in college. They became strippers and have a soft-core sex act they perform in Reno. They call themselves *Twin Skin*.

Billy remembered Julian Federer. Julian might have eventually become Billy's best and only real friend. They really hit it off the couple times they talked. But Julian, for reasons Billy never found out, was suddenly pulled out of school and sent to a mental institution. Within six months, as the result of a toxic reaction to heavy doses of anti-psychotics, he had taken his own life — hung himself with the extension cord attached to the reading lamp in his room. Billy cried for someone he barely knew.

Billy remembered them all. But what he couldn't remember was himself having any personal interactions with any of them.

Maybe he never had any.

The Bunker

There was one thing Billy did have. And that was his own room — his bulwark against the incomprehensible, his survival sacristy, his temple fortress at the center of his Universe.

He called it The Bunker.

Now *that* was truly the heart of his world during his high school days — not the classrooms or halls at school, not the gym or the football field, not the mall or the movie theater or the ice rink or church or any other room in the Green family dwelling. His room was the place where life really happened, where he was in charge, where he wasn't just a sidelined spectator for the endless nonsensical whirl that constituted the frivolous, frantic days of his contemporaries at Troy Junior-Senior High School. There alone at his desk or on his bed, Billy was in the thick of the action — the player.

His room was definitely tricked out. His mother took care of that. Great sound system, VCR and 23" television, more books on every conceivable topic than he could ever read, maps of the world and the solar system, a rudimentary

Dell computer, a punching bag, an aquarium, three posters of his favorite female rock singers — Gwen Stefani, Ani DiFranco, Tori Amos — a 1999 *Shipwrecks of the Seven Seas* wall calendar, and a small assortment of pretty tame soft-core girlie magazines.

Yes, good old mom had pulled out all the stops and provisioned him well. Except, of course, the girlie magazines, which he had gotten surreptitiously on his own by looting the bottom drawer of his father's unused workbench in the corner of the garage. Almost everything else, he and his mom had gone out and bought together, or Billy had been turned loose at one of the area shopping malls to select himself. Billy kept his door shut at all times to keep his dad from seeing how "spoiled" he was, though the man's lethargy and palpable indifference to anything that wasn't fermented from hops or didn't have three sports channels, probably rendered the secrecy unnecessary. Nevertheless, Harold most certainly would have gone postal if he had seen the steadily increasing stockpile of life's luxuries and comforts in Billy's room.

Billy wasn't spoiled by all of this. Not at all.

Nor was it all fun and games in the bunker. If there was one word which summed up Billy in the solitude and solace of his room doing his Billy thing day after day, week after week, throughout these formative years, it was ...

Purposeful.

He was a serious young man. Always doing something, head buried in a book, eyes focused on his computer monitor, writing away in one of his dozens of notebooks, scribbling calculations and formulas, head down, working away.

In spite of all of this intellectual intensity and focused energy, there was one question which Billy never seemed able to answer.

To what purpose?

What exactly was the point of all of this searching and finding, curiosity and imagining, thinking and dreaming?

He felt like a jungle explorer who didn't know where he was going or what he was looking for. He was a hunter driven by hunger who had no idea what the prey was or even which direction he was pointed.

Sometimes in his reflective musings, he would come up with plausible pearls of youthful insight, little philosophical bumper stickers which were clever and revealing, but not particularly useful.

Detroit ...

Anywhere but here.

Isolation ...

Loneliness is a prayer for tomorrow.

Integrity ...

The search for truth is a walk through a minefield.

Fate ...

Coincidence is what's left when everything else doesn't happen.

Futility ...

The things that go right are merely the ones that slipped our attention.

And his most frequently repeated mantra and prayer of hope ...

There has to be something better than this. There has to be something better than this. There has to be ... !

But Billy never could come up with that one big hook, the one he could confidently hang his hat on and joyously yell to the world: THIS IS IT, FOLKS! THIS IS WHAT IT'S ALL ABOUT! THIS IS WHAT I'M DOING HERE!

Of course, the more Billy isolated himself in his own corner of the Universe, the more his curiosity about the outside world deepened. As he tried to imagine all of the great unknown that existed outside his room, he fashioned greater and greater expectations for himself and for the future. He wanted to know everything, see everything, and be everywhere. His longing to escape the limited trappings of his pathetic and impoverished life in suburban Detroit, the gnawing hunger inside his belly, the desperate burning in his soul, to escape the aching void of his present circumstances, began to torment him his every waking hour.

The only relief from these smoldering, persistent cravings was sleep and masturbation.

He could never get enough of either one.

At night he never slept more than two hours without being woken by a dream. To add to his frustration, he could never remember his dreams. Back to sleep. Two hours later, he would bolt upright, mind instantly alert and receptive, reaching out into the darkness of his bedroom. Nothing there. Never a clue as to what eyelid movie he had been watching — his nocturnal visions always just out of reach.

Masturbation was great up to a point. That point was usually right at the very end when in his mind's eye he would suddenly see his father's face imposed on his own, his own slim youthful body morphed into the hairy corpulent ape man sitting downstairs zombied out on television and beer. Major bummer. If he did manage to bring his whacking to a happy ending, he couldn't feel all that good about it. It wasn't Catholic guilt as much as familial self-loathing.

There appeared to be no relief in sight.

Not yet anyway.

But he refused to lose hope.

His slumping spirits would just often enough receive a rejuvenating shot of hope. Across the vast range of possible human events, these always came from the same place.

Girls.

Roxanne Whittier would be bent down in front of her locker — his was only a few feet away — and he would glance over and get a mesmerizing view of her beautiful breasts through the unbuttoned top of her blouse. Though she had been reprimanded repeatedly by her ogling counselors and other school fashion police — the men only gave her transparently half-hearted rebukes — Billy could never remember her wearing a bra.

Squeaky-clean but sexy Missy Cordakis, full of nervous energy and bubbling with cheerleader enthusiasm for life, seemed to always be wiggling her legs back and forth under her short pleated skirts. Billy still used the dropped pencil move from the 4th grade at St. Jerome's. With discrete peeks Billy always got an eyeful. Her panties always had cutesy pink teddy bears, the ubiquitous Playboy bunny logo or playful cartoon characters — Mickey Mouse or one of the Simpsons separated by a thin layer of silky cotton from her labia.

Then there was the time Billy was studying in the school library. He looked up and saw that Darlene Thomas, who was sitting across from him but at another table, was looking directly at him. She coyly reached under her dress and slid off a tiny strand of sheer material — he would some day find out it was called a g-string — then sat quietly and wrote a note. She stood up and gathered her books to leave. On the way out, she playfully dropped the note and the dainty underthing in the middle of the book Billy was reading. The note simply said ... *Let's go out sometime for a hot fudge sundae. My treat. Darlene.*

There was a huge body of truth contained in that 1982 Marvin Gaye song, *Sexual Healing*. The power of love — pure or carnal — or the promise of it, cannot be underestimated.

Girls. Girls. Girls.

Everything about girls strapped Billy to a mammoth torturous roller coaster. First plunged into the suicidal depths of futility and despair, then at the last possible second snatched from the lethal jaws of wretchedness and rocketed back to a flower-crested summit, now staring at a distant blurry vista of hope — the flight-of-the-angels ascent purely the result of seeing the tender delicate curve of a young girl's breasts or imagining the soft inviting down between her legs.

This fascination with feminine beauty and female sexuality didn't mean that he was misogynistic or shallow. Quite to the contrary, Billy if anything was truly and remarkably sensitive. Yes ... sensitive. Not a word most guys his age would proudly wear as a badge to define their nascent masculinity.

But he was what he was.

No rape fantasies. No hustling. No games or conquests.

Despite his precocious start — a tender kiss at age 12 from an atheist nun and an excellent blow job at 13 by a riot grrrll — Billy was a virgin and would be for some time. He would remain ensconced in a rich world of his erotic fantasies, dreams of explorations which would serve to both frustrate and ennoble him.

Who is to decide with what currency a young man purchases hope? A lovely girl real or imagined meant ...

He could look at the seemingly unyielding stasis of life in the Detroit suburb of Troy.

At the heartbreaking pathos of his mother and the aggravating torpor of his father.

At the tragicomedy of his classmates and everyone around him.

At the Pavlovian acceptance and allegiance to the treadmill of life.

At the tackiness and sad lack of beauty of his surroundings.

And draw the ironic conclusion that kept him going ...

There has to be something better than this.

The Devil Wears a Jockstrap

It's actually hardly surprising that Billy grew up thinking that women were beauteous angels — gentle, caring, comforting, giving, nurturing, affectionate, appreciative. And that men, in vulgar contrast, were heartless beasts — crude, competitive, aggressive, ruthless, mercenary, vengeful, covetous, mean.

This started at home with his parents.

But then in school, this lesson was reinforced on a daily basis.

His female teachers praised his intelligence, encouraged his scholarship, pushed him to new levels of achievement, even laughed along with his jokes. When they were critical, Billy never took it personally. He always could tell their criticisms were offered constructively, that they viewed him as a promising student, and therefore had his best interests at heart. When they teased him, it was never mean-spirited or demeaning but affable and respectful. They treated him as an equal. There were even a few occasions when some of his younger female teachers seemed to be flirting with him, which he found flattering, even valuable as a starting point for some interesting new sexual fantasies.

With the men teachers, it was a completely different story.

His math teacher in his freshman year was intimidated and horrified by Billy's quick grasp of mathematical principles, his ease at constructing creative solutions to problems that should have been beyond his age. Feeling that Billy was upstaging him, he stopped ever calling on Billy for the solutions to assigned problems. Toward the end of the school year, Billy would sneak into class beforehand and post on the blackboard the arduous proof of the most difficult homework problem for that day's lesson, then sign it 'A. Einstein'. Everyone in the class knew who the real author was.

The next year he took Journalism as an elective. Second semester he was allowed to contribute to the school paper, the Troy H. S. Student Inquirer. No matter how well-written and thoroughly researched his articles were, his teacher Mr. Gleason ripped them to shreds. He always returned Billy's drafts with massive amounts of red ink, making changes that without question made the articles worse. He loved to humiliate Billy whenever he was within earshot of other students.

"You seem confused, Green. This is the Student Inquirer, not the National Inquirer."

Not a single of Billy's excellent articles ever made it into the school paper.

His junior-year world history teacher seemed obsessed with the cruel lessons of war and mocked Billy's lack of enthusiasm for the gory details of plunder, mutilation and conquest. It was what came before and after the gore that most fascinated Billy. But Mr. Hutchinson's denigration of him was relentless and his sarcasm thick with contempt.

"Perhaps Billy Green could tell us what flowers were growing in the royal garden during the Battle of Trafalgar. Were they daffodils, Mr. Green? Orchids? Perhaps begonias?"

"There were probably no flowers in the garden during that battle, Mr. Hutchinson. It took place late October of 1805. During the long reign of King George the Third. Bad time of year for spring flowers."

"And there you have it. Mr. Green here would have it that the singular tragedy of this brutal campaign, this bloody clash between the navy of England and the warships of France and Spain who had joined forces for the battle, this pitched struggle which by the way claimed the lives of 3,692 men and seriously wounded Lord Nelson, Great Britain's greatest naval hero — the real calamity, mind you — was that there was nothing blooming in the palace garden, so poor King George III could not sniff his favorite floral scents. It wasn't a good time of year for flowers. Is that how you see it, Mr. Green?"

"Not really."

"By applying Billy Green's Disney-Channel logic to a more recent time in history, we might similarly conclude that the real tragedy of World War II, after over 72,000,000 deaths and the slaughtering of 6,000,000 Jews in the Holocaust, was how difficult it was to get a good plate Wiener schnitzel in Muncie, Indiana during the war."

"I haven't been to Muncie, sir. But I hear they have great public schools."

Billy often wondered in situations like this: Why did he bother?

But he continued to plug away.

His art teacher in the 11th grade — a very effeminate, though not openly gay man in his early 30s — took a special dislike to Billy almost from the beginning. It was only the third week of the new school year. After Billy's disturbing encounter with Mr. Rogers, not so very long ago, he was never comfortable being touched by unfamiliar men — any men for that matter. Mr. 'just-call-me-Michael' Dubbs tended to be very physical with the boys in his classes, as he made the rounds to check on the progress of their masterpieces.

"A Matisse in the making, Billy!"

Dubbs had walked up behind Billy to look at his sketch. Billy pulled out from under the hands the teacher had placed on his shoulders, and said only two words which permanently poisoned the air between them for the rest of the year.

"Please don't."

After that, Billy could have outdone the ceiling of the Sistine Chapel and Mr. Dubbs would not have been able to find any redeeming qualities in his work.

"What is this? A Rorschach test? This is art class, Green. Not Psych 101."

Things deteriorated from there and Billy ended up getting his only C in all of high school.

Billy's absolute worst teacher, however, was Mr. Sandoval Zenas.

Sandoval Zenas was Billy's gym instructor for three years running. From his very first physical education class in his sophomore year, it seemed to Billy that Mr. Zenas was bent on humiliating him, constantly reminding him that he was not physically gifted, and without reservations, a pathetic embarrassment to the male gender.

Mr. Zenas. You could write a book on the guy. A classic case of someone trying to work out his own issues at the expense of his students. He was the last person you would expect to teach phys-ed or coach any sports. Here was a man — half a man would be more accurate — who wouldn't survive two minutes doing any of the stuff he required of the boys in his class. He was weak, puny, probably uncoordinated — hard to call that one since he never demonstrated anything himself. His muscles and skin had the tone of a chronic shut-in, and on the rare occasions he was caught with his shirt off, his flesh looked like wet wax paper. Not in the least handsome, he was prematurely bald, a fact which he unsuccessfully tried to hide by wearing a baseball cap 24/7.

Most revealing of the utterly unfortunate, twisted nature of the man was the look in his eyes. Under the little-man bellow and bluster was an obdurate core of insecurity — the expression on his face was open reading on the defeats, belittlement and missed opportunities which had whittled his ego to that of a frightened child. He naturally thought he could bury all of this. Now that he was armed with a whistle, an oversized cap that said *Coach*, and empowered with his official, if undeserved, title of Instructor of Physical Education, yes now after all those years of humiliation at the hands of other boys — even girls! — who could do all of the things he had not the physical gifts or the basic talent for, he figured it was finally payback time. He was the big man now. He could strut his stuff, even if he didn't have any to strut. He could call the shots. He could show these little maggots who was boss.

To add to this perverseness, Zenas had his favorites in each class. Out of a class of thirty to forty kids, there were usually five or six of them. Everyone called them the gym jocks. These were the pathetic dumb hulks who despite their size advantage and self-proclaimed athletic prowess, couldn't make the cut in real athletics, either failing to make the team or reduced to warming the benches for the football and wrestling squads. Maybe they couldn't experience the glory of victory on the field, the adoration of the crowd, the fawning of the easily impressed coeds in the school. But at least here in Mr. Zenas's class, they were the king's royal circle. It would have been easy to laugh at the lot of them, except that would have been suicidal.

Zenas played them like his own personal fan club. They sucked up to him and he doled out the favoritism of a vassal lord. It was almost comical. Here were these big tough guys hovering around this pathetic little shrimp. Any of them could have balled him up like a wad of newspaper and tossed him away. Yet he strutted around like he was General Patton. And the gym jocks polished his stars.

Zenas didn't start out as rotten as he eventually ended up. As a damaged, fear-driven person, he naturally had to feel his way along to see what he could get away with. Gradually over the years, however, he evolved from being merely tough to being a card-carrying sadist. Once he got tenure and had the protection of the teachers union, there was no stopping him. By the time Billy first walked into his class, Zenas didn't even attempt to hide the buzz he got from arbitrarily inflicting physical and psychological anguish on the kids who were ill-fated enough to not be gym jocks.

"Give me fifty, you candy-ass little wimp!"

"For what?"

"You were thinking about talking."

"But I—"

"I told you to shut up. Now give me a hundred."

If you couldn't do the required number of pushups, then you had to run the gauntlet.

The gauntlet was a very special innovation which Mr. Zenas introduced to instill some respect for his authoritarian rule and maybe give a needed boost to a boy's tolerance of pain. He would make the rest of the class form two lines facing each other about three feet apart. As the person being punished made his way between the two lines — trying desperately to get through as quickly as possible — everyone would whale on him. He got pushed, slapped, punched, kneed, kicked, gouged. The gauntlet was where the gym jocks really got to shine. They always lined up at the very end and salivated at the chance to pounce on the poor victim. If the others at the head of the lines were easy on the poor kid, they were especially brutal, thinking they had to bring of the total amount of abuse up to the required minimum.

Mr. Zenas had other innovative phys-ed activities. One was his own brand of dodgeball. Normally the ball is thrown at the opposing players. Either the person catches it and stays in the game, or he is hit and has to leave the court. For Zenas this was way too tame. The object of his dodgeball was to knock the opposing players out. He allowed the ball to be kicked, often at very close range. Nose bleeds, black eyes, even surface cuts were not uncommon.

Another cruel innovation was his version of the fairly pleasant game of basketball. He dispensed with all of the normal rules. No dribbling. No fouls. No boundaries. No barred passes or illegal shots. None of that stuff which normally made the game one of great skill and finesse. He called it rough-house basketball. The main idea was to get the ball. Possession of ball could be achieved by any means whatsoever. No holds barred. The game consisted of beating the shit out of whoever had the ball until it came squirting out of his hands. The object supposedly was still to try to put the ball through the hoop. But rarely did anyone ever get around to that. It was pretty difficult getting off a nice jump shot when you were on the floor and six guys were all over you like a gang of rabid gorillas. If a person was even remotely sane, he didn't want the ball at all. Therefore everyone usually tried to avoid it at all costs. The gym jocks were particularly adept at forcing it on some poor kid and then going at him with their fists and feet flying. And if someone tried to pass it to one of them, the big jock stood there casually holding the ball, while his buddies beat up the kid who passed it.

Both of these games — much to the chagrin of both Mr. Zenas and the gym jocks — were brought to a screeching halt by the School Board of Education. Parents of a boy whose two front teeth were knocked out playing dodgeball, and those of another who ended up in the hospital with big painful contusions to his ribs as a result of a severe stomping during rough-house basketball, brought their grievances to the attention of the Board of Education at the same monthly public meeting. Mr. Zenas was called in and told to cool it or lose his job. He complied.

"If you want me to crank out a bunch of wimpy girlie-boys, then I guess I'll have to do as required. But don't come back to me when half of these young punks turn out to be poofs."

This, of course, did not put an end to other cruel antics of the gym jocks, activities which while not officially organized by Zenas were given his tacit approval by his never objecting or interfering. His blind eye frequently was not all that blind, as he could often be seen watching from the sidelines and getting a huge bang out of their brutal harassment of the others in class.

They had a bag of unimaginative but annoying stunts — all painful to one degree or another — devised and crudely improved as they lumbered through the four years of high school.

Sometimes it was just standard-issue beating. They would be waiting in the narrow stairwell which led from the gym to the lower level of the locker room and showers. There was no way to avoid them and no escape, other than running through the gymnasium itself and into the adjoining parking lot. Most kids took their knocks and showered.

Regularly they would lock a kid in one of the large equipment lockers, usually reserved for football helmets and padding. One boy was discovered by a janitor several hours after classes ended. Knowing the rules of survival, the kid said he had accidentally locked himself in the locker.

Often they would force-feed a bar of soap to a gagging, sometimes vomiting victim while he was trying to take a shower. A homo-erotic variation occurred later in the year when they force fed the other end of a victim's gastro-intestinal tract. In his struggle, he farted a bubble. That gave the gym jocks weeks of *homo erectus* guffawing, lasting into summer vacation.

Sometimes the gym jocks resorted to lame fraternity-type pranks, more designed to inflict mental anguish than physical pain.

One time when a boy had inadvertently left his locker unlocked, two of the gym jocks took his clothes and threw them out in the hall outside the gym, a hallway which was heavily trafficked by hundreds of students at each bell. They left a note telling him where his stuff was, then waited out of sight in a doorway down the hall. After returning from the shower soaking wet and anxious to get dressed, he found the note and peeked through the locker room door. Sure enough, there were his pants, shirt, shoes, and so on, across the hall opposite the door. There was still ten minutes before the bell and the hall was completely empty. He figured he could get his stuff without being seen. Buck naked he dashed across the hallway. Another gym jock closed the door behind him and locked it. The two down the hall then set off a fire alarm. Almost instantly the hall filled with kids, some screaming because they were excited about the prospect of fire, many girls screaming because right there in front of them was a completely naked boy banging on the gymnasium door, shouting at the top of his lungs to let him back in. An especially shy young man, from a conservative Muslim home, he was never seen at school again. Rumor had it that the following summer he had committed suicide.

As another weapon for severe humiliation and something the gym jocks were the undisputed champions at was spitting. The velocity and sheer volume of their hockers was awe-inspiring. There was an area of wall in the far corner of the basketball court tucked beside the bleachers, where they did their target practice. Some unfortunate boy was the preferred target.

"Whaddya think? What's the bullseye?"

"Let's make it his big dick of a nose."

"Nah. How about those girlie lips."

"A buck for a bullseye."

"Let the games begin."

They weren't very accurate. But they scored somewhere on the kid often enough. And since they always stood their victims in exactly the same spot, the wall had a reverse silhouette in the shape of a human body — kind of a crime scene outline drawn in a nimbus of phlegm. The gym was Zenas's exclusive domain. That wall was never washed and layers of filmy dried sputum continued to accumulate over the years that Billy attended school there, proof positive if any was needed, that Zenas got some sort of unsanitary macho thrill out of the sickening game.

Another stunt they cleverly named the 'lynch mob'. A couple of times a year, the boys were required to climb a thick rope, preferably all the way to the ceiling. It was a difficult challenge — only about of a third of the class could do it. Of course, all of the gym jocks could, muscle-endowed great apes that they were. For the lynch mob, they would randomly choose one of the weaker boys and tether him to the climbing rope by one ankle, leaving him hanging upside down and helpless.

Zenas always got a big kick out of walking in and finding some poor kid in this condition.

"What is this? Have you developed a whole new approach here? I can see why you don't want to use those spindly noodles you have for arms. But I don't think you're going to make it up on one foot."

Zenas and his jocks all laughed. It wasn't quite as funny the time when hanging upside down triggered an epileptic attack and the kid started convulsing. But Zenas covered his tracks.

"Some of these wimps will do anything to get out of gym."

Because of the gym jocks and the autocratic sadism of the man himself, it was in Mr. Zenas's phys-ed class that Billy's deep distrust and core disdain for chest-beating macho types in particular, and the male gender in general, took firm root. One incident crystallized these feelings into a lifelong bias.

Billy had been thoroughly briefed by experience as to the danger which hovered around the gym jocks, like a lethal cloud of radioactivity, wherever they moved. He had been clever and stealthy enough — and maybe just plain lucky — to avoid being in the wrong place at the wrong time. Despite a couple close calls, they hadn't cornered him all year.

Until now.

Billy had just gotten dressed. He still had five minutes before the bell and had to go to the bathroom. He was in the stall finishing a sit-down and had not heard them come in.

"Hey! Billy Buttboy!"

He knew immediately who it was. The last people in the world to be trapped with in an otherwise unoccupied bathroom.

It meant big trouble.

He nervously rushed to pull up his pants. He gathered his books, then opened the stall door to see what he was up against.

Four of them leaned against the sinks with their arms folded.

"Our good friend, Billy Buttboy! So good to see you, Billy Buttboy."

They laughed raucously at his new nickname. They felt so clever.

He turned towards the exit door to the hallway but two of them quickly grabbed his arms. Danny Seitz and Tom 'Killer' Killion each had fifty pounds on him, of meaty unfettered muscle. He wasn't going anywhere.

"Billy. Are you sure you got everything? Maybe you better look and see if you left your Raggedy Ann Doll or your Kotex back there."

They all laughed and he was forcefully guided back into the stall.

When Billy first heard the 'Billy Buttboy!', he knew he was in for some harassment or maybe a beating. But he couldn't have imagined or bargained for what was about to happen.

The gym jocks had only tried this a couple times before. They saved it for the ones they thought really deserved it. Billy's successful evasions to date and his reputation as an all-A student made him a perfect choice.

It was a cruel and frightening stunt which was a variation on what later became widely known by the general public as waterboarding, typically associated with torture inflicted by mafia-style mobsters and international terrorist groups. The idea was to submerge a person under water until he almost drowned, then pull the victim out just long enough for him to get a breath and some of his bearings. This was repeated as desired or when the intended results were achieved — a confession, some valuable information, agreement, a bargain, surrender.

The gym jocks preferred using a toilet to dunk their victim as he begged for mercy. They really loved it when the previous person forgot to flush. In his haste and panic, Billy for the first time in his life forgot to flush.

They made him kneel down facing the toilet. Danny Seitz held Billy's arms behind his back, painfully wrenching them when Billy squirmed or tried to put up some resistance. Tommy Killion had one hand on the front of Billy's chest and the other on the back of his head.

"Whaddya think, Killer? Should we off him?"

"Nobody would miss the little fuck."

"We'd be doing the school a favor."

"They'll probably give us a reward. Maybe a trophy."

Billy wanted to think they were just cruelly adding to his terror, but since these guys were individually and collectively incredibly stupid, he began to fear they might be serious.

The whole thing only lasted about five or six minutes. But that's a long time when you are fighting to stay alive.

In one forceful thrust, they pushed and held his head under the water well over a minute. Billy thought his lungs were going to burst. They pulled him out in the knick of time but slapped his face and head repeatedly. Then before he had enough time to recover and get a decent breath, they shoved him back under. Now a full-blown panic started to consume him. Another full minute under. While submerged, his gag reflex at being immersed in his own urine and feces caused him to exhale prematurely, then suck back in some of the fetid contents of the bowl. Choking, he struggled violently to come up for air. He was completely powerless against the enormous strength of the two brutes.

They violently yanked his head up and out of the toilet the second time. Coughing and gagging, he tried to yell for help. To silence him, immediately back in he went. This time he was sure it was all over. He hadn't gotten any breath at all. Despite a Herculean effort to keep from inhaling, his body's survival breathing reflex won out and into his mouth and throat came the foul liquid.

This time not even the colossal strength of his assailants could hold him as his body convulsed in one arching thrust out and away from the toilet bowl. He reared up spitting and gagging and retching all at the same time. He eyes were the color of radishes from all of the broken blood vessels.

"Jesus Christ! Look at this loser."

"This is disgusting!"

"What a little pussy. I think maybe he's had enough."

"For today anyway."

They let go of their grip, stood up and left Billy laying on the bathroom floor, still gasping and puking. The other two gym jocks who had been howling encouragement and gawking at the spectacle over the shoulders of the two who had actually put Billy through the horrible ordeal, were laughing and high-fiving.

"Good days work!"

"I guess we showed that motherfucker what good all those brains do him."

"Billy Buttboy, the brain who eats his own shit!"

That brought out a round of boisterous haw-haws and fraternal shoulder punching, as they strode apelike and proud out of the restroom.

It took fifteen minutes but Billy eventually stopped crying, stopped gagging and vomiting. He sat there on the tile floor with his head propped against the edge of the toilet, head, hair and clothes wet and soiled, stinking with the foulness of his own piss and excrement. He was still breathing hard but the hysteria and fear which had before gripped him finally passed.

Still somewhat shaky, using the toilet paper dispenser and door handle to steady himself, he stood, then staggered over to the sink to clean up. He removed his shirt and pants and attempted to rinse them the best he could, at least enough to get him home where he could change clothes. His text and note books were ruined. He just tossed them in the waste basket.

He made his way out and down the hall to the nearest exit.

At he walked he wasn't sure how he felt. He was at first understandably violently angry. Full of vindictive rage. But the desire to kill the bastards — put them out of their misery and everyone else out of their reach — rather quickly dissipated. It was replaced by some sort of vague but gnawing malaise. He couldn't quite pin it down. He couldn't put a name on it.

Then it slowly came to him what he was feeling.

It was pity.

Genuine pity.

But not self-pity.

Rather it was pity for the gym jocks themselves. Their parents. Their grandparents. Pity for their brothers and sisters, if they had any. Pity for their neighbors. Pity for the whole community, the entire city of Detroit, the state of Michigan.

Pity for the country, the great U S of A. Pity for the proud nation that had to accommodate and tolerate them — and disingenuously perpetuate the myth that we are somehow all equal.

Pity for the God that everyone seemed to believe in — who Billy assumed must be appalled and ashamed of what had become of his well-intentioned and noble experiment.

Pity at how we all fell short, how we all failed to measure up to our potential.

Pity at how pitiful it all was.

Scholastics

Billy loved taking tests. He literally thrived on them. Normally considered the bane of students far and wide, the batteries of tests — aptitude, benchmark, personality, intelligence, career preference, achievement, subject proficiency, college entrance — to which students were subjected to over the course of junior and senior high school, were his extracurricular playground. It was a delicious alphabet soup. WAIS-III, WISC-IV, MMPI, MCMI-III, SAT.

Billy's comfort with taking tests and general self-confidence in all things academic, coupled with his natural intellectual gifts, meant that on aptitude tests, he always performed in the top five percentile of his peer group. His scores on the SAT test were no exception.

Writing	781
Mathematics	773
Critical Reading	764

Coupled with his 3.85 GPA at the end of his junior year meant that Billy could get into just about any university in America.

The problem was not going to be academics. It was going to be money. Billy would in all likelihood get scholarship aid. But as outrageously expensive as college had become through the 80s and 90s, that probably wouldn't be enough. His parents could contribute some to his education. But the family income had been taking a big hit in recent years. Harold had actually seen his earning power go down. More and more manufacturing jobs were being exported overseas, where labor costs were cheaper, unions non-existent, regulations on workplace safety and pollution laughable. The U.S. automakers used this as a stick to beat back any attempts for better wages in contract negotiations with the unions. While wages were going down, living was getting more and more expensive. The upshot was that the money Irene had been able to tuck away for Billy's college fund was not going to be enough to allow Billy to attend any of the Ivy League or similarly expensive schools.

Billy's parents, of course, wanted him to attend a local campus and continue to live at home. That meant one of three in the surrounding area which were commutable — Wayne State, University of Detroit and Oakland University. Oakland was a commuter campus, which would offer none of the atmosphere of college life. University of Detroit was Catholic. Wayne State was a fortress of academic aspiration in the midst of an urban wasteland.

Regardless of the individual merits or drawbacks of any of these schools,

Billy was certain of one thing. None of them accomplished what was at the very top of his priority list.

That was to get out of the house and as far away as possible from his father.

He loved his mom and had let her know over the years how much he appreciated all that she did for him. But one more day unnecessarily spent under the same roof as his father was one day too many.

He couldn't come right out and say this. Not without risking some outrageous tantrum from Harold, or even worse, breaking his mother's heart. While she had in recent years — actually for as long as Billy could remember — given up actively defending Harold or trying to play peacemaker between the two of them, it was clear to Billy that she was in total denial the extent to which Harold resented Billy and how much Billy in turn loathed his father.

Over the course of fall and winter, as the application deadlines approached for the various campuses that had caught Billy's eye, he was able to lay out an increasingly clear path, pointing to the college experience he hoped to be having the following autumn.

Discussions about his attending college were usually at the dinner table, since once Harold got in front of the TV, all bets were off for any communication with the protoplasmic lump. To put it mildly, these mealtime discussions were more histrionic than constructive.

"What about Wayne State, Billy?"

"Mom. Five students got shot there last year. Are you going buy me a gun?"

Harold with blindside insensitivity. "None of them died."

"I think I'm allergic to bullets. Actually one did die. And there are a lot of muggings."

"I can't believe this! How did I end up with such a bedwetting wimp-ass sissy for a son?" He pointed threateningly at Billy. "You know, Mr. Afraid-Of-Your-Own-Shadow. A lot of my buddies died in 'Nam just so you and your pussy willow friends could go to college."

"Dad. Is that supposed to make sense? Besides, from what I understand of the Vietnam war, your buddies died for no good reason whatsoever."

Irene to the rescue. "What about University of Detroit?"

"They don't have the program I want. Besides, it's run by Jesuits."

Harold elicited a snorting laugh.

"They don't even have a football team! Whoever heard of a college without a football team? What the hell do they play there? Badminton? I do know one thing. Them priests play pocket pool. When they're not fudge packing the boys."

"Harold! Clean it up!"

"Anyway, mom, I think I've narrowed it down to three. University of Massachusetts, Cornell and Penn State."

"Oh, Billy. They're so far away."

White lies. "Gosh, mom. I hadn't really thought about it. But actually, they're not that far. I mean, like California is far."

"We'll never see you."

Empty promises. "I'll come home whenever I can. On all my breaks. Summer vacations."

Billy felt guilty. Like he was abandoning her. Condemning her to a life alone with his father. But she had made her choice long before Billy arrived on the scene. Realistically it was a burden she heaped on herself, though Billy was sure that way back then, his mom had had no idea it would turn out the way it had. Does anyone? Marriage is a crap shoot. Unfortunately, his poor mom lost every roll of the dice with Harold.

At last, Billy arrived at a decision. As he looked at the letter of acceptance from the school, he smiled from ear to ear and raised his hands high in the air to thank the heavenly powers.

In September of 2001 Billy would be starting at Cornell University in Ithaca, New York. He was to report last week of August for freshman orientation.

Billy's mom shared his excitement tearfully and made him promise to be sure and come home for Christmas and Easter. She told him protectively she intended to visit him as often as she could. She would bring him whatever he needed — as if this distant and mysterious Ithaca, New York did not have stores and other outlets for the basic necessities of life.

When his father got the news at the dinner table that night, he grunted, then went on to offer some rambling fulmination, mumbled through the mastication of several mouthfuls of head cheese and ground beef casserole. Billy was only able to catch a few key phrases — 'keep your trouser mouse in its cage', 'high falutin college boy', 'don't bend over in the shower', and 'damn place crawling with commies'.

Harold crowned his invaluable contribution to the occasion by holding his beer glass up in front of himself and staring at it expectantly. Billy thought he was going to propose a toast. But Harold just glanced over and gave the evil eye to Irene.

"Doesn't this look empty to you? It sure looks empty to me."

She jumped up and scrambled to the refrigerator for more Pabst Blue Ribbon.

Billy looked at the disgusting figure of his father and at his endearing but pitiful mom as she poured his beer, then glanced around the room, and found a measure of reassurance in the hopelessness of it all.

Homesickness would be the least of his problems.

Chapter Three

INTRODUCTION TO REAL LIFE 101
2001 – 2002

Perspective

Changes were in the air.

Big changes.

A vast and triumphant precognition built and came to possess Billy, as the summer following his uneventful graduation from high school dissolved into autumn. It was a sense of destiny unfolding. The chrysalis breaking the prison of its sheath, expanding into the boundlessness of the world, the new unbound butterfly then stretching its wings in a grand, epic arc that somehow embraced all that was possible.

He felt he was now approaching one of life's summits. That until now he had been struggling to climb the rocky, nearly impossible backside of life, but soon would stand on the summit and begin finally journey the frontside of the future.

The summit came when Billy and his bags had been deposited at Jameson Hall, the freshman-year student residential building that would be his new home. Billy waved to his mom and dad pulling away, as the family automobile turned onto the public street intersecting the North Campus exit drive.

Where previously each day's events conspired to drag him backwards into the inauspicious cul-de-sacs of suburban Detroit entropy, here he was in a new state (New York), in a new town (Ithaca), at a new school (Cornell University), starting a whole new chapter in his life — as a college student.

A brand new beginning.

The promise of a new life.

As he unpacked his meager belongings, then took his first exploratory stroll through campus, a phrase repeated itself in his head over and over again.

Nothing will ever be the same again.

As fate would have it, this indeed was a monumental point in history for him and many others, as they embarked on a voyage into a world transformed.

Nothing will ever be the same again.

Only 13 days after Billy plopped his suitcase and duffel bag down in his new dorm room, these became the same seven words trumpeted over and over again by politicians, pundits, preachers, talking heads, spokesman, men in the street, men in the alleys, men and women in their homes, at the dinner table, praying at their various houses of worship, all pleading for hope and struggling to comprehend what had happened to their old world.

Nothing will ever be the same again.

September 11, 2001.

Frankly, Billy didn't get it.

The entire student body and faculty, from what he could see, sat glued to every television screen on campus, watching the latest developments and the continuous looping of frightening but riveting video footage — the same scenes over and over again. The planes flying into the buildings; the fires in the buildings; desperately trapped people preferring a quick death to incineration, thus jumping from the upper floors of the World Trade Center; the scrambling of fire and emergency equipment and personnel to the area; the collapse of each of the buildings; footage of the damage and fires at the Pentagon; on and on and on, over and over and over.

As some new scrap of footage became available — a different angle, a different aspect of the multi-site, multi-faceted tragedy — it would take its place on the continuous loop of ongoing video imagery.

Then came the mini-movies of the heroics. The word hero was bandied about so frequently and with complete abandon that it completely lost any meaning. Not that the public seemed to notice.

Billy just didn't get it.

The problem with the entire self-obsessed, self-indulgent, self-congratulatory, self-promoting, frantic orgy of media coverage and public hysteria was rather straightforward and quite obvious to anyone who had a clear head and just took a few moments to think about it. Missing from the picture was the single most important ingredient needed to process what had just happened.

That something is called perspective.

Missing from all of the narration and analysis, commentary and speculation, monologues and dialogues was some prioritizing mechanism, clarifying standard, a normative concept which might function as an organizing principle. Something which would inject some sense into the hundreds of hours of verbiage and opinionating and horrifying video footage played ad nauseam. Something which would distill meaning from the heart-wrenching, mind-numbing, obsessive media coverage and counterbalance the nightmarish montage of gruesome imagery.

Unfortunately, the public — shaken to its visceral core and frightened like helpless trembling children — never asked for it.

So it was never offered. Not by the media. Certainly not by the government.

In fact the government, dealt from the bottom of the deck and played the fear card. It played the fear card ruthlessly and blatantly. It made sure that people were scared, uncertain as to the future of the country, uncertain as to the safety of their families, uncertain as to the security of their homes and their communities. It made sure that people knew that the merciless perpetrators, men with dark skin and angry bearded faces and towels on their heads — men who subscribed to an un-Christian faith that rejected the love and kindness and charity of our own religious beliefs, men who embraced a violent and remorseless creed of cruelty and the killing of innocent civilians, cold-blooded madmen bent on destroying the American Way — the government made damn sure that people knew these terrible, heartless, conscienceless, savage terrorists still lurked out there in untold numbers, conniving and drawing up plans for their next assault on our sacred God-fearing Christ-embracing freedom-loving homeland.

Nothing will ever be the same again.

Billy didn't get it.

Billy certainly didn't buy it.

But the vast majority of people fell for it hook-line-and-sinker.

George W. Bush and his band of closet tyrants had people right where they wanted them. *Put* people right where they wanted them. Cowering in their rooms, hiding under their beds, crouched behind their locked doors, waiting like terrified pre-schoolers for daddy to protect them, waiting for big bad Uncle Sam to make the big bad boogie man go away.

Billy just didn't get it … or buy it … or understand it.

Because if that missing concept, that sense of proportion, that sorely needed perspective which was never requested and therefore never supplied, if it had been there, people would have had to see how bogus and childish and truly *embarrassing* all the hand-wringing and heart-wrenching and torrential downpour of tears really was — how infantile and cowardly the collective response of the American people was to the events of September 11.

What would perspective have looked like had anyone had the presence of mind and the courage to drag it out of the back of the closet?

Start with the claim that America had never before been attacked on its home soil. What was the War of 1812 then? What about the attack on Pearl Harbor? This catastrophic assault killed 2,402 men in their bunks or while they scrambled around the tarmacs trying to get some of our planes in the air, *and* this massive air raid by the Japanese temporarily destroyed most of America's naval fleet.

The attack on the World Trade Center destroyed three buildings which were losing their corporate landlords money, and the attack on the Pentagon suspiciously occurred in a section of the building which was undergoing construction. As a result, it didn't hamper the ongoing functions of the military in the least.

Perspective.

Initial estimates of deaths resulting from the fires and collapse of the twin towers were in excess of 6,000. The real total turned out to be 2,753. Of course, each and everyone of those 2,753 individuals were important, and the loss and sorrow visited on each of their families and friends was a horrible and tragic thing — made more so because their deaths seemed to be so random and unnecessary, victims arbitrarily slaughtered by psychotic terrorists with an unfathomable political agenda. But …

Perspective.

Over 425,000 people die every year from using tobacco. Just lighting up.

Perspective.

Over 195,000 people die every year from human error while getting treatment in a hospital. Nurses reading the wrong chart.

Perspective.

Over 63,000 die every year from excessive use of alcohol. Nothing like a few cocktails.

Perspective.

Over 40,000 people die in traffic accidents every year. Wrong intersection at the wrong time.

Perspective.

Over 16,000 people are murdered every year. Guns and knives and hammers and saws.

Perspective.

Around 6,000 people die in workplace accidents every year. Just trying to make a buck.

Perspective.

2,753 people died in an attack on the World Trade Center by a handful of political terrorists.

They showed up for work and got caught in the crossfire.

Perspective.

Lamentable. Tragic. Horrible. Sad. Heartbreaking.

But taking another logical step further, going to a whole other level and looking at the *really* big picture — comparing the death tolls resulting from other political clashes and ideological conflicts — really puts it in perspective.

World War II	72,000,000 dead
World War I	37,000,000 dead
Stalin's Forced Famine	7,000,000 dead
Nazi Holocaust	6,000,000 dead
Korean War	2,800,000 dead
Pol Pot Cambodian Terror	1,650,000 dead
Armenian Genocide	1,500,000 dead
Vietnam War	1,200,000 dead
Rwanda Tribal War	800,000 dead
American Civil War	600,000 dead
World War II (U.S. deaths)	418,500 dead
World War I (U.S. deaths)	117,465 dead
Vietnam War (U.S. deaths)	58,198 dead
Korean War (U.S. deaths)	54,246 dead
World Trade Center	2,753 dead

It's a dangerous and violent world we live in. Always has been. People are going to get hurt. People are going to die.

Perspective.

The brutal and coldly calculated truth was pretty simple. For George W. and his merry band of control freaks, perspective would have been very inconvenient. If significant numbers of the American population had perspective, then the tyranny of the subsequent months and years would not have been possible. Americans would not have been running around like frightened children, stocking their basement caches with survival supplies and having rolls of tape handy to seal their windows and doors against nerve gas attacks which never would arrive.

Billy's fellow Cornell students would not have been glued in a glazed stupor and rubberneck paralysis to those television sets for hours and days on end.

As Franklin D. Roosevelt so famously said: *"The only thing we need to fear is fear itself."*

Too bad no one remembered FDR's advice. Instead, the President and the media just kept repeating the new mantra.

"Nothing will ever be the same again."

And as with all self-fulfilling prophecies, this empty formulation, purely as a consequence of its universal thumbs-up acceptance by a numb and misled public, would become the defining theme of life in America for many years to come.

Too many people believed that it had to be true, for it to be false.

Nothing will ever be the same again. And so it was.

Billy refused to watch television. It was almost two years before he ever saw any footage of the twin towers being hit by the planes and their eventual collapse.

Rather than sitting immobile in a fixed stupor staring at a television, Billy walked.

He walked across the eerily deserted campus — through the gardens, on the pedestrian walks, the bike paths, the various grounds with empty benches.

He walked alone lost in his own thoughts.

He attended classes where only a handful of other students had shown up. Sometimes the lecturer wouldn't even be there.

He would spend hour upon hour thinking about one thing.

Lost opportunity.

Actually, if people believed that things *should* never be the same again, it could be the most powerful force for positive change in human history. Billy surmised that if people believed that there was no place in the world for war anymore, or that mankind could never again allow a human being to go hungry, or if just in the U. S. people truly accepted the principle of total equality for every person living on American soil — if that was the way that things would never be the same again — what a bold transformation of our mean-spirited, divisive, avaricious world it would be.

Unfortunately, that's not what happened.

That wasn't in the script.

Americans instead adopted a whole new set of narrow-minded, paranoiac, sometimes just plain nutty ideas which ate like acid through the fabric of the country's core principles.

It's us against them.

The terrorists hate our freedom.

The U. S. must conquer and run the world.

Muslims are all ruthless and determined to destroy us.

We are in a clash of civilizations, which *our* God will help us win.

Billy was determined to not get pulled down into this gummy self-loathing morass. He had had enough of it on a personal level at home growing up.

Billy noticed that after the first week of the crisis, gradually more and more people were seen wandering about campus, and classrooms were more likely to be near capacity. Instead of staring dumbfounded at a TV screen, they stared dumbfounded at the person behind the lectern in the front of the lecture hall.

After about three weeks, things started to return to normal — if you could really call it normal. For indeed nothing would ever be the same again. All sorts of changes were afoot. Changes that would eventually prove to be anathema to the Constitution and the principles and traditions which had for over two hundred years defined the greatest experiment in self-rule in all of history. America would see abuses of power which were an affront to all thinking Americans.

Freedom of the press. Gone. Freedom of speech. Gone. Freedom of movement. Gone. Freedom of privacy. Gone. Freedom of political dissent. Gone. Freedom from unwarranted search and seizure. Gone. Freedom of assembly. Gone. The right to a free and fair trial. For many citizens gone.

Billy didn't get it.

He never got it.

What he did get — down the road a couple years — was the irony of it all.

A handful of terrorists attacked U. S. soil to allegedly destroy the American Way — as if taking down a few buildings could undermine all that great minds had wrought and built over a glorious two hundred plus years.

In the end they didn't have to destroy the American Way. We did it for them.

They just had to show up.

If it hadn't been for 911, Billy probably would have been political. He had the ingredients. He was smart and he cared.

But the collective cowardice of the country, and the futility of fighting what appeared to be mass insanity and deference to brainwashing, undermined and destroyed his budding political conscience. Of this he was not and never would be proud. But that was how it turned out. That's the way it was.

Like millions of Americans all across the land, but for entirely different reasons, Billy pulled into himself. He decided he would just tend his own private garden. Like a whole nation in the tidewaters of change, he shrunk the perimeters of his world to a tiny zone around him, something he felt he could manage. Some little piece of the chaotic whole, where he thought he could make a difference.

Billy became one of almost 300,000,000 separate little nations within the borders of a once-great country, united not by a shared sense of greatness or destiny, but united by fear — at the same time divided by fear.

Things definitely would never be the same again.

And Billy himself didn't have to change.

Everything changed around him.

Skin Deep

Billy was a pretty decent looking young man. Not devastatingly handsome or head-turning.

But good on the eyes.

He was lean and moderately tall — just under six feet — muscular but not bulky. He had fair complexion, brown hair, thin graceful eyebrows which arched slightly to give a hint of levity to his otherwise fiercely intelligent, piercing blue eyes, a masculine but not unwieldy chin, full lips which turned up slightly at the extremes to herald the onset of an impish knowing smile, a fine almost feminine nose with small delicate nostrils, a fairly sparse beard which completely disappeared when he shaved, revealing the porcelain youthfulness of his skin. His face embodied a beautiful contradiction. It was a portrait of furtive calm.

Billy moved with a smooth but potent grace. He was neither laid-back nor was he rushed. He seemed purposeful but not frantic. He was a welcome contrast to most eighteen-year-olds, whose shared affliction — especially the boys — is to always have to impress, to draw attention to themselves and make sure everyone knows just how cool they are. Billy had never done this in high school and certainly felt no need, and frankly had no expertise, in doing it as a freshman in college.

When Billy came into a room, his long strides were fluid and confident. He seemed quite at ease with himself. Though somewhat detached, never gave the impression that he was unsociable or threatening.

All of which made him very approachable.

Approached he was.

Girls — almost all girls — found Billy fascinating. The only exception to that were the ultra divas who were driven by their own hyper-inflated sense of self-worth and entitlement, self-adoring princesses who exclusively sought the brutish arms of Type A mega-macho men. Billy found these Pamela Anderson wannabes repulsive, so he was relieved to never draw their attention. More accurately, he never gave any of them a second thought. He was too busy with the other 99% of the female population at Cornell University.

What most fascinated the young ladies who would watch him eagerly at a distance before making their moves, was that Billy never was the aggressor. Unlike just about all of the other boys on campus, Billy never ever approached girls, never even seemed to notice them. He certainly was not a member of the deplorable peanut gallery that sat in little groups at the tables in the cafés and other public gathering places, or lined the walkways and hallways, ogling, rating, wiggling their eyebrows, making obscene gestures with their hands and tongues, pointing out some coed and then sharing some predictably lewd comments.

For one thing, Billy was a loner. Not a loser. But a loner. Which ironically made him even more attractive and approachable. The losers, which comprised about 99% of the freshman boys, in their individual insecurity and complete ineptitude with the opposite sex, typically banded together in small tribal units of three to six individuals, hoping that clustering would either disguise or remedy all that they individually lacked. Billy just went it alone, went on with the business of being Billy, of being grateful beyond anyone's comprehension to be there on campus, living on his own, finally far away from home town Detroit.

His solitary man modus operandi provided a wide range of opportunities for girls to come up and introduce themselves. To say hello to the mysterious boy, who seemed so preoccupied with his books or whatever it was he was doing. Billy would be sitting in the cafeteria alone, ignoring his meal but totally wrapped up in reviewing his notes. Billy would be in the student lounge, all by himself in a cozy corner, poring over a text book. He would be in a coffee shop, the dorm café, on a bench outside the library, on the grass under a tree, in a hall waiting for his next class. Because he wasn't in a cluster of cub scouts, there would conveniently always be that space next to him, that chair opposite, that place on the lawn, a body-width of room on a sofa, empty and inviting.

It couldn't be better if he planned it. He wondered sometimes if he subconsciously did. Maybe his love-starved brain had secretly fashioned behind the scenes the perfect pick-up technique for him. Whatever was going on, the results were spectacular.

"Is that *Comparative Cultural Studies* you're reading?"

"Uh-huh."

"I'm Marcie. I'm in your Anthro 1400 class. Monday, Wednesday, Friday. Right?"

"Right. Uris Hall. I've never seen you there."

"Actually, I sit behind you. Right behind you. You may have felt me kick your seat. Accidentally, of course.

"Of course."

"Do you want to get a Coke somewhere?"

This went on for most of his first term of college.

As any boy would be at his tender age, hormones surging through his body like beer at a bottling plant, Billy was flattered by all the attention. But one glaring anomaly prevailed the whole time.

He never asked out a single girl. Not one.

Some girls would come back time and time again, tracking his movements, stalking him like he was jungle prey, making sure to be in the right place at the right time. They plied their best — if somewhat immature — tricks and teases and temptations. Billy got a kick out of it. But his record remained intact. He still never asked one of them out.

To some degree, it was economics. Billy was broke. He had enough to pay his tuition, dorm fees, books and assorted and sundry minor personal items. But there was nothing left over. He had no intention of getting a part-time job unless he really had to. Somehow, working as a custodian or in the dorm grill just so he could take a girl for a movie and a pizza did not add up in the greater scheme of things.

But to the greater degree, it was something else.

The simple fact was he found these excitable little coed cuties boring.

Really boring. Or stupid. Sometimes stupid can be interesting. But their stupid wasn't even that. It was just stupid.

No doubt about it, they were sexy and appealing on a raw, purely carnal level. His eyes took in their fresh, lovely, often beautiful young faces, their firm delicious breasts, the hypnotic curve of their necks, their tight perky butts, their lean legs of different musculatures and alluring lengths, legs which met and formed the provocative Y below the zipper of their skin-tight jeans, behind which he knew from the aching burning craving lust inside his own pants, was the fulfillment of all of his nocturnal fantasies.

Yum said his body.

But …

Yuk said his mind.

Unfortunately, Billy couldn't shut off his mind, not even for a moment. And when these girls, from the first to the last, opened their mouths, he could not believe or stomach what he heard.

"I hate smoking. It's really bad. But I have to do something with my hands. Do you like my hands? You think they're ugly, don't you? I really hope you like my hands. I just did my nails. Do you want a cigarette?"

"Like you are so cute. You're cuter than my last boyfriend. He was a football player. Italian. But not a smelly Italian. I mean, he was like really clean. He tried to rape my younger sister. That was icky. So I told him, you're outta here! She's only fifteen. Does that suck or what?"

"My roommate thinks you're gay. I said, no way! No way is Billy gay. Right? You're not gay, are you? I mean, it's okay to be gay. But you gay? No way!"

"I want to get a tattoo. Do you have any tattoos? Like maybe where I can't see them. Can I see them? Sometime maybe? Should I get my belly button pierced? I knew this guy that got his nipples pierced. He wanted me to put a ring in my vagina. I said, back off on that, dude!"

"I was going to do pre-med. Then I find out you have to cut up these dead people. Cadavers! Can you imagine? And where do they get them. Like you're riding a motorcycle and hit a tree. Next thing, there I am cutting you up like we're in a butcher shop. Screw that!"

"I hate my parents. I say I want a car. They get me this old clunker. It was like two years old! I was so embarrassed. One time they went out of town. So I took their car. That's when I lost my license. My girlfriends and I were so wasted! We drove into a 7-11. I mean we literally drove into a 7-11. Right through the front window. It was so funny!!"

"I'm not really a blond. Here. Look in my pants. That's my real hair color. Of course, it's not that curly. Do you like my hair like this? I'm blond but I'm not just some stupid bimbo."

"So, Billy. What kind of girls do you like? I can be anything you want. Just name it. Cutesy. Sexy. Bitchy. A slave. Just tell me and I can do it. I'm like a really good actress. I think I might change my major from education to theater. What do you think? What's your major?"

"Ever see that show Beverly Hills 90210? That's what it's like. Only I'm from Orange County. I want to get implants. I'm too flat. A lot of my friends got them. My mom says I'm too young. What's that all about? Hey mom. Hello! This is like the 21st Century! Just because you have no tits doesn't mean I can't have any."

And this was Cornell. Wasn't this supposed to be one of the premier academic institutions in America? Where did all of these airheads come from? Are the CIA or the CDC secretly breeding them somewhere to create a super race of imbeciles?

Billy decided there must be some truth to that idea, as far-fetched as it might be. Maybe it's about the economy. These girls would make good shoppers. But nothing else. Between the visits to the salon and the local shopping mall, it wouldn't register with them if their brains were impounded, unless it spoiled their hairdo or made their eyeliner run. Or somehow corrupted the magnetic strip on their Visa cards.

So despite the persistent grinding all of this female attention caused in the dark recesses of his J. C. Penney Fruit-of-the-Looms, the lack of discernible cerebral activity in the girls themselves only assured the continuation of his celibacy.

Which brought up another issue.

A lot of other guys in the dorm bragged about prolific sex lives, huge numbers of sexual exploits and conquests. It really put Billy on the defensive. How horribly humiliating it would be if any of his dorm mates found out the truth.

Billy was still a virgin.

Granted, he had been kissed at 12 by a nun. An older man had tried to molest him — if that's something even worth counting. Then at 13, a sexed-up partially psycho 15-year old punk rock babe had gone down on him. But that was it. Within a short couple years very early in his adolescence, a lot had happened. But then it all stopped. Stopped short of where he supposedly needed to get.

So here he was, still a virgin.

As much as he tried to avoid listening, he would overhear the braggarts and blowhards talk about how they had done this to some girl, and some girl had done that to them. On and on they carried on. He truly hated the way they talked. It seemed cheap and demeaning to the girls and only heightened his contempt for the misogynistic showboaters themselves. But it still created this agonizing feeling in him that he was somehow inferior. That he had been left behind.

He still couldn't make himself do anything about it.

It turned out he wouldn't have to.

The matter would be taken care of for him.

Date Rape

Kristin, Angie, Erin, Julianne and Tanya all lived in the same area of campus, where most first-year students were housed. Angie and Kristin roomed together on the 5th floor of Jameson Hall, the same high-rise dorm where Billy lived. Tanya and Erin shared a room on the 3rd floor of nearby Mary Donlon Hall, where Julianne also lived on the 2nd floor with a nerdy computer science major from Minnesota.

Without a doubt, they were the five hottest looking girls on North Campus. As such, it was no surprise that by the end of August freshman orientation and registration week in September, they had found each other and formed their own unofficial sorority. They were subsequently always seen together in various combinations, and when schedules permitted, as a unit. They never tired of hanging out in very public places — the student lounges, cafés, multi-purpose

TV rooms, study halls, the library — attracting the salivating oohs-and-aahs, hoots-and-hustles, catcalls, and come-ons of the braver upper class boys, the inevitable disdainful and envious snipes of other girls who they totally outclassed, and of course the dazed-and-distant drooling of freshman boys who cowered behind plants or viewed them from a distance through windows and glass doors.

They all had noticed Billy about the same time, during the second and third weeks of October, when the 911 turmoil had calmed a bit.

Billy had become a hot topic.

They each had given him their best shot. Put their best foot forward. Pulled out all of the stops. And now as they compared notes, shared varying degrees of confusion, frustration and rejection.

It was inconceivable. This had never happened before. All of the girls were each in her own unique way extremely attractive. Sexy attractive. Any one of them could have been the original inspiration for the phrase *drop-dead gorgeous.* None of them had ever had trouble getting with a guy. In fact, they frequently shared stories of being pursued by several guys at once, and what a pain it was sometimes to shake a fellow-in-pursuit when he was very bound and determined. Now they themselves had effectively been blown off by this one particular dude. This was a slap in the face, something completely new and rather disconcerting.

They spent many hours, sometimes late into the night trying to make some sense out it, licking their wounds, comforting one another, and trying to figure out what made Billy tick.

"He's not gay. I know that."

"That's for sure. I know how gay guys act. They don't look at you that way."

"He's always looking at my tits."

"Yeah. Me too. And I've checked him out. I've looked down there. He definitely not gay. I'm not tooting my horn but the guy always has a major woody when he's talking to me."

"I've seen the bulge."

"Me too."

"Yup."

"Definitely."

"Okay. So the guy is on some weird trip. Maybe he's just shy."

"Not a chance! He's totally got it goin' on. If he was shy I don't think he would have talked to the five hottest babes on campus."

"Right about that!"

"Well then, maybe he likes ugly chicks."

"He's got a lot to choose from on this campus."

"That's for sure."

"Have you ever seen him with an ugly girl? Not!"

"Listen! This is a matter of principle. We can't let him get away with this."

"He's probably laughing at us. Like we're a joke. This is a sick game for him. We can't let him win."

"You are *so* right. And we're smarter than any dude on the planet. Let's figure this out."

It took a whole week of late night brainstorming but the girls hatched a plan.

Erin was in Billy's Introduction to American Government and Politics class on Monday, Wednesday and Friday. Neither of them had to be anywhere right after and would typically go back to their dorms. She was in Mary Donlon Hall, which was right on the way to Jameson, where Billy lived. Erin scooted on up next to him a few times for the ten minute walk. In one of their conversations, she navigated the chitchat around to his birthday.

"I hate that class."

"It is what it is."

She held up a charm bracelet for him to see.

"Hey! I'm a Leo. See? I'll bet your a Scorpio. Right?"

"I'm not sure I know my sign."

"Well, when's your birthday?"

"December 18th."

"That makes you a Sagittarius. Excellent!"

"Whatever you say."

December 18th. Perfect.

The 18th was during finals week, but things would soon wind down and by December 22nd, everyone would be heading back home for the holiday break. This would be an opportune time to throw a little birthday party for Billy.

Now they had to choose who should give him his birthday present.

Erin: "I found out his birthday. It should be me. It's only fair."

Kristin: "I'm the fairest of them all."

True. Kristin was a Swedish blond and had the white flawless complexion of fairy goddess who had never been in the sun.

Tanya: "Totally irrelevant. We're all in this together. All for one. All for me."

Julianne: "I think we should just draw straws. That's the only really fair way to do this."

There were no straws. Everyone drank straight from the can or the bottle.

"Here. Let's do this."

Angie removed her beret. They each took a sheet of cigarette rolling paper from a Zig Zag packet which she had in her backpack.

"Got anything to go with those papers, Angie?"

"You could wish. I'll be reloading this weekend."

"I've never seen you without your beret. I thought maybe you were bald on top."

"Only bald on the bottom."

They wrote down their names and dropped them into Angie's hat. She stirred them around, as Tanya turned off the lights.

"Okay, Erin. Give me your hand." She found Erin's hand in the dark and guided it into her beret. "Now choose."

"Okay. Got one."

"Lights."

Erin held the selected name against her chest as the lights came back on.

"I just want you all to know that if this is not my name I am holding here, I am very pissed and will hold it against you the rest of your lives."

"Okay, Miss Congeniality. What does it say?"

"Julianne!"

Julianne smiled brightly, way too brightly, then mockingly started to act like she had just won the Miss America pageant.

"Oh my God! Oh my God! I think I'm going to faint. This is the best day of my life. Thank you all. Thank you so very much! I'm so happy! Thanks, mom. Dad. Theodore."

"Who's Theodore?"

"My Rottweiler. Actually, I hate him."

Kristin might be blond. But she wasn't a bimbo. She was very focused and methodical in her thinking. A born leader among leaders. She pulled the meeting of minds back to order.

"Listen girls. We know what we're going to do. But we still haven't figured out how to get him here. I don't think he'll come here for a birthday party. Especially if he knows we're all going to be here at the same time. Just my gut feeling."

"Where's he from?"

"He told me Michigan. Near Detroit."

"So what do they do in Detroit?"

"They used to build cars. Now I think they just shoot each other."

Kristin's face lit up even more than it usually lit up.

"Okay, that's it. Julianne, do you have a social science or a sociology class?"

"I do. Introduction to Sociology 1101."

"Is Billy Green in that class?"

"No."

"Perfect. Here's what you do …"

Kristin's plan was brilliant. Julianne would find occasion to explain to Billy that over the holiday break she had to write a extra credit paper for her sociology professor. It was to be about an area of the U.S. she was unfamiliar with. The paper required her to do an extensive interview with someone, to find out what it was like growing up in that part of the America. She was to compare the story the person shared with her — the anecdotal evidence — with statistical data she got from scientifically collected sources to identify correlations and contradictions.

Julianne was perfect for the part.

In the first place, she was incredibly smart.

And while all five of them were outgoing, at times effervescent to the point of bubbling over, Julianne had a calm coquettishness about her. This charming dimension of her personality was an amalgam of her incredibly high IQ, an alluring and ironic smile, and the naturally cool inquisitiveness which lived in her piercing hazel green eyes.

Of course, she was beautiful. Or she wouldn't have been one of the Fast and Foxy Five, the moniker they later were given by the MC of an off-campus wet t-shirt contest, held as a charity fundraiser. She was the tallest, with long slender athletic legs, narrow hips, broad shoulders, full pert breasts below a thin elegant neck and sensuous collar bones. She looked a little younger than her 18 years and had an innocent, optimistic face. People often told her she reminded them of

Claire Danes.

Julianne was excited. This was going to be fun. She'd have no problem tracking him down. They were in the same Introduction To Statistics class two days a week, Tuesday and Thursday 1:00 - 2:30 pm. He never missed.

"Listen, Julianne. You should probably wait until the week before."

"Then I could act panicky. Say that I had had someone else but she backed out, and now I really had to find a good replacement in order to do the project. I'll act desperate."

"Ask him if it's alright if you tape record it. Tell him you'll probably need like a couple days. Of course, try for the Tuesday evening — 'cause that's his birthday — and then maybe one other. I hope he doesn't have any evening classes. Anybody know?"

Angie jumped in. "He doesn't. I always see him evenings. The library or the study lounge. Sometimes he eats at Ezra's or Bear Necessities."

Three of them said it at the same time: "Stalker!"

Kristin smiled as she looked at the other girls. She was confident they had come up with a good plan.

"I'm sure he won't suspect a thing. He'll just think he's being a Good Samaritan for our lucky little princess Julianne here."

Of course, once she got Billy to the room, it would be a whole different story. He would see he had walked into a very special surprise birthday party. None of them could imagine, as elusive as he had been with them individually, that he could resist spending a couple hours celebrating his birthday with some fun-loving girls and getting a birthday present he would always remember and cherish.

Everything went very smoothly. They decided to hold the party in Tanya and Erin's room, since Tanya had a killer stereo system. Angie would provide the special birthday cake — actually it would be her favorite recipe for brownies — because she had a friend off-campus who would let her use his kitchen. Kristin knew a couple guys who would buy some champagne for the occasion. A couple of bottles of $3.98 André should do the job. Bubbly on a budget.

As planned, Julianne waited till the week before final exams to approach him. Until then, she had just casually nodded and smiled in passing. But today after class, she walked directly up to him and suffused her usually calm demeanor with a strained look of anxiety.

"Hey Billy."

"Julianne. It's Julianne, isn't it?"

As if he didn't know.

"Good boy. I like a guy who remembers my name. Listen, I need a favor. I'm really in a bind. Do you think you could help me out?"

"Did you want me to do your laundry? I'm a gold medalist with an iron."

"Really? You'd do that for me? Just kidding. No, it's something else. This is really important, Billy. You see …"

Billy agreed to get together with her Tuesday and Thursday evenings the following week. She explained that she had to do an interview for an extra-credit sociology project.

This worked out fine in terms of his finals schedule. He had two exams on Monday, two on Tuesday, then one last one on Thursday. Thursday's was a snap — Calculus I, which was pretty much a review of what he'd gotten in high school — so he wasn't even planning on studying for it. He might be a little burned out Tuesday night but figured he could handle mumbling through the uneventful years of his life in the Midwestern wasteland without batting an eye. It would probably be a great way to wind down.

"Hey, Julianne. Did you ever see that movie *Polish Wedding*? It was out a couple years ago. They filmed it in Detroit."

"Why?"

"Has anyone ever told you that you look like Claire Danes?"

"Never. Has anyone ever mentioned that you look like Matt Damon?"

"Can you keep a secret? I *am* Matt Damon."

"I knew that. Don't worry. Your secret is good with me. See you next Tuesday night, Matt. Eight o'clock sharp."

As the final week of official classes moved along and quickly approached the weekend, Billy started to really knuckle down. He was a solid and disciplined student and had kept on top of his studies throughout the school year. But it was extremely important for him to do well on this initial set of exams — after all, this was his first term at college and first impressions are lasting impressions. He wanted to kick things off the best he could.

Those first four exams at the beginning of the week, were going to be a bear. After that, he figured he could kick back.

Friday, Saturday and Sunday nights, Billy got only a few hours sleep. He pored over his class notes, reread important passages from the textbooks, drank a lot of coffee. Review. Review. Review again.

Both exams on Monday went well. He felt pretty confident he had done the best he could. But Tuesday he had two much more difficult ones to tackle — Comparative American Literature at 10:00 am and Introduction To Statistics at 1:00 in the afternoon.

On his way back to his room, Billy grabbed a tuna salad sandwich, a bag of pretzels and two liters of Coke — Coke Classic, of course, because it supposedly had the most caffeine — and rode the sugar-caffeine high well into the evening. He crammed as much information into his cerebrum as his cranium would allow. He was in overdrive. But it had to be done.

Later, during a late dinner break at the Bear Necessities Café, as he wolfed down a greasy hamburger and what only barely passed for macaroni and cheese, Billy could only think how glad he'd be next week when this first term of college was behind him. He had decided to stay in Ithaca and work over the Christmas break. He needed the money, that was a given. But it also gave him an excuse for not going home and having to endure another orgy of belching and snide remarks from his father. The only Christmas spirit the old man had was the one in a bottle of 80 proof. He wouldn't mind seeing his mom but even that had its risks. He knew he could only handle maybe a day or two of the constant attention, pampering, mothering, questions and concern she would heap on him. This was much better. Stay in Ithaca. Make a few bucks. Hang loose. Start the new school term with a clear head and some dinero. Maybe he could afford to actually go out on a date.

He did have some mild anxiety — was it clairvoyance? — about the temp job he had landed from a notice on the *Student Employment Opportunities* bulletin board at the Campus Community Center. Typically, the jobs off campus that were put up for grabs by students were ones that no one else would take. This one definitely looked like one of those.

Billy had landed nine hours a day as a department store bunny. He wasn't sure what relevance a rabbit had to Christmas but he would be handing out promotional coupons for a cosmetic gift pack. He was the Clinique Bunny. With college students gone, he wondered what kind of cosmetic shoppers he would be seeing. And greeting. Wiggling his bunny nose at. They would obviously be local ladies. Maybe professors wives? Homemakers? High school girls?

It definitely would be a change of scenery.

Life sure could be weird sometimes. Eh, silly wabbit?

After he scooped the last forkful of inorganic chemical-macaroni into his mouth and washed it down with a double espresso gritty with four lumps of sugar, he made the short dash back to Jameson.

As he scurried down the hall to his room, it suddenly popped into his head that tomorrow night he had agreed to help that brunette — what was her name? A real looker! She was in his Intro to Statistics class. He had talked to her a number of times, most recently just last week. What *was* her name? Christ! Where was his brain? He felt punch-drunk from all this studying. Ah! Julianne. That's it. He was supposed to help Julianne with some sociology project. Eight o'clock sharp.

Yes! There was a reason to live after all.

But for now … back to the books.

Billy fell asleep shortly after 2 am, face down in a text book, nose pointing at a passage about the stylistic differences in the use of irony by Mark Twain, Henry James, and by F. Scott Fitzgerald, a half cup of coffee getting cold next to his halogen reading lamp.

Early Tuesday morning his room phone rang. It never rang. He never got any calls and his roommate, who was a third-year physics major and never around, was from Israel. Did they have telephones in Israel?

"Vatican Bowling Alley."

"Happy Birthday, birthday boy!"

"Mom. Is it my birthday? I'll be darned."

"How is my favorite son?"

"Your only son is a year older and deeper in debt."

"Get used to it, Billy."

"So how are you, mom? Everything okay?"

"I'm fine but your father broke his ankle."

"His foot got stuck in his throat?"

"You are so funny. No, he was outside shoveling snow—"

"Wait! Are we talking about the same person here? He didn't make the neighbor kids do it by threatening them with an ax? When was this?"

"Just a few days ago. Saturday afternoon he was out there for about an hour.

Then I hear the door open and he's cussing up a storm and groaning and moaning. I thought he'd been hit by a car. I says, 'Harold! What happened?' But you know your father. Talkative as a tamale."

"So what happened?"

"He wouldn't tell me but Mrs. Tedesco — you remember Mrs. Tedesco? The lady across the street with the diabetes? She told me that he fell down really hard. It was very icy. She said he laid there for more than ten minutes. He had a heck of a time getting back on his feet."

"Did you take him to the hospital?"

"He wouldn't go. Just kept on saying it's nothing, I'm telling you. It's nothing. But he never moved all evening and wouldn't talk."

"Sounds normal to me."

"Well, it must have been hurting because he drank twice as much beer."

"Any excuse is a good excuse."

"Anyway, next morning his ankle was swelled up like you wouldn't believe. Like a watermelon. It was the color of an eggplant, purple! And he couldn't walk. We couldn't even get his pants on over the thing. So I called an ambulance."

"Dad rode to the hospital in an ambulance? With no pants? This is truly a historic occasion! Did you call the New York Times?"

"He kept saying 'I'm fine I'm fine, it's just a little twist' but by the time the ambulance arrived his attitude had completely changed. So off he went. I've never seen him in so much pain."

"So he's in a cast?"

"And on crutches. But I have to hand it to him. He's sturdy as a bull. He went right to work yesterday and today."

"That's stubborn as a mule, mom."

"And your father actually cracked a joke. At the hospital."

"Dad? A joke? He must have been high. What kind of drugs are they giving him?"

"A lot of painkillers. He can't drink either. Not and take the painkillers. Anyway, after the cast was on, the doctor — a bright young fellow who seemed way too young to be a doctor — he's telling your father it was a clean break and it should heal just fine."

"And the joke?"

"Well, your father kept looking at the guy like 'what does some young kid like you know about anything'? You know how he is. So then he says to the doctor, 'Hey, doc. Will I be able to run the marathon when this thing heals?'"

"I think I see where this is going."

"And the young doctor says, 'I don't see why not.' Then your father says, 'That's great! Because I've never been able to run more than fifty yards without collapsing.' I wasn't sure I was hearing him right. Then I looked at your father and he was actually smiling. Billy, I laughed so hard I almost peed my pants!"

"Mom. You can spare me some of the details. That's amazing. When do you think he'll be on Jay Leno?"

"Billy, you're the one who should go on Jay Leno. I miss you. I'd better go. One thing hasn't changed. Your father is still tighter than a garter belt on a blue

whale."

"That's very funny, mom. Let's all go on Jay Leno! Thanks for calling."

"Happy Birthday, my favorite son! Don't do anything crazy."

"Believe me. You don't have to worry about that. Bye mom."

"Bye bye, Billy. Be a good boy."

Billy went in to the bathroom. Peed for five minutes. God bless Coke and coffee. Washed his face. Brushed his teeth. Swallowed the toothpaste in his mouth. That would have to be breakfast. No time to think about eating until the ten o'clock exam was behind him.

He studied till the last possible minute, threw on his clothes and waterproof boots, strolled at 10:01 am into the hall where the teaching assistant was handing out the exam questions, blew through the exam in less than an hour, and was the first to leave. He knew he had nailed it. Aced it. A hole-in-one. A bases-loaded home run. He felt good.

Only two more to go and he wasn't worried about Thursday's in the least. But the one coming up in a couple hours made him nervous.

On the fly, Billy grabbed five jelly donuts and a extra-large cup of black coffee, and carried them back to his dorm room. He had about an hour-and-a-half to stuff his face and cram into his brain any last minute data and formulas which might be useful for his statistics exam.

It was obvious that the prof didn't expect anyone to finish. There were about twice as many questions as could possibly be answered, even if textbooks and class notes had been allowed. They weren't. It was a test of pure brainpower.

At the end of the 90 minutes, Billy was totally exhausted but satisfied he had done alright. Depending on how it was graded, Bell curve versus some absolute scale, he thought it quite possible he had aced it. He'd know in a couple weeks.

He was out the door and looking forward to crashing for a few hours of much needed sleep. Then maybe getting some real food in him.

"How far did you get?"

"Julianne! How's it going? I made it to question 83. But didn't have time to finish it. You?"

"86. But I skipped a few along the way. Like the one about randomizing related sample sets. I never quite understood it."

"Well at least it's over. It's all in the hands of a higher authority now. I just hope the gods are in a good mood."

"Tonight? Still on, I hope."

"Absolutely. Eight o'clock sharp."

"Thanks, Billy. You're a lifesaver."

"Orange or lemon-lime?"

"Cherry would be my guess. I guess we'll have to see."

Julianne turned and crossed the street. She must not be headed back to her dorm. Whatever. All he could think about now was how good his bed and pillow were going to feel.

He woke to the distorted thumping of a boombox going by out in the hall — Savage Garden's "The Animal Song" — and voices. The party train must be leaving early. He looked at his wall clock. 6:30 on the button. He felt like he had been drugged.

As the fog cleared, he started to get ready. Plenty of time. Shower. Pick up a sub sandwich. Head over to Mary Donlon Hall. Julianne said she'd meet him in the lobby. 8 o'clock sharp.

When he breezed into the lobby, sucking the last few swallows of a sugary strawberry milkshake, Julianne was waiting. She looked great. She always looked great. Nice smile.

"Am I late?"

"Right on time. Thanks so much for coming, Billy. I owe you."

"Put your checkbook away. I haven't done anything yet."

They went up the elevator to the 3rd floor, and Julianne led the way to the end of the corridor. She was a couple steps ahead of him, for which he was extremely grateful. Julianne offered a very good view.

She stepped into Room 348 and left the door open for him. He walked in.

"SURPRISE!!"

They were so loud, Billy almost jumped back into the hall. But they weren't about to let that happen. They surrounded him, and amused by the startled look on his face, escorted him to the place of honor, a spot in the center of the room. There were several chair cushions on the floor, a couple throw rugs, a few ashtrays, several bags of snack food — potato chips, cheese puffs, chocolate pretzels, red licorice. Except for the bed, which was shoved against the far wall, the only furniture in the room was a small low table, which supported an excellent stereo system and two Elevation Audio speaker cabinets.

"I'd say we got you good, Billy Green."

"Kristin! How did you know?"

"We have our ways, Billy."

"Oh I got it. Erin! I'm a Scorpio. Very sneaky girl."

"Make yourself at home, Billy. Just remember to put up the toilet seat."

"Angie! We meet again. I swear, I seem to run into you all the time."

"Stalker!"

The other four girls all yelled it at the same time again.

"Stalker?"

"Private joke, Billy."

"Tanya! You are looking mighty good tonight. What's the occasion?"

"As if you didn't know."

Billy was now sitting. The girls arranged themselves around the room. Tanya hit the play button on her stereo. The intro to Prince's *1999* came pumping out. The party was underway.

Kristin sat on one side of Billy, Julianne sat on the other.

"So Julianne. I guess we won't be doing your special project tonight."

"Don't rule anything out, Billy. You just never know, do you?"

He smiled, though he didn't know what he was smiling about. He smiled because she did.

Kristin reached over behind her and came up with some glasses. "Let's break out the bubbly."

Erin went to the other room of the suite, then excitedly returned with a bottle of champagne in each hand. She planted her feet and did a hip-grinding hula.

"Whoo hoo!!"

They popped the plastic corks and started to pour. Billy tried to pass.

"Come on Billy, lighten up. It's your birthday."

"No no. Really I don't drink. I've never had a drink. Ever."

"Billy Boy! There's a first time for everything. You only turn 19 once, you know."

Okay. How could he resist? And what was the point? He was outnumbered. Overwhelmed. Flattered. They poured him the biggest glass. He timidly tasted it. Not bad. Kind of tart. But not bad at all.

Billy glanced over at Angie. She was rolling joints and passing them out. When one came to Erin, she offered it to him and had a butane lighter in her left hand ready to light it.

"No. No thanks. There I draw the line."

Erin lit up while Kristin leaned into Billy.

"Good for you, Billy. It's bad stuff. I myself *never* indulge."

Erin was holding in her toke and rolled her eyes at Kristin. She handed the lit joint to her.

"But … tonight, since it's your birthday, I'm going to make an exception."

"Kristin, the only time I ever saw you turn down ganja was when you'd already passed out."

"Busted!"

Everybody laughed. Billy took another tiny sip from his glass of champagne. Vinegar with sugar and bubbles, from what he could tell. But it tasted better than it was. The good vibes and the incredible view worked their magic and made for a splendid time. His best birthday ever for sure.

Angela slipped into the other room for a couple minutes. When she came back she was carrying a fudgy square pastry of some sort, centered on a cake platter. It was aglow with 19 candles. Tanya hit the wall switch to kill the lights and the girls all broke into a spirited if somewhat untuneful rendition of "Happy Birthday".

When they finished singing, Billy blew and blew but the candles wouldn't go out.

Trick candles.

Julianne leaned over and blew. They all went out. How did she do that? She just gave him an enigmatic smile.

"Some people got it. Some people don't. Right, sailor?" She kissed his cheek.

Angela came over to him with a knife. "Here. Would you like to do the honors?"

Billy started dividing the thick gooey square. "Brownies?"

"My own special recipe. I think you'll really like it."

Billy passed the plate back to Angie but she held it out to Billy.

"Honored guest first."

Never shy about eating sweets, he took a big bite. Then another and another.

"This is incredible."

She handed him another piece.

"It's your birthday. It only gets better."

They all giggled. There was a hint of a conspiracy but Billy just dismissed it. He figured they probably just felt like they were being bad girls. Drinking champagne and smoking marijuana was not exactly within the guidelines of Student House Rules everyone was given when they signed up for on-campus housing. Though from what Billy had seen in his own dorm, this behavior was more the rule than the exception.

Tanya hadn't put the overhead lights back on but instead had gone around the room and switched on a couple tiny night-lights and lit five or six candles. The room was now bathed in a soft glow which seemed to only enhance the air of conviviality and the incredible beauty of the five girls. Tanya slowly increased the volume of her stereo. It was a high-end system of some sort — Billy couldn't quite see what brand of components she had, but he thought he spotted the trademark Audio Pulse and deHavilland corporate logos in the dim light. It even had sub-woofers. It was by a long stretch the best sounding music system he had ever heard. She again increased the volume and the more he focused his attention on the music, the better and better it sounded.

Tanya had eclectic tastes which leaned towards dancey pop. He didn't listen to commercial music much — actually, since he had started college, he barely had time to listen to music at all. But he still recognized many of the tunes. Dee-lite's "Groove Is In The Heart", Technotronic's "Pump Up The Jam", "The Sign" by Ace of Base, OMC's "How Bizarre", Janet Jackson's "Escapade", "Tubthumping" by Chumbawamba, Peter Gabriel's "Steam", UB40's "Higher Ground", "You'll Be Mine (Party Time)" by Gloria Estefan, "All I Wanna Do" by Cheryl Crowe.

When C & C Music Factory's "Gonna Make U Sweat (Everybody Dance Now)" came on, all five girls jumped up and went nuts. It was like being in a Miami disco during Spring Break. They pulled Billy to his feet and made him dance. He was a horrible dancer but it didn't seem to matter, either to him or to them. They were all just having a good time.

As he made his own epileptic gyrations in some approximate relation to the thump-thump of the song, Billy watched his harem of girls-gone-wild. Kristin was probably the best dancer. But to try and rank them was splitting hairs. They all looked great, and were able to do some amazing things with their bodies. They were totally uninhibited and seemed unaware of what effect their blatantly suggestive moves might be having on the young man in the room.

Or were they? Whenever he was in this situation — rare as it was — he could never decide just how "innocent" girls were. Was this sort of display a dance of seduction, or were they simply just having a good time? He could never decide. Maybe it was both. Whatever their ultimate motive was, they definitely "knew how to party", as the stock expression went.

It was evident they liked one another.

Whether they were up dancing or just sitting on the floor, all of them were extremely chatty. It was obvious that these five girls had in the short span of a single term become closest friends. He didn't sense any competitiveness among them. No one seemed to play favorites but seemed equally at ease with one another and the conversations bounced back and forth with a carefree abandon. The five were definitely some kind of unit. It may have occurred to him at some prior time that two or three of them were buddies, though he wasn't particularly inclined to track that sort of thing. Now he tried to recall if he had ever seen all five of them in the same place at the same time. It seemed like he would have noticed.

What Billy found especially curious was that they all seemed so happy that he was there. Whether it was his birthday or not, it occurred to him that they could have fun with or without him, or with just about any other dude they chose to similarly include. Why him? He had talked to each of them separately on various occasions — he shared classes with Erin and Julianne and he seemed to run into Angie an awful lot, especially in the evenings — but here he was and here they were all together. How did that come about?

There was little opportunity to think very deeply about any of this. Nor did he even want to try. He felt like he was on a wildly whirling carousel. They sort of randomly rotated from one sitting spot to another. Angie would be on his left. Erin on his right. They'd talk and laugh. He'd turn back to say something and Angie would be gone and there would be Kristin. Then Erin would have moved on and there would be Julianne. Then Tanya would come up behind him and say something to him and the other two would laugh. Very physical laughs. Lots of hands on his shoulders, fingers in his hair, elbow nudges and bumping knees.

He could really get used to this.

His face was hurting from smiling so much.

And his mouth was so dry. Maybe he needed to try to keep it shut. Or have a little more champagne, which actually was starting to taste really really good.

And talk about really good. Those brownies!!

"Angie. You were right. You win the Grand Prize. Best brownies in the entire Universe!"

"Oh Billy. You're just saying that because you know it's true."

Besides all of the attention he was getting from his new best friends — or more accurately his birthday party playmates — the other thing that preempted his analyzing the how and why of this particular event, was the music. Not the songs themselves. But the sound.

It was completely overwhelming and nearly shut down all his other cerebral functions.

Billy had always gotten into music. Certainly he had compiled his own esoteric collection of CDs and spent many hours listening to his favorite artists. He was never as obsessive about it as were many other kids in his high school, but he knew what he liked and always made time to immerse himself in music. He loved the separate space that could be created in a darkened room with speakers pumping at such a volume, they shut out the chaos of the outside world, and subdued the anxieties of the inner one as well.

But what he seemed to be experiencing tonight went way beyond anything that had ever happened before.

"This music sounds phenomenal! Absolutely incredible! Whose system?"

Tanya scooted over next to Billy and smiled. "Mine." She reached for the dessert platter. "Here. Have another brownie."

He was famished.

"Don't mind if I do."

Julianne and Kristin were watching him and whispering. Giggling.

"What?"

"Billy. You are one of a kind. Truly innocent as a lamb."

"Am I going to a slaughter?"

"Not quite."

He munched. They smiled. He finished his champagne. They toked. The dimly lit room seemed to expand into an infinite cave of sound and deep wonder.

A new song pulled Billy tumbling into a different swirling galaxy of sonics.

"Oh my God. What is that? Who is this?"

Tanya knew her music.

"Savage Garden. Big hit early 1998. "Truly Madly Deeply." Hey Billy. You really want to get into this? Come here."

She stood up and took him by the hand over to the bed, then had him lie down. She reached under the table and pulled out headphones. AKG 240s. Nice. She put them on Billy's head.

He was instantly transported. Tanya put her fingers lightly on his eyelids to indicate he should close his eyes.

He did.

Suddenly the entire space inside his head was filled with images. Floating shapes, structures, faces, bodies, winged creatures. Tumbling and dancing in a spatial ballet that seemed to swim through the invisible fluid of infinity. Deep pulsing waves of energy propelled giant jellyfish and buoyant translucent filaments. Ghostlike apparitions floated and changed the color and intensity of their inner illumination.

The other girls came over and watched. Then Julianne sat on the edge of the bed next to Billy. She put her hand on his chest. To Billy it was a huge gust of galactic wind against the escarpment his body had become in the vast planetary shear of the Universe.

With the headphones on, Billy couldn't hear what Kristin said.

"I'd say he's ready. Have fun Julianne."

The other girls left them alone. On their way out, they snuffed all but two of the candles.

The song changed.

"Kiss From A Rose" by Seal. Billy got pulled into the waltz-time and deep orchestrations. Renaissance images. Ballrooms full of gowns and jewelry and powdered hair. He smelled the deep redolence of perfume and skin. Tasted lips and licked the slippery lotion of a tongue as it explored the inside of his mouth.

He opened his eyes.

Julianne.

She was kissing him. Unbuttoning his shirt. Reaching in and caressing his nipples.

"Julianne. Should we be doing this?"

"What do you think?"

"I can't think."

"Then I'll decide."

There is a first for everything.

As it was on Billy's 19th birthday. December 18, 2001.

It was the first time he ever got stoned.

And the first time he ever got laid.

She Walked into the Room

That night was the first time Billy ever saw Natalie.

He was still laying on the bed, not quite passed out, but very relaxed. His head was floating in some space between Heaven and Earth, and whether he could move his body or not, he certainly didn't choose to. Julianne was sitting there next to him, one hand on his knee, the other holding a paperback book on Etruscan excavations, which held her captivated.

He no longer had the headphones on but was still lost in the music — a song by Smashing Pumpkins, "Tonight Tonight." The symphonic vastness of it was giving him visions.

Erin, Angie, Tanya and Kristin had returned and were cleaning things up, putting the room back together. Kristin and Angie were picking up the glasses, bottles and ashtrays. Erin and Tanya were in the midst of bringing the desk and chair back into the room and restoring the feng shui of Tanya's half of the suite.

There was a knock on the door but before anyone could answer it, she walked in — Natalie.

"Girls! What have we here? Late night cram session for exams?" She spotted Billy on the bed. "Or maybe a kidnapping. A hostage situation."

Still carrying the desk, Erin sprang to their defense.

"Just setting things right. The editorial staff and a filming crew from Architectural Digest are coming in the morning to do a feature story on the splendors of Mary Donlon Hall."

"As you know, I try to look the other way. I am pretty blind most of the time. But you're pushing things — putting my job on the line here." She picked up a champagne bottle. "Maybe a little discretion is called for. It smells like Bob Marley's bedroom in here."

"You've been in Bob Marley's bedroom?"

"Burn some incense or use that illegal hotplate there to stir fry some garlic. Something!"

She walked over to Billy and glanced at the book in Julianne's hand. "Not Danielle Steele. Refreshing." Looking at Billy. "I'm Natalie. Local gendarme. You have the right to remain silent. Or you could introduce yourself."

"Billy. Billy Green. I'm from Jameson. 4th Floor."

"Nice to meet you, Billy Green. Are you okay? Your eyes look like tomatoes. Are you here of your own volition? Or are you being held against your will by this surly group of lesbian jihadists?"

Right then, Billy noticed another girl standing at the door.

"Everything's fine, Natalie. Actually I've never felt better."

"I can imagine."

She gave Billy a thorough once-over, nodded, then headed back toward the door.

"Just bring the music down a bit, please. Maybe we can get through this week without the DEA landing helicopters on the roof. Oh, I'm sorry. How rude of me ..." She took the hand of the girl at the door. "... this is my best friend in the world. Pam. We've known each other for a gazillion years."

They each said their names and gave Pam warm sorority-sister smiles. Pam didn't seem impressed. She nodded politely but seemed somewhat distant. Not at all the gregarious type. Serious bordering on severe.

Natalie put her arm around her waist.

"While you party animals are globe hopping in your Lear Jets, Pam and I will be in DC for the holiday break. National Gallery of Art, Smithsonian, National Air and Space Museum. Might stop and visit our congressman if his favorite escort service will tell us what hotel he's at."

"Don't forget the Holocaust Memorial Museum."

"We won't, Julianne. Everything we can cram into ten days. So girls, rumor has it that this is still finals week. A time to maybe crack some books. Books? You do remember books. Arrivederci."

As soon as they left, Tanya turned off the stereo. The party was over.

Angie and Kristin gathered their things and headed for the door.

"Happy Birthday, Billy Green. See you on the other side."

"Mmmwah, you hunka-hunka burning love."

They left.

Julianne stood and held up the book she was reading.

"Can I borrow this?"

It apparently belonged to Erin.

"Knock yourself out. I had no idea I had it. Keep it."

Julianne took Billy's hand as he managed to upright himself.

"Going my way?"

"Unless you're jumping out the window."

As they approached the door, Tanya came over and gave Billy a big, tits-first Hollywood hug.

"Don't be a stranger."

Erin joined them.

"Don't get any stranger."

"I yam what I yam. Me and me cans of spinach."

Billy walked Julianne down the flight of stairs to the 2nd floor. When they got to her door, he felt his first moment of awkwardness with her. After all, they had just had been as intimate as two people can be. Now here they were, two ships setting sail in opposite directions. What do you say?

"Billy. I enjoyed myself. One thing."

"What's that?"

"Always keep a condom in your wallet."

"Right. You never know."

"You never know."

She held up the book on Etruscan archeology.

"I have a hot date. See ya."

"Right. See ya."

She closed the door.

He heard the lock click.

He suddenly felt desolate. Abandoned. Empty.

Billy walked leisurely back to Jameson. It was only a little before 11 pm. The sidewalks were deserted. But lights lit up every dorm room he could see. Everybody was still hitting the books hard for their remaining exams.

By the time he got to his room, the evening seemed like a distant dream. He flopped on his bed and slept almost twelve hours. A dreamless sleep. A catatonic void.

Next day he flipped through his Calculus book, barely paying attention to what was on the pages. His last exam was Thursday. He really couldn't concentrate but knew the stuff cold. He finally just tossed it aside and went to a movie — some mindless Bruce Willis chase-em, sock-em, shoot-em flick at a Cineplex in town.

On Friday, three days after his birthday party, something completed unexpected happened. His phone rang. While that was unusual enough in itself, the truly unexpected thing was what followed.

"Norwegian Embassy."

"Billy Green? This is Natalie. I met you briefly the other night. On the way out of that party the girls threw for you."

"Yes. I remember. You're the 3rd floor Resident Assistant. Right?"

"Do you have some time this afternoon? I'd like to get together. Just talk."

"No problem. What about?"

"Things. Campus. You. We have the same major, you know. Let's just talk about it then."

They agreed to meet in the Atrium Café at five o'clock. Billy was done with his exams but Natalie had one at 3 o'clock near the Pew Engineering Quad.

He got there a little early and she came flying in at 5:05, looking a bit stressed. She plopped her things down on an extra chair, took off her coat, and sat down.

"Remind me never to take a computer science course again. That stuff is so left-brain those guys have side-cars to haul around the extra gray matter."

"What course was that?"

"Geek 1610. Computing in the Arts. It was 99% computing and 1% arts. Rather skewed, as far as I'm concerned."

"It's the digital age. Art is dead."

Billy wasn't really interested in what courses she was taking. But as soon as she walked in, he had immediately become very curious about her. Obviously, he wondered why she had wanted to get together with him. It must be a matter of some urgency. Exams were over and everybody else had left or were trying to get out of there as soon as possible to get on with their little holiday break. But she had insisted on meeting with him.

The other thing was Natalie herself.

He frankly was in a bit taken back. The other night through the fog of intoxication — both the chemicals and the sex — he had not really gotten a clear perspective on how incredibly attractive she was. Maybe not the hot-babe, Sports-Illustrated-swimsuit-edition beauty of the five hostesses who entertained him that night, but the kind of deep, exotic beauty of a woman behind a veil. Her face hinted of secret worlds and unspoken promises. Layers of complexity and nuance. More questions than answers.

For several long moments, neither of them talked.

Billy studied her.

She let him.

As if she had planned it.

He was trying to guess what her ethnic mix might be. Certainly not boilerplate Euro-Saxon. Maybe some Italian, Eastern Europe. The Middle-East? Could she be Jewish? Amazing. Whatever combination it was — and he was certain she was some rare blend — the final product was breathtaking.

Natalie was short. Maybe 5' 4" if she was balancing a book on her head. But her compact frame embraced an intense physicality and heightened sexual energy. She had narrow hips, a slender waist, thin shapely legs, a tight gymnast's butt, perfectly proportioned shoulders and arms, and beautiful hands. On her petite frame was densely-packed muscle without an ounce of fat. Except for her breasts. Some guys might think they were small but from the brief glimpses Billy got those first few minutes, they were just right. He imagined she had small, lively nipples. The kind that kiss back.

A huge part of her beauty was her eyes, which close-up drew him in with their deep intelligence. But there was her mouth as well. Asymmetrical and enchanting when she talked. Full lips. Lovely white teeth.

No doubt about it. Up close and personal, she was a stunning beauty.

He started to say something but hesitated.

He couldn't remember exactly when, but sometime in high school, he had made a vow to never ever compliment a girl. In the first place, the ones that really craved compliments usually didn't deserve them. And the ones who didn't need them, got more than their share. In the second place, it seemed to him that flattery actually had nothing to do with showing appreciation. It had to do with power. One person or the other gaining some advantage.

The Plain Janes wanted assurance that they weren't as bad looking as they suspected. But as soon as a plain girl signaled her need, she became a member of the slave class. Throughout high school, Billy would see guys turn these pathetic self-esteem challenged girls into their personal little servants, get them to loan money, do their homework assignments, run petty errands. He thought it was disgusting how the cool boys would so callously manipulate a little personal insecurity so ruthlessly to their advantage.

For the hotties, it went the other way. They already knew they were hot. They knew guys wanted them. When a guy couldn't stand it any longer and lacked the imagination to come up with some more interesting way of letting a babe know he was interested, he would state the obvious. Something brilliantly original — *"You are so beautiful!"* Now the girl totally had the upper hand. Complete control. And just as it was with the boys, Billy watched with amazement and awe at the way some girls would turn a guy into a pathetic little puppet. Her little valet to do her bidding. Some real lookers had a small army of grovelers at their beck and call.

Power. Advantage. Manipulation. It was just so predictable.

So he had made his solemn vow. Never compliment a girl.

Unless she's your mom, of course.

Billy continued to study Natalie.

"You are *so* beautiful."

"That's what they say. And?"

Damn. He should have stuck to his vow.

"Roses are red. The chemical valence of Magnesium is +2. There are more than twice as many sheep in Utah as human beings. Just stating fact."

She stood up and turned her backside. Looking over her shoulder at him.

"I've been told my ass is my best physical feature. Is that another fact that gets your nod of approval, Billy Green? What do you say? Thumbs up?"

She sat back down. She stared intently into his eyes and smiled impishly. Obviously she was really enjoying this. Fine. He could play the game too.

He shrugged. Tried to look unimpressed.

She squinted her eyes.

"So they popped your cherry the other night."

That did it! Wham!

Billy wanted to hide under the table. Better yet, completely evaporate. Vanish into vapor. His face felt hot. He was sure he was blushing like a school girl who'd just wet her panties.

Natalie laughed, then suddenly got serious.

"I'm sorry. Really. I'm not trying to bust your balls."

She seemed sincere. But Billy was wary. After that, could he could trust her?

He definitely couldn't figure her out. Or think of anything to say. It had been a while since he felt he had so thoroughly lost control of a situation. Here he was thinking he finally had his game together. Now this major curveball.

He was *really* certain now he never should have told her how beautiful she is. Big mistake.

She reached over and put her soft fingers on his hand, then lightly caressed it. Her touch was warm and friendly. A comforting sensation spread up his arm and through his whole body. Kind of like champagne.

"Here's what we do. Let's get some food and we'll start again. Okay?"

She had spinach salad and herbal tea. He had a mushroom burger with fries and a coke. Both of them were still hungry. Natalie got a fruit salad and Billy a hot fudge sundae.

"Natalie. Listen. I just looked at you and said it. You are beautiful. It's not a pick-up line."

"Too bad. Don't you like me?"

She was at it again.

"Well … uh … I … I don't know you."

"Look Billy. You are very charming. But actually, I have a reason for getting together with you today. See, as a Resident Assistant, I have certain privileges. So I looked at your file. You are a very bright guy. A lot of potential. You have a Soris Foundation scholarship. Those are really tough to get. Great test scores. Excellent grades in high school. All very impressive."

"Right. I guess. I mean, thanks. But I think I'm still missing something here. What did you want to talk about?"

"Just to tell you not to blow it. You've got a lot going for you. But if I had been one of the other play-it-by-the-book RAs who walked in on your little drug and sex orgy the other night, you could have been in some big trouble. Just don't blow it. That's my advice."

"I had no—"

"Those girls are warped! I know that. I took it for one of their stunts. Shake a tail feather. I suspect you had a *very* good time. Boy gets lucky. It was your birthday, right?"

Billy nodded. He looked away to hide his discomfort. Catholic guilt never completely dies.

"Julianne is brilliant. I'm not sure why she hangs out with the others. They're just party girls. Their daddies have a lot of money. They probably won't make it past their sophomore year. And what difference does it make, eh? Enough said. So. You grew up in Detroit?"

"Yes. A suburb of Detroit. And you?"

"Indianapolis. I'm not sure which one of us was worse off."

"It's probably a toss up. Either city would be ideal for storing nuclear waste."

"Or testing nuclear weapons."

"Even better yet."

Natalie took the last sip of her herbal tea. She glanced at her watch, then abruptly put on her wool coat, grabbed her book bag, her purse. She stood up.

"Don't mean to be rude but I better go. Think about what I said. Have a great Christmas. Don't stand under the mistletoe with anyone you don't know."

Billy stood up and started to gather his belongings.

"Say hi to George W. and Laura for me. They make me damn proud to be an American."

"Me too. That's why I tell everyone I'm Canadian."

Something was bothering Billy. He felt this last bit of repartee was a little too clever. Very unsatisfying. He didn't want to end on this note.

"Natalie, can I ask you something?"

"Fire away. As long as I don't have to answer."

There it was again. That smugness. That cutesy bit of provocation. The cat toys with the mouse. Again that Cheshire cat smile.

"I really do have to go. What's the question?"

"I just want to know. Do you do this all the time? I mean, let's face it. You don't even know me. But it sure seems you've gone way out of your way here."

"I've never done it before. Why should I care if some loser wants to hang himself?"

95

"But here we are."

"Exactly, Billy. Exactly. And how will it all end?"

She came around to Billy's side of the table, put her bags down, turned and wrapped her arms around him, sliding one hand up to the nape of his neck and the other to the small of his back. Then she went up on her toes and kissed him like they had just exchanged wedding vows.

"Bye for now. You know where to find me."

Only a moment later when he opened his eyes, she was already threading her way through the tables and out the café's double doors. He hadn't even had a chance to say good-bye.

He stood there in the center of the café. A busboy was off to the side, his back to Billy, wiping the condiment counter. There was no one else around. Thank god.

He wasn't sure how he felt. Enchantment and disappointment were in opposite corners of the ring and confusion was the referee.

Billy put on his down jacket and wool-lined gloves, then made his way out into the cold air. There were a few snow flurries and abrupt gusts of wind. He bundled for the long walk back to his dorm.

How did he feel? Not turned off. Not turned on.

Anxious. Like he was waiting for something. But what?

Maybe waiting for something to make sense.

And how will it all end?

How will what end?

She said she was from Indianapolis.

If being enigmatic was an Indianapolis race car, she went from zero to 60 in two seconds flat.

At the outset, she played the silent seducer to Shakespearean levels of perfection. She let Billy fall deep and hard into the cracks between his imagination and her taciturn hush. Taunted him with her physical assets. Then whacked him with the 2-by-4 of her mockery.

So they popped your cherry the other night.

Now there was a bucket of cold water in the drowsy face of self-delusion. *That* was probably the *real* deal on Natalie Jeckyll-Hyde, or whoever she was.

Or was it?

She did seem genuinely concerned that Billy stay out of trouble. She had gone out of her way to give him some solid and heartfelt advice on surviving there at Cornell.

What had she said?

You are a very bright guy. A lot of potential. Very impressive.

Natalie didn't seem at the time to be stroking him. Why would she bother? Why would she make the effort? She was beautiful, smart, sexy. She could have anyone she wanted.

What about the kiss? That was an entire conundrum itself. Not only wholly unexpected but even more puzzlingly, it was completely unsexual. It was an amazing kiss in every way that a kiss can be amazing. But there was no physical reaction on his end. Nothing. Not even a twinge. Not a single paltry throb from that part of him which always leaped to a soldier's rock-rigid attention every time he got within ten feet of a girl.

Very strange. Very *very* strange.

Then there was that last dash of arrogance.

You know where to find me.

How could she be so sure he would *want* to find her? After bitch-slapping him, mothering him, coming on to him, bitch-slapping him some more, then kissing him, she left without another word. Ran out like someone had just yelled, *Fire!* At he end, he was left standing there as numb as a eunuch. At the same time, full of raw curiosity and anticipation.

Natalie was a beautiful riddle — engaging and manipulative, sexy and unnerving, alluring and daunting, clever and calculating. Where did he stand? That was a riddle in itself.

Should he even care?

He couldn't begin to guess why he should.

His head was starting to hurt from thinking about it. Or was it the blustery assault of the December air? Well, that's just great! He couldn't even figure out if the storm raging around him giving him brain freeze, was internal or external. He was maddeningly frustrated and hopelessly confused.

Billy yelled at the top of his lungs.

"I give up! I give up!"

Three passing male students embroiled in an animated discussion of a thermodynamics exam test question, all stopped in their tracks and gave him a strange look. From their expressions, they seemed to be waiting to see if he was going to pull a gun out from inside his thick coat and start shooting infidels.

He didn't pull out a gun. But he did give up.

He just pushed it out of his mind.

At least for the time being.

Maybe not gone but …

Forgotten.

How will it all end?

How will what all end?

The Invisible Man

For the week-and-a-half Christmas holiday school break, starting the day after his fast-food dinner with Natalie, Billie spent nine hours a day as the Clinique Cosmetics bunny rabbit.

They basically hired him sight-unseen for the job. A pulse and being able to stand upright seemed to be the only requirements. He must have been the only primate to respond to their job posting.

He didn't know what they were possibly thinking when they designed the ridiculous-looking white bunny suit, but it sure couldn't have been the comfort of the person who had to wear it.

The costume was as huge as it was heavy. The bunny head towered above Billy — he looked and breathed through a white gauze hole under the bunny chin.

The weight of the entire superstructure, including the giant oversized head and floppy ears, had to be carried on Billy's shoulders. There were thick foam shoulder braces on either side of his face, holding the whole thing upright. But they were flimsy and would frequently collapse, causing the bunny to slump over like it had had too much to drink. The whole thing weighed over eighty pounds and after only a couple hours, Billy's back screamed for relief.

Moreover, no matter what the temperature was outside, it was so hot inside the suit, Billy could barely breathe. Other than the gauze viewing window, no provision had been made for ventilation. Billy's own body was like a furnace, from which there was no escape.

The heat and lack of ventilation caused another problem. Billy always considered himself a reasonably clean person. He showered both before and after his shift as the Clinique rabbit. But he had no prior inkling of how much he apparently off-gassed in a typical day. Now he knew. Inside the suit he had to live with the entire copious cocktail of noxious odors his body created, odors which normally would be dispersed undetected into the surrounding atmosphere. Body odor, breath odor, butt odor, foot odor, crotch odor. The accumulated stench inside the bunny suit by the end of his shift was overwhelming.

His job was to hand out promotional coupons advertising a very special Limited Edition Holiday Cosmetic Gift Kit, containing an array of Clinique products — a cleansing masque, anti-aging cream, waterproof mascara, skin rejuvenating base, sculpting blush, non-smearing lip liner, glossy lipstick, and samples of their most expensive perfumes.

Limited edition? As in you better buy now because you don't want to miss out. What a joke! One lunch break Billy went back to the area of the warehouse where they stocked them and found enough of the cosmetic kits for the entire population of Ithaca and then some.

The promo coupons for the three days before Christmas, touted what perfect gifts they would make for the special lady in your life — girlfriend, fiancé, mother, daughter, grandmother, niece. A different set of coupons for the Limited Edition After-Christmas kits, which mysteriously dropped in price for the exact same package by half, had a new spin. These told the shopper to spoil herself: *For the lady that deserves only the very best - YOU!*

People really didn't want any more coupons or advertisements shoved in their face, and Billy frankly didn't want to give them anything, if he could help it. It should have worked out fine. He and the customers had an understanding.

Unfortunately, his in-store boss for the holidays, the Clinique Regional Sales Manager, was pretty gung-ho about selling every last kit. Consequently, he was always on Billy's case to chase down even the most unlikely prospects and insist they take a coupon.

Billy was like a one-man border patrol. No one was to pass Checkpoint Clinique without being approached and shaken down by the Bunny Guard.

It could have been fun in a parallel universe. But in this one, it was a major drag. After only a day on the job, it became so predictable it hurt.

People were like walking VCRs, all playing back the same worse-for-wear, pathetic one-liners.

Look, it's Bugs Bunny. Not!

Do you know Hugh Hefner?

I'll bet you fuck like a bunny.

Here comes Peter Cottontail.

Ha ha. Take that, Silly Wabbit!

The last one was always accompanied by the person firing an imaginary shotgun in his face. Brilliant.

Listening to the same stupid, completely unimaginative tripe over and over again destroyed any hope for the human race Billy might have entertained — as if there were any there to begin with.

It also amazed Billy how crass people were. Customers who were quite fancily dressed — this was a very classy department store — presumably shopping for some member of their family, employees, or maybe a close friend at church or Kiwanis Club, would say the most vulgar things.

The men always seemed to assume that it was a girl inside the suit.

One barrel-chested business man really laid on the smooth-talk, obviously a dude who knew how to score the chicks.

"Hey, bunny. I've got something better than a carrot to stick in your mouth."

Billy replied: "Thanks, but my girlfriend really hates it when I suck dick."

Another actually tried to feel Billy up. He was a tall, demented looking man with craters in his nose that suggested smallpox was still an active threat. Billy noticed him ogling as he passed by. Apparently the guy made a U-turn, then slid up behind Billy, reaching around with both hands to grab some nice young titty. Billy lowered his voice as much as he could and said, "Is that a cucumber in your pocket or do you just like boys?"

The guy ran off like Billy was radioactive.

The women always assumed it was a guy — a handsome young college guy, hungry to jump the bones of a bloated over-the-hill ostrich slathered with paint-roller makeup and coifed with badly dyed hair.

One such beauty rolled up to Billy like a cement truck. Her front teeth were caked with maroon lipstick, a catastrophic clash with her greenish-purple gums.

"Oh my! What a very big rabbit. If your cock is as big as I think it is, why don't you come home with me? I like big cocks."

One lady whose face was pulled so tight from repeated facelifts she actually looked Chinese, sidled up next to him, reeking of acrid Sunday services perfume and bilious cigarette breath, and whispered confidentially.

"Maybe big bunny would like to meet nice pussy."

Billy couldn't let that one go by.

"Maybe big bunny would like to tell rich hubby that spoiled wifey is a slut."

She huffed off like someone had just accused her of shopping at Walmart.

The only good thing — other than the sluggardly caching of the minimum wage earnings he was receiving — was that no one knew it was him inside the bunny. At least he was spared that humiliation.

He was the invisible man.

There was almost some twisted joy in being submerged in the anonymous persona of a corporate bunny costume. As a consequence, in the same way many of the department store's customers were comfortable saying just about anything to him, by the end of his first week, he likewise started to feel at ease sharing with them anything that just popped into his head.

> *"The Mona Lisa has no eyebrows. And she never had chemotherapy. Do you believe in astrology?"*

> *"You can win a pet rhesus monkey from Clinique if you can explain why couples who marry in January, February, and March have the highest divorce rates."*

> *"Last year, Pope John Paul II was named an 'Honorary Harlem Globetrotter'. To be blunt, I don't get it. He's kind of short, from what I've read."*

> *"Do you do your own makeup? I heard over 2500 left handed people each year are killed from using products made for right handed people. Kinda sucks, eh?"*

> *"Clinique makes a line of long-lasting highly durable nail polish. Personally, I think that really rocks, since human nails continue to grow after death."*

This was fun! Well, maybe not fun. But it made his meaningless temp job at least bearable. So for the next few nights after work, he spent more than an hour looking on the internet searching for more and more obscure things he could befuddle the customers with the following day.

> *"Did you know that when glass breaks, the cracks move faster than 3,000 miles per hour? What a crack-up, eh?"*

> *"Bless you! Hey, I heard that every time you sneeze, some of your brain cells die. Quick: What's the square root of 256?"*

> *"Scientists say that butterflies taste with their feet. Which is probably why they don't wear sandals."*

"I see you smoke. Here's something to think about. Most turtles can breathe through their butts. Now that's one sure fire way to avoid lung cancer."

"A pig's orgasm lasts for 30 minutes. But they have no sweat glands. That explains why they typically don't use bed sheets."

"Armadillos are the only creatures other than humans that can get leprosy. Hey, I don't know about you, but that sure makes me feel special!"

Somehow his boss got wind of Billy's surrealistic running commentary.

"Listen, joker. I know this job gets a little boring. But we don't need you to embellish things here with whatever goddamn weird thing you feel like saying. The product speaks for itself. So button it up."

Billy certainly did not want to screw up such a promising entry level career opportunity — being a promotional hare for women's cosmetics. After all, who knows what it might lead to. Valentine's Day he might be Cupid or Godzilla. Next Christmas maybe Elvis. Or Big Bird. Or King Kong!

He toned it down considerably. The customers no longer looked so totally confused, his boss smiled from ear-to-ear, and the store racked up sales of the cosmetic kits well into the hundreds. Billy now amused himself by making weird faces and obscene gestures. After all, they couldn't see him. Sure, it was childish, but at least it made the interminable hours inside the suit crawl along a little more quickly.

Time still didn't exactly blaze by. It was like what they said about dog years. The three weeks of Billy's Christmas vacation equated to thirty in bunny weeks. At least that's what it felt like.

The only highlight of the holiday break was when Billy talked long distance to his mom on Christmas Day.

He had just the previous evening received the snorkel and flippers she had sent him — what was she thinking?

"I knew you wanted them. You know, Billy, when you were just a boy you used to constantly watch Jacques Cousteau. We couldn't tear you away from the TV set."

He of course thanked her and told her it was the best gift ever. With lots of tears and Christmas cheer, they spent almost 20 minutes on the phone together. Naturally, Billy's dad was at his holiday best.

"So how is your ankle?"

"Broken. What? You think it heals in a week?"

"I mean. Does it hurt?"

"Oh no. It's so much fun that when this one is better, I'm going to take a sledgehammer to the other one just to keep the party going."

"Well anyway. Merry Christmas, dad."

"Right. Here's your old lady."

"It's me again, Billy. Your father didn't mean anything. He's just a little upset this year."

"He was the same last year. And the year before."

"He loves you, Billy."

"Don't threaten me, mom. It's Christmas."

"You are such a funny boy. Hey, how is that job?"

"It's great, mom. I'm thinking about quitting school and becoming a full-time rabbit."

"Billy, you make me laugh so crazy sometimes. I swear, I'll be doing something when some goofy thing you said just pops into my head, and I get laughing so hard I practically—"

"Don't say it! I get the picture. Much too vividly."

"Uh-oh. Your father is pointing at his watch. You'd think we were poor."

In the background, Billy could hear his father shout: *"We are poor, Irene. For Christ's sake, get off the phone before I have to get a second job."*

"Merry Christmas, mom."

"Merry Christmas, Billy. Be a good boy."

Maybe he could snorkel in the Olympic-size swimming pool over at Teague Hall. Better yet, outdoors in the center of campus there was lovely Beebe Lake. The visibility underwater must at least be six inches on a good day. Hypothermia is probably treatable.

Mom. She was a good lady. A really good lady. And a great mom. She did everything she could for him. He felt blessed. At the same time, he could feel a distance slowly opening up between them. It really had accelerated over the last three months, especially on his end. Being away from home, immersed in a completely different environment.

Be a good boy.

She had taken to closing all of their conversations with that. Billy wondered why. And then he wondered what would constitute a *good boy* in that completely disconnected mind of hers. While he really didn't want it to happen, he realized that it was probably inevitable that the minor and infrequent differences between them would grow into a vast chasm of unshared experience and unshared ideas. Very sad but certainly inevitable. The generation gap. The values gap. The music gap. The technology gap. The dreams gap. The expectations gap. The trust gap. The willingness-to-believe-anything-is-possible-so-keep-on-trying-regardless-of-the-inevitability-of-failure gap.

Yes. He could see it coming. The arrival of that day when, despite 18 years of living under the same roof, despite all of the trust and the love and the bonding which came from the habitual routine of shared day-to-day living, they would be viewing one another through the wrong end of the binoculars.

Be a good boy.

His parents would eventually become as incomprehensible and invisible as God. And he would probably appear to them as strange and inscrutable as an alien from another planet.

Actually his dad had always viewed him that way. And with his mom, there was always some degree of disconnect. It came and went but never totally disappeared. What can you say? The gap between parent and child is probably as inescapable as death and bellybutton lint.

These were Billy's thoughts on his final, seemingly endless day on Earth as the supersized, fake-fur, fluffy-white, anatomically-incorrect, corporately-owned Clinique Promotional Bunny.

His last nine hours of polyester and foam incarceration as ...

The invisible man.

Please consider buying our exclusive gift sampler of fine Clinique products.

The invisible man.

Did you know the first contraceptive was crocodile dung, used by Egyptians in 2000 BC?

Father Knows Best

Finally, Billy's last day as a bunny rabbit was over!

As he climbed out of the suit, changed out of his sweat-soaked clothes, gulped bottled water and took long deep breaths to try to clear the Billy stench from his nasal passages and lungs, he realized he really wished he could maintain this cloak of invisibility when he went back to classes. Despite his best attempt to avoid recalling the encounter, he was still smarting from Natalie's jibes and confused by her enigmatic behavior. Did he need distractions of any kind at such an important stage in his life? He couldn't help but think he would be much better served by cutting back on what little social life he had trifled with first term. Keep life simple. No more "birthday parties". Eliminate the silly mating dances, no matter how persistent or attractive the coeds were — after all there would be plenty of time for that later. Just really knuckle down on the academics.

Billy had signed on for a very challenging second term. Nineteen credits. If he was going to survive it with good grades, he couldn't allow diversions of any kind. He needed to lay low. Fly under the radar.

It turned out he didn't even need to try.

Events and the unfolding order of things conspired in his favor.

During his three-week Winter Session COGSTI 1101 — Introduction to Cognitive Science class — and for the opening weeks of Spring Term, he didn't run into any of the usual suspects, not Kristin or Erin, and as unlikely as it would seem, not even Angie or Tanya, who lived in the same dorm as him. With just a hint of disappointment, he didn't see Julianne or Natalie, with whom he had had more than just casual contact. And though they had similar academic programs and all of them were freshman, quite surprisingly he had none of them in any of his six classes.

Probably for the better.

Then there was the weather. It was brutally cold these three months of winter and everybody tended to cocoon in their rooms more and spend less time congregating in public places, especially if it required going outside.

Finally after three weeks, he did run into Tanya on his way back from his

Introduction to Art History class. He was power-walking head down into a brisk wind. She spotted him first.

"Rupaul!"

He looked up. Then looked behind him to see who she was talking to. There was no one behind him. She gave him the okay sign with her hand.

"It's all good, my man. Keep it smooth."

Two days later, he was walking out of Jameson as Kristin was coming in.

"Rupaul!"

He tried to hide his confusion.

"Princess Diana!"

Who or what was Rupaul?

He just wrote it off as more girlie stupidity.

But a week later he was on the way to the convenience store at Appel Commons to buy some toothpaste and shaving supplies, when he saw both Tanya and Erin coming toward him on the sidewalk. He put his head down and started to cross the street to avoid them but they spotted him anyway.

They both shouted loudly.

"Rupaul!"

He waved and kept crossing.

Now their little game was starting to grate on him. The Fab Five were up to something and he was against his better judgment curious to find out what it was. He suspected there was something insulting about this pet name they had chosen for him. Even so, he wanted to get to the bottom of it — just to know — regardless of how mean or pointless it might be.

He did an internet search. Several entertainment sites filled him in. Rupaul it seemed was quite the show business item. How did he manage to miss him? Or her? Depending on how you looked at it. He/she was the world's most famous drag queen, creating a lot of buzz with an expansive career that included acting, modeling, singing, and writing songs. Rupaul's debut album was *Supermodel of the World*, which spawned a number of huge hits and resulted in appearances on the most popular television talk and variety shows in America and England, even the MTV Music Awards. He/she even landed a very popular show on VH1.

But what in the world did this have to do with him? He pondered all possible angles and came to the conclusion that it was just some catty, irrelevant stunt which he shouldn't dignify by responding to or even thinking about any further. Life had been simple and his devotion to his studies completely unencumbered until he began running into them again.

This new stupidity underscored the commitment he had made the beginning of the term to avoid these bimbos at all costs. He didn't have the time or patience to play their insipid games. He had much bigger fish to fry.

He did indeed.

Saturday morning, the phone rang. Amazingly, his roommate was there — Billy typically only got brief glances of his shadow or silhouette early in the morning, late at night — and got to it first.

"Shalom. Aah. Yess. Ukay."

He turned to Billy.

"Eet iss foor you."

"Hi Billy. How's my boy?"

"Fine mom. How's it going there?"

"Not as good as I would like. I mean, there's nothing to worry about. But I'm calling from the hospital."

"Dad? Something else happened?"

"No, Billy. It's me. I'm in here for something."

"You? Mom, are you okay?"

"I'll be fine. Yes. I'm going home today. I didn't tell you. But I had a lump in my breast. They removed it yesterday. And everything came out fine. They're sure they got it all."

"Oh mom. I'm sorry. Do you want me to come home?"

"No no, Billy. Really. I'm okay. I ... I just was thinking about you. I miss you. And I wanted to let you know. Everything's going to be alright. Promise."

"Just let me know if I can do anything."

"Maybe say a prayer for me. Bye, Billy. Be a good boy."

Whew! That came out of nowhere.

His father with a broken ankle. His mom with some kind of tumor or whatever lumps were. How strange to be suddenly confronted with … with their mortality. He always assumed they could drop a bomb on his dad and he would brush off the dust and ask for another beer. His mom from what he could recall had never been sick a day in her life. Now this.

But she sounded good. Confident.

Everything's going to be alright.

Unfortunately, it wasn't. Just before midterms week, he got another call. This time she didn't sound so upbeat. They had done some tests. The lump had been malignant. They thought they had gotten it all but were concerned that if they had missed any, it might metastacize. They did a microprobe to take samples from the area of the one breast where they had operated. Mammograms for both. Blood tests. Ultrasounds. An MRI.

His mom hadn't filled Billy in on any of this while it was going on. She knew he was very busy with school and didn't want to worry him. Now it was time to be worried.

She was scheduled to go in for surgery the week after his exams. Monday morning at 8:30. The only good thing about any of this was that it was during the scheduled midterm spring break and that meant he could be there.

Billy hadn't planned on being home during this breather from school. He needed to make money and had lined up a temp job for the nine days he had off. No bunny suit this time. He would be working on the campus grounds crew helping groom gardens, plant trees, seed lawns, sweep bike and pedestrian paths, in preparation for spring. He called and apologized for not being able to accept the job, citing a family emergency, then bought a bus ticket for Sunday of the following week. He was leaving a little after 10 am and would arrive in Detroit just before midnight, after almost 14 hours on three different buses. It was going to be a grind but he couldn't afford a plane ticket. His mom had not offered to buy him one. She probably didn't think of it. She had sounded very flustered on the phone.

His dad picked him up at the Greyhound bus terminal. When they finally pulled up to the house, Billy was exhausted and hungry. As they walked from the car, Billy noticed that his dad was limping slightly, favoring the ankle he had broken.

His mom was already at the hospital, staying overnight in preparation for the early morning surgery. His dad had negative cooking skills. Tearing open a bag of potato chips was the extent of it. Billy made them both some pasta with Heinz ketchup and melted American cheese. Much to Billy's surprise, his father drank a glass of milk with his meal.

"So dad. What are they doing tomorrow?"

"I don't know. Cutting her up."

"Come on! You must know more than that."

His father didn't say any more. He turned up the volume of the television and only got up to get himself another glass of milk. He never looked at Billy even in passing.

Unable to keep his eyes open any longer, Billy went to bed.

The next morning they waited together at the hospital. Not two words had been exchanged between them since the Hooverville spaghetti meal Billy had made them. Billy tried to read the magazines that were provided in the waiting room but couldn't concentrate.

Finally, the surgeon accompanied by an assistant came out to talk to them.

"Everything went according to plan. She's still unconscious and probably will be for an hour. You are welcome to see her when she comes out of the anesthesia. But she's going to be groggy for quite a while. You might want to wait until this afternoon. Any questions?"

Billy's father just shook his head. Billy spoke up.

"What did you do?"

"And you are?"

To Billy's surprise, his dad spoke up immediately. "This is our boy. He's Irene's son."

"Well, I assume you know then. We did a complete mastectomy of both breasts."

Mastectomy! Oh my God! Billy couldn't speak. He couldn't breathe. He heard a loud buzzing in his head and was afraid he was going to faint. He felt his own hands tightly gripping the sides of his face but didn't know how they got there.

The doctor and his assistant just stared at him. Finally, the doctor filled the awkward silence.

"The surgery was a complete success. We don't think any of it has spread to her lymph nodes or any other part of her body. But we will be doing extensive tests to make sure. At some future date, after she has recovered, we can discuss the possibility of reconstructive surgery. Here is my card. Please feel free to call if you have any questions."

The doctor offered to shake hands. Billy's arms hung lifelessly at his side. Billy's father had turned and walked away and now stood staring at the items in a candy vending machine.

When the doctor and his assistant had left, Billy walked over behind his father. His dad was addressing no one in particular but Billy heard him.

"She never had any tits. How could she have cancer?"

Billy was immediately filled with a blinding maniacal rage. A nauseous belly of disgust. A hatred that could be spooned from every cell in his body and flung like napalm at the man. He eyed a chair within arms reach and was so incensed at his father's insensitivity, he was sorely tempted to pick it up and smash it over the man's thick bullish head.

Then he noticed his father's shoulders quiver slightly. His head hanging down on his chest. One of his hands going up to his eyes.

His dad was crying.

His dad was crying.

His dad … was … crying.

Billy came up next to him. He put his arm around the man's huge shoulders. Brought his hand down between his shoulder blades. Patted his back. Reached across and pulled his father toward him. He felt the massive bulk of the man against his own slender ribcage. He couldn't remember the last time they had touched, except when his dad had been hitting him.

Billy had no idea how long they stood there like that.

Finally they sat down, each in his own private space. Each in his own private hurting place.

Thinking about the special lady in the other room.

After 19 years Billy finally felt something in common with his father.

Irene came home from the hospital a few days before Billy went back to school. It was a somber time. Not the kind of visit he had ever imagined or certainly had ever wanted. But he was there for her. She was alive. And there was hope.

Irene was weak. There was fear in her eyes.

Her aging face was a portrait of betrayal.

Of violation and irretrievable loss.

Of confusion and unknowing.

Words and empty phrases are bandied about at such times. The colorless salve of nonsense.

The Lord works in mysterious ways.

There's a reason for everything.

You just have to have faith.

All's well that ends well.

He could almost bite into that last one.

Fast food philosophy.

The problem with cancer was never knowing if the story had ended. It was a waiting game. Nothing could be done. The doctors could test and tinker and probe and prognosticate. Ultimately, it was in the hands of whatever arbitrary mechanism decides who is cured and who must continue to wage a fight for life itself.

All is well that ends well.

And how will it all end?

Hmm. Natalie's words.

How will it all end?

There was one mildly encouraging and rather unexpected side note during Billy's visit. Before sinking back into the oblivion of his deeply entrenched beer-potato-chips-TV routine, for three nights running Harold came home from his shift at the nearby Chrysler assembly plant with bouquets of flowers. He had started working afternoons at the beginning of the new year, which meant he got in shortly after 1:00 am. Billy and his mom were both asleep, so they never actually saw the flowers in Harold's big calloused hands. But in the morning, there they were on the night stand next to Irene's bed. He had even put them in whatever he could find in the kitchen to hold them. One time it was a cookie jar. Another it was a stainless steel thermos bottle. Then he actually found a vase.

But by the end of Billy's stay, the familiar anti-iconic shape of the Harold they had known for at least a decade — his bulk heaped on the La-Z-Boy chair in the living room, beer in one hand, remote in the other, bloated face rendered inert and lifeless by the taxidermy of the television screen — materialized from the temporary hiatus occasioned by Irene's surgery.

What would life be without the well-worn and predictable?

It was depressing. He wished he could do something. But before he even began to blunder into thinking that he could make any difference whatsoever, he looked at the hand he was dealt.

Like that old Kenny Rogers song went, playing on the only cassette his dad ever listened to in the car: *Know when to hold 'em and know when to fold 'em.*

It was time to fold 'em.

He packed his duffel bag, said a long and tearful good-bye to his mom, then rode silently in the family's 1987 Plymouth Reliant as his father drove him to the bus station. If his dad was feeling anything, he certainly hid it extremely well. The man wasn't exactly big on sentimentality.

They pulled up to the drop-off curb at the Greyhound Bus Terminal.

"Don't fuck anything I wouldn't fuck."

Good thing he didn't write Hallmark cards for a living.

"Thanks for the advice, dad. Send me a list when you get a chance."

"List? Of what?"

"Of what you wouldn't fuck."

His father glared at him. Billy was out of the car before his father could take a swipe at him. As he walked away, he saw the driver's side window roll down halfway. Billy could just make out the parting shots over the traffic noise as entered the terminal.

"Smart ass little cocksucker. For starters I wouldn't fuck any of your fudge-packing college butt-buddies."

He loves you, Billy.

Right, mom.

Chapter Four

DANCING ON BROKEN GLASS
2002

Welcome Home!

Billy spent that entire Sunday before classes resumed, riding the bus back to Ithaca — another thirteen hour plus ordeal — then caught a taxi to Jameson Hall. Interestingly, the trip back had the opposite affect on him as the bus ride had in the other direction just nine days ago. Instead of being exhausted, he was pumped up and full of energy.

He made the short dash from curbside through the blustery cold of the evening air.

As soon as he walked into the lobby of his dorm, it felt like he had entered a twilight zone of surrealism.

Lots of unseasonably nice tans. Sunburns. High fives and chest bumps. Self-satisfied grins. Exchanges of knowing nods, winks and oscillating eyebrows.

Apparently a sizable portion — certainly a highly visible portion — of the underclassmen at Cornell had experienced a very different spring break than he had. Following the established migratory habits of college students over many previous decades, they had gone to Florida, Texas, Cancún, Acapulco, Mazatlán, Puerto Vallarta, Jamaica, and the Bahamas, for nine days of wild abandon. Beach parties, night clubbing, dancing, flashing, streaking, anonymous fucking, licking, sucking. All of it fueled and lubricated with massive quantities of alcohol, reefer, cocaine, acid, MDMA, and whatever else would render them out of control, insensate and uninhibited.

Billy enjoyed a bit of voyeur's fascination by virtue of the eavesdropping he did over the next few days.

"Me and my two best friends like go to Jamaica, and there's this really cool Jamaican guy with a whistle, two bottles of Tequila and a funnel. First he poured it all over my tits. Then some guy licked it off. We're completely wasted and going from one hot spot to another. Anyway I hook up with this awesome Sigma Chi from Ohio State. I can't remember his name. We just go out behind this club and while we are in the middle of it, the lawn sprinklers like come on. We're laughing and wet and going at it. Totally trashed. It was so amazingly awesome. It was the best ever!"

"So I'm sittin' there in this way cool club. Jimbo is like dancing his ass off with some sorority slut from Louisiana State. So these two girls go by and I stick my tongue out like I want to lick them. They stop, push my table back and start lap-dancing me! Both at once! Pretty soon the tops come off and I got a face full of the most beautiful titties, man."

"I can't believe it! I'm going to be in this awesome video. It's called 'Girls Gone Wild'. Margie and I got to know the director. He's like going to feature us. We even went back to our motel and did some stuff you won't believe! Like she went down on me. And check this out. I got a Girls Gone Wild t-shirt and cap."

For some reliving the orgy of sun and hot young flesh was remembering that they were so fucked up they couldn't remember anything — except of course how fucked up they were.

"Whoa, I was so hammered. I wake up seven miles from my hotel and look over at this chick and say, 'Who the fuck are you?' And she says, 'Who the fuck wants to know?' Fucking awesome! I end up taking a shower with her AND her two roommates. My dick never got so clean."

"Cancun rocks! There's this club called Fat Tuesdays and we're all drinking this red drink. I have no idea what it was. Whatever! But I'm like totaled. Next thing I know I wake up with this black guy named Cassius. And he rips my panties off and says like, 'I'm going to fuck you like it's the last game of the World Series.' So the next day, Suzie comes by with her camera and shows me the pictures. I won the spanking contest at the club, she won the wet t-shirt contest. Then she shows me these pictures of me at the club with two guys and my top is off. One guy is taking me from behind. Like I don't remember any of this. I can't believe these photos. You want to see them?"

The more innocent forms of exhibitionism included, as a bare minimum, the revealing of a young coeds breasts.

Billy was no prude. For as long as he could remember, if a girl wanted to show him her breasts, he had no problem with it whatsoever. Full speed ahead. All systems go.

But after spending over a week with his mom after her mastectomy, there was a bittersweet pique to the whole proposition. And a reminder of how fleeting all of that youthful perfection ultimately was. What a delicate barrier stood between any of them — male or female, young or old, everything in between — and some esteem-shattering disfigurement.

He thought of the Foxy Five, of Natalie, and of some of the prettier girls in his high school. How lucky they were. How much they took it for granted, or if they didn't take it for granted, how they used their beauty as a cheap bargaining chip to attain status, power, control, leverage. Born with a gift of extraordinary beauty, which in the microseconds of a car crash, less than a minute of a fire, some random act of violence with a knife or a bludgeon or a splash of sulfuric acid, or the horrifying disfiguring potential of a disease like cancer, any of these girls could be thrust into a lifetime of hiding and apologizing and rationalizing. Of humiliation and self-pity.

Maybe it was better to be ugly. But then, of course, you wouldn't get to be on America's Next Top Model. Or get to flash your tits and your vulva for a *Girls Gone Wild* video.

Could life be worth living then? Apparently not, for the growing segment of the population who had so much invested in being sexy and beautiful.

It was ironic, Billy kept thinking. These playful little tarts think they're so liberated and free. That they've arrived at some sort of feminist Amazonia where they are so comfortable with their bodies, that modesty and discretion are laughable antiquated concepts which belong in their grandmother's crocheting basket. But the truth was, this was the opposite of freedom. In fact, they were slaves to their youthful beauty. Slaves to the easy attention and cheap approval they got from playing into male tyranny. And when those breasts started to sag, or when like his mom they faced the ever-increasing possibility of breast cancer, then what? Will that be the end of their lives? Will they be able to face themselves? Or will they live out their lives in misery and shame, calling up distant fond memories of a wet t-shirt contest in Mazatlán or dancing naked in a bar in the Bahamas?

He thought with an aching melancholy about his mom. He tried to imagine what she must be going through.

Was his mother's image of herself so mutilated by the mutilation of her body that she would never be able hold her head up again? Would she be so deafened by the screaming emptiness of the space her breasts once occupied, that she wouldn't be able to hear Billy when he told her what an amazing mother and great person she always had been and still was in his eyes?

There would be no comfort from his father, that was a given. His mother had some friends. She still played Euchre a couple times a week with the "girls". That was encouraging. It at least was something. But was it enough?

It hurt thinking about it. Things in life came and went. Some good. Some bad.

It seemed so random. It *was* random. That was the truth of the matter.

God doesn't work in mysterious ways. He doesn't give a shit.

Everything doesn't happen for a reason. Shit happens.

Having faith doesn't make any difference. It's just something to do while you go from point A to point B. You could just take up juggling. That would work too.

All is *not well* even if it ends well. Because there will be something else.

Always something else. That much you can count on.

How will it all end?

Will it *ever* end?

Thursday night. 8:24 pm. His phone rang.

"Welcome home! It's me. Natalie."

Shadowboxing

Welcome home.

She was right. This was home. Home is where you are. It's where you brush your teeth. Home is where you leave your dirty socks on the floor.

Natalie said she just called to say hi. The whole conversation lasted less than a minute.

It was two weeks before Billy talked to her again. Again, she called him.

"Hey Billy. It's me again. How's it hangin'?"

"Like Julia Roberts on the end of a bungee cord. How's it with you?"

"Busy. Classes. The RA thing. Did you know that Julianne didn't come back from break? There was some trouble at home. Nobody can tell me anything. Of course, it's none of my business. But I like her. She's so brilliant."

"No. I haven't talked to any of them. I'm sure they're struggling to somehow survive without me in their lives. But they should have no problem making friends. They don't seem like the brooding lonely types."

"I know you're being cute. But you would be surprised. Sometimes the hottest ones are the most desperate. That's why they can't be alone."

"How about you?"

"You think I'm a hot chick? Ohmigod! I'm so flattered! Do you want to talk dirty to me?"

"You know. I can't keep up with you. You throw more curve balls than Pedro Martinez."

"Listen. I'm slammed all this week. But do you want to get together this weekend? Saturday? Sunday would be good too. Something easy. Picnic. Walk down to the lake. Hitchhike to Mexico City? Start a commune in New Guinea?"

"The commune idea sounds inviting. Should I bring my allen wrenches?"

"Bring Allen if you can. Can he do the electrical for a mud hut? And cable TV?"

"I think he's booked. Something about putting motion detectors in all of the pyramids."

"Okay. Let's scale it back down to the picnic. By the lake. Sunday at noon."

"I like your take-charge approach. Okay. I'm there. What should I bring?"

"A dozen condoms and your favorite Dr. Seuss book. Nothing, Billy. My idea. My treat."

"Even the condoms?"

"No worries. I have no ovaries."

"Really?"

Natalie started laughing so hard, Billy was afraid she wouldn't stop until Sunday had already come and gone.

"Billy. You are tragically innocent. See you Sunday. I'll come by around noon."

Sunday was one of those days Billy would never forget.

The morning started cloudy, threatening to rain on their picnic plans. But by 11 am all of the grey had cleared and the sun lit the campus in a brilliant spring solarity that brought the temperature into the 70s and set the campus aflame in the rich floral colors of blossoming fruit trees and early flowering perennials.

Billy dressed casually in white painter pants and a red Cornell University wife-beater, while Natalie arrived ready for a remake of the Sound of Music. She looked so wholesome in her light blue spring dress and her hair banded with a white scarf, that Billy did a double take in the lobby to make sure it was really her waiting for him.

"Natalie?"

"Billy."

"Natalie?"

"Did you want to see some ID?"

They walked to the lake, chose a charming spot under the trees by the shore. Natalie had brought a blanket which together they spread out. It was perfect.

With the picnic basket sitting next to her, he was tempted to ask her if she knew how to sing *Edelweiss*. Instead he opted for something less obtuse.

His voice squeaked like he was still going through puberty.

"You look so … so nice."

"Were you expecting the little girl from The Exorcist?"

Damn! She was so quick. It seemed she never was at a loss for a wise crack. By the time they got around to the lunch she'd packed for them, Billy's stomach was starting to hurt. Not from hunger but from laughing so hard.

Natalie brought everything for an ideal picnic. She had several different kinds of sandwiches, chips and pretzels, juices, trail mix, fruits, barbecued finger food, and even two delectable slices of cake she picked up at the deli, carrot with almond cream frosting and lemon with white chocolate frosting.

"Well, Natalie. We have a problem. That's a tough choice. Both of those cakes look really really good."

"Choice? They're both for me."

Fortunately for Billy she was bluffing, and they both dug into each of the cakes, savoring each bite and praising the unrivaled talent of whoever made them. When they were finished, they simultaneously collapsed on their backs, bellies bursting, bodies surrendering to the soothing sedation of the meal. They lay there inches apart, sighing contentedly, as they looked into the deep azure of the sky, and let the gentle breeze bathe them with the natural fragrances of new season.

Natalie woke up first. How long had they been asleep? She didn't have a watch and to keep the sanctity of their picnic free of technological incursions had left her cell phone in her room. She leaned over Billy to see if he was wearing a watch.

Just as she got directly over him, he opened his eyes.

"Are you robbing me?"

"I can't seem to make ends meet on my salary from the university. What else can I do?"

"Kiss me."

"Does it pay well?"

"No."

She leaned down and kissed him. It was brief and delicate.

"Yes it does."

Natalie leaned back and lay down again on her back.

Billy thought of pursuing it. Then he thought better of it. No need to rush. Good things come to those who wait. Is that how the expression went? He would wait.

Plus he didn't have that balls-to-the-walls craving. That overwhelming need for release. That rutting dog response of free-flowing libidinal juices.

Billy thought about it. It was both puzzling and a relief.

This was exactly what happened before. That first time she kissed him when they met in the Atrium Café. Interesting. What was going on?

It wasn't that he didn't find her attractive. Good grief! How could he not? She was absolutely stunning. Her face. Her body. He frankly could hardly wait to put his hands on her breasts and butt. Explore her whole body with his fingertips and eyes. His tongue? Yes, definitely his tongue. He had no experience with that but somehow knew in his gut, the tongue was a very important item.

But all of this "desire" and curiosity was coming from such a different place. It definitely wasn't coming from between his legs this time. He wasn't even hard.

So where was it coming from?

His mind? His heart?

"Billy."

"Natalie."

"I really want to fuck you. But we can't. Not today."

Billy was not entirely comfortable with her bluntness. Maybe that was her intention.

"That's so beautiful. Has this got anything to do with your not having ovaries?"

"What's my last name?"

"Your last name?"

"Yes. Me. I assume you know your last name. And you're the only other person here. So ... me. What's my last name?"

"Um ... I don't know. Sorry."

"Diamond. Natalie Diamond."

"That's an interesting name. Are you related to Neil Diamond?"

"Did you want to fuck me today?"

Billy thought for a moment.

"Actually no. Not really. I was more thinking of you as a salt lick."

Natalie broke out in such a hardy laugh, Billy was afraid all the leaves on the tree they were under might shake loose and bury them.

"We'll have to check your blood pressure first. But I might be into that."

She continued to giggle. It was obvious she was trying to stop, but couldn't.

"Natalie. Can I ask you a personal question?"

Giggle. "Sure." Giggle. "I don't have to answer it." Giggle.

"Does insanity run in your family?"

Giggle. "Hmm." Giggle. "Not any more than yours." Giggle.

"Should I go for help?"

Giggle. "I think we can handle this." Giggle.

She abruptly stopped giggling.

"Billy, before you remove all of the salts from my body with your tongue, there are some things you should know."

"I'm here. You're here. The day is still young. Are you radioactive?"

Natalie started talking and didn't stop for almost an hour.

She told Billy all about herself.

She was the daughter of a Methodist minister in Noblesville, a suburb of Indianapolis, Indiana. Actually, now an ex-minister. But until she was 16, she was a member of a model Christian family, in a very close-knit, ultra-Christian community — fanatic in its devotion to Christ, generous in its charitable works, militant in its efforts to expand the congregation of believers, frantic in its intolerance of any who strayed from the Good Book, vigilant in its monitoring everyone's obedience to the Ten Commandments, self-righteous and judgmental, dogmatic and insular, conservative and obdurate. It was the worst possible world for a curious, creative, questioning, critical-thinking, intelligent young lady like Natalie Diamond.

She survived it by constructing a completely fictional person — the one that everyone in Noblesville saw and waxed lyrical about — and completely suppressing the real one, the one the entire world beyond the city limits of Noblesville saw — the one Billy was seeing now.

There were two advantages to her seemingly impossible situation growing up. First, she never had to keep track of who she lied to. She lied to everyone except herself. Second, she learned and practiced the rare, nearly lost art of relying entirely on herself for entertainment. She developed her brilliant imagination and quick wit in order to survive the drab, banal and completely unfulfilling life she was expected to live, and on the surface did live, for the edification and approval of those around her.

She had two brothers, one three years older and the other two years younger, and a sister four years younger than her. Though they lived in the same house, they were complete strangers to her, as she was to them. She felt a closer affinity with people she met for the first time than with any members of her immediate family.

It both amused and amazed her that in Noblesville, to the very last one, not a single person ever showed the slightest suspicion that anything was amiss with her. Either she was one of the world's greatest unheralded actresses, or everyone around her was so immersed in the fog of their ignorant and prejudiced perception of the world, they didn't take any notice.

Then again, she gave them little to work with. While inside her was a whirling dervish, a frenetic and crazed mind which never rested and was secretly feeding itself with fresh and innovative books, art forms, alternate paradigms and metaphysical concepts, and always flying to new created landscapes of her own imagination's making, on the outside was the quiet, subservient little minister's daughter, towing the line, walking the straight and true, an exemplary illustration of how a young girl could and should be, given the right upbringing, values, and roll models for living a good Christian life. The main role models, of course, were her mother and father, but especially her father. A devoted man of the cloth. The man who selflessly gave his energy, love, prayer, and counsel, to the needy souls of the First Methodist Church of Noblesville.

The Reverend Alphonse Worthington Diamond was a sight to behold. Unlike the rest of Natalie's family and Natalie herself, he was quite tall — 6'4" tall. He had a broad, handsome face, Nordic complexion, high cheekbones, strong chin, blond hair combed straight back from his high forehead, the large athletic frame and musculature of a footballer — indeed he was the varsity quarterback for his team three years running in college — the erect confident posture of a leader, and piercing, deep-set blue eyes which were simultaneously both judgmental and compassionate, tenacious and gentle, righteous and forgiving.

For Natalie, her father's larger-than-life persona, galvanizing charisma, physical gifts, and lofty position of respect, were a blessing. It allowed her to easily blend into the background, assume the meek role she had chosen and perfected for herself, move easily through the tight circles which constituted the community of her father's ministry, relatively unnoticed and unanalyzed.

It allowed her to be both invisible and visible.

Visible she certainly was.

She was a team leader in the *Youth Carry Jesus' Love To Others* workshop. On Saturday mornings, she was a discussion facilitator for the 8 to 10-year-olds class of her father's Junior Bible Study program. She was a Nature Usher for the Christian Seniors Walk In The Park two or three days a week after school, held on the grounds of a local convalescent home. In the summer, she was a coach for both the Christian Children Soccer Camp and the church's popular Summer Youth Sports Festival. Even though she was not a great singer, she was always front-and-center for Sunday services as a member of the all-congregation choir.

At the same time she was invisible.

Invisible when she wanted to be. When she needed to withdraw into the private world she had so painstakingly constructed, sequestered beyond the prying eyes of everyone in her family and in the congregation.

Natalie relished this secret private life, as much as she hated her public one.

She understood all along that while she was praised for her contributions to her father's ministry, she was but a mirror for the spotlight on him. All of the adulation and gratitude reflected off her and ultimately found its way to the great man at the head of his inspired community, the great man at the head of his glorious church, the great man at the head of his model family.

The great and unanimously respected Reverend A. W. Diamond.

The man who joined new couples in the holy bonds of matrimony and consecrated their union with God's divine blessing. The man who graveside offered inspiring words of comfort to the bereaved and held the Holy Bible high into the air as he spoke of God's divine wisdom and infinite mercy. The man who truly cared about each and every member of his extended family of Christ and gave counsel to young and old alike. The man who every Sunday to the standing-room-only pine and glass First Methodist Church of Noblesville delivered rousing Scripture-filled, thundering orations of such majesty that everyone agreed he stood shoulder to shoulder with the likes of Reverends Billy Graham and Oral Roberts. The man who was adored by his congregation as their own inspired agent for the divine word of God Himself.

The same man who when Natalie was 15 took a special liking to an attractive young woman who sang in the choir, was less than half her father's age and only three years older than Natalie herself. The same man who a year later would manufacture scandalous rumors about his wife's infidelities and use the pulpit to attempt to turn the tide of opinion against his own wife, and drive her in shame from the graces of the community she had served selflessly for over 20 years. The same man who would deliver the eulogy and blessing at Natalie's mother's funeral after Natalie came home from a Senior Walk In The Park and found her mother in the bathtub sitting in her own blood, wrists slashed with a steel kitchen carving knife. The same man who would stand before his congregation and in the same breath, disingenuously declare his grief over the loss of his wife and genuinely offer his gratitude to God for sending in such a time of personal suffering someone to comfort him and be his new partner in life, the nubile 19-year old Cynthia Scallon.

To the credit of the members of the First Methodist Church of Noblesville, they saw what their great minister was up to and weren't buying it.

That was when Natalie's life completely changed.

Changed very quickly.

Despite the powerful sway Reverend Diamond had long held with a loyal core of the church membership, once a few highly conservative and watchful individuals — people who were active on a day-to-day basis with the various committees and volunteer outreach teams headquartered at the church's administrative offices — once these straight-arrows suspected his dalliance with the young soprano in the choir, the whispering began. They were more loyal to God's law, especially the Sixth Commandment forbidding adulterous activities, than they were to the Reverend himself. Almost from the beginning of the affair, they started to take special note of Cynthia's comings and goings. Considering choir practice occurred only once a week on Saturday morning, she sure seemed to be around a lot. At first, just slipping in and out of the Reverend's office, then eventually seen openly in his company.

When the Reverend made the tactical error of airing his suspicions that the good Mrs. Diamond was having an affair, they knew it was a case of the frying pan calling the kettle black. It was time to prepare an appropriate response. They saw what was coming. This type of sinful, scandalous nonsense was not the sort of thing which had ever taken place at First Methodist, and they were not about to let it happen now. Very discretely, they went about circulating petitions among the congregants, which once supported by a sufficient number of signatures, would at an appropriate time in the near future be presented to Bishop Anthony Pulfer at the North Central Episcopal Area headquarters in Bloomington. The petitions demanded that Reverend Diamond be replaced as their head pastor.

Unfortunately, everything happened too fast and events got ahead of this vigilante group. The much-loved and respected Mrs. Diamond killed herself. A short time later, the Sunday worshippers sat stunned as the Reverend seemed to have entirely gotten over the grief of losing his wife, and now stood at the pulpit with little Cynthia Scallon at his side, she humbly smiling and blinking at her good fortune, unaware of the outrage simmering among the congregants. Sprinkling his pronouncements with generous doses of Scripture, he turned this special sermon into an embarrassing public spectacle, attempting to replace the real first lady of the church, his deceased wife — someone who had become regarded as a saint — with a hot young piece of ass who happened to sing well.

The good Reverend was so pumped up on love or lust or both, he failed to notice the frowns, grumbling, and general ill humor he had unleashed.

But the mechanism for his removal was in place, and his behavior was such

117

an outrageous and crass affront to the respectability of the Methodist Ministries, it took no time to implement it.

Within only two weeks of submitting the petition, Reverend A. W. Diamond was relieved of his responsibilities with First Methodist Church. Natalie, her sister, and two brothers, with the desultory assistance of their future step-mother, found themselves urgently packing boxes and getting ready to move.

At first they lived at a Residence Inn on the northern perimeter of the Indianapolis beltway. The first few days, her father drove Natalie and her younger brother and sister to and from school. Natalie's older brother was attending junior college, had his own car, and fended for himself. The following week she missed school entirely, when her father and Cynthia disappeared, merely leaving a note.

Kids,

We're going to Vegas for a few days. Big surprise when we get back.
God bless and keep you.

Love,
Dad and Cyndy

God bless and keep you? That was sure a bit difficult for Natalie to swallow. Was her father still planning on being a minister?

Apparently he was. Because when they got back from Las Vegas, all he could talk about was getting a new church and was constantly asking all of them where they wanted to live. Indiana still? Ohio? New York? California? Florida? Pennsylvania?

A whole month passed. The Residence Inn was set up to look like apartments. But they were still living out of their suitcases. It certainly didn't feel like home. But truthfully, could any place feel like home without their mom?

During that month, Natalie's father had numerous meetings with the hierarchy of Methodist Ministries. She overheard a lot of very tense phone calls. Eventually the verdict came in. Reverend Diamond's charm, good looks, persuasive powers and plain good luck had finally hit a wall. He was not under any circumstances going to be assigned another church. In fact he was barred for life from serving in any official capacity for any Methodist ministry-related activity or organization. His preaching days were over.

The surprise he promised — as in *'Big surprise when we get back'* — probably sealed his fate.

Natalie's father and Cynthia had gotten married. Natalie was able to both hide the horror and suppress the desire to laugh in her father's face as he went on and on about their Church of Elvis Wedding Chapel ceremony — with two inebriated strangers as paid witnesses — and the uncanny resemblance to the Big El himself which the minister performing the ceremony bore.

What a pathetic, self-deluding, shallow hypocrite this man had become. Or perhaps always had been. There he sat across from her, Natalie's mother only two months in a grave where the sod cover had barely taken root, with his little teen bride at his side, one hand holding his, the other playing with his ear. Talking about their future as a family.

Family? Right.

What a dandy step-mom she had. At nineteen, just out of high school herself. How perfect! They could go shopping together. Trade make-up tips. Hang out at the mall. Sneak ciggies. Maybe check out boys. Take turns reading *Seventeen Magazine*.

Of course, Natalie didn't herself do any of these things. But if she did.

The point was, this little slut had better never even *try* to order her around, or think for one minute she could fill the shoes of her real mom. If dad wanted a young fuck-buddy, that was his business. But Natalie didn't need a mom-buddy. Her mom hadn't even filled that role.

The family that never was. The family that never would be …

Billy had not moved for over an hour.

Natalie stopped talking. She stared off to the side, maybe overwhelmed by her own candor with a young man she barely new, maybe just needing to take a breather, ponder what all of this must sound like to Billy, coming completely out of the blue, so harsh, in such sharp contrast to the splendor of their surroundings.

Something suddenly struck Billy really hard. Until now, Natalie had spoken evenly and dispassionately. She almost frightened him with the cool detachment with which she was able to describe everything about her troubled upbringing. But as soon as she started to talk about her step-mom, some intense emotion built and he could feel a powerful tempest engulf her. It was an angry and tumultuous side of Natalie he had never seen. Of course, he hadn't seen much of her period. He hardly knew her.

"Do you still speak to this Cynthia step-mom?"

"I don't speak to any of them. Are you thirsty?"

"You must be."

"Miss Blah Blah Blah."

"I am completely riveted, Natalie. I want to know everything you're willing to share. Seriously. But this must be very upsetting …"

"Like anyone has control over their lives?"

They drank some lemonade and Natalie continued.

For the first time in her life, she saw her father dejected. Defeated. Miserable. Though she had never discussed his vocational choice and had no idea what his true motives were for becoming ordained, it was very evident that he had a genuine passion for the ministry. It was now nearly impossible for him to accept his fate, and face the mortifying humiliation of his self-inflicted fall from grace. But the simple, unalterable truth was, that life was forever behind him.

After several weeks, a time when her father was extremely withdrawn and given to piteous brooding, he finally sprang into action. Again, she had no idea how or why he pursued the new path he did — or if he merely stumbled onto it by chance — but within only a few days, he secured a job as a new car salesman. He reported for work and to this day is employed at Gleason Oldsmobile, Pontiac and Buick, in Zionsville. Confident that his new career would prove successful — it has and he is now Assistant Manager there and makes a nice six figures annually — he bought a four-bedroom ranch house in the nearby bland but upwardly mobile suburban town of Carmel. There he has a swimming pool, two dogs, two snowmobiles, two Jetstreams, two SUVs, two of everything.

Natalie recently heard that her step-mom — she really has to force herself to call her that — still looks like she's nineteen and has gotten breast implants. She didn't need them but apparently it seemed like a good idea, based on the trashy magazines she reads.

As far as Natalie can tell, none of them go to church now. Natalie's extremely religious grandparents on her mother's side tried to visit one Christmas but were treated so rudely they never came back. They called her a couple times but they live in Oklahoma, so Natalie hasn't seen them since her mom's funeral.

Natalie doesn't miss her mom any more than she did when she was alive. She wishes she could feel something normal about her mother's death. She has a sense of loss but it is abstract, like the way you feel when a celebrity dies. You know who the person is and you feel bad but it's not real grieving because you share no history.

If Natalie sat on a jury, she would insist her father be convicted and sentenced to life in prison for killing her mom — he was the cause of her death. An open and shut case of murder. Even so, she doesn't hate him any more for that heinous act than she does for him just being who and what he is.

She would totally cut off her ties with her family-in-name-only, but her father is still paying for her college education. She makes token contact on the recognized days for token contact — birthdays, Christmas, Easter, Father's Day.

Natalie smiled with not a little irony.

"And they lived happily ever after."

It had started raining. Not hard. But a steady drizzle.

Neither of them had noticed. Billy looked up and blinked.

"I think our picnic may be coming to an end. What do you think?"

Natalie playfully mussed up his hair.

"I think our picnic is moving to my room."

"Maybe I should stop at Jameson and get some dry clothes."

"Why do you need clothes?"

"Right."

It was amazing how much she had packed for them to eat. So after Billy licked her from head to toe and back again, they enjoyed some barbecued chicken, potato salad, carrot and celery sticks and salt-and-vinegar kettle chips.

"Billy. What's my last name?"

"Diamond, of course. How could I forget?"

"Exactly. And that means the rules have changed."

"I hated those old rules. Even if I have no idea what you are talking about."

They made love late into the night. They each missed their morning classes, a first for both of them. When they finally woke up tangled in each others arms, it was 10:55 am.

Billy stretched and struggled to his feet. He bent over and looked in the picnic basket.

Finally, it was empty.

"You're out of food. I can't see you anymore."

"Okay. Bye."

Billy had two classes that afternoon. Natalie had one, then an administrative meeting early in the evening for all of the Mary Donlon Hall RAs.

Billy waited to call until he was sure her meeting was over. It was shortly after nine.

"Hey."

"Why, it's Billy Green. How are you Billy Green?"

Crazy Natalie. Ha ha ha.

"Not quite the man I used to be. Not quite the man I will be. Taking my vitamins, though."

"That's very nice. Glad to hear it. Listen, my friend Pam ... you remember Pam. She was with me the night you lost your virginity. Anyway, she's here right now and I need to go."

"Right. I understand. No problem."

"So I'll talk to you later. Okay, Billy Green?"

Click.

Whew! That was cold. Maybe she was just joking around. Doing a little skit for her friend. But he felt like he had been rabbit-punched in the heart.

The night you lost your virginity.

Ouch! That was a head butt.

Okay. Fine. It was probably just a moment. An anomaly.

But it was the same the next night. And the next. And the next.

Natalie was busy. And playfully distant. Each time he was sorry he called.

As the week wore on, Billy reassured himself with the certainty that Pam's little visit — from which he was beyond a shadow of a doubt excluded — soon had to come to an end.

But Friday afternoon's conversation sank his hopes further.

"Sure sure. Of course I want to see you. But listen, Billy. We're heading into the city for the weekend. In fact I have to leave right this very minute or we'll miss our bus."

"The city?"

"New York City, goofy boy! I'll call you as soon as I get back. Gotta go."

Click.

Okay. Billy had plenty to do. Most people wouldn't consider even sleeping if they had his six-class load. So this weekend, it was a date with the books straight through. College was no picnic. At least it wasn't supposed to be.

Billy's phone didn't ring. Of course, it never rang. So what was new?

But Tuesday night he couldn't stand it any longer. He dialed Natalie's number. Actually, he walked over to Mary Donlon and called from the lobby on the house phone.

"Billy!! I have missed you so much. Can you come over right now?"

"I can be there in ... actually I'm here. Downstairs."

"Thank God. I can't wait to see you. I'm coming down."

Within two minutes she was sprinting at him from the stairwell door, nearly knocking over two coeds walking in the opposite direction in the process. She looked great!

She literally leaped into his arms and smothered him with kisses. Then she

121

stepped back and gave him a good once over, smiling like she was looking at her newborn baby.

"You look so good!"

"So do you, Natalie. So do you. When did you get back?"

"Sunday."

Sunday? It was Tuesday.

"Sunday?"

"Hey. It's a beautiful evening. Let's go for a walk."

Out they went. Natalie was practically skipping like a young school girl, alternately hugging his arm and putting her hand around his waist. It slipped down on his butt a couple times, and she gave him an affectionate squeeze on the underside. Natalie definitely knew how to make him feel good.

They returned within a half-hour, made love twice and fell asleep in one another's arms.

They didn't miss classes the next day. In fact neither missed another class for the rest of Spring Term.

But they spent a lot of time together. As much as Natalie's busy schedule and Billy's heavy class load would permit.

They were realistic. If either one of them had an important paper due, or a test to prepare for, they respected that. Cornell was still the top priority, for both of them in terms of scholastics, additionally for Natalie in terms of her job as a Resident Assistant. It trumped their desire to be together, no matter how acute.

Whatever the demands of campus life now, they promised one another they would have time this summer. Indianapolis wasn't all that far from Detroit. Maybe a six or seven hour drive? It was doable.

Only two things interrupted the blissful flow of their budding, building romance over the remaining four weeks of classes.

The last week of April, Billy decided to find out what was happening with his mom. He called during the evening on a Wednesday, knowing his father was still working afternoons and wouldn't be there.

"Hey mom."

"Oh Billy. It's so good to hear your voice. If I sound funny … I'm a little out of it right now. It's very painful. They have me on chemo."

"I thought they got everything. The doctor sounded confident."

"It's always something. They keep running tests. It seems like they say something different every time I go in."

"Are you … has it spread?"

"They don't think so. But they want to make sure. It's no fun. I'm tired all of the time."

"How long will this go on?"

"Till my hair falls out, I guess. Just kidding. They're monitoring my progress. When they're absolutely positive that I am out of danger, the treatments stop."

"You kidding about your hair, right?"

"Well, no. If they keep up the chemo long enough, that's what happens. But it grows back. Pretty funny when you think about it. Your dad was the one always so worried about become a billiard ball. But it might end up being me."

122

"Don't worry, mom. You'll be beautiful anyway."

"I'm looking at wigs. I'm got my eye on a couple from a mail order catalog. Whaddya think? Should I go Marilyn Monroe blond or maybe Katherine Hepburn brunette?"

The thought of his mom as a blond bombshell really broke Billy up. They both laughed hysterically.

"That's a tough call, mom. How about an afro?"

"That's it! There was this group. Sly and the Family Stone. All of the girls had these afros wider than their shoulders."

"Or Diana Ross and the Supremes. There are kids here at school that are crazy about that old Motown music."

"How is school? Do you have a girlfriend yet?"

"How did you know? You must be psychic."

"I dunno. Just had this feeling. It's good to have someone. But you're young. Don't go getting too serious. Just have fun ... while you can. The years just run away, Billy. Have fun while you're young ... and healthy."

Billy knew what his mom was really saying.

"How's the old man?"

"Old and cranky. But still my Prince Charming."

"Mom, you could find something good to say about anyone. You'd probably find something nice to say about President Bush."

"His daughters are quite pretty. Very sweet looking."

"Yeah, for a couple of airheaded party girls. Anyway tell the old peckerhead his son says hi. Is he still limping?"

"No. He's pretty much back to normal. He healed pretty fast. He told his doctor that drinking beer helps to speed up the healing process. And he doesn't need a prescription for it."

"Is he still planning on running in the Detroit City Parks Marathon this summer?"

He could hear his mother's feeble laugh segue into a breathy cough.

"Oh my! Sometimes you are so funny, Billy. Your dad running the marathon. Not likely. Maybe no more limp. But the man gets out of breath just walking from the bathroom to the kitchen in the morning after taking his buffalo-size dump."

"Spare me the visuals, mom."

"Okay Billy. I better go. Right now I feel like I just ran the marathon myself with your father on my back. I sleep twelve hours a day. In bed before nine. I'm becoming an old lady."

"You'll be fine. Just give it some time. Love you, mom."

"Love you too, Billy. Be a good boy."

He was worried. But what could he do? What would happen would happen.

Billy never was tempted to discuss any of these particulars with Natalie. Of course, if things worked out between them, at some point she would see the dirty laundry of his family life. At least for now, he preferred to keep his time with her unsullied. As much as he loved his mom, as close as they still were even with him away at college, it just didn't feel right getting into any of this for now with his new "girlfriend".

Despite his frantic class schedule and enormous amounts of homework, he saw Natalie every day. Sometimes, as it was the evening of his call to his mom, it was just a brief rendezvous midway between their dorms, for some playfulness and a goodnight kiss. At least three evenings a week, usually including both Friday and Saturday, they spent an extended amount of time together, with Billy staying overnight in Natalie's room. She never said one way or another, but Billy assumed that her feelings like his were deepening with each and every moment they shared. He found now that whenever he wasn't immersed in his studies, his thoughts went to her, filling him with a warm contentment, an intoxicating anticipation for their next meeting.

Then, just over two weeks after the call to his mom, right before study week and then final exams for the term, Billy got a rather awkward, somewhat frantic call from Natalie. This was just as he was heading out the door to spend the evening and the night with her. Apparently, some crisis manufactured or real had put her friend Pam in a frightful state.

"I don't know what's going on yet. She just got here. I had no idea she was coming. But I really need to spend some time with her. I'll call you tomorrow and let you know."

"Tell her I said hi. I ... I love you."

That was the first time he had said it. Maybe she didn't hear him. Or maybe she didn't think she had heard it right. Those three foreboding words tended to be a no-mans-land for most guys — certainly it was uncharted territory for Billy.

"Bye."

It was disappointing not seeing her tonight. But a mixed blessing. Billy was rationalizing when he claimed he had the time to be with her this evening. Sure, they would have done some studying but most of the time would have been we-really-should-be-studying foreplay, decathlon-level lovemaking, and at least one reprise to make sure they had gotten it right. And he had two papers due by the end of the week. So he definitely could put the time to good use. But it sure hurt down there in the achy-breaky part of his body to not have a go at it tonight.

Billy by now realized he had reached some addictive level with Natalie. It wasn't just the sex, though it did seem that that's where the withdrawal pains surfaced when they weren't together. The truth was she was the whole package. She made him laugh. She made him cry. She was his friend, his mother, his muse, his confidant, his shrink, his guru, his counselor, his fix. She was his religion and his inspiration.

It had happened so fast. Nothing he had been looking for, that's for sure. In fact, he vaguely remembered swearing off women back about a thousand years ago right after the Christmas holiday break.

How had this come about? In the tumbling free fall of the past seven weeks, he really couldn't reconstruct how this beautiful lady had gone from being a stick in his eye, taunting him about the cherry-popping party the girls had arranged for him on the very same floor where she was an RA, to being ... being ... *the one.* The one he was increasingly feeling he could not live without. The one who filled all of his idle thoughts. The one who intruded on his productive moments. The one he always now found center stage in the theater of his imagination. The one who he didn't have to stop and think about. Because she was always there.

Billy threw himself at his school work. He finished one paper that evening. The next night, after a demanding day of classes, he got a good head of steam going on the second paper. The entire time, he kept turning around from his desk to glance at the phone. No call.

A little after midnight on Wednesday, the second paper was nearly complete. He needed to clean up some of the writing, double check his references, fill in the footnotes, and format the short but impressive bibliography.

Two more days passed. No call. It was Friday. This had a familiar feel. Was she going to disappear for the weekend again? Right before finals?

Should he call?

No.

Even if the dead air, the silence, the separation, the wonder, the worry, was killing him.

No.

Something told him to wait it out. Don't call her. Give Natalie the time and space she needed with her mysterious friend Pam.

Billy ejaculated into a wad of Kleenex and went to sleep.

Girls in White Dresses with Blue Satin Sashes

Except when he was extremely tired — when studying for final exams, for example — Billy had always been subject to what would be diagnosed as a sleeping disorder. Nevertheless, he never sought any professional help. It just was the way things were, so he toughed it out. Truth was, ever since he started high school, he never slept more than two hours without awakening. The kicker being, though he was quite sure he had them, he never remembered his dreams. A blank slate. He would go back to sleep and no more than two hours later, again his eyes would pop open or he would literally bolt upright in bed. But no matter how hard he tried, without fail, he could not remember a single detail of any dream he might have been having.

Suddenly one night, midway in the second half of Spring Term, he again abruptly woke up. He had fallen asleep at around 11 pm and sure enough it was just before 1 am. But this time he remembered the dream. He was at first startled but too exhausted to keep from going back to sleep. Then when he awoke again, he realized that he had just had a continuation of the previous dream. And so it went. Four times in a row.

Finally he got up at 6:15 and got ready for his 8:00 am class.

On his way to class he had time to think about what had happened. It began to sink in what a breakthrough it was. He was actually able to recall in broad terms the content of the dream. Overall it was a pleasant, if somewhat surrealistic garden-like landscape with ethereal music playing, and a seemingly endless parade of young ladies all attired in identical white flowing dresses.

The next couple nights, Billy's sleeping routine reverted back to what it had been for years.

Then a few nights later, after staying up late studying for an announced quiz in his Statistical Theory class, he awoke and fully expected it to be 2:30 or 3:00 in the morning. It was 7:30. He had slept the entire night through, for the first time in five years.

And he remembered the dream.

Vividly.

It was the one he had started a few nights ago.

He was in a vast borderless park, one which stretched from one edge of the world to the other. The lawn was intensely green, an endless rolling sea of clover and grass with patches of ankle-high flowers and floral groundcover. The colors of the flowers were breathtakingly bright, almost as if they were illuminated from within. There were occasional trees of modest height spread out throughout the park, as far as he could see. On some of the trees were perched large heron-like birds with long graceful wings that they stretched and waved. They looked like huge feathered angels.

Billy could smell a quartet of scents, one blending into the next. The sticky sweet smell of marshmallows warming on a stove — one of his favorite smells from childhood when his mom would make s'mores at home — a honey and vanilla scent, pure jasmine, and lastly a spicy combination of honeysuckle and saffron.

Music was playing, a soft airy mixture of male voices like a Gregorian chant, but with symphonic orchestrations and modern melodies.

There were young girls strolling across the entire expanse all wearing identical long white dresses, made of some airy chiffon-like material which alternately billowed and clung to their young graceful bodies. They all had sandals which laced up their calves, and had long hair variously tied with white ribbon bows. Each had a blue satin sash around her waist.

The sky was pale pink and powder blue with long wispy tendrils and eddies of white clouds which arose from one horizon and raced across the sky to the other at breathtaking speed. These translucent fibers and taffeta clouds sped along a jet stream at a very low altitude, maybe only a few hundred feet. In contrast to the epic rush across the sky, the air on the ground was completely still. However, if any birds got to close to the racing wind they would be pulled in and swept along, then discharged some distance away unharmed. The rushing fibrous clouds would sometimes descend very close to the ground. Usually they never got lower than twenty or thirty feet. Even this low, they were completely silent. But the effect was so startling that anyone on the ground would out of reflex duck down, usually more playfully than actually frightened. Very rarely, the cloud stream would come down to within ten feet of the ground. Now the silent wind carrying the clouds could be felt. The girls all would crouch on their hands and knees, while their hair and gowns would tangle and billow. It was great fun and they all laughed with delightful ease.

The lowering of the cloud stream was always preceded by a blend of very high-pitched female voices — young girls singing in a euphonius language he didn't recognize — joining the airy male voices. They combined in sharply ascending and descending microtonal melodies, creating pleasant but unusual and sometimes dissonant harmonies. This sonic whirl increased in intensity as the luminescent jet stream got closer, and would soften and disappear as the jet stream rose to greater height.

Billy would be wandering about — it was effortless and felt more like floating than walking. When any of the girls passed near him, they would acknowledge him with a pleasant smile and nod of the head, sometimes just a friendly wave of the hand. Then as the dream developed, one would come directly up to him. She would bend down and sinking her fingers into the earth, pick up a rectangular plot of grass, which would immediately begin to transform into a mirror mounted in a sinewy gold frame, which shimmered and undulated. She would hold it up to him and Billy would look straight into the mirror. He would see a female face he recognized. After a few moments that face, in a watery rippling of the reflective glass, would morph into himself, hold his reflection for a while, then his face would dissolve into another female face.

The females were a random assortment, all different kinds, different ages, friends, family, recognizable strangers, from various periods in his past, up to the present. His mother, Sister Mary, maybe a high school teacher, girls from junior high or high school — once it was Jackie the Ripper — Kristin or Erin or one of the other Foxy Five, sometimes a movie star like Natassja Kinski or Nicole Kidman, an Olympic figure skater, news anchor Connie Chung. Sometimes he didn't know the female in the mirror by name, but remembered that it was someone he had seen, like a cashier at a campus deli or a department secretary.

Each of the females mimed some inexplicable or silly facial expression. They winked, frowned, mocked, flirted, taunted, appeared angry, showed approval and disapproval, laughed, gestured for him to come closer for an unheard whispered secret, licked their lips seductively, yelled, looked bored, snarled, put on lipstick. One picked her nose and flicked it at him. There was no particular order or discernable reason for whatever they were doing, or the implication that any of it was important or meaningful. Usually after one round of girl-Billy-girl-Billy-girl-Billy-girl morphings, the blue sash girl would put the mirror back down, where it would dissolve back into the lawn. Then she would merely walk away, looking back over her shoulder smiling. Or she would raise her arms high, look heavenward, close her eyes and surrender to a deep rapture, as she was abruptly sucked into the overhead cloud jet stream to instantly vanish.

The dream was both pleasant and unpleasant. Dreamy and intensely real. Buoyant and sad.

There was an innocent fairy-tale quality about the park. It was airy and optimistic, capturing the kind of dreamscape utopia of a modern-day Garden of Paradise. The blue sash girls were all playful and engagingly cheerful. Despite this, Billy would often feel a tugging at his insides, not so much a frustration as a sadness, of the sort one feels years after the death of a loved one. The initial grief might be gone but there remains a lingering sense of loss, of never being able to talk to this person again and say things you wish you had said when the person was alive — a poignant impotence.

Moreover, he found himself pulled into the faces of whoever was in the mirror, and he would try to communicate with them. But he could form no words. He could feel his throat constricting and his lips moving but there would be no sound. It was especially difficult when he was looking at himself in the mirror. This would momentarily drive him to tears. He'd see himself as this helpless mute, struggling to speak, but not even know what it was he was trying to say.

The dream recurred a number of nights running. It was pretty much the same each time. Some nights there more of a playful air about it. Other times it was quite somber, harshly focused on his alienation and his inability to communicate.

Two of those nights, he was with Natalie. In the translucent jelly of his senses as he transitioned from sleep into consciousness, it was disorienting and surreal for him to open his eyes and see Natalie right there, the starkest element of his current reality, juxtaposed over the dissolving images and subsiding surrealism of the dream.

Both times she was still sleeping when he awoke. He could hear her slow, deep breathing. She was worlds away deep in the yawning caverns of her own sub-conscious. She didn't stir as he pressed his face against hers, turned his head slightly and brought his lips to her ear.

"I love you, Natalie."

Billy appeared to have conquered his sleeping disorder. He now regularly slept through the entire night.

Some nights he would either not dream or not remember having one. Often, he would again be immersed in the fairy tale world of girls in white dresses with blue satin sashes.

There were only two dramatic departures from the set format of the dream.

One time as the jet stream got closer and closer to the ground, the microtonal vocal music built and built, sounding not pleasant but increasingly ominous. Mimicking the girls around him, Billy got down close to the ground. This time he found himself looking into the mouth of a round well, sunk so deep into the earth that nothing could be seen but the blackest of black voids. There was no way to tell how deep the well was, but Billy got the sense that it went down thousands of miles. Concerned that Billy was thinking of entering the well, he was immediately surrounded by five or six of the blue sash girls, who grabbed him and pleaded with him to stay with them on the surface. They literally held on to him for dear life, pinned him down so he could not move. Finally the jet stream rose back skywards and the black hole of the well evaporated before his eyes. Though in the dream no one told him, and therefore he had no way of knowing how he knew, immediately after the well had disappeared, Billy was certain that at the bottom of the well was Natalie's deceased mother. He woke up crying.

The other variation happened the very last time he had the dream.

It occurred at the tail end of Pam's most recent surprise visit.

A blue sash girl held up a mirror and Billy could see the face of his mother. This time, instead of morphing into himself, the lady in the mirror morphed into Natalie. She studied Billy intently for a long time, then laughed and playfully blew him a kiss. The blue sash girl then kneeled and put the mirror down, where it was absorbed into the earth. But when she stood back up, the girl had become Natalie's friend Pam. Pam blithely looked him up and down kind of smirking. She then said, *"Is this how you want to be remembered?"* Billy glanced down and saw that he was completely naked. Pam laughed tauntingly, waving her index finger back and forth as if saying '*shame on you*', the way you would tease a child. Then she brought her other hand up, turned her palms upwards and reached both hands toward him, offering her fingertips for him to smell. Billy leaned forward slightly and the bouquet of a tauntingly familiar odor filled his nostrils. It was both sweet and sour, not pungent but slightly sharp, and it caught in his throat. It was an earthy smell he couldn't quite identify, but which seemed intensely feminine — natural secretions which were distinctly female. Billy to his surprise and embarrassment could feel he was getting an erection. He could also in the dream sense how desperately he hoped Pam wouldn't notice his arousal. Shame spread across his skin like hot steam. Pam glanced down only briefly but registered no emotion. Her steely gaze fixed on Billy's eyes, as she put her hands back up to her own face. She closed her eyes and inhaled deeply. Her smile became intense, animated. Her face dreamy. Then she again extended her hands palms up in front of her and blew across them. The air between them filled with a shimmering silver-and-purple vapor. The soft translucent pall was beautiful, almost hypnotic to watch. But as it reached his face, it slammed him with the violence of an explosive shock wave. He instantly grabbed his throat, choking on the poisonous plume, then collapsed to the ground. His eyes burned as if acid had been thrown in them. His nasal passages were on fire and he wanted to scream but he was completely paralyzed. No matter how desperately he tried, he couldn't breathe and knew in the next moments he was going to die.

That was when he woke up.

Gasping for air. Trembling. Heart pounding.

Crying out loud in terror and pain: "No! No! Please no!"

Briefs soaking wet with the warm slime of a nocturnal emission.

Billy soon calmed down and got his bearings. It was 5:20 am. He cleaned himself up. He couldn't go back to sleep and didn't want to, fearing that the dream would repeat, or worse, continue. He'd be forced to witness his own death.

Pam.

It was so weird how vividly he was able to see her. He had only met her once and that was some time ago — the brief encounter at his birthday party when Natalie had stopped by to caution the girls about the noise and using controlled substances. Clearly she had made quite an impression on him. Of course, Pam had come up a number of times since. She and Natalie had been best friends for most of their lives. Didn't she say they went back to the third or fourth grade?

He wondered if he should mention it to Natalie. No, he definitely shouldn't. Way too morbid. Way too psycho.

Billy made himself a cup of coffee and thought about it. He finally decided the whole thing was a fluke. Some insane brain fart. The mind sure likes to play games, especially when a person is under pressure.

It now occurred to Billy that he had never brought up to Natalie his sleeping difficulties, or the dream with the blue sash girls he had been repeatedly having. Or more importantly, how he was after so many years finally sleeping through the entire night. It seemed like too much to explain. Too much to burden her with. All the same, he had no doubt that she was responsible for this phenomenal breakthrough. It was her gift to him, even if she was unaware she had given it.

But this thing last night! This truly bizarre nightmare. Where does *that* fit in?

No, even if he if he did get around to talking to her about any of this, he certainly would not bring up this last dream — the Pam dream. It was irrelevant. An anomaly.

Besides. How could he go about telling her? When would he see her again? *Would* he ever see her again? What was he supposed to think? It was several days running now, this latest mysterious unforeseen gap in their communication.

Where was Natalie?

Still with her friend Pam?

Billy was exhausted. After all it was barely six in the morning and that meant he had only gotten four hours sleep. He couldn't make himself go back to bed. He was just too agitated.

He gulped down the remaining cold mouthful of his coffee, got dressed and went for a walk. When he came back, he figured he would start the study blitz in preparation for exams.

And try not to look at the phone and wonder why Natalie hadn't called.

Billy started wandering. It was a splendid late-May morning. In a few hours, if it didn't cloud up and rain, it would probably get uncomfortably warm. But right now it was absolutely perfect. The air was completely still, there were a few wisps of cirrus clouds on the farthest reaches of the sky. Some early birds were full tilt into the chipper melodies with which they greeted the new day.

He headed south directly past Mary Donlon, threaded his way through Clara Dickson, Court and Bauer Halls, crossed Cradit Farm Drive, over to Beebe Lake. No one was out and about yet. It was too early and a Saturday — a sleep-in day for most everybody.

As he walked along the north bank of the lake he saw the very spot where he and Natalie had had their first picnic. Billy sat down for a while and just looked at the glassy surface of the water and thought about her. He was sure she was not trying to intentionally hurt him, but this disappearing act thing was driving him absolutely crazy. Twice now. Twice because of Pam.

He tried to put it in perspective. Okay. He was the new kid in town. They went back. Way back. The majority of their lives. He could only wish to have a friend like that. But it still bothered him. What was it? Simple. He missed her. Ached for her. Things had happened quickly but they ran deep.

He got up, walked a little ways east along the shore. Then headed back north toward his dorm. This time he went around Kay Hall and thought about going over to Purcell Community Center to get some breakfast.

As he strode up the street, he casually glanced to his left toward the east entrance of Mary Donlon.

He nearly fainted.

Talk about a weird coincidence.

There was a taxi out front and who did he see leaving the lobby? Natalie and Pam!

Pam had an overnight in one hand. They walked slowly with their arms around each other.

They hadn't seen Billy and he didn't want to create the impression that he

130

was spying on them, though he inadvertently was. He stepped behind a tree and watched.

It took them a few minutes to say good-bye. Hugs. It looked like Pam might be crying. She wiped her eyes a couple times.

Pam then got in the taxi and Natalie waved as it pulled away. She turned and walked leisurely back into the dorm. She seemed pensive. Lost in thought.

Billy still feared if he made his presence known, it might be misinterpreted. So he just continued on his way to pick up something to eat. He grabbed some fast-food pastries, Gatorade, and a giant bag of popcorn at the Bear Necessities Convenience Store, then quickly returned to his room in Jameson.

The phone was ringing as he walked in the door. His Israeli roommate looked up briefly from his bed through bleary eyes, then rolled over and went back to sleep.

"Tomb of the Unknown Soldier."

"Billy. Did I wake you?"

"No. I'm still asleep."

"I know you're busy. But can I see you?"

"Let me think about this for a while. Hmm. Okay."

Billy went directly to her room. She opened the door completely naked, closed and locked it. They made love for two hours, then took a short break to eat his junk food.

"Billy. You're going to kill yourself eating this stuff. Look at this label. There are more chemicals in this so-called fruit strudel than the chemistry lab."

"Want some popcorn?"

They then spent another three hours in, around, under, and beside her bed in every shape and variation of lovers' embrace and entanglement they could devise, before hunger finally made a non-negotiable demand that they put some real food in their bodies.

On the way over to the North Star Café, they agreed that after lunch they both really had to hit the books. Their resolve wobbled a bit after the meal, so they ended up taking a long walk through campus before finally heading back.

"If we can just get through the next couple weeks, we'll have the whole summer."

Natalie didn't say anything.

"I can probably borrow my family's car a few times. How about you? Do you have a vehicle back in Indianapolis? It's 280 miles. With a tailwind, maybe 4½ or 5 hours tops."

"Billy. I'm not going to go home this summer."

"Not going home?"

"No. Big change of plans. Pam and I are going to travel. Just in the western half of the U.S. Camping mostly. Her parents are loaded. But I have to watch my money."

Billy was having trouble wrapping his mind around this. He wasn't sure it made any sense. First of all, based on little comments she had made along the way, he assumed that Natalie had to supplement what her father was contributing toward her education, therefore would have to get a job for the 3-month break.

And maybe he had read her wrong, but it had certainly seemed like she was looking forward to seeing him this summer. 3 months? No Natalie and Billy? Could this really be happening?

"So … uh. Does this change things? I mean … is it over?"

Natalie stopped walking and turned Billy to face her. She gently pulled his face down towards her, so that their foreheads were touching. Her hands softly caressed the back of his neck.

"What do you think, Mr. Billy Green? Do I look like some silly school girl to you? Do you think this is just a Spring Term dalliance? Have you so little faith in me, Mr. Billy Green?"

Before he could answer, she brought her hands around to the sides of his face and kissed him. Tenderly. Affectionately. Running her fingers over his ears and through his hair.

"Now you remember that, Billy. Anytime we can't be together, whether it's just for a few minutes, or if it's the whole summer. You think about this very moment right now. Carry it in your heart. Your mind. Every cell of your body. This feeling. Because this is how I feel."

"I'm going to miss you."

"Yes, you will. And I'll miss you."

"Natalie, I love you."

"You should."

Billy walked her back to Mary Donlon then headed back to his own dorm to crack the books. For the first time since they had been seeing each other, he couldn't concentrate. He read the same passages in his text book over and over, without knowing what he had just read. Finally, when he couldn't take it any more, he went to the phone and dialed Natalie's number.

It rang and rang and rang. No answer.

Oh my god! The whole summer.

The whole *fucking* summer!

Summer of Discontent

Freshman year was over. It was middle of June and time to go back home for nearly three months.

Billy couldn't dispel the gloom that settled into every pore of his skin, every cell of his body, as he got closer to Detroit. He was back on a Greyhound bus, suitcase in the belly of the metal beast, duffel bag stored above his seat.

Throughout his entire life, Billy would experience no small amount of wonder at what a gray wash-out all his memories of Detroit were, what a homogenous void the years he had spent there seemed to be. And now, the closer the bus got to Michigan, the more he dreaded the blurred vision and the numbing insensibility that the next three months would be.

He had to go back. He had to make some money. Poverty struck no bargains.

His father had arranged for him to work at the same assembly plant he himself had been working for the last eight years. Billy was a temporary hire and wouldn't be required to join the union. Which begged the question: Why would they want to keep around some worthless college punk who didn't know which end of a broom did the sweeping?

He arrived at home on Sunday and went to work on Monday.

The good news was that during his eight-hour shift, Billy never saw his father. The factory was monstrous, taking up half of a square city-mile, and his father worked off in some other section, buried behind enormous machines, conveyors, robotic arms, hoists, and other complex bulky mechanisms. Thus he only had to endure the short but conversationless ride to and from the plant, circumscribed by his father's lobotomous stupor and his own private meditations.

Billy's job was boring, thankless and numbing. Once he got familiar and comfortable with the cavernous, lifeless facility, with its 110 decibels of clanking, motorized churning, its unabating industrial redolence of oil and ozone, its Planet-of-the-Apes citizenry — an environment he certainly had never been in before and frankly couldn't have imagined — it was all he could do to keep his mind from turning to an inert bowl of mush.

His duties consisted of sweeping the shop floor, collecting metal shavings, curlicues and granules of metallic waste. These were the debris created by dozens of lathes, mills, drills and shapers, aligned in row after row in the custom metal working area, the section which made iron and steel prototype components for future versions of the engines, transmissions, rear axles, and other mechanical units they would eventually pump out by the thousands when put into full production.

Billy, in his heavy work clothes and apron, filthy with shop grime, slimy and wet from the splattering of oil and the dingy gray lubricating fluid that poured over and cooled the metal parts being machined, would go from workstation to workstation and using a narrow pitchfork and shovel, scoop out the tangled clumps of curly metal vines, scoop up the flakes from the catch pans, then sweep the area of any other waste. The work itself was monotonous and mind-numbing, but not the primary source of Billy's annoyance.

What became a dreary and aggravating ritual was dealing with the men.

Billy had never been and wasn't now elitist or condescending. He didn't think that just because he was attending college, that meant he was somehow better than the guys who worked in the thousands of factories in and around Detroit. As he saw it, these men put in long, hard hours to eke out a living in order to support their families and have their little piece of the American Dream. He could respect that.

He had every expectation that he would somehow fit right in for the short duration of his summer job, be a member of the team, be just one of the guys. Chuck and jive. Crack a few jokes. No problem.

Unfortunately, the men didn't see things that way.

From the get-go, he was treated as an outsider, an intruder, a mutant strain, a smarty-pants college boy. When they did pay attention to him, they often made him the butt of a lot of crude and lame jokes. Often they ignored him, making it *really* obvious they were ignoring him. Either way, Billy was never able to let his guard down and just be himself.

He became defensive. More often than not, he couldn't for the life of him come up with anything to say. Which just confirmed in their mind that the smart-aleck, sissy college boy thought he was better than they were.

They were relentless in their antagonism. He was rendered speechless by the bottom-feeding level of their ignorance.

> *"After you become a fancy lawyer, are you gonna turn around and sue your own mother like those kikes in New York do?"*

"Well ..."

> *"If there ain't no God, how the hell you think you got here? In a fucking space ship?"*

"Hmm ..."

> *"You gonna tell me my great grandfather was a monkey? What about Noah's Ark? Was Moses a monkey?"*

"Golly ..."

> *"Fuck these immigrants. If English was good enough for Jesus, it's sure as hell good enough for them."*

"Uh ..."

Actually Billy had the perfect rejoinder to that one but he likely would have gotten his ass kicked the length of the huge factory.

The men were long on confrontation but short on actual conversation.

In his sixty-nine days working there, he never once had what might be called an actual dialogue with any of the 'lifers'. Not even small talk. Not even a slight opening into which he could insert some sports trivia, a joke, a weather comment, anything to establish a foothold and start to build the simplest camaraderie.

Maybe they were threatened by him.

Or maybe they were just as plain stupid as they seemed.

After a couple frustrating weeks, Billy realized he should have expected this. After all, he had spent 18 years under the same roof as his father. And in terms of having a coherent discussion, this same impregnable wall of ignorance and idiocy was all he knew at home. He mistakenly assumed his dad was an anomaly.

How very wrong.

What routinely really got to Billy was how single-minded most of them were. The bulk of men in his section — who Billy found out were something of an "elite" corps of highly skilled journeyman, all of whom had gone through long and arduous apprenticeships to qualify for their current jobs — never seemed to tire of warning Billy and giving him sage advice about masturbation ...

> *"Listen son. You're gonna get hair on your palms, you keep spankin' the monkey the way you do."*

"The trick is to sit on your hand till it falls asleep before you jerk off. Then it feels like someone else is pulling your pud."

"If you keep jacking off in the shower, you're gonna get a hard-on every time it rains."

… or making crude jokes about college coeds, homosexuals or AIDS …

"Hey! You know what AIDS stands for, don't you? Asshole Injected Death Sentence."

"Do you know what you get if you cross a homo Eskimo and a nigger, don't ya? A snow blower that doesn't work!"

"You wanna know why the Mafia and eating college pussy is the same? One slip of the tongue and you're in deep shit!!"

"So Einstein. You know why scientist's can't discover a cure for AIDS? Lemme explain it to ya. It's because they can't get the laboratory mice to fuck each other up the ass!"

Hand-jacking seemed to have totally replaced the friendly wave, pleasant smile, or simple handshake as the standard form of greeting. He couldn't remember a single time that any of the men he worked beside just simply said, "Good morning" or "How are you?" Maybe they didn't know how. And though Billy had heard them talk among themselves — actually conducting something resembling conversations, as pedestrian as they might have been — with him, no one ever mentioned the news, sports, their jobs, families, or even the weather.

It was all jack, whack, fudge-pack.

There were only two men who deviated from this formula.

One was a complete loner. Moses Hamilton was an older black man, reputed to be just six years from retirement, who ran a iron casting shaper. He did the crude rough-cut on raw castings, machining that didn't have tolerances which would demand his constant attention. After setting the machining parameters, Moses would set the machine on automatic, then read his pocket Bible. Over and over again. He never spoke to anyone, and was reputed to be a weekend minister at a downtown African-American Baptist church.

The other guy was a younger fellow — maybe in his late 20s — who was in charge of the tool crib. Kip Jenkins presided over a caged area which housed all the various custom and replacement drills, jigs, bits, threaders and other cutting tools that the men needed from time to time to do their jobs. For some reason, right off he took Billy under his wing. They became buddies and often talked or played cards during lunch break.

When Billy knew that his area foreman wouldn't be hovering around looking over his shoulder, he took the opportunity to slip into the tool crib for twenty or thirty minutes and hide in the back. Kip typically joined him and smoked a joint, while Billy kept an eye peeled for anyone approaching the service window to check out tools, or more ominous, for a surprise appearance by a supervisor. Billy kept a book, typically a light novel, stashed back there. Most times he was too distracted to get much reading done. He couldn't concentrate both because of his anxiety about being discovered goofing off, and from the deep-lung inhalations and explosive coughing of Kip trying to suck in an entire shift-worth of cannabis in only a few tokes. But it was a nice break from the other seven-and-a-half hours of hand-job and homo jokes.

The only thing that Billy learned to enjoy about his job came toward the end of August, with only a few weeks left in his 3-month term of service. That was when they let him drive the lift truck. After Billy collected all the metal scraps and wheel-barrowed them to the rear of the shop, they had to be hoisted into a monstrous dumpster the size of a flatbed 18-wheel truck. When the dumpster was full, every few weeks or so, it was hauled away to some foundry for recycling. Hoisting the containers of scraps, each of which probably weighed half a ton, required a lift truck. Billy thought operating it was great fun!

Unfortunately, the fun came to an abrupt end. With just a few days left to go, Billy got a little careless and backed the vehicle into a large work bench which contained three enormous tool boxes. Over went the bench, sending hundreds of wrenches, pliers, screwdrivers, calipers, levels, rulers, files, punches, chisels, hammers, clamps, and so on, tumbling into a huge chaotic pile.

He was permanently relieved of his lift truck driving duties.

Through the monotonous ordeal of stockpiling money for 48 hours a week over the slightly less than 13 weeks of summer employment, Billy lived for one thing and one thing alone.

That was his calls to Natalie.

As she had unceremoniously announced to him at the end of Spring Term, Natalie was for the entire summer traveling cross-country with her friend Pam. Somehow she was making the finances work out. Her father was earning good money and with her RA job, she apparently had just enough to take the time off. She had never been west of the Mississippi River and told Billy she was planning to live in the wild, and camp her way through a number of western states she always dreamed of seeing. Billy himself had never had the opportunity to travel. He couldn't really blame her. You're only young once.

As the school year was winding down and the time came to say good-byes, Billy knew he was really going to miss her. But it was all still so new. He was as crazy as crazy can be about her, but didn't know where things officially stood on her end. He certainly didn't want to blow it by coming off as possessive, or by being melodramatic. He secretly wished she'd throw him in her backpack so that he could spend every minute with her. But that wasn't going to happen.

The last week of Spring Term, Natalie had just gotten a cell phone. After his last final exam — the day before he would get on the bus and head home — she wrote down her new number for Billy, and made him promise to keep in touch. He later copied the it five times and put it in five different safe places, to make sure he wouldn't lose it.

"I know you'll be working, Billy. But have a great summer. I'll be thinking of you."

"I'll call. Just don't loan your phone to any bears. They never give anything back."

All summer, Billy was good to his word. As soon as he got home from work, he started dialing. Again and again. By end of August, his right index finger had a callous on the tip. But he could practically never get through to her. It drove him nuts. It seemed eleven times out of ten, he got a *'We're sorry but this number is not available at this time'* message. Sometimes he panicked and thought she was avoiding him.

Natalie and Pam were doing a west coastline, Arizona, New Mexico, Colorado jaunt for the better part of three months. They flew to Seattle, rented an SUV, bought a tent, some cooking utensils and other necessary gear, which they hadn't brought along with them. After five days kicking around Seattle, including a two-day trip up to Vancouver, British Columbia, they started down the coast. They made a brief stop in Portland, Oregon where they visited a girl they had both gone to high school with. Then it was off to San Francisco.

During these ten days or so, Billy was able to talk to Natalie every day. One time she even called him. She was always in a hurry and Pam didn't seem to place much value on their phone calls, interrupting Natalie more often than not. Billy hated it when Natalie would divide her attention, to make some comment on what Pam was wearing, or to help her locate the hair dryer or a missing sock, one of numerous things which seemed to go into hiding every time Natalie got on the phone with him. But at least he got to hear her voice.

However, once they headed east from San Francisco toward the Sierra Nevada Mountains — the onset of the camping segment of their trip — the communication blackout was almost completely total.

On the rare occasions he got through, the reception was horrible, and Pam would of course be there. Which only made sense, since close proximity went with the territory when sharing a small tent and campsite.

Without fail, Pam would be chattering away. Continuously. The whole time he and Natalie were on the phone. Who was she talking to? And if she was talking to Natalie, why did she have to yap during his all-too-infrequent and precious few minutes on the phone with the girl who he fantasized about practically every waking moment?

Billy didn't want to cause problems. But he was often tempted to ask Natalie what the hell Pam's problem was, that she couldn't give them a few moments of privacy on the phone. However, each time when he came close to blowing his cool, he pulled himself back, deciding he would come off as whining, and it would cause more hard feelings than it was worth. Billy realized that in some sense, he was still on a test drive. Their relationship was still quite new and he had no idea where the boundaries were. He certainly didn't want to screw it up. At this point, Natalie meant everything to him. If she had an annoying friend, it was a small price to pay for the future he envisioned for them.

As the summer rolled along, Billy had been giving it a lot of thought.

There was only one conclusion he could draw.

Natalie definitely was the one.

If he could just hang on until they were back together again at Cornell.

Billy had always judged that the way service providers were littering the landscape with cellular relay towers was a disgrace, that they were an eyesore which only reflected the greed of the telecommunication companies. Now he wished there were hundreds more. At least along the route that Natalie and Pam were taking.

Even just barely hearing her voice through the electronic tsunami of static and the popcorn crackle of an unstable connection worked wonders. He felt like he had been rescued from a black cesspool of gloominess and uncertainty, been slingshotted into a brilliant arc of hope and euphoria. The glow of these all too brief audio ops would illuminate him for several subsequent days.

There were two occasions during this camping phase of their trip when Billy and Natalie took advantage of excellent connections and had a real conversation. She seemed genuinely happy to hear from him. Thus beyond the volatile thrill of feeling some visceral connection with the lady he hoped to make love to the rest of his life, beyond just the sheer excitement of enjoying the specter of someone who was figuring in his every plan, fantasy and expectation, Billy heartily embraced profound relief and rejuvenation. He felt whole again. He savored the reassurance that Natalie indeed seemed to be on the same page as he was. These two relatively brief talks, unlike their typically superficial exchanges, renewed his optimism and helped allay the fears tended to mount between calls, that she would lose interest in him over the summer and that by autumn all would be lost.

By the middle of August, he no longer worried that she was avoiding him. They were by circumstance cut off from one another — simply because of a lack of phone connectivity.

Nevertheless, the last two weeks before summer break finally ended, turned out to be the most frustrating. Billy couldn't get ahold of Natalie at all. Then, just a couple days before he was supposed to return to Cornell, she called, but unfortunately he was out running some errands for his mom and didn't get to talk to her. His mom gave him the message the next morning.

"That girl Natalie? She called last night. She's home now and getting ready to go back to school. She said she'll see you there."

"That was all?"

He wasn't sure what else he expected.

"Nope. Nothing else. She sounds very nice, Billy."

"You're right about that. Real nice."

His mom broke out in a gaunt but joyful smile. The kind of joyful smile only a mother would so unabashedly give.

"Oh-oh. My Billy Boy is in love."

If she only knew.

If *she* only knew.

Natalie.

The Greatest Gift of All

It was the day before Billy would be returning to Ithaca. Friday evening a little after seven. They had just finished dinner. Harold was working the night shift. It was just the two of them.

His mom had prepared Billy's favorite, homemade pizza with mushrooms and pepperoni. They topped off the meal with Häagen Dazs Cookie Dough ice cream drowning in chocolate and caramel syrup.

They both looked very content with the meal, and frankly were too content to make themselves move from the kitchen table. Billy nursed a lemon-lime Fresca and his mom sipped Earl Grey tea.

She didn't look very good. The doctors kept extending the duration of her chemotherapy and radiation treatments, assuring her that the end of the punishing program was soon at hand. Billy had watched her lose weight, noticed her skin become pale and lifeless, had seen the fine lines of age in her face deepen, now looked into eyes which seem to sink deeper into her sockets as each day passed. Most dramatically, he witnessed over the course of the summer, the loss of her hair. She apparently wasn't kidding when she had claimed months ago to be shopping for wigs. Now she never left her room without one of the four which she kept on manikin heads in her room.

But Irene was not the kind of person to let any of this get her down.

With the inner strength of twelve people, she was able on almost any and all occasions to rise above the pain and intense fatigue which constantly plagued her, and put on a happy face.

Tonight was a very special occasion, the last night she would be spending with her Billy for probably nine months, if he stayed at school and worked through his breaks as he had intended to do last year. So she was, at least on the surface, in pretty high spirits tonight. The Häagen Dazs had helped a lot.

After several minutes of blissful silence, she started talking somewhere in the middle of a train of thought she apparently had been quietly riding.

"Billy. I think your father wants to love you. But his pride won't let him."

"What are you saying? He's too proud to do what comes natural to practically every father on the planet? I don't understand."

"Billy. This is really hard. But you're a big boy now. You're practically a man. And you should know the truth." She paused and took a long deep breath. "Oh god! This is so hard." She started weeping so hard it took several minutes for her to get her composure back enough to be able to talk.

"It's alright, mom. If this … whatever this is you want to say. If it's so difficult, maybe I don't need to hear about it right now."

"No no, Billy. You have to know. It will help you understand. Everything about your father will make more sense. I mean, it's very hard for me to talk about. But here goes. About three years after we got married, we went through a very difficult time. We started fighting."

"From what I've seen, you've always been fighting."

"Oh no, Billy. When we first got married, it was absolutely incredible! Really. Your father was such a handsome man. We were so in love. I know it's hard to imagine. But Harold was special. He was so dynamic. And funny. Yes, he was the life of the party. People loved his sense of humor. And he could sing. People would ask him to sing songs. He had this beautiful baritone voice. You know, he used to be slender and muscular. Just like you. When he put on a suit and tie, people would stare at him like he was some big shot or celebrity. Do you know what they used to call him back then, Billy? Duke. Everyone knew him as Duke."

"Duke?"

"Your father always hated his name. He used to say that he could never forgive his parents. 'Harold' was an old fuddy-duddy name. Sometime in high school everybody started calling him Duke, because he reminded them so much of John Wayne. Mainly his cocky attitude."

Billy was reeling. Suit and tie. Handsome. Funny. Dad? Singing? Duke? John Wayne? Was his mother actually saying this or would he wake up any moment now and realize he had just had the weirdest dream of his entire life?

"Anyway, he got elected as a union official at the plant. Which was very unusual because he was the youngest union official on the board. But the men loved him. Your dad really got into it and would be out every night with the boys. I don't know what they were doing. Naturally, he used to say it was union work. But then it got so bad, I started to worry he was out chasing other women. I mean, for a long time, night after night, he'd come home late. And that's when he really got into drinking. He'd come home very drunk and stinking of beer. This went on for almost a year. I was going crazy. I really loved your father and here he was ignoring me, treating me like dirt. Like some old girl friend he had gotten tired of. And that was when … this is so difficult."

"It's okay, mom. Just take your time."

"Billy. I met this man. His name was Peter Loy. And well … we got very close. I was sick of being … being home all alone."

"Are you saying … ?"

"When I found out I was pregnant, Billy, I didn't know what to do. I didn't say anything for the longest time. Finally, I couldn't hide it any longer. I was showing. Harold knew it wasn't his kid. We hadn't, your father and I, you know, been doing anything for months."

"Mom? This is … I … are you sure you want to—"

"Billy. My beautiful son. Peter Loy was your real father. Not … you know, your father … not Harold."

Bombs exploded inside Billy's head. Or was it fireworks?

What was he to say to his mom? What he was really feeling? That to find out that Harold was not his real biological father was the greatest gift of all. He knew that would hurt her. He knew she wanted Billy to accept Harold in some sense as his real father. After all, this was the man she chose to spend her life with, and for better or worse, was the man who had raised him — if you could call alternating between indifference and abuse raising someone.

He looked at his mom more intently than he had ever looked at her before. Her face was so drawn, her skin so sallow. She looked sad. Frightened. Fragile.

Billy felt he had to say something. To reassure her. Give her strength. Give back to her some long-forgotten much-deserved dignity, and some small piece of the love and nurturing she had so unselfishly given him over his entire life.

He was at a loss. He was fumbling for words.

"You say that … uh … Harold is not—"

"He's your father, Billy. And you should call him that. He's been here for you."

Right. Been here to physically and psychologically abuse both Billy and his mom, to dish out on a daily basis unconscionable cruelty and moribund rejection.

"But you say … dad … was this handsome, dynamic man. I never thought ... I've never seen a picture of him back then. Or you. Most people have wedding pictures. Do you have anything I could look at? I'm just trying to put this in perspective. It's hard … very hard."

"Your father destroyed everything, Billy. To spite me. To punish me. He grabbed every last picture, memento, anything he could find which had anything to do with him and I, then he threw it in a big pile in the back yard, poured gasoline on it. He burned everything."

"Mom, I don't know what to say. I can't imagine what you've gone through. So … ever since, he's been trying to punish you. And me."

"He was so hurt, Billy. I've regretted this every single day of my life. I mean, I don't regret you. You are … you have always been everything to me. But … but your father never forgave me. He has made me pay for my mistake every day of my life. And that's why he treats you like he does."

"What happened to this Peter guy?"

"He moved away. Your father never found out who he was. He told me he would kill whoever it was, if he ever came within a mile of me again. I told Peter. I don't blame him. He had his own family, you know."

"He was married?"

"Yes, he had a wife a three children. He was a little older than me. Maybe five or six years."

"I … I am having trouble. This is so incredible. So overwhelming. I … I have a question. Is that why you never had any other children? This little affair?"

"Billy, I shouldn't tell you this. Your father would kill me. But we did try. A few years later when things had cooled down a bit. But nothing ever happened. So we got tests. Harold insisted it was my fault. He called me a whore and said that was why we couldn't have kids. But it turns out that it was him. He's sterile. He can't make babies. Which is another reason he resents you so much. You are the boy he was not man enough to make himself. That's how he sees it."

"Ohmigod. He's so hung up on the macho thing. He hates gay people so violently. But it's his own manhood that's the issue."

"He's a real mess, Billy. And it's all my fault."

"No no no, mom. How can you say that?"

She started crying again. Crying so hard that her nose started to bleed. Billy ran upstairs for a washrag and towel. When he came back, his father was standing there staring at her. He had just gotten home from work.

Billy rushed over to the sink and dampened the washrag and handed it and the hand towel to his mom.

Harold walked over to get directly into Billy's face.

"What's going on here? Did you cause this?"

They were standing toe to toe, glaring at one another, neither giving an inch.

141

"No. You did."

Billy turned around and went back up to his room, two steps at a time. It took him less than five minutes to gather his things. He half-walked half-ran down the stairs with his suitcase in one hand, duffel bag in the other.

"Bye mom. I love you."

He was out the door before either Harold or Irene knew what was happening. Irene got up.

"But Billy—"

"Fuck him. Let him go."

Irene started crying again. Harold got a beer out of the refrigerator and carried it unopened into the living room. After about ten minutes, Irene's nose stopped bleeding. She looked in on Harold. He just sat there staring at the blank television screen. Irene reached over and picked up the remote.

"Don't you want to turn it on?"

No reply.

"I'm going to bed. Are you coming up, Harold?"

No reply.

The next morning when Irene came down stretching and yawning, she found Harold still sitting there, staring at the television. He still hadn't turned it on. Without even turning to look at her, he held up an empty Pabst Blue Ribbon bottle.

"I could use some more suds here, woman."

Chapter Five

LOVE IS A TRAMPOLINE
2002 – 2003

Yet Another Surprise Party

Billy caught a ride from a taxi driver who happened to be loitering at a 7-11, reading sports magazines. He then spent the night half propped up on a bench at the Greyhound Bus Station, before leaving early in the morning on his usual marathon bus trip back to Cornell.

All he thought about the first half of the journey was how much he hated his father.

All he thought about the second half was Natalie.

His excitement built as the taxi from downtown Ithaca approached his new residence on the very north end of campus. He had switched from Jameson to the Townhouse Community, where he would be sharing an apartment with another sophomore from Gainesville, Florida. A nice fresh start on the new year. New term. New location. New roommate. New digs. Anything which would help to put Detroit behind him and out of mind would be welcome.

"Dude! Your mother has left like seven messages for you. I'm Gil Skidmore, but my friends just call me Skid. I was just rolling a doobie. You wanna smoke some great shit?"

The invisible Israeli with the incomprehensible accent suddenly seemed like the dream roommate. The luck of the draw. Bad luck this round.

"Thanks anyway, Skid. But I only have one lung and it's filled with mucous right now."

"Bummer."

Billy really wanted to talk to Natalie but thought he'd better call his mom first.

It was a short call. She just wanted to make sure he was safe and let him know everything was fine at home. That the other night his father was just in a bad mood.

"Dad sends his love."

Right. Attached to a grenade with the pin pulled.

"Take care of yourself, mom. Please let me know what's going on with you. I worry, you know."

"I know, Billy. I'll be fine. You be a good boy and make sure you use those thingies you put over your you-know-what. I'm too young to be a grandmother."

"Bye, mom."

When he repeatedly tried to call Natalie, her room phone just rang. He tried her cell phone. *'We're very sorry but this phone is not in service at this time.'*

Was it starting all over? This on-again-off-again game of hide-and-go-seek? Maybe Pam came back with her. Christ, it was frustrating sometimes trying to figure her out.

It was three days later, the day after classes had started, that he finally caught up with her. He reached her on the regular phone in her room.

They met in the lobby of Mary Conlon Hall, where she was again a Resident Assistant.

There was a disconcerting awkwardness for the entire first half-hour they were together. Since they were both hungry, they had decided on the phone to head over to Temple of Zeus in Goldwin Smith Hall for one of their renowned mega-meals. It was a twenty minute walk and it was only after they had started eating that they both relaxed a bit.

He didn't want to bring it up, but it should have been obvious that the major source of tension for Billy was how difficult it had been to connect with her, all through the summer and even now, the first few days back at school. It raised all sorts of doubts and fears in his mind. Was she still serious about him? Were things still on? It was hard to read but he feared that she was nowhere near as obsessed about him as he was about her.

In addition to his anxiety, there was the unwieldiness of having been apart for three whole months. It almost felt like they were strangers again. Objectively, they were. The amount of time they had been apart was actually longer than the few weeks when things had been hot and heavy between them. While Billy's feelings for her, and presumably her feelings for him, might still be very real, they had been strangers far longer than they had been lovers.

He was determined to get beyond it. What did he have to lose?

Just everything.

"How's Pam?"

"The trip was fantastic. It was just what I needed, Billy. Just what I needed. And you?"

"I worked in a factory, watched my mom disintegrate from chemotherapy, and lived under the same roof with the biggest, dumbest macho pig on the planet. It was Paradise."

"Your mom's not doing well? I really hope I can meet her."

"You want to meet my mom?"

"Of course, Billy. Don't you want me to meet her?"

"I hadn't thought about it."

"Billy. I missed you so much. You have no idea."

"You're right about that."

They ate the rest of the meal in silence.

Natalie cuddled up next to Billy all the way back to Mary Donlon. He finally let his guard down. Things started feeling right again.

Neither had early classes the next day. Whatever had gone down earlier in the evening was deeply submerged into the background noise of oblivion, as they made love late into the night, falling asleep in one another's arms just before the sun declared a new day.

From that day forward, they settled into the familiar pattern of the previous Spring. They saw each other whenever possible, even if only for short but passionate embraces and a good-night kiss.

Billy had carved out for himself another grueling class schedule. 19 credits. Six classes. Which meant devoting a lot of time to studying, preparing for tests, writing papers. This also meant that Billy typically stayed overnight only two, or at most three times a week, in Natalie's private room in Donlon.

About a month after classes started, there was a surprise visit from Pam. But this time the surprise was on Natalie. Billy got the call just before going to sleep. He had been up studying hard for a test early next morning in his very difficult Social and Political Philosophy class. He was exhausted.

"Hello, Billy? I'm sorry I'm calling so late."

"Who is this?"

"It's Natalie's friend Pam. How are you?"

Pam! Billy immediately felt strange. Suspicious. What did she want?

"Fine. Tired. You know. College. Is everything okay?"

"Yeah, Billy. Great. Listen. Natalie's birthday is the 20th. This coming Friday. I want to have a surprise party for her and I need your help. If you're not too busy."

Natalie's birthday? Billy was filled with a sense of relief. He could handle this just fine. Plus now he wouldn't have to admit that he had no idea Natalie's birthday was coming up.

"Sure. Sounds great. I'll be glad to help."

They talked for almost a half-an-hour and came up with a good plan. Billy needed to discretely contact the girls on Natalie's floor and let them know. Pam had the name and numbers of a few other friends and close acquaintances, who she herself would contact. Pam would be coming into town Thursday night and wondered if she could stay in Billy's room. That could be arranged, though he obviously was a little uneasy about exactly how that would work out. Maybe she liked dopers from Florida and it would just fall in place.

The main thing was for Billy to make sure that Natalie was out and about Friday evening, away from her room for a couple hours before the party. Pam and whoever she recruited to help, could then put up decorations and get ready to surprise the bejesus out of Natalie when she finally walked through the door.

They agreed the party would start at 9 pm and be held in Natalie's own room. Billy either had to get a key or in some way make sure Natalie didn't lock up when he took her out that night, on whatever pretense he came up with. He felt confident he could easily come up with accommodating plans for the evening. They had been regularly getting together on Fridays anyway.

After Billy hung up, he felt really good. First of all, since he had had no idea that Natalie's birthday was coming up, he would have felt very foolish if he had not done something for her. Now he was in the thick putting together a very cool party, so that his potential blunder, intended or not, was excised.

Secondly and probably more importantly, he was being thrown together with Pam, at her initiative no less, as her co-conspirator. He sensed — hoped — this would be an opportunity to get to know her, maybe get a better understanding of hers and Natalie's friendship, perhaps break some of the ice he felt had encrusted him, and her also, with respect to one another. He certainly couldn't claim up to this point to have warm fuzzies about her. This past summer, there were times he wished he could have reached through the phone and strangled her.

But it was clear that Pam was here to stay for the near and probably far term. She and Natalie had been friends forever and there was no hint that this would change any time soon. They shared a lot of history and made a point of seeing one another as often as possible. Even if at times it interfered with him and Natalie, he was in awe of their friendship, and certainly had nothing in his own life to compare to it.

Everything went smoothly. He put some well-disguised invites in the mailboxes of the girls on the floor where Natalie was a Resident Assistant. RSVPs came pouring in.

Even getting Natalie's key was a snap.

Three nights before the party, he was walking her back to the dorm after their final classes for the day, which were in adjacent buildings in the Arts Quad.

"Natalie. Maybe I can catch up with you later for dinner?"

"I wish I could. I'm going to grab a quick bite, then I have to go to a staff meeting. I hate these things. Usually it's a lot of whining. And they go on forever. I probably won't be back until after ten."

The light went on in Billy's head.

"Could you do me a big favor? I've really got some serious studying to do tonight. And my suitemate Beavis always has the TV on the whole time on Tuesdays."

"You want to study in my room?"

"You read my mind. I could wait for you, then maybe hang for a little while after you get back. If you're not in too bad a mood."

"I can't say I won't be in a bad mood. You'll just have to take what you get. Why don't I give you my key? Just come by whenever it works for you."

Bingo!

While Natalie was at her drudge meeting, Billy hurried into town. After trying three different places, he convinced a hardware clerk to ignore the 'Do not duplicate!' warning on her key and run him a copy.

On Friday, he passed it along to Pam on his way out the door. He would have liked to stay for a little while and talk it up with her, but Natalie was expecting him to come and pick her up to see a movie in town. *Star Wars Episode II - Attack of the Clones* had just opened nationally and was causing quite a buzz.

As they left the theater, Billy was first to voice what they were both thinking.

"Well, that was stupid."

"I don't get it. I guess special effects have replaced substance. How much could it have cost to make that piece of tripe?"

"I heard over 115 million. They could have made 20 good independent flicks for that."

"Are you hungry?"

"For you. Let's go back to your room."

They got there about 9:15. There was no sign that anything was up. But when she opened the door, over 20 people packed into her very modest quarters all yelled as she flicked the overhead lights on.

"SURPRISE!!"

A *Happy Birthday, Sexy Girl!!* banner was stretched across the wall above her window. There was a ice chest full of soft drinks, wine coolers and beer, and a folding table with bowls of chips and other snack foods, a pan containing Angie's popular marijuana brownies, and a punchbowl full of what Natalie and Billy would later learn was LSD-spiked lemonade.

As overwhelmed and excited as Natalie was, she almost immediately spotted Pam.

"Pam! Ohmigod! So it was you. I can't believe it!"

They hugged and yukked it up, Natalie repeatedly declaring how she hadn't had a clue about the party, and expressing amazement that Pam could pull it off so perfectly.

Billy let them carry on like crazy school girls and decided to mix. It wasn't hard to do, since they were all sandwiched in shoulder-to-shoulder, hip-to-hip, sometimes pelvis-to-pelvis.

All of the usual suspects were there. The girls who had joyously deflowered him — Kristin, Erin, Angie, Tanya, even Julianne. He had occasionally run across them from time to time on campus but had kept his distance. There had been their weird head games with him, which he had neither time or patience for. But this evening it was actually fun to see them again, given the occasion and everyone's evident good feelings for Natalie.

All but one of the girls living on Natalie's floor popped in and stayed for varying amounts of time. Some of them came in with a guy, either their boyfriend or a Friday night date. They gave her silly gifts — ranging from worthless but cute knick-knacks, to confectionaries including one pair of edible panties and a lemon-flavored sucker shaped like a penis — to pricey condoms: *'Scientifically designed with maximum pleasure in mind.'*

At one point, Billy spoke briefly to Julianne. She came up behind him and flicked his ear.

"Hi there, you clever young man."

"Julianne. I heard you were missing in action Spring Term."

"You watch CNN?"

"No, actually Natalie told me."

"My mom died."

That hit way too close to home.

"Oh … Julianne, I'm sorry. You were close?"

"She was my mom."

She looked away. It was clear she didn't want to talk about it.

"Hey Billy, this is a good thing. You and Natalie. You guys are great together. I mean, at least that's the way it looks."

"That's the way it looks to me."

"I like you, Billy. You are a very sweet boy. I hope we'll become friends. Especially since we've already slept together."

It could have been a sarcastic swipe. But as Billy looked deeply into her eyes, he saw both the sadness of her recent loss and a profound sincerity about what she had just said.

"Natalie really respects you. Everyone knows you're extremely brilliant. As the superficial male that I certainly am, I can say that you're good on the eyes. Friendship? Nothing less would do the situation justice."

Julianne couldn't help but to smile. Billy's reply was a refreshing departure from the usual simple-minded drivel guys came on to her with. Being beautiful seemed with only rare exceptions to reduce every male in her proximity to drooling monosyllabic baboons. Billy was one of those notable exceptions.

An enormous guy — football lineman huge — with two bottles of beer in one hand, stumbled into Billy and put his other arm on Billy's shoulders. As he leaned into Billy, it felt like someone had dropped a huge pile of logs on him.

"Hey Dude! I'm Peter. So you're the lucky guy. Man, I've wanted some of *that* action for the longest time. But Natalie just keeps saying, 'Fuck off , I've got a boyfriend.' Let me know if she boots your ass, eh Motown?"

"Motown?"

"Like you're from Detroit, aren't you? That's the word. Stay cool, man."

High five. It was like being slapped with a two-by-four. Peter stepped away, then slid up to a girl Billy didn't recognize, then threw one arm around her as he tweaked her tit with the other hand. She giggled and smiled.

Deep.

Then Billy recalled what stud boy had just quoted Natalie as saying. *I've got a boyfriend.* That felt good. Real good.

"Hey, is your dance card full?"

It was Pam.

"There's always room for a girl from Indiana."

Billy hadn't had any opportunity to talk to her until now. There was the brief hello-goodbye exchange when she arrived to sleep in his room. But he had gone immediately over to Natalie's to spend the night.

From what he gathered, she would be leaving Sunday. Billy assumed Natalie would probably want to spend time with her alone, if this visit followed suit with the previous ones Spring Term. Meaning, if they were going to talk, it was now or never. She seemed to be in an ecstatic state. Maybe she had had the lemonade.

"I really like you, Billy. Natalie has told me so much about you, I feel like we're old friends. You've been really good for her. I can see the changes already. Good changes."

"Well, Pam. I have to say that comes as a bit of a shock. I'm not trying to be humble. I frankly didn't know I was even on your radar. Thanks!"

"Natalie and I had a great summer. But I could tell she missed you."

"Let's sit down. I'm tired of grazing."

They found a spot in the corner. Natalie looked over and smiled, apparently pleased that the two special people in her life were finally getting to know one another. Then she went back to chatting and giggling with two girls who lived on Natalie's floor, giddy types who Billy had seen a couple times in passing.

"What do you do back there in Indianapolis, Pam?"

"Oh. I'm not there anymore. I'm in Chicago. But I'm thinking of moving. I'll probably wait until Natalie graduates. We were talking about maybe hooking up somewhere for a while. Unless, of course, a certain someone … you know …"

He didn't know. But he sort of knew. This thing with Natalie was all still so new. He was trying to keep his head screwed on straight, but he had to be honest. He had already been fantasizing quite a bit about a permanent future with Natalie. Mainly because he couldn't imagine a future without her.

"You know, Pam. I feel so stupid sometimes. I get so overwhelmed by her. In a good way. But I honestly sometimes forget the essentials. Like I didn't even know it was her birthday. Embarrassing. And now that you're bringing it up, I have no idea when she'll be graduating."

"End of the Summer Session. She's taking either 6-week or 8-week courses. Or both. And then she's done."

"*This* year?"

"This academic year. Next calendar year. But yes, she'll be completely finished by first week of August. A little over ten months from now. You know, she started college a year early. She hated living at home and had enough credits to graduate high school, so off she went. She was only seventeen."

This landed like a bomb. Billy had never really stopped to think about it. He knew she was a year older than him, but he assumed they would still be at Cornell together at least the next couple years. He tried to cover his panic.

"That makes sense. She told me about her father. And all about that young sleaze her old man married after her mother committed suicide. Man, what a screwed up family!"

Pam visibly tensed and didn't say anything for a while.

Billy studied her face. She was a very attractive girl. But there was something about her that made her seem a bit older. Certainly older than him. And really analyzing her, older than Natalie as well. Was it her features? Or was it the way she carried herself? She definitely wasn't frivolous or superficial, from what he had seen so far. Of course, he wouldn't expect Natalie to hang out with someone who was. But Pam had a *gravitas*, and a subtle but sure assertiveness. Her eyes were resolute. She had a genuine strength of pride which Billy never saw in anyone his age. It was easy for Billy to imagine a strong, enduring friendship with her, such as the one she and Natalie apparently shared.

"How about you, Pam? Messy home life?"

"No. Not really. More of a model Christian family. Boring. Very boring. I'm kind of the black sheep."

"Why?"

"I just am. I can't live that way. And I certainly won't bring my kids up that way."

"Do you have a boyfriend?"

A familiar voice from behind him.

"Billy! I have to watch you every minute. Putting the make on my innocent friend Pam. Does she have a boyfriend? Are you applying for the job?"

Natalie had slipped up behind and now sat down next to him.

"That's not what—"

"Isn't that what they all say? Bill Clinton ... R. Kelly ..."

Pam had the inside scoop. She was apparently a subscriber to perverts.com or got home delivery of the National Inquirer.

"Kelly is more of a pedophile. But a nascent filmmaker. Only uses Super-8."

"What other philanderers immediately come to mind, Pam?"

"I think 'male' and 'philanderer' are synonyms."

"Who can argue with that?"

Natalie and Pam were getting a big kick out of all of this male-dissing and laughed heartily. Billy was slowly coming around to realize that Natalie was just teasing, and cautiously joined in the hilarity with a somewhat forced chuckle. Natalie stroked the back of Billy's neck.

"So I assume there has been more to this discussion than just trying to get into Pam's pants. I'm just glad you're finally getting to know one another."

Natalie then sidled up close to Billy, picked up his arm from his lap and placed it around her.

"Now give me some lips, big boy. After all, it is my birthday."

Without any further encouragement, Billy gave Natalie a long sensuous kiss. When the spell was finally broken, he opened his eyes, glanced over and saw that Pam was staring at them. Actually glaring at them. It was a combination of fascination and something else.

Alarm? Anger? Jealousy? Billy couldn't read it.

He didn't have time to analyze it because suddenly her face broke into a big theatrical pout. With her best intentionally worst acting, she pleaded her case like a spoiled little brat.

"Hey! What about me?"

"No way, girl. He's all mine."

"Now that's cosmically unfair. Come on, Nat. Just one little kiss. I won't hurt him."

Pam grabbed onto Billy's other arm and the two girls conducted a mock tug-of-war with him. Now both giggling. Throwing in some jabs at one another. Even tickling him as well.

Finally, Natalie relented.

"Okay. Short and sweet. No tongues, Pam. Are you listening? No goddamn tongues."

Maybe Pam was listening but was more concentrating on plying her feminine charm on him. Her index finger behind his ear. Nice caresses to the inside of his elbow. Then she leaned over and planted a big wet slobbery pulsating kiss on his lips, the kind of overbearing, overwrought, over-the-top kiss that Billy absolutely hated. Plus she was entirely ignoring the tongue prohibition. Billy felt like she was trying to lick his Adam's apple from the inside.

After less than ten seconds of the lips-and-tongue military assault, Billy managed to wrench himself free. He wiped his mouth with the back of his wrist as discretely as he could. It was an awkward moment. While he didn't want to offend Pam, he was having difficulty hiding how totally repulsed he was by the experience.

"Nice, huh? I've been told I am the best kisser this side of the Rocky Mountains."

She was either gloating or provoking him. Maybe the whole thing was just a mind-fuck.

"That's a lot of geography."

Billy glanced over at Natalie. Her expression was equally as enigmatic. Was this all a joke?

"Pam and I usually share everything, Billy. But I'm thinking in your case, I'll just keep you for myself."

Pam laughed. To Billy's ears, it had a sinister overtone. Or was he reading into it?

She then got a mock serious expression while she looked directly at Natalie and winked.

"Your turn, sister. After all … it *is* your birthday."

Pam started to lean over Billy, presumably to land one of her octopus kisses on Natalie. Natalie just laughed and pulled away. Then she got to her feet, excitedly yanking Billy by both hands. He didn't have much choice but to get up.

"Let's dance. Yes, it's my birthday. It's my fucking birthday! Time to party!"

And so it went. Until about one in the morning. Fortunately, it was a Friday, so no one had to get up for classes the next day. And equally convenient was the fact that the person who would normally tamp down the level of noise and substance abuse was the person for whom the party was being held. Natalie cut everyone a lot of slack. Herself included.

After all, it was her "fucking birthday".

As things were winding down, Pam came over to Billy, wrapped her arms around him and gave him an affectionate sisterly hug.

"Thanks so much for your help. I think this turned out really great. Natalie's the best and she deserves the best. In this case, I think that's you."

"And you, Pam."

"Listen. Change of subject. No offense. But I would prefer to not spend another night with that drug-addled swamp rat you have for a roommate. That guy is so lame. Or psycho. Maybe both. I would have thought that Cornell would have some minimum standards for admission. There's no way that dude could possibly have a high school diploma."

"They've expanded the affirmative action program. It used to be just for African-Americans and Hispanics. Now it includes retards."

"That explains it. Anyway, I think I'll just crash here with Natalie. Sorry. I don't mean to push you out. But three's a crowd, eh?"

"Yup. Three's a crowd. Even two-and-a-half's a crowd."

"What's that supposed to mean?"

"It means I've had too much to drink. Have fun. If you want, I can come by for breakfast."

"We'll be eating at the Y."

"The Y? Where … uh? What do you mean?"

Pam laughed and gave him another athletic hug, briskly rubbing him like a big teddy bear.

"Nothing. It doesn't mean anything. You really are, aren't you? Just like Nat says."

"What? I'm what?"

"Tragically innocent."

"Yes. I guess I am."

No Pain No Gain

Natalie saw Pam off on Sunday night. This time Billy joined them.

No tears. A lot of laughs and good will. Except for a brief parting glance from Pam.

Just as the cab pulled away, Billy caught it. It was directly aimed at him. Not actually meant to communicate anything. Just an expression which crossed Pam's face at the last moment as the taxi started to move.

It was a dark expression. Envy? Resentment? Some emotion attached to the inequality of the equation. Pam had to leave. Billy got to stay.

Were they competing for Natalie's love? It had never seemed that way. Yes, competing for her time. Up till this most recent visit, it was either-or. Either Billy or Pam. At least they were in the same room for Natalie's birthday. And now here curbside.

While Billy had no particular fondness for Natalie's and Pam's friendship, he accepted it. Respected it. Understood it. Friends are a good thing. Billy certainly had at times wished he had a real solid friend. Just a person to spend time with. Share thoughts, ideas, feelings, frustrations, triumphs.

But at no point had it occurred to Billy that he and Pam were competing.

Not until that glance.

He liked Pam. At least now he did. She seemed to like him. At least that's how she acted.

But he still had to wonder? Would there always be some underlying tension? Some sub-text of resentment now that Natalie had a man in her life, a serious boyfriend?

He would have to wait and see.

Bye-bye Pam. Back to the studies.

The term turned out to be more difficult than Billy had imagined it would be. His freshman year was hard work, but he had come out with flying colors. A 3.8 grade-point average. Plus favorable first impressions on three of his professors, with whom he had been able to meet face-to-face and get positive feedback and generous encouragement. That would be important down the road, if Billy opted to go to grad school. But that was a long way off.

For now, he really had to knuckle down. He could tell that his mid-term exams were going to be a real bear. Two of his professors clearly had an attitude toward underclassman. Not only did they seem to resent having to teach the more fundamental classes in their respective fields, but they seemed to assume that freshman and sophomores were completely unworthy of being in the same room with them. That meant, from what Billy surmised, and what he had heard through the grapevine, their tests were more instruments of humiliation than tools for gauging knowledge and mastery of subject matter. It's not easy to predict the mind of a supercilious asshole bent on confirming the vast chasm that exists between him and the pathetic numbskulls who make up the rest of the human race. How do you study for that?

The ongoing reward for all of the time and energy he put into his books, was whatever time and energy he could devote to the love of his life, Natalie. Billy increasingly found that just thinking about her, picturing her face, imagining the phantom memory of her touch, breathing the recollection of the distinct and beautiful smell of her body, which he now could call it up in his mind at will, any of these could provide a temporary respite from the labors of his academic work, and bridge the time they inevitably had to spend apart. They had no classes in common, very different schedules — though they still had four evenings free to spend together when they could — and of course, Natalie had the responsibilities associated with being the Resident Assistant on her floor of the dorm. This year brought an influx of fourteen new freshman, with the attendant duties. Answering a lot of the same questions all freshman had, providing a minimum of guidelines so that their new freedom from the constraints of living at home with their parents didn't turn into a wild and self-destructive plunge into chaos. She had to be available to listen to a predictable laundry list of complaints and immature nitpicking, and sometimes just to provide an ear and a waterproof shoulder as homesickness set in. Those duties and "boy talk", which for many of them would continue with varying degrees of sophistication and self-fulfilling pessimism over the rest of their lives, made enormous demands on her time and energy.

As Billy came and went, he was often there in Natalie's room when one of these freshman girls stopped in for a quick chat. He increasingly became a familiar item and all of the girls on Natalie's floor liked him. Some really liked him and were not very subtle about flirting with him. They made a point of coming by on some patently contrived excuse, to discuss some improbable or lame problem which they insisted needed Natalie's sage advice, just because they knew Billy was there.

Natalie was becoming more comfortable sharing with Billy some of the insider information of her position as an RA — maybe not the really personal, confidential stuff — but at least the harmless and funnier tidbits that seem to crop up daily.

"Hey, Billy. You know that little red-haired Irish girl who always wears Christina Aguilera t-shirts? Shannon?"

"Yeah, I know. She has freckles on her legs."

"Hah! Looking at her legs, eh? Anything else? You know, the girl has a major crush on you. I'm surprised she's not here right now asking me if I know the capital of Bolivia or where she can get a copy of Andrew Jackson's first inaugural address."

"It's nice to be loved."

"Actually, to be more precise, so far *this week* she has a crush on you. It's always changing. Sometimes daily."

"Will I break her heart if I stay here the night with you?"

"You've already broken her heart, silly boy. That's the point."

"A broken heart? That's the point?"

"In spite of receiving top-notch social sexual education via such credible and respected sources as daytime soap operas, People and Seventeen magazines, and movies like *American Pie*, some of these girls — at least at this stage — can only relate to the drama. Not the sex. Not the romance. Just all the camera angles and photo ops that go along with their ..." Natalie made air quotation marks with her fingers. "... 'idea' of romance. They live these fantasy lives inside of the lyrics of popular songs."

In terms of exposure to the traumas of high-drama post-pubescent romantic entanglements, Billy's exposure and comprehension amounted to little or none. But listening to Natalie talk about all of this gave him a keen appreciation for what he had now and what he had been spared. Even if unawares and without intention, he and Natalie were actually doing something constructive. If indeed the "boy problems" of the young girls under Natalie's care were as profound and intractable as they seemed to think they were, she and Billy at least offered a model for just how good having a relationship could be.

They were constantly amused and flattered at both the doleful envy and elated praise heaped on them as a couple, even if it was only coming from wide-eyed, unloved 18 year-old girls.

"I just want to be like you guys."

"I sure wish my Prince Charming would parachute into my life."

"If I had a boyfriend like Billy, I'd be the happiest girl in the whole wide world."

"You are the perfect couple! I hope some day I can just be half as in love as you guys."

Of course, appearances are often deceiving. It may have looked great from the outside, but none of this was easy. Not for either Billy or Natalie.

Yes. It was great. But it could be hard work too.

On Natalie's side — though Billy didn't know this — he was her first real boyfriend. She had occasionally been on dates in high school. But they were always within the strictly patrolled police state of her church community and parents' watchful eyes. Most of her time in the company of boys was at priggish church-sponsored activities, hardly occasions for either healthy or unhealthy exploration and experimentation.

Then when the bad stuff started to happen — the accusations of infidelity fabricated by her father and her mother's subsequent suicide — all of that normal adolescent boy-girl curiosity and activity came to a halt. This hiatus continued through the pandemonium of her father's losing his ministry, his re-marriage, their moving to a new home, and his finding a new job to support his reconfigured family. There was no time or desire on Natalie's part for frivolities. In fact, it was all she could do to get used to the "new man" her father had become, and deal with the extreme attention her new step-mother, only three years older than Natalie herself, lavished on her. Ironically, Natalie grew to really like her. By the time she went away to college, Cynthia was spending more time with Natalie — aggressively courting her affection — than she was with Natalie's father. He was pre-occupied with becoming "salesman of the year" for the car dealership where he was employed, and worked very long hours.

On at least one level, Natalie's bonding with her new step-mom actually made sense. They were, after all, nearly the same age.

Natalie hated her father more than ever during this period. Rather than being disposed to trust or seek the affections of any other male, she spent the bulk of her emotional capital on fantasizing ways to humiliate, even destroy her father, to avenge her mother's death, to punish the man, who with little doubt or hesitation she held responsible for the loss of her mother, and all of her subsequent misery. To her eternal regret, she never entirely completed this task. To her ongoing humiliation, she accepted the money her dad gave her so that she could attend Cornell. It was a compromise that deepened her desire and resolve for revenge.

When Natalie arrived at Cornell, she was a very pissed-off 17 year-old. A very *attractive* pissed-off 17 year-old to be sure. The boys took special notice. Her anger and intransigence they brushed off as mere adolescent feistiness, the kind of feral wildness that one encounters in an unbroken mare. Pluckiness which made the thought of conquest even more delicious.

But as any of those trying to woo Natalie into the sack quickly found out, they weren't dealing with just another chick who with some smooth talk and clever manipulation, they could add to their fuck list. They were dealing with a one-woman army, well-equipped, savvy and indomitable.

She went out on many dates her first two years on campus, setting the stakes high and constantly upping the ante. Never did she actually deceive any of the over-confident jerks she went out with. She merely let their imaginations do her work for her. She let them assume that if they spent enough money and poured on enough charm, she could be theirs and somewhere down the road there would be a happy ending — their eager dicks slick with the lovely juices of her vagina.

Of course, that never happened.

'Ballbuster' was usually the term most often applied to Natalie by the end of a string of expensive dinners, lavish skiing weekends, great fraternity parties, rock concerts, ballets and plays. Ballbuster. Or cockteaser. Because she never slept with a single one of them. Her seducers were universally left with a lot less money in their wallets, scratching their heads wondering where they possibly could have gone wrong, and ultimately depending on the services of the ubiquitous friend of the sexually frustrated male. Left staggering across the sprawling plain of female rejection, it was time for the mistress of last resort — Rosy Palm.

But rebuffing horny males wasn't the whole story.

Natalie had slept with two young men. Mostly out of curiosity. And neither of these blokes had spent a cent on her. Moreover, they were entirely of her own choosing.

They were both quiet, studious types. Gentle. Shy.

They were both one-night stands.

She never regretted either one.

Nor did she pine about either of them. Or consider going back for seconds.

Both times it was okay. Decent. Not quite what sex with a guy had been trumped up to be in the movies and by girls around her who could — or at least did — claim experience and expertise in the matter. But it was okay.

Then along came Billy.

She never let him know what an apprentice she was in terms of men. And she never would. Let him think what he might. Imagination is much more exciting, if sometimes slightly more cruel, than reality anyway.

From the first time she saw him laying there in bed with Julianne at his side, she knew she wanted to get to know him. The sheepish look on his face alone was reason enough. Most guys would have been gloating, looking like they had just climbed Mount Everest in the nude. Billy looked like he'd just wet his pants in full view of the audience while making his Valedictorian speech in high school.

Very cute.

Very funny.

She could also sense there was something very special about him. A depth. Intelligence. Trustworthiness. Morality.

Yes. Even morality, though the occasion of their first meeting would on the surface seem to mock that idea.

As soon as she walked into Tanya and Erin's room that night of his birthday party, she knew what was up. She took a good look at him and was sure that this was not the real Billy Green. This mini-orgy was some anomaly. The girls were experts at these kinds of hijinks. So even if he was high on dope, frothy with champagne, and sticky with recent random sex, she still sensed that this Billy guy was a person who at his core was a person she wanted to and would get to know.

Love at first sight?

Probably not. More like that item in the window of a department store you see and know you're going to come back and try on — so it's best not wait too long and risk that someone else buys it first.

When she arranged their first meeting at the Atrium Café, on the very real pretext of giving him advice, she knew this was a breakpoint evening. Within a few minutes of their sitting down, their fate would be set. Either she had misjudged him or had gotten it completely right. And if she was right about him, she knew she would kiss him. A kiss that would reverberate down through time for many years to come.

She didn't know how she knew any of this. She just knew.

Natalie's only concern was Pam. How would Pam fit into all of this?

Pam wasn't her real name. She had just left Indianapolis and was hiding. Hiding from her past and rebuilding her future. Therefore she had a new name. Pam Fullbright. She had new ID. Everything she needed to get a fresh start. The only thing she would carry forward into her new life was Natalie. In fact, part of the reason she had made a break and was starting all over was Natalie. She desperately wanted them to be able to continue being friends, and share the love which had borne both of them through the desolation of their lives to this point. The bond which had given them the hope and desire to go on, when everyone else had betrayed and abandoned them.

Natalie had transplanted herself to Cornell.

Pam now had a new career and a fresh start in Chicago.

They would have to see where that went. How their friendship would survive the changes.

Pam's reinvention of herself had only just received the final touches during the week prior to Billy's birthday party. When Natalie walked into Billy's birthday soiree with Pam at her side, they had just spent hours talking about it. Pam had shared all of the details of her preparation and escape from Indiana. Told Natalie about her new job, and the tiny apartment she had found in Chicago. Toward the end of this very intense chat, they decided that they would celebrate by spending the 10-day Christmas holiday together in Washington DC.

Billy, of course, had no knowledge of any of the behind-the-scenes things that were going on that night with Natalie. She breezed in, made some funny comments to the girls in the room, gave Billy some flak, introduced the girl she was with — who Billy surprisingly remembered but who made no specific impression on him — then left the room, after which the girls cleaned up and the party abruptly ended.

Beyond the marijuana-alcohol fog and post-coital euphoria, which certainly precluded a very detailed reconstruction of Natalie's brief visit, he was left with the general impression during her brief visit that he was completely mortified, that he must have looked like a complete idiot, and the sooner forgotten the better. He did recall that Natalie had a sharp wit, and it was obvious she wasn't afraid to turn it on someone to amuse herself and those around her.

If he were to draw the most logical conclusion from that night, he would have inferred that Natalie thought he was a superficial dope, thus he would probably never see her again.

Nothing, of course, could have been further from the truth.

In fact, December 18, 2001 turned out to be a very momentous day — an inauspicious beginning for big things to come. Not that Billy could have known at the time.

When he got Natalie's call three days later and agreed to meet with her for a quick bite and a talk, he was not a little shocked and confused. By the end of their little dinner date, his head was really spinning. Natalie was all over the map, showing a deep and sincere concern for his future, ridiculing him like he was a silly delinquent child, sexually taunting and teasing him, humiliating him about the loss of his virginity, then capping it off by giving him a good-bye kiss that he would remember for the rest of his life. As a postscript, she hinted there would more of her craziness and abuse, if he were interested.

How will it all end?

This rousing but unpredictable dynamic defined their relationship to this day.

While Billy knew only the gas pedal, Natalie fortunately knew the brakes. She periodically applied them to keep their relationship from spinning off into wild uncontrolled flight. Of course whenever Pam was around, the brakes were firmly applied in an annoying screeching skid. But even when it was just the two of them — just Billy and Natalie locked in a seemingly indestructible embrace — Billy always sensed that behind those hypnotic eyes, beyond the breathless abandon that Natalie abandoned herself to when they made love, beyond her total surrender at the heights of their amorous exultation and the depths of their erotic passions, down in the impregnable center of her being, there were calculations always being made. That their relationship was subject to some set of controls — Natalie's controls — which he couldn't fathom much less apply himself.

This probably should have concerned Billy.

But it didn't. He took it all in stride.

They say love is blind. But it's not. Not at all.

In fact, your vision is never better than when you're in love.

Things are bright, focused, full of color, dazzling, stark and hyper-real.

The problem is you don't always know what you're looking at.

Sometimes Billy wondered if he was chasing an illusion.

He had never played mind games with himself before — especially about matters of the heart, since he had no experience. As a result, he had no reason to believe that what he had with Natalie was merely a product of his imagination — his fantasies gone wild.

But reality was reality and it was uncompromising.

Nothing was simple. Even the simplest of emotions.

Nothing was pure. Even the purest intentions.

Everything was somehow tainted. Compromised. Multi-layered. Elusive.

Pure and simple love was apparently not so pure and simple after all.

It was a road with unexpected twists, slippery turns, potholes, falling rocks, dangerous curves, unexpected obstacles and sometimes traumatic fender benders. It even had speed limits.

Billy didn't want to slow down.

But as the blurred road rushed by beneath him like a grey, streaking charcoal sketch of a trail to an indistinct future, and the scenery slipped past his peripheral vision in nondescript fragments of the present, which often could not be wholly grasped or even remembered — all in pursuit of that single enigmatic point of light on the distant horizon — one question remained unanswered.

Where was he going?

Or yes, as Natalie liked to say …

How will it all end?

Does Anybody Really Know What Time It Is?

Fall Term itself was racing by like a nitro-methane gulping fuel dragster. Accelerating faster and faster as each day passed. All of the particulars of life shrouded by the shriek, smoke and flames, the dash to a checkered flag which offered the promise of more checkered flags.

This extreme warpage of time started for Billy the moment Pam mentioned to him at the birthday surprise party that Natalie was graduating in less than a year. He tried not to think about it, but it was there all of the time somewhere in the back of his mind.

That looming deadline was at the root of his skewed temporal perception — making their days together a blurred trail of quickly evaporating mirages.

What should have been gourmet meals were just fast-food eat-on-the-fly moments. No time to stop and savor. Just enough time to stuff the pie hole and swallow partially-chewed, barely-tasted morsels of who-knows-what. No time to stop and smell the coffee. Not even to taste it. Gulp and run.

At least that's how it seemed.

It affected every area of his life.

Billy would just finish taking one exam and it seemed another one was right there on him again. He would turn in a term paper for one class, only to realize he was woefully behind preparing one for another class. He would fall asleep at his desk night after night just trying to keep up. Then trying to catch up.

With Natalie, there never seemed to be enough time.

Especially with Natalie.

Then they had a big fight.

It probably wasn't really a *big* fight. But the fact was, they had never fought before.

Period. Not once.

And this one certainly should never have happened. It wasn't actually about anything. Like many arguments, it was more a symptom of other tensions and anxieties than about what was actually said. Fights of this sort have a logic of their own and they're certainly not logical.

It was the week before the short Thanksgiving holiday break, essentially a four-day weekend, which most students just used to study and get a jump on their final exams, which would be coming up in a little over three weeks.

Billy saw no reason to make a big deal out of it, though people, especially the older generation, seemed to think it was a momentous occasion. Back home in Detroit, they certainly pulled out the stops. His mom had invited him for turkey and stuffing, but it was out of the question. Four days just wasn't enough time to make it home and back, without ending up completely exhausted and upset about all the time he had wasted. And what for? Just to see his mother completely bust her ass to create an amazing feast, then watch his father belch and fall asleep without showing one iota of gratitude. Frankly, if he never had to endure another Thanksgiving dinner at home again, it would be too soon.

He had tons of studying to do, but that aside, he was looking forward to spending the four days with Natalie, without the pressure of attending classes. Maybe they could conjure their own mini-Thanksgiving — a Deluxe Turkey Mega-Sub from Subway and some chocolate-dipped donut holes from Mr. Donut, a couple wine coolers and cranberry belly-jellies.

That sounded like the perfect ticket!

Then came the bomb.

"Pam is heading to New York City for ten days. I'm going to spend the weekend with her, Billy."

Fuck!

Billy slammed his fist on the nuclear launch button. Missiles away.

"Sometimes I really think this whole thing is a big game, Natalie. You don't really love me. I'm just your on-again off-again fuck-boy."

For only a few milliseconds, a look of pain — genuine hurt — flashed across Natalie's face. But almost immediately it was replaced with the hot flush of poisonous rage.

"Like I couldn't have practically any dude on this campus on his knees begging to fuck my brains out with a snap of my fingers? Grow up. Pam is my best friend. Deal with it."

"Somehow ... somewhere ... I thought I played into that equation. I thought maybe I held that coveted place in your life."

"It's apples and oranges, Billy. Get a fucking clue. If you want to, go and fuck whoever you want. I don't care what you do."

"See. See. Right there. You don't care. Maybe I will. Maybe it'll put things in perspective. Then I can be as indifferent as you are."

"Fat chance."

"Fat chance what? That I can be that indifferent. I think I already am."

"No. Fat chance you can get laid. At least by someone that looks human."

"Right. What does that say about your taste? Hey! What about Julianne? Does she look like dog meat to you?"

"Oh ... yeah. Now I remember. You're right. Julianne. One of the most beautiful chicks on campus. She couldn't go another day without you. She was talking suicide. I think she had even bought the rope already."

"She fucked me, didn't she?"

"I don't know, Billy. I wasn't there. If you say so, then she did. But probably on a bet."

"A bet? What bet?"

"How should I know? I can't see into the demented minds of those girls. Maybe they had a bet that you didn't have a dick. Or that you couldn't get it up. I have no idea. But it wasn't love. And it sure as hell wasn't lust. But give her a call. Maybe it'll work out for you."

"What are you doing in New York? How about if I come along?"

Natalie turned around, walked over to her desk and sat down. She lowered her head to her chest and gripped the bridge of her nose with her finger and thumb. Then she started to rub her eyes. She hadn't, but Billy thought she had started crying. She just took a moment.

"Billy. Whether you choose to believe it or not, I really really love you. I have never loved a guy before. Ever. Not even a crush. I used to think there was something wrong with me. But I don't anymore. I know exactly how I feel. I also know that sometimes I need space. So that ... so I don't lose sight of who and what I am."

"Pam gives you space?"

"Being with a girl is a whole different thing, Billy. She's ... she's my friend. A girlfriend. It's completely different. Completely different."

Billy thought for a while. He was grateful that things had calmed down a bit. At least they weren't screaming at one another.

There was something that had been bothering him. Something he had wanted to bring up for a long time. He couldn't be sure but maybe this was as good a time as any.

"Natalie. When you told me about your past, that first time we really got together. When we had the picnic down by the lake. You remember?"

"Of course, I remember. It was one of the most special days of my life, Billy."

"Well, I remember it too. Very well. And there's something that's been bothering me."

"Knock yourself out. You couldn't piss me off any more than you already have."

Billy collected his thoughts. He didn't want this to come out wrong. Like he was calling her a liar, or nitpicking what she had said. But there was something odd about it.

"You basically told me about ten or twelve years of your life. Everything that was going on. But you never once mentioned Pam."

"She was in there. What do you mean?"

"You never once mentioned Pam. Your best friend. The person you would turn to in a crisis. The one I assume you would confide in."

"She was there, Billy. Of course, we talked. But what are you getting at?"

"I ... I ... don't know."

"You've really gone off the deep end. I don't know what triggered this. All I know is right now I don't give a shit. I'm spending a couple days with my friend. When I get back, I'm going to believe none of this ever happened. You'd be smart to put it behind you, too."

"I'm sorry."

"Fuck 'I'm sorry'. You better go."

He went. He felt like a complete jerk. A total fuck-up.

Worst of all, they didn't see each other till Pam finally left New York and headed back to Chicago.

Ironic. How completely ironic.

He was all bent out of shape about missing out on a few days with Natalie, and because of this argument, it cost him over ten. Ten days without a single moment with her.

Billy had a lot of time to study over the next week-and-a-half.

And think. If you could call it thinking.

It was more playing over and over in his head how he had screwed up, how he should have handled it, what he should have done, what he shouldn't have.

Not very productive. Painfully unproductive. Pure torture.

How many times did he look at the phone on the wall wondering if it was ever going to ring?

Ring for him, that is.

His roommate had seemed to have made an awful lot of friends in the short time he had been there at Cornell. Maybe he was a drug dealer. He was coming and going so much, he could have been running a courier service out of their suite. And the phone seemed to be going day and night. When Beavis wasn't there, Billy felt like he was the desk clerk for a 24-hour home shopping channel.

He felt pretty desolate without his regular calls and get-togethers with Natalie — regardless of how brief they often had to be. It was the first time he realized that loneliness could be physically painful.

Billy decided to call home.

He waited till Tuesday evening. He couldn't remember what shift his dad was on. Last he knew, it was afternoons, meaning he wouldn't get home until late. If the old fart wasn't there, his mom could talk more comfortably.

His father answered on the first ring.

161

"Yeah?"

Billy was so shocked at hearing his father's voice, he was speechless.

"Uh ... well ..."

"Spit it out! Who is this?"

"Dad. You're home. Is mom okay? Is there something wrong?"

"No, I took the evening off so we could go roller skating. I'm here because she's sick, son. She feels like shit. Whaddya want?"

As he would expect. Just because the old man stayed home to help, nothing really changes. What an asshole!

"Well ... I ... I ... tell her I hope she feels better. Oh ... and tell her to call me when she feels up to it. Bye."

"Bye. Just like that. You have nothing to say to me?"

This was a new twist. After two decades, now he wants to chat. Okay. He'd try.

"How's it going, dad? Are you holding up okay?"

"Tough as nails. You know me. But sometimes I worry. Your mom doesn't look too good."

Buy a Playboy if you want good looks. What does he expect? *She* doesn't look too good. Look in the mirror fat man.

"So the chemo and all that ... it's ... has her hair fallen out?"

"In clumps. She looks like Sinead O'Connor."

Sinead O'Connor? His dad knew who Sinead O'Connor was?

"You know Sinead O'Connor?"

"Not personally. But she's the bitch who tore up a picture of the Pope. I thought that was rich. She can sit on my face any time after that stunt."

"Is mom going to be okay?"

"Who knows? These fucking doctors should carry pompoms. They're a bunch of shit-grinning cheerleaders. They're always cautiously optimistic. That's their favorite phrase. Cautiously optimistic. Who can tell what the hell's really going on? But your mom's hangin' in there, I have to say that. I'll tell her you called."

Click.

She called the day after Thanksgiving. Friday.

"Billy. How my number one son?"

"Singularly okay. How was Thanksgiving, mom? Did you make your usual feast for twenty people and their best friends?"

"Funny boy. You know it's only been just you and me and your dad."

"But you still always cook enough for twenty people. So he said you weren't feeling well. I called Tuesday evening."

"I've been a little under the weather."

That meant she had been having near death experiences.

"But I'm fine. I'll be okay. We didn't do anything yesterday. Just relaxed."

Didn't do anything for Thanksgiving? The first time in twenty years. Things must be bad. Relaxed? That meant she was in a coma and dad was drunk as a skunk in front of the boob tube. Billy was really worried. He made an on-the-spot decision.

"Mom. I think I want to come home for Christmas break. Is that okay?"

"Oh Billy! Is that okay? That's great. It would make us both so happy."

Both? The old man couldn't care less. Maybe she meant her and Billy.

"Okay. Plan on it. Don't do anything special. Just rest. Take care of yourself. It'll be great just to be there and spend time with you."

"I can't do much right now, Billy. I'm so weak. I feel so tired all the time. But having you here ... well ..."

Billy could tell she was crying and doing a poor job of hiding it.

"... it will mean so much to me right now."

"Okay. Just rest. I'll see you on the 21st. Bye, mom."

"Be a good boy, Billy."

Time.

What a crazy subjective thing it was.

Sometimes it just crawls by so painfully slow, like when you're waiting for something and you're too fidgety and distracted to get your head into anything. Each second ticks off with the lumbering thud of a giant, striding in slow motion over a bleak and colorless landscape.

Tick tick tick.

Like it had been the last few days without Natalie or any classes to go to — or even anyone to talk to.

Tick tick tick.

Then other times the ticks are a rapid fire blur of a machine gun. Hours disappear. Days. Months. Years. Where did they go?

That was the mantra of people when they got older. *Where did all those years go?* It hadn't made much sense to Billy for most of his life. Old people always carrying on about how time flies by faster and faster the older you get.

But now he was beginning to get it. Just barely. Just enough that he was getting an inkling of how someone later in life might say that.

This term at school came to mind. It just seemed to blaze by. It seemed like only yesterday that he had arrived and registered for classes, then there was the surprise party for Natalie, and here he was now sitting in his room during Thanksgiving break. Finals were just around the corner and then Christmas and blam it would be 2003. All in the blink of an eye. How did that happen?

And looking back on this past summer it was both fast and slow. He spent nearly three months working in that damn factory, never getting to do anything in the evenings because of the shift he was on. He arrived and did the same thing every day for 69 days and then it was over, just like that. The whole summer just seemed to have evaporated into thin air.

But he also remembered how at certain times, it crawled by so slowly he thought he was going to go crazy, and his reward for devoting three months of his life trying to build up some cash reserve for school, was going to be a permanent home in a padded cell.

And waiting to talk to Natalie! That was whole other level of getting stuck on the slow boat through hell. Trying hour after hour, day after day, to call her. Never knowing when he would be able to get through to her. He remembered dialing her cell. No answer. Telling himself that he'd try again in another hour. But being so restless and impatient, watching the seconds tick off one by one, that he'd couldn't wait a full hour. Sometimes it would be a half hour. Or fifteen minutes. Or ten. Or five.

Tick tick tick.

At least for now he couldn't complain about time racing off and leaving him scratching his head, a victim of amnesia. No. Sitting there in his room with the best intentions of studying, the seconds were crawling by like little drunk ants across a window sill.

Natalie would supposedly be back in two days. This was Friday. Classes were back up and running on Monday.

When would he hear from her?

How would that go after their fight?

The envelope, please. And the answers are.

Not very soon.

Not very well.

There were three weeks left in the term. Another whole week passed before Billy heard from her. He knew better than to call her so he didn't. He immersed himself in his classes. It paid off. Before heading into the weeklong study period in preparation for exams, he was finally caught up. Which meant he felt really good about school. This at least partially compensated for how lousy he felt about things between him and Natalie.

By Friday he was convinced it was over. Not a word. Not a single word had passed between them for over two weeks.

Billy was coming back from his last class on Friday, PSYCH 2610, Development of Social Behavior. This had turned out to be his most interesting — and favorite — class of the current term. He realized he had grown up a social mutant in Detroit, not just because of the community and family life he had experienced, but because by his own choice had been so removed from the kind of normal social situations which develop ones perspective on man as a social animal. Not only was the subject matter interesting, his professor was a real rarity. An astute scholar but with excellent lecturing skills and a wild, unpredictable sense of humor. Dr. Joseph Miller was his name. Billy had even bought two extra books by Professor Miller, with the intention of reading them over the Christmas break.

Today was the final scheduled class of the term for Miller's course and the good professor had been in rare form. Billy was still smiling about a very funny game they had played involving pairing off all of the students. He had been partnered with some girl named Rose, a little cutie from Queens with a quick wit and a ton of attitude. It had been great fun.

As he came around the building and approached the front door to his apartment, he stopped dead in his tracks. There was Natalie sitting on the stoop. Bundled up against the cold.

"Hi, Billy."

She never came over to his place. Mainly because it was so uncomfortable with Beavis there, his druggy roommate, who was only tolerable when he was completely unconscious.

Billy finally managed to make his mouth work.

164

"Hello stranger. How is it?"

"I've been very pissed at you."

"Hey. Don't mince words. Just get to the point. Is my fuckwad roommate in there?"

"I don't think so. I'm half frozen to death. Can we go inside?"

"That's why I'm here."

He unlocked. Natalie followed him in. He put down his stuff and took off his coat. He was having trouble looking at her. He had missed her so much and spent so much time waiting for this moment. But now that she was here, he felt a burning resentment at what she had put him through. It shocked him how cold he felt toward her right now.

"But I'm not mad at you anymore."

"And the skies opened up and beamed the light of love on the happy couple. They embraced and strolled hand-in-hand into the burnished blue valley of contentment."

"I can imagine how you feel."

"At one time, I could have believed that. How's Pam?"

"Don't change the subject. Please. I'm not here for small talk."

"Pam is hardly small talk. She is ... she's a major thorn, in my view. I mean, she shouldn't have to be. But that's the way it seems to work now, doesn't it?"

"What are you doing over Christmas?"

"Now look who's changing the subject. I'm going home. My mom is in a bad way."

"Can I come with you?"

Billy reeled. That was the last thing he ever expected to hear. Particularly right now.

"No. I don't think it's a very good idea. Why would you want to do that? Would you be bringing Pam? Maybe the two of you would get a kick out of seeing how pathetic Billy's family situation is, eh? Lots of good rollicking laughs there. No doubt about it."

They were still both standing. Without making a conscious effort or even noticing, they had worked their way from the living area into Billy's room.

Natalie suddenly moved quickly. She stepped right up to him and wrapped her arms around him in a big needy embrace. Her face was turned sideways and down away from his, so he couldn't see her expression.

He could just barely hear her. She was whispering. Over and over.

"Billy Green, I love you. Billy Green, I love you ..."

Cream Colored Ponies and Crisp Apple Strudels

Slowly ... very slowly ... things returned to normal for Billy and Natalie.

Too slowly.

There were only two weeks left. Study period — four days of intense preparation for final exams — then the finals themselves spread over ten days.

The pressures of cramming and then taking these critical tests normally left little time for romance, much less time to repair one which had been recently damaged.

The good news for Billy was that during his hiatus with Natalie, he had truly gotten on top of things. This time around he didn't have to stay up late into the night, only to awaken next morning and find himself slumped at his desk using a textbook as a pillow.

Natalie had nowhere near the demanding classes Billy had assigned himself. She had five exams to prepare for, but they were easier classes, and like Billy, she had done her homework. Since her exams were nicely spread out, giving her time to prepare adequately for each one, she was not under as much pressure as she could have been.

So they weren't completely shut off from one another by schedules. There was time for them to try to put things back together.

What slowed things down was them. Both of them were shaken by the confrontation and the two weeks apart which had followed. Both were tentative, more unsure of themselves than they probably needed to be. Neither wanted to make a misstep, something which might trigger another fight and throw them back to the starting line. Or worse, blow the whole thing completely apart. For the first time in their relationship, that was a real possibility.

There was too much to lose.

Baby steps. Baby steps.

The Friday Billy came back from his psych class and found Natalie waiting for him, they had parted as secure friends but insecure lovers.

It was a full week later that they finally revisited the hotbed of their still fiery passion, and enjoyed the erotic bliss they had often shared before.

Today was the third day of exams and Billy had returned to his apartment, after taking his Computing in the Arts final. Skid — aka Beavis — was smoking a big fat joint and drinking a Coke.

"Hey, Skid. Getting ready for your next exam?"

"Aw man. I can't cut this shit. I really bombed out this morning. I think I'm going to pack it in."

"What's that supposed to mean?"

"Shit. College. I don't think it's for me. Like what am I going to do with all this stuff they're trying to cram in my head?"

"Harry Truman only had a high school diploma."

"Who?"

"Harry Truman. He was President of the United States back when. After World War II."

"I ain't gonna be no president. Why did you bring that up?"

"Just shooting the shit, Skidmore. Just shooting—"

The phone rang. Billy was standing right next to it, picked it up and handed it to Skid.

"Yellow! Oh ... it's for you, dude."

He handed the phone back to Billy.

"Can you come over? You're done today, right?"

Natalie.

"What's the occasion?"

166

"You."

How could he have a problem with that?

"Be there in fifteen."

Beavis looked at him enviously.

"You are one lucky dude."

"I guess I am. Especially if you say so."

"Hey Billy. I won't be here when you get back. I'm blowin' this pop stand. My bus for Florida leaves in a couple hours. I think."

Skid looked at the ticket that was laying on the table.

"What day is this?"

"Friday. The 13th."

"That figures. Wow! That's so fucking *real.*"

He got up and low-fived Billy, then gave him a big hippie-brother hug.

"Good luck, Skid. You are one of a kind."

"You're right, dude. I am."

Skid headed for his room. Billy put his coat back on and was out the door.

Natalie's door swung open before his third knock. She must have been standing right there or be capable of space-time travel to have gotten to the door so quickly.

"I have a surprise. Close your eyes."

"I don't think you have enough room in here for a firing squad."

He closed them and she led him like a blind man to a table, where she guided him to sit down on a wooden chair.

"Okay. Now open."

His face lit up like he was looking at the spaceship from *Close Encounters of the Third Kind.*

"I have arrived in Heaven!"

Billy loved white chocolate. While elsewhere others might be putting white powder up their noses or injecting melted sienna-colored horse in their veins, those things didn't have any special appeal for him. But what could evolve into a full-blown addiction, one which if he ever became impoverished might drive him to mugging old ladies and fencing stolen televisions, would be his love for white chocolate.

In front of Billy right now was a huge silver serving platter covered with candy and pastries. Very special candy and pastries. Animal figures, mostly horses and other domesticated farm creatures, posed in the center like trick ponies in a circus, surrounded by at least a dozen fruit-filled confections.

Natalie just stood there and grinned ear to ear.

"Those are apple and raspberry strudels."

"And are those little animals made of what I think they are?"

"Yes. White chocolate."

"Do you have an IV drip of insulin ready? I think I'm going to need it."

"Whatever it takes to keep you alive, my good friend. My ... boyfriend."

Natalie looked at him with a tiny dollop of insecurity he had never seen in her eyes before. As if she were asking, are you? Are you still my boyfriend?

"You are the best girlfriend money can buy. How much do I owe for this?"

"Paid in full. Let's eat."

It didn't take much persuasion on her part. Somewhere between the 'ea' and the 't' Billy had already dived in and was savoring the creamy melting on his tongue of the head and front legs of a delectable equestrian figurine. It was a spunky pony, who had just moments before been rearing up on his hind legs as if to celebrate or challenge Billy's arrival. Within thirty seconds, he was no more. Billy was a very happy young man.

So it went, until they fell into Natalie's bed, their bellies bloated and their entire beings in the throes of sucrose saturation — the ache and nausea of their pancreases working at 120% of capacity, combined with the jagged exhilaration sugar euphoria.

Full-blown sugar shock almost immediately set in and they fell asleep in one another's arms.

When they awoke in the middle of the night — somewhere around 3 am — without ado or hesitation, they made love long and hard, the animal intensity of which was driven by their self-imposed and long-suffering abstinence. It had been way too long.

When the faint glow of dawn just began to pull into relief the trees and buildings visible through Natalie's window, exhaustion trumped desire and they slept until just before noon. Finally they stirred and woke up.

"Good morning, Billy. What do you have to say for yourself?"

"Is there any white chocolate left?"

Just the Two of Us

Billy and Natalie would spend this Christmas holiday apart.

They vowed never again. But this particular time Billy would take the bus back to Detroit and Natalie would fly back to Indianapolis.

Neither one was very thrilled about going home.

Billy of course wanted to be with his mom. But prospects of making any money there were little and none. Meaning he would really be pinched toward the end of the next school term. Moreover, he wanted to be around his dad as much as he wanted to be dropped in a vat of molten iron. He assumed he'd be gritting and grinding his teeth down to stumps by the end of the holiday break.

Natalie had since high school made a point of using home purely as a quick, brief stopover. Usually two days maximum each time, as had happened this past summer when she came off her camping trip. Obviously that wouldn't be the case this time, as she would be spending the entire twelve or so days with her family.

It was pure tokenism. She couldn't stand any of them and still looked at the day she left home to go to college as the great turning point in her life. But her dad was footing part of the bill — a sizable part of the bill — so she had to make cameo appearances and push her acting skills to their limit. If she didn't make a big show out of her gratitude for his help, as well as how much she loved being with them all, she wouldn't put it past her father to cut her off. Her visits were entirely mercenary but quite necessary.

Natalie's exams were done on a Wednesday. Billy's on the Friday.

He saw her to the airport.

Things between them weren't quite back to normal. Or more like it, not back to the innocent uncluttered heights they had been before their recent quarrel.

But it was still a very sad parting. They arrived at the airport early, which meant that after Natalie checked in, they had at least an hour to turn on the faucets and leave one another's shoulders sopping with tears. They also had time to repeatedly declare that nothing should ever come between them and promise to never fight again.

Just before entering the maze for the security checkpoint leading to her gate, Natalie turned to give Billy one last kiss good-bye.

"Hey, Billy. I didn't forget…"

She reached in her pocket and pulled out a small package, gift-wrapped with a bow.

"… I couldn't fit Julianne in there, so it'll have to do. Go ahead. Open it."

Billy blushed at the reference to his last birthday. Then he suddenly realized, it had only been a year since he had first seen this young woman, who was now at the center of his life.

One year.

And here he was, a year older. Twenty. No longer a teenager.

In love.

What a difference a year can make.

Billy tore off the wrapping. It was a beautiful Cartier watch. Elegant deep-blue facing and wrist band, perfectly machined white gold casing, thin stylish hands and numerals. He had never seen a watch of this quality on anyone, much less owned one.

"Natalie, I—"

"Happy Birthday, Billy! I better go."

Two days later — a very cold Saturday — Billy reprised his fare-saving but arduous bus trip back to Detroit. Late that evening his dad was waiting for him at the Greyhound terminal. Billy threw his small suitcase and satchel in the back seat. There was another suitcase and a small carry-on back there as well, but he didn't give it any thought.

He did notice that his father was driving a different car. It looked brand new. Some kind of Chrysler product he guessed. These days cars were beginning to look all the same to him.

He climbed into the passenger seat and closed the door.

"Hi dad. New car?"

His dad didn't reply, nor did he say a single word for the thirty-five minute drive home.

It was a lot of dead air space, so it felt like it took forever to get from the main bus terminal downtown to the north side of Detroit.

They finally pulled into the drive. Uncomfortable and slightly annoyed, Billy couldn't get out of the car fast enough. As he grabbed his bags and turned to head into the house, he noticed his dad had not gotten out and the car was still running. As soon as Billy kicked the passenger door closed, his dad put it in reverse and backed out of the drive.

Billy didn't know at the time, but this would be the last time he would ever see the man.

His mom was waiting in the kitchen.

Billy leaned over to kiss her on the cheek.

"What's going on? Where's dad going?"

"Las Vegas."

"Las Vegas? You're putting me on."

"He and a few of his buddies at work are heading out there. He's taking the red-eye tonight and won't be back until after New Years day."

This shock postponed the shock of registering how badly the anti-cancer therapy had ravaged her. Not that he could avoid noticing.

She looked terrible.

She had always been lean with very little to spare, so it was very obvious that she had lost weight. Her skin was loose and shriveled and was the color of sepia parchment. Her clothes barely hung on her scarecrow-thin body. Partly out of self-consciousness about her surgically-flattened chest, she slouched and defensively crossed her arms in front of her. With the strength drained from her, it was easiest just to keep her center of gravity low in a submissive slouch.

She was wearing one of the wigs she had bought. Billy remembered how her getting them initially was in a spirit of playfulness, and how she had joked about it then. Well, it was no laughing matter now. Because of her deteriorated state, the one she had on now was a mocking affair, rather than an effective means of disguising the hair loss.

Right now, he didn't have the stomach to talk about anything to do with her health, or lack of it. He'd get to that later.

"Dad has buddies? Hard to imagine."

"Billy. He's not a terrible person. Okay … he is with you. I'm sorry. It's the way it is."

"He's actually flying to Las Vegas. Flying!"

"He's a pretty normal guy."

"Then the world is in big trouble."

"He used to fly all the time. Well, not all the time. But a lot. When he got the union job. The union officials always had to be somewhere for some important meeting. This was before you were born."

"Is he flying cargo class?"

She suppressed a smile at that one.

"Stop it, Billy. There's nothing wrong with your father that a few sit-ups couldn't fix."

"Plus liposuction, then stapling his stomach. Maybe wiring his jaw shut. Finally sending him to the Mahatma Gandhi weight-loss clinic. So, mom … how are you?"

"Fit as a fiddle. I'm thinking of teaching aerobics. Maybe enter the Miss America contest."

"You'd win. At least the senior division."

"Think so? Oh, Billy. It's been very hard. I'm always so tired. I can't keep anything down. But only for a couple more weeks. That's what they say."

"So it's just you and I."

"Just you and I."

"What do you want to do? Anything special? Shopping? Anyone you want to visit?"

"Nothing, my Billy Boy. Just having you here is enough. Do what you want. Just come and go as you please. The old car is in the garage. The keys are right there …" Pointing at a set of keys hanging on a bulletin board next to the door to the garage. "… and if you need gas money, just ask. And really. Just having you around is perfect."

"I don't have to go anywhere. I came home to see you."

"You have no idea how much that means to me."

Billy looked at her. She was making a great effort to smile. He could tell just a few minutes talking with him was already wearing her down.

"Mom. You don't deserve this."

"Billy Boy. I'm fine. You learn as you go along. It's not what you deserve or don't deserve. You just get what you get. The important thing is to live. Live your life like every moment counts. Because whether you know it or not, every single one does."

Billy thought about that a lot while he was laying in bed that night. He thought about it eating a bowl of Cheerios for breakfast the next morning. He thought about it the entire rest of his visit. The more he thought about it, the more it he became convinced she was right. What a huge body of wisdom was contained in those simple words.

Live your life like every moment counts.

Starting right now.

As bad as she obviously felt, as bad as she looked, and as bad as it made him feel to see this wonderful woman suffer, this lady who had given him so much, his mom unlike any other mom in the world — if for no better reason than she was *his* mom — as sad as he could have allowed himself to be, Billy made his time with her count. Maybe the pain and weariness of her illness was written all over her face, but her smile could light up the universe.

His universe anyway.

Billy hardly went anywhere the whole time he was in Detroit. To the store to buy groceries. To the mall to buy his mom a couple of Christmas presents. That was it.

They talked and laughed. They watched TV and movies — he went out and bought a VCR and hooked it up, then got a family membership at Blockbuster. In the evenings, they would watch old Alfred Hitchcock classics or contemporary romantic epics like *Titanic*, quirky fun films like *High Fidelity* and *Wonder Boys*, or Hugh Grant feel-good movies like *About A Boy* and the one with Julia Roberts, *Notting Hill*. His mom loved Hugh Grant.

Some afternoons her friends, a few of the old gang and a several new ones, came by and they played Euchre. He still kicked their butts after all of these years. They were always reminding him of how he used to clean them out of their mad money when he was a boy.

Of course, he drove her for her appointments at the clinic. Waiting in the lobby he tried to read the books he had brought home with him. It wasn't easy. He felt very uncomfortable, cancer patients everywhere. Everyone so grim.

Sometimes he and his mom would just sit quietly in the living room together. Especially after the chemo treatments. She would be so exhausted. She napped. Billy would read. The house was pleasantly quiet. It felt good being there.

Then holiday vacation was over.

It tore him up inside when the taxi pulled up early the morning of January 2nd. He had been there a full eleven days, but he still felt like he was abandoning her. Fortunately, she would be there alone only part of the day. Her newest good friend, Phyllis, was coming over around noon. Then his dad was supposed to be back from Vegas sometime that evening.

The night before Billy had cooked them dinner. It was his first attempt at making lasagna and frankly, it didn't turned out too well. The resemblance between the charred dish he served up and edible food was purely coincidental.

Naturally, his mom gushed over it and assured him that what he had done was a cutting-edge improvement on the traditional recipe. After a couple of glasses of wine, he almost believed her. They finished some Sara Lee cheese cake and then his mom became very serious.

"I think I did a bad thing."

"What bad thing?"

"I told your father."

"Told him what?"

"That you knew. About your real father. And that … you know. I was really afraid he was going to totally go nuts and kill me. But I thought it's only fair. We've never had any secrets. Not after what I did. Since then, I've always tried to be honest with him. It's not easy, that's for sure. He has a bad temper."

"Believe me, I know."

"But he took it pretty calmly. For him. He's been different since I got sick."

"If I were you, I wouldn't have said anything. But you have to do what you think is right."

"But that's why … at least I think that's why he left. He couldn't face you."

"Don't blame yourself. It's not worth it. Besides, this has been great. Just the two of us. Like it used to be when I would come home from grade school."

"Yes it has. It's been great. You're my favorite boy, you know."

"As an only child, it's hard to argue with that."

It was this last conversation that Billy was mulling over as the taxi took him to the bus station. That and the expression on his mom's face as they waved good-bye.

It was such a sad expression. But at the same time hopeful.

Parents really do live through their children. Sadness at how their own lives have fallen short of their youthful dreams and expectations, is displaced by the hope they hold out, that their children will fulfill all the promises they had made to themselves when they were young. That their children will find and experience the love that never quite arrived for them, at least not the love they had imagined and dreamed of in the floating fantasies of youth.

Billy tried to picture his mom as a young woman. Maybe twenty or twenty-one years old. When everything was possible and each handsome young suitor held in his eyes the promise of a lifetime of perfect love, companionship, devotion, marriage, children.

Then he tried to picture his dad as one of those promising young suitors, charged with optimism, ready to conquer the world, eager to please and impress, ready to dazzle, full of enthusiasm for the same possibilities of life, excited at the prospect of a smile or a simple kiss from the lovely young girl before him.

Whew! Trying to imagine this was really difficult. He just couldn't get there. It felt like such an impossible leap. Billy just couldn't picture it, no matter how hard he tried.

What he could imagine with little effort, was how his dad had probably been behaving in Las Vegas over the past eleven or so days. He could picture that with great ease. Sickening ease.

Grabbing the asses of the sexy young waitresses. Slugging down copious amounts of booze. Bleating and bellowing obscenities. Sitting at the foot of a stage in a strip club sticking his tongue out and making repulsive remarks to girls one-third his age. Even hiring one of the thousands of street-meat hookers you could find anywhere in Vegas and take back to your room with you, like picking up a bag of potato chips at a convenience store.

Yeah. He could picture that. No problem at all.

Did his mom see his dad the way he really was and just ignore it?

Or did she still carry those early idealized impressions of him as a young man, somehow thickly superimposed over reality, completely blinding her to what he had become?

It was impossible for Billy to get his head around.

There was his mom, loyal in every respect to the very end. Trying to be honest. Fair. Loyal. Even protective. Always trying to do the right thing by the undeserving old bastard.

What would it feel like to love the man who he had been told to call 'father'?

What does it feel like, mom? Please tell me. What does it feel like?

January 2, 2003. Bright and early Thursday morning.

The taxi pulled away and there she stood waving.

Sad. Frustrated. Lonely. Perhaps even dying.

But still hopeful. Still capable of smiling.

Still there to light up Billy's universe.

Living each moment as if it counts.

What a truly amazing woman.

Billy was her favorite son.

"Be a good boy, Billy."

I'll try … really try.

I promise, mom.

Chapter Six

LEAPING OFF THE MÖBIUS STRIP
2003

Welcome to the Motel California

When Billy got back to his apartment very late Thursday night, Skid's stuff was indeed gone. No one else had been assigned to share the place. Billy had it all to himself, at least for now.

Perfect.

His three-week Winter Session cram course started tomorrow — PSYCH 2140 Cognitive Psychology — and he would not have a minute to spare on social niceties or adjusting to new patterns of roommate behavior. In some twisted way, he had really had it made with Beavis. Though the phone rang a lot, the guy was practically never around and even when he was, he was usually passed out cold. Overall the guy was more like having a fish than a dog for a pet.

Billy called Natalie.

"You wanna come over? I have the honeymoon suite all to myself."

"Should I bring the Maid of Honor?"

"Only if she's willing to do guard duty on the porch all night."

"That was the right answer. See you in a half-an-hour."

They spent a couple hours describing their holidays, since they had only talked a few times during the Christmas break. Natalie was never alone in Indianapolis and the curiosity of her family was less than healthy, so their short exchanges on the phone for the past couple weeks had sounded to the big ears around her — and even to Billy — more like she was fielding a sales call from a stranger than having a personal conversation with someone she truly cared about. It made the whole attempt to keep in touch pretty pointless and very unsatisfying.

Fighting exhaustion — Billy had just spent 13 hours on a bus, and Natalie had only arrived a couple hours before, after six hours on three planes stopping in four airports — they jabbered away excitedly as long as they could hold out. Neither had anything majorly exciting to tell but they were certainly jazzed to see each other again. It had been almost two weeks.

They both had to be at class very early. Just before 3 am they were sound asleep in one another's arms. Four hours of shut-eye would have to suffice.

Long class schedules took up both Friday and Saturday.

Sunday they hit the books hard and were back at the tortuous class schedule every day for the next two weeks.

Finally Winter Session ended, but Spring Term began only two days later.

It was a real grind. In fact, the next five-and-a-half months ended up being a real grind.

For Spring Term, they each had five classes but Billy's were a lot less difficult than Natalie's. She was forging ahead at full speed fulfilling the rigorous requirements for an early graduation that coming August. Plus she still had her duties as a Resident Assistant.

On his end, Billy was really strapped for cash. Not working during the Christmas break guaranteed he would run out before the end of the regular school year. Moreover, in the back of his mind, he was thinking he would like to take classes the coming Summer Session, both to speed up his own degree program and to be on campus with Natalie till she graduated. After that, he didn't have a clue what might be happening.

Whatever the case, it was going to take money.

To pick up some extra cash, he took on two part-time jobs. One was doing some digital archiving data entry for the main campus library. The other was as a custodial assistant three nights a week cleaning the Computing and Communications Center, typically the top floor where there was a cluster of offices and small computing labs.

They were fairly mindless jobs, which didn't particularly tax his brain. But while they didn't compromise the energy and concentration needed to study, combined they lopped about twenty hours out of his schedule each week. This was both time he would normally apply to his books and time he would spend with Natalie. But he had no choice in the matter.

Spring Term ground along like a large earthmoving machine, carving a huge swath through their waking hours, crawling steadily and methodically towards some sort of closure in June.

Billy and Natalie toughed it out, grabbing fast food on the fly, exchanging drive-by hellos and good-byes barely applying the brakes, and surviving on abbreviated nights of sleep, further truncated once or twice a week by some hard and fast lovemaking.

By the time the eight days of spring break finally rolled around middle of March, they both were suffering from a severe case of burn-out. They were more than ready for a serious respite from the daily grind of campus life, both longing for a dramatic change of scenery from Cornell.

Regardless of what Natalie did — and she had not said anything one way or another — Billy had originally intended to just stay around Ithaca and try to pick up some full-time temp work, either on campus itself or in town. But now, for the first time ever, he was being confronted by an overpowering urge to escape. He just couldn't face anything resembling mindless work. More of the same ol' same ol' was out of the question. He needed a break. Eight days sounded like a decent start and a gift from the gods.

It was late Sunday evening, and spring break was only a week away. Natalie was on her computer and Billy had appropriated her bed to organize and review his lecture notes for his Contemporary Moral Issues class.

"I haven't even started looking for a job."

"I had a feeling. And I didn't see a rabbit suit in your closet."

"Ah yes! The rabbit suit. Such fond memories. I just can't make myself go look for a job. This place is getting to me. I need to get away from here."

"Detroit?"

"I'd rather take a bullet."

"Okay. I was going to surprise you. Come here and look at this."

Billy came up behind her and looked over her shoulder. He loved the way her hair smelled.

She minimized the page she was working on and pulled up the internet. Apparently she had put some time into this. There were several bookmarks in a folder named 'B&N/SB-2003'.

Point and click.

A webpage sprang to life.

WELCOME TO THE MOTEL CALIFORNIA

A touch of the West Coast right here in the Poconos!

"Could I love you any more?"

"I'm feeling the same way as you. I mean, it makes no sense. I sure don't have the money. But I'm about ready to explode. And I thought—"

"Whoa! Hollywood Boulevard. Suite on the Beach Boys. Beverly Hills 90210. Surf City. Sunset and Vine. Castro Street San Francisco."

"I think that's for gay couples."

It was a theme motel. The decor of each room was designed around some motif which in the public mind was 'typical California'.

"The rooms must not have any windows because the Poconos are about as un-California as it gets. But this looks fantastic. Spring break with surfers and movie stars. And no jet lag."

"They must have a huge arc lamp in the corner of each room. Hey! We can get a tan and never even go outside."

"Do they pipe in smog for the L. A. rooms?"

Almost arbitrarily they chose the Disneyland Suite. Amazingly enough, considering the late date, the room was still available. An online form and a telephone call later, they confirmed their reservation.

In only a week, Billy and Natalie would be heading to *"the happiest place in the world"* for eight days and seven nights.

The Great Escape

Sexually, what Natalie occasionally lacked in hedonistic wild abandon, she made up for with flexibility.

Billy remembered, sometime in high school, seeing on TV a spectacular and highly unique circus act out of Montreal called *Cirque du Soleil*. Many of the acrobats were from China and were these petite little Asian girls who could tie themselves up like shoelaces or human pretzels, into practically any tightly wound, contorted configuration imaginable.

That was Natalie.

The sexual possibilities were infinite and Billy seemed bent on exploring them all. She was the perfect and willing accomplice.

After the first few times the slept together, it was not only the passion but the sheer mechanics which drove them. It was the challenge of gymnastics and the spirituality of yoga fused one into the other. As Natalie's and Billy's skin tones and body parts mingled and merged into one another, they became a single two-headed multi-limbed organism.

There was only one problem with this scenario.

That was the limitations intrinsic to a single bed. Both Natalie and Billy had narrow single person mattresses in their campus quarters. Single beds packed tightly in the corner of a room which also hosted desks, bookcases, computer stands, and so on. For Olympic-level lovemaking gymnasts like themselves, this was like asking Tarzan to show his stuff on a toddler's portable jungle gym.

But!

One of the great selling points of the Motel California — aside from the in-room theater-size movie screen, a selection of Hollywood's best flicks, a Dolby Digital 5.1 Surround Sound music system, and a fully stocked wet bar — was the conspicuous presence in every room, of a plush kings-size bed.

For Billy and Natalie, this was like taking two porpoises who had been bred and raised at Sea World and dropping them in vastness of the Pacific Ocean.

Finally — at least for seven nights — the carefully cultivated promises of their prior sexual acrobatics could reach their full supranatural and superphysical potential.

The first night, they both became obsessively fascinated with the pure architecture of their lovemaking. It was as if there were two parallel universes — physical and metaphysical. The fluid dynamics and solid-mass mechanics of the act in the physical world were but a nuts-and-bolts mirroring of the energy dances and deep-space seraphimics of the metaphysical.

They seemed to be able to read one another's minds. They spontaneously improvised exotic figurations of coital choreography, ones which under other circumstances would require teams of anatomical experts, gymnastics coaches, dance captains, and orthopedic specialists to engineer, if such calculating professionals even had the imaginations to attempt to work at this level.

By the third night, they could have appended several awe-inspiring pages to the Kama Sutra.

The tangled clashing of their bodies sent shards of lightning, peals of silent shrill bells and high-mass ecstatic screams of shared bliss ripping through the cosmic ether of their pleasure.

After each orgasm, they locked eyes in the awe of mutual astonishment.

They pleaded with each other in disbelief.

Is this possible? Could this really be happening?

Then to make believers of one another, they began the slow-building erotic dance over again.

Again and again and again.

With Natalie, there was the coolness, the disciplined steadiness of a sculptor's model. Even when she climaxed, which was at least three times every time they made love — one time it was either eight or nine depending on which of them you asked — there was a controlled, balletic discipline, which frankly drove Billy crazy and multiplied his own pleasures many times over.

By contrast, Billy's orgasms — even the third and fourth in several hours of continuous lovemaking — were the messy, earth-shattering, mind-numbing, cannon-roaring, sawed-off shotgun announcements characteristic of a healthy, virile, oversexed, perpetually horny young man of twenty.

Not that good old fashion romance was lacking.

Billy was never entirely comfortable with the guttural grunting, the violent animalistic rutting, that most other guys seemed to think was the essence of sexual union. While the man in him told his body to go for the obvious parts, the holistic human in him insisted on embracing the sum total of Natalie. Which meant that her ear or her little toe or her fingers or her shoulder blade all were coequal participants in the pursuit of their mutual pleasure. He left not a single square inch of her body ignored or unattended.

Moreover, with Billy there was a patient gentleness that belied his youth. A deeply erotic aesthetic sense, which measured and savored every step in scaling the sensual heights, as much as the breathtaking splendor of the climactic summit.

Their kisses sometimes lasted for more than a half-hour. Billy would have to remind himself to keep moving forward, that indeed as perfect this particular moment might be, there were new levels of perfection just a short journey ahead. Natalie always knew the ideal moment to urge them onward, the best possible pace, and most pleasurable path for that journey.

They never talked about their lovemaking. Billy never asked her how she felt about it or him. He didn't have to. There were no games, no insecurities, no jealousies, no silly contests. What she shared with him sexually was as much a part of the totality of her person, as her brilliant mind, her irreverent sense of humor, her mystery, history, persona, and her unique physical beauty. Each gift discrete but inseparable from the whole. Each appreciated on its own merits and beyond question and analytics.

Predictably, as each moment and hour passed of the spring break that would on some level, live on forever, Billy was falling deeper in love.

It was not so long ago that he was merely a boy in his room, pounding the thick surrounding walls of hopelessness with a battering ram of dreams, fantasies, and agnostic prayers.

There has to be something better than this.

Billy was now becoming convinced that Natalie was the answer to those prayers, those lonely desperate pleas. She was the missing silhouette in those fantasies, the haunting center around which he had circled but could never reach, the mystery behind Door #3.

As they made their way to the rental car to start the drive back to Cornell, Natalie with elliptical exactitude summed up their amazing week together.

"I can hardly walk."

"We need wheelchairs. But then, who would push?"

They moved like two bowlegged cowpokes who had spent the week riding wild horses.

In some surrealistic sense, they had.

Indeed they had.

Surrogate Bride

The taxi from the car rental office dropped them in front of Mary Conlon. Billy couldn't fathom being apart from her any more than he had to. Especially after this past week.

He walked her up to her room.

Natalie noticed when she turned her key, her door didn't appear to be locked. She stepped in cautiously.

"Pam! Wow! What a surprise."

Billy saluted facetiously, winked at her, and forged a credible grin as he stepped through the door.

"Hi, Pam. How are you?"

"I've been good. Real good. I missed you guys. I just wanted to say hi. Hope you don't mind, Nat. I let myself in. You know. The key from the surprise party."

Pam stood up and handed it to Natalie. They hugged. Billy stood back but then Pam came over and gave him a big long-lost-brother hug. His initial apprehensions melted in the buttery warmth of her embrace. Quasi-sibling qualifiers in place, Billy had to admit that her full breasts against his chest and the gentleness of her palms on his back filled him with a creamy comfort. It was the first time he had felt anything like affection from Pam.

"We just got in from the Poconos. Long story. But it was so great. Billy here is a fucking machine. He should be on TV replacing the Ever Ready bunny."

Billy felt like he had been slapped in the face. Is that what he was? A stud monkey?

Pam came to his rescue.

"Natalie! You are so cold sometimes! I can see just from looking at Billy's face the boy is mortified. You want to reduce the miracle and magic of love to mere fucking? Is that what you had in mind? Hmm? Don't be so freaked out, Nat. I've never seen you look so good. Except for the way you're walking. Did you sit on a hot plate or a clothes iron or something?"

Natalie ignored her remark and turned to Billy. She looked flustered.

"That was wrong. I'm ... I'm just not good at this. I guess I'm a little off center. Sorry."

Her eyes teared up. Billy and Pam came over to her. They sat on the bed, Pam on one side of Natalie, Billy on the other. They both hugged her. Their arms kind of met in the middle. They glanced at one another and discreetly shrugged.

Natalie uncharacteristically seemed deflated and was hunched over slightly, to avoid looking at either of them. She continued sniffling, dabbing her nose and eyes with a Kleenex.

Natalie's mood swing seemed as inexplicable as it was drastic. What had just happened wasn't really that serious. Just a tasteless, offhanded remark. But not that big of a deal.

Billy and Pam glanced at each other, as if to ask, what should we do?

Natalie still didn't look at them. Billy started to feel like he was in the way.

"Natalie. Maybe I should let you girls talk. But make sure you get some rest. I don't think we slept very much this last week. Not that I can recall anyway. I'm gonna head home."

He lightly kissed Natalie on the top of her head, then turned to leave.

As Billy and Pam stood up, Natalie lay back and stretched out on her bed.

Pam looked anxious, like she had something to say. There was a discernable twinkle in her eye.

"Before you go, Billy. Maybe this isn't the best time to mention this. But listen you two. There's a reason … a bigger reason for me being here. I know you've got classes tomorrow. But if you could make time for me, maybe tomorrow afternoon. I mean both of you. Together. I fly back to Chicago early Tuesday morning. So maybe dinner? Yes? My treat."

Natalie seemed to brighten up a bit at the suggestion. She looked at Pam curiously.

"That's very sweet, Pam."

Dinner it was. They agreed to pick Billy up between 5 and 5:30 at his place.

Billy headed out. He had three classes on Monday, the first starting at 9:00 am, the last ending at 4:00 pm. As far as he knew, he didn't have to work tomorrow. He would swing by to check the manpower assignment schedule to make sure. Natalie only had two classes, both in the morning. She could spend almost the entire afternoon visiting with Pam.

On his way back to his apartment, it occurred to him he should have offered to let them stay in his place. It had two beds and he still had not been assigned a roommate, so they could have had the entire place to themselves. He could have stayed in Natalie's room. One night probably would have been fine. If anyone knocked, he would just not answer the door. Because of his thoughtlessness, one of them would be sleeping on the hard floor. Too bad.

It felt both familiar and strange to return to the routine. But it was what it was and had to be done. Billy liked all of his classes this term, despite the superhuman challenges they potentially posed. Two of his classes — PHIL 1450 Contemporary Moral Issues and SOC 1150 Utopia in Theory and Practice — had professors who were pure inspiration. Not only did he look forward to each and every class, but when time permitted, he read independently any books or journal articles mentioned in the lectures. He found them all to be both informative and fascinating supplements to his understanding and appreciation of what he was learning from the required reading and the lectures.

His only regrets came from having to work. Now, after he and Natalie splurged on their little retreat to Disneyland in Pennsylvania, he was really in a money pinch.

Monday shortly after noon, he went into the individual offices for his two part-time jobs to check the work schedules. After seeing they had him on the exact same routine as before — adding up to 20½ hours total each week — he put in requests at both locations for any additional work they could throw his way. He figured he could handle at least five more hours, maybe as much as ten.

It had to be done, barring a C-130 flying over campus and dropping several gunny sacks stuffed with $100 bills in front of his apartment. Odds seemed solidly stacked against that happening.

Right on time — 5:00 pm according to the Cartier that Natalie had given him — a taxi pulled up at his townhouse. Billy ran out and could see immediately he was underdressed. Apparently, dinner was going to be something fancier than Two Naked Guys Café or the Big Red Barn, both renowned for grease float fast food and speedy service.

"I'll be right back."

He slipped on slacks and a shirt, both with hanger creases from not having seen action since he started college, then jumped in the backseat of the cab.

They looked great. He couldn't complain about being on a double date with two absolutely stunning ladies.

Pam found a great Italian eatery in town called Lucatelli's Ristorante, and had made reservations for 6:00 pm. They arrived a little early and sipped cocktails in the bar while their table was being prepared. Only Pam was old enough to drink but they weren't checking IDs, so he and Natalie went for it.

Billy opted for one of the featured high-priced bourbons. He was hoping it would grow on him by the time he finished it. So far there was no progress.

"So, Pam. Did you win big at the track or find a suitcase full of money since I last saw you?"

"Things are looking up. I was telling Nat here about my new job. Quite a bit of a raise. And they're really great to work for. I was in Philadelphia just before I flew up here to barge in on you guys. I had a presentation to make before a bunch of bloated, stuff-shirts who had apparently not had a young woman in their board room since before Woodrow Wilson. I seriously doubt if they heard a thing I said. I played the sex card just by being there."

"Congratulations! Are we a line item on your expense voucher then?"

"Yes. No. You're my best friends. I've been thinking a lot about Natalie. You. Things. Chicago is a lonely town … for someone like … for me."

Their table was ready, so said the debonair maître d' whose precise and poetic enunciation was perfectly matched to the balletic shimmer of his gambol to their booth in the corner of the restaurant.

The meal was everything they could have expected and more. From the Grand Marnier aperitifs, through five courses, a toast of champagne, spumante ice cream and carrot cake, they ate and drank their way to bliss.

Pam looked glazed and dazed. Happier than Billy had ever seen her. He had to be honest. She was not the person he thought she was. Maybe she was shy that first time they met briefly at his deflowering birthday party, or put off by the circumstance of being dragged along for what might have been a tense disciplinary action. Then too, she was in the middle of some serious life changes. Whatever, his initial impression was that she was a hard-as-nails, cold, tough gal. She frankly scared him. Then subsequently, she always seemed to be in the way whenever Billy wanted to be close to Natalie. In fact, she literally shoved him aside a number of times, episodes when Pam's visits created the impression that Natalie was off-limits.

The surprise party for Natalie smoothed things a bit. But tonight was a complete turnaround.

This evening he could now see, as the two of them laughed and so thoroughly enjoyed one another, not only the depth of their friendship, but what it was that Natalie saw in Pam. Whether he knew the particulars of their long history together was irrelevant. There is no way he could from the mere telling of a story appreciate all they had gone through together and what they meant to one another. It had been impossible for him to see what qualities drew Natalie to her. Now finally, he was getting a true sense of Pam as a person.

It had taken over a year-and-a-half.

He felt good about her.

He trusted her.

"So. Natalie. Billy. This is going to seem a little bizarre, what I'm about to propose here. But understand where it's coming from." She pointed at her heart. "Billy, Natalie means more to me than anyone else in the entire world. What is it you boys say? I'd take a bullet for her. Weird expression. But you get what I mean."

Billy smiled.

"I'm not exactly full of bullet holes for all my buds. But I hear you."

"I hope I am not embarrassing you, Nat, but for many years, Billy, she really had an unbelievably tough go of it. Her father. Losing her mom. There were many times if I wondered if she would ever really be happy. But now … "

Pam seemed to searching for the right words, or needing to reach deep for some stock of emotional strength. The pause made them all a little uncomfortable. It wasn't like her at all to be circumspect. Where was this going?

Natalie jumped in to fill the vacuum.

"My knight in shining armor rode out of Detroit in a Greyhound Bus, drove through the front lobby of Mary Conlon Hall, then defying the laws of physics and the rugged construction of the building, drove the diesel-powered steed up to the third floor and in a huge arcing gesture of devotion and chivalry, rescued me from the desolate chambers of my room, and here we are, stuffing our faces on your Visa card. Is that basically what you're trying to say?"

"I think that pretty much gets us to this particular moment in time."

"Listen, ladies. If it's about the structural damages, call my attorney."

The silly, alcohol-fueled repartee seemed to loosen Pam a bit. She stopped fidgeting, and finally smiled at her two companions.

Then she reached into her handbag and produced a small, unwrapped jewelry box, which she put directly in front of Natalie.

"Nat. Really. There's no commitment implied here. Just do what your heart tells you to do. If and when, of course, it feels right. This is from Billy to you … you could say through me. Yes. As your dear friend and someone who wants the best for you."

Natalie picked up the box. She hesitated. Then finally she opened it.

It was a 1½-carat diamond engagement ring.

"Billy. Natalie. Like I said. There is no pressure. No obligation. If it's what you want, it's what I want. For the two of you."

From the expression on her face, Natalie could have been staring at Kurt Kobain's eyeball. Not that she was horrified. More just completely baffled as to how this had materialized unannounced from out of nowhere.

Billy, on the other hand, was entirely disoriented. Was Pam asking Natalie to get married? Billy's blurted reaction was embarrassingly inappropriate and came off as an insult.

"Is this real?"

"Are you asking me if it's cheap costume jewelry or the real thing? You can have it tested."

"No no no! I didn't mean that. I mean ... does it ... what does it mean?"

"Billy. You're struggling for money. You can't afford this. But I have gotten the feeling that you've been thinking along these lines. If fact I'm sure of it. Personally, I think you guys should get married. I really do. But that's just me. It's obviously entirely up to you. But, if I'm right and you wish to take my dear friend Natalie as your duly chosen wife in the holy institution of marriage, there you have it." She tapped on the jewelry box with her index finger. "A ring which should make any future blushing bride happy — with the exception of maybe Paris Hilton and Madonna, and any number of spoiled rotten Hollywood bitches. But who cares about them anyway. Right?"

Pam's joke fell flat. Natalie was in her own world and wasn't listening.

"I can't accept this. This is ... I don't know what to say. I ... listen Cyn ... I mean Pam ... this is too much. I—"

"It's not too much or it's not too little. Just think about it for a while. If it works for you, if it makes sense, I'm all for it. It's that simple. This is the least I can do."

Billy took the box from Natalie and studied the ring like it was a wood chunk from Christ's Crucifix. He seemed to be afraid to be touching it and warily slid it back in front of Natalie.

Natalie appeared to be emerging from the initial shock. She removed the ring from the box and briefly looked at it under the light of the candle on the table, before putting it back.

"It's really beautiful. I don't know what to say. I guess ... just thanks. I'm so overwhelmed. And I guess I can understand where you're coming from. I've ... well ... you know ..."

"Enough. Natalie. Just put it away. Think about it when you feel like it. I am sure that you and Billy will do what makes sense for the two of you."

Pam abruptly looked up. Followed by Billy and Natalie. There stood their at-your-service, Mediterranean-skin, college drop-out waiter. How long had he been listening? Despite an attempt to feign total discretion and a cool air of professional indifference, he was obviously aware that some unusual transaction had been taking place at the table, though he had no clue as to what it might have been. In an attempt to move things along, he looked at Billy.

"Can I bring you anything else? Would you like to look at our menu again?"

"Do you have cotton candy?"

"No, sir. Just what's on the menu."

"I see you have fruit shakes. And rack of lamb. Would you be willing to have the chef make me a mango-mutton shake?"

"I'll check, sir. It's highly irregular. But for you I'll look into it."

There was an impatience in the waiter's mincing shuffle back to the food preparation area which betrayed what he was thinking: *Cotton candy? Mango-mutton shake? Why do I always get stuck with the non-tippers? This fucking ménage à trois is worth 10% if I'm lucky.*

He returned with the bill tucked in an elegant stitched-leather holder, embossed with the Lucatelli's Ristorante logo.

"The pastry chef said that meat and dairy are not kosher. Yahweh be upset with the three of you."

Pam put a 20% tip on top of the exorbitantly-priced meal and beverages, and charged the whole thing on her company Visa card.

Natalie and Pam laughed and sang in the taxi all the way back to North Campus. It was a hymn they used to sing in choir back in Indianapolis called *The Good Lord Is My Shepherd.* Naturally they added their own touches.

> The Good Lord is my Holy Shepherd
> Under skies of blue and fields of grass
> He loves each one of His little lambs
> As he shoves His big cock up its ass

They pulled up to Billy's townhouse and all three got out.

"Hey Billy, do you want to stay with Nat tonight? I mean, I hate to horn in all the time."

"I ... that's very thoughtful. Maybe—"

"Maybe Pam and I need to catch up on our girl talk, eh? They did teach you to share your toys back in Detroit, didn't they?"

Pam and Natalie each gave Billy a good-night hug with cutesy instructions to count some sheep, don't let the bedbugs bite, and so on. There was the shared air of good will and random mirth all around — as well as matching blood-alcohol content — so smiles and giggles substituted for any chagrin at the parting.

Billy could see the tail lights of the taxi round the corner as he closed his front door.

He fell into bed without taking off his clothes, then lay back to think about the evening.

For the first time in his twenty years, he felt really young. Like some pathetic clueless kid.

Get engaged? Was he ready for this?

Pam of course was right. He had been thinking a lot about what it would be like to marry Natalie. Having that permanence. Knowing their lives were eternally intertwined. Never wondering again how things were going to work out.

As a fantasy it seemed so real.

Now that it might be a reality it seemed like a fantasy.

Of course, nothing had been decided.

What would he say?

What would it be if it came right down to it?

Yes or no?

A scarier thought. What would Natalie say?

He loved Natalie as he could never have imagined loving anyone ever.

But marriage. Playing for keeps. The real world. Forever.

Yes, he felt so young.

So very young.

So overwhelmed.

So completely and thoroughly overwhelmed.

Just before he fell asleep, he heard floating through the soft echo chamber of memory those words Natalie had spoken to him so long ago.

And how will it all end?

Friends Are Forever

Natalie had just finished brushing her teeth and now it was Pam's turn.

"Do you think he had a clue?"

"Nope. Not a clue. Thank you, Pam. For everything."

"If you're sure this is the way to go, I don't mind doing my part. But I just hope this never changes things between us. Does it? Will it?"

Natalie came up behind Pam and kissed her on the back of her neck.

"Diamonds are dust. Friends are forever."

More Books by John Rachel

If you were dazzled by what you just read, please check out these other fine novels by this author and political blogger.

"The Man Who Loved Too Much"
Books 2 and 3!

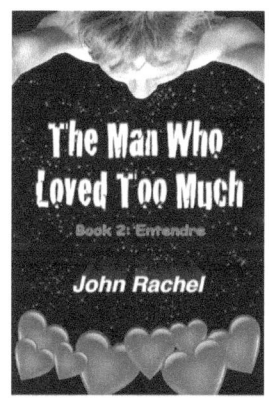

The Billy Green saga continues! . . . a complicated, joyful, twisted, sometimes humorous, sometimes tragic, always unpredictable journey. As we all must do, Billy wrestles with the questions which have haunted humans from the beginning of time: How do we function in a world which is both as randomly and intentionally cruel, as it is randomly and intentionally kind? How can we make sense of our lives when so much around us makes no sense?

Book 2: Entendre

Amazon (Kindle): amzn.to/18x1ZnS
Amazon (Print): amzn.to/1xfmjp3
Barnes & Noble: bit.ly/18OGY85
Apple iBook: apple.co/1bkFQe7
Smashwords: bit.ly/1AMUCPz
Kobo: bit.ly/1OS86XB

Book 3: Oxymoron

Amazon (Kindle): amzn.to/1LJnMcX
Amazon (Print): amzn.to/1NZPU9Y
Barnes & Noble: bit.ly/1fvzxXD
Apple iBook: apple.co/1DfoG9g
Smashwords: bit.ly/1LJnRgJ
Kobo: bit.ly/1mL5zld

• •

"Petrocelli"

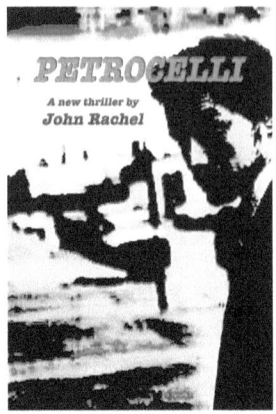

Lenny Petrocelli had it made until his gangland bosses decided to set him up as the fall guy for a child prostitution ring. This crime thriller confronts the horrifying and taboo topic of sex slavery and human bondage. There are over 35 million slaves in the world today. It's a multi-billion dollar business, subjecting females, many of them barely in their teens, to the worst kind of savage exploitation. If this gritty novel rings true, it's for good reason. Petrocelli is based on actual stories from the violent and gruesome world of human trafficking.

Amazon (Kindle): amzn.to/1XIWg2I
Amazon (Print): amzn.to/1GHrkMb
Barnes & Noble: bit.ly/1PktCnc
Apple iBook: apple.co/1S7P6F7
Smashwords: bit.ly/1RntW2h
Kobo: bit.ly/22PZogH

• •

"An Unlikely Truth"

In this political drama, a bright, young, idealistic, Green Party candidate in his bid for the congressional seat of a very conservative district in Ohio, teams with a beautiful, fiery African-American intern to combat the slick deceptions and ruthless tactics of a sweet-talking right wing incumbent.

Amazon (Kindle): amzn.to/1jetpiY
Amazon (Print): amzn.to/1lddvsp
Barnes & Noble: bit.ly/1l5FmuG
Apple iBook: bit.ly/1gT2O7w
Smashwords: bit.ly/1fIU3Mq
Kobo: bit.ly/1PTaKeG

• •

"Blinders Keepers"

In this dark comedy, a young man who escapes his hopelessly hayseed home town in Missouri is mistakenly labeled a terrorist and must survive a manhunt by government security agencies, as the President of an America in chaos and collapse perpetrates an end-of-the-world hoax, in a desperate attempt to regain control and get himself re-elected.

Amazon (Kindle): amzn.to/1IiodLp
Amazon (Print): amzn.to/1Ohf9T7
Barnes & Noble: bit.ly/1mPC6a5
Apple iBook: apple.co/1JmzENg
Smashwords: bit.ly/1kb5Axk
Kobo: bit.ly/1OET2qg

• •

"11 - 11 - 11"

Noah was turning 23 and desperate to get out of town. Pulnick, Missouri had always been bland and soporific, but now it was now being invaded by white supremacist meth heads, plagued by an unprecedented crime wave, exploited by spiritualists and local politicos, and driven to hysteria by paranoid rumors that the world would end on November 11th.

Amazon (Kindle): amzn.to/1RQzupo
Amazon (Print): amzn.to/1krreNU
Barnes & Noble: bit.ly/1nlgS2Z
Apple iBook: apple.co/1JeJlTb
Smashwords: bit.ly/1PwjEN8
Kobo: bit.ly/1JIdpRQ

• •

"12 - 12 - 12"

Welcome to the parallel universe of "12-12-12". This not what actually happens during 2012. But what unfolds is not more implausible. Nor is it less implausible. It is dark satire, a portrayal of reality with healthy doses of surreality and comedy, spawned by the tragic absurdity of our times. One reviewer calls it "laugh-out-loud brain food for hungry minds."

Amazon (Kindle): amzn.to/1R75rYT
Amazon (Print): amzn.to/1UfOpHb
Barnes & Noble: bit.ly/1wD1izo
Apple iBook: apple.co/1R776xp
Smashwords: bit.ly/1NUVFVn
Kobo: bit.ly/1JeLNJg

• •

<u>Coming Soon</u>

[2016 and beyond]

"Love Connection"

"The Last Giraffe"

"Happy Happy Dreaming Girl"

"13 - 13 - 13"

"The Naked American"

"Sex, Lies and Coffee Beans"

"St. Jerome's Home For The Sexually Insane"

About The Author

John Rachel has a B.A. in Philosophy, has traveled extensively, been a songwriter and music producer, and is a bipolar humanist. He has spent his life trying to resolve the intrinsic clash between the metaphysical purity of Buddhism and the overwhelming appeal of narcissism.

In October of 2008, while living in Japan, he completed his first novel. It unfortunately was hijacked by an unscrupulous publisher and never released in its entirety.

In November of 2009, he completed his second novel, *The Man Who Loved Too Much*, written over ten months, as he lived in and traveled through Japan, China, Nepal, India Thailand, and Malaysia. It follows the convoluted life of a young man from age 4 to 28, as he tries to find his place in the world. The story is set in Detroit, upstate New York, and New York City. At 800+ pages, it is an epic. This encyclopedia of white trash pulp fiction plotlines has been split into three volumes, the novel you have just read being the first book of the series.

While writing his third and fourth novels in 2010 and 2011 — *11-11-11* and *12-12-12* — which track two years in the life of a young man, a hapless victim born in a hopelessly hayseed town in Bible-belt Missouri, the author hopped around between Japan, Taiwan, Indonesia, South Korea and the Philippines. Those two efforts evolved into the short and snappy adventure, *Blinders Keepers*, both as a novel and a screenplay. Combining plot elements from *11-11-11* and *12-12-12*, *Blinders Keepers* is social-political satire in the tradition of Jonathan Swift, Kurt Vonnegut and Joseph Heller, but revved up and spit-shined to take on the historical new levels of absurdity and dysfunction of the 21st Century. It was published in 2013, after which the author bounced between Japan, South Korea, the U.S., and nine countries in Europe.

He then became somewhat rooted in a small traditional farming village in Japan near Osaka. It was there, immediately after poking himself in the forehead with chopsticks, that he was inspired to plant soybeans and sweet potatoes in his small but promising vegetable garden, and to write *An Unlikely Truth*, published March of 2014. In this political drama, a bright, young, idealistic, Green Party candidate, in his bid for the congressional seat of a very conservative district in Ohio, teams with a beautiful, fiery African-American intern to combat the slick deceptions and ruthless tactics of a sweet-talking right wing incumbent.

After the publication of the entire *The Man Who Loved Too Much* trilogy, he has two more novels in the pipeline: *Love Connection*, a drug-trafficking thriller set in Japan, and *The Last Giraffe*, an anthropological drama involving both the worship and devouring of giraffes. It unfolds in sub-Saharan Africa.

Also in the works is a creative non-fiction work, *The Naked American*. It is allegedly an account of his travels since leaving America August 2006, but more likely the product of the voices in his head which have plagued him since puberty. Several publishers have declared that they will do everything in their power to make sure this book never sees the light of day.

The author's last permanent residence in America was Portland, Oregon where he had a state-of-the-art ProTools recording studio, music production house, a radio promotion and music publishing company. He recorded and produced several artists in the Pacific Northwest, releasing and promoting their music on radio across the U.S.

• • •

You can follow John Rachel's adventures
and developing world view at:
jdrachel.com

• • •

Since the open mind recognizes no borders, you are also
invited to join us in the ongoing dialogue about
literature and the writing arts here:
literaryvagabond.com

Legal Notices and Disclaimers

Three adapted excerpts from *The Man Who Loved Too Much, Book 1: Archipelago* have appeared as short stories in online and print publications: "Just the Two of Us" was published in the Scottish print magazine Ranfurly Review, September 2010 issue; "Balloons" appeared in the American magazine The Toucan, the January 2011 issue; "Cream Colored Ponies and Crisp Apple Strudels" appeared in the Midwest Literary Magazine, November 2011.

The Man Who Loved Too Much
Book 2: Entendre (Excerpt)

<u>Chapter 1:</u>   THE HABITS OF CREATURES GREAT AND SMALL

Dear Ann Landers

Billy had a quirky professor Spring Term for his PSYCH 2800 Introduction to Social Psychology class. Her name was Dr. Phyllis Hargus and in spite of the fact that her physical appearance placed her somewhere around 110 years old, she had the enthusiasm and energy of high school cheerleader.

Billy found her classes, if not informative, at least entertaining. Professor Hargus had a good sense of humor, a sharp tongue, which she was routinely inclined to turn on herself in a hilarious bit of self-mockery as to her sex appeal and 100% failure rate with the opposite sex, plus a seemingly infinite number of personal anecdotes to draw from for her often risqué lectures. It was clear that Professor Hargus thought that the psychology of social interactions 99.9% of the time revolved around sex but never bothered to identify what that other .1% might be. No one seemed to care.

She also had a nearly pathological obsession with the personal advice columns that typically appeared in daily newspapers, and had over the years become more of a staple in magazines as well, especially men's and women's monthlies — like Playboy and Cosmopolitan — or targeted niche publications — like Seventeen and Ebony.

She had apparently grown up reading the advice columns of Ann Landers and Dear Abby. They were twin sisters who competed fiercely for popularity and syndication in newspapers all across America during the last half of the 20th Century, and made no secret how much they hated one another.

These two legends had spawned a whole industry, so that now there was a vast number of personal help pundits, each with a following and distinctive style. Dr. Hargus had enormous respect for the whole range — Dr. Ruth, Miss Manners, Dr. Tracy, Dr. Joyce Brothers, Carolyn Hax.

But Professor Hargus also enthusiastically embraced the new breed of irreverent, caustic, outrageous writers who delivered advice and abuse in equal proportions. Whereas Abby and Ann were gentle and genteel, Dan Savage, The Love Doctor, Dog, and a host of new print and online counselors were more pop pugilists than pop psychologists.

Of course, Billy thought all advice columns were crap. What little exposure he had to them, browsing through the occasional pop zines and now going online as part of his class assignments for Hargus, only made him wonder what was so special about these editorial psychologists that they were now in a position to be telling others what to do. Plus he had the suspicion that they themselves were probably pretty screwed up, further prompting him to think they should deal with their own issues before tackling those of everyone else.

But Dr. Hargus was convinced that advice columns were insightful portholes into the psyches of the public, and if that's what the professor had decided, Billy would surely go through the required motions and make believe something valuable might come out of it.

One thing Billy couldn't deny. Her classes were a lot of fun and never predictable. The most comical, sometimes heated discussions would arise out of some silly, seemingly innocuous question, and the reply offered by the columnist.

"Okay, class. We have an interesting one today. I'll hand these out. Please pass them along. We can read this together." Dr. Hargus took a couple big handfuls of the printed questions and responses and gave them to students in the front row to distribute. "Now do not, I repeat, do not turn these over to look at the advice until we come to that. Okay. Everybody's got it? Let's go over the question and see what we think."

Professor Hargus read aloud.

Dear ———— :

My girlfriend acts like a dude. It didn't bother me when we first started dating but it's getting to me, more and more, lately.

How can I get my girlfriend to act more feminine?

- Guy Who Wants A Real Lady

"Alright. I see a number of hands already in the air." Pointing at a hard-looking blond with tattoos and a leather jacket. "Yes? You there. Courtney Love."

"This guy's the problem. Who is he to tell her how to act?"

Groans from some of the guys.

"Yes. The guy with the Hard Rock Café shirt."

"If the guy wanted to date Tom Cruise, he'd be a homo, right? So he wants a girl who acts like a girl. But Lizzy Borden over there might be right. He's probably a wussie boy who would be better off with some cuddly kewpie doll instead of the dyke he's with right now."

That brought a lot of laughs.

"Okay, class. What's the advice we give him?"

Courtney Love again.

"The guy needs to get a clue. He should cancel his subscription to the Disney Channel and start going to strip clubs."

"Hard Rock Café?"

"He should sign up to become a pen pal with a bunch of Japanese high school girls."

A girl a few seats over shouted. "Is that how you got started?"

"Anyone else want to venture advice to our poor femininity-starved boy?

Billy stood up.

"Masculine and feminine are artificial categories, solely made up by human beings with a lot of time on their hands and too many products to sell. Either the guy finds his current girlfriend attractive or he doesn't. If he doesn't, it's time to move on. Unless she looks like Marlon Brando, some other guy will think she's a dish and she won't have to waste the time and energy trying to match up to this guy's comic book idea of femininity. The guy should have no problem finding someone. He should just start hanging out in the cosmetics and perfume department at Macy's or Walmart."

There seem to be unanimous approval from the girls in the class. The guys offered polite nods of assent. There were a lot of why-didn't-I-think-of-that expressions, probably at losing a great opportunity to impress the girls, who now thought Billy had it pretty much together.

Dr. Hargus loved it when the boys got slapped in the face by one their own. She always stressed in her lectures that male competitiveness was one of the primal forces driving civilization building, matched only by female competitiveness, both of them trumped by the ongoing age-old battle between the sexes.

"Nice work, young man. That pretty much agrees with the columnist's reply. Flip over your sheets and check out the response given by the advice professional."

> *GWWARL:*
>
> *How does she act like a dude? Spitting, cursing, scratching her balls in public? And she pees standing up? What? Don't tell me she's finally beating you in Guitar Hero and your ego is being bruised?*
>
> *She is who she is and your asking her to act more feminine around you will result in you playing Guitar Hero on your own.*
>
> *If the attraction isn't there anymore … well, then it just isn't there … She prancing around, following a script (if she went there), would only work for so long.*

"Let me ask you this. With a show of hands, please. Is this columnist male or female?"

The class decided almost unanimously it was a male. Only two dissenting votes.

To the raucous laughter of the rest of the class, she pulled two dunce hats out of a large bag she always brought to class with her, then had them passed up to the two students — one male and one female — who had guessed wrong. They had to wear the hats for the rest of the class period.

"Yes, class. He's pretty gnarly. But he knows the subject matter. It was probably himself he was describing there. Spitting. Scratching his crotch. But I love the guy. He really nails it. Besides, I don't know any girls who play Guitar Hero. Okay. Hopefully you didn't peek at the reply to the next one. Let's go back to the front of the page. This is a broken-heart letter. This young man got dumped.

I can't imagine that happening to any of the handsome, well-mannered, highly intelligent lads in this room."

The girls got a big hurrah out of that one. Choruses of *'Oh no, never'* and *'Not them'* went up all around. The guys were good sports and took it in stride, having often been the butt of Professor Hargus' taunting.

"Here we go." She read aloud.

Dear ——————— :

In October, my college girlfriend ended our relationship by email within a week of our year anniversary, my longest relationship to date. She said a lot of stuff about us living too far away (30-minute drive) and that she needed time to be alone.

Not three weeks later, I found out she was dating some other guy.

I never contacted her after the first month of being broken up. When I got the email, I called her and told her how much she meant to me, but she insisted that the distance wasn't working, and that she needed to be alone. A week or two later, I called to just say hello because I was feeling pretty low (I didn't tell her that) and she got off the phone pretty quick. I never contacted her since, because I knew that would only be bad for me.

I've been doing everything to get over it; taking her number out of my phone, getting rid of anything she gave me, all mementos of the relationship.

But yet I'm having a hard time forgetting her. I've gotten to a point where I know that if she wanted me back, I'd even say no to her, because I see now that it wasn't like the relationship was working so great by the time we broke up. So it's not like I feel like she was the only one for me. But I can't forget the good times, and I can't forget the way she just left me like that. I've been on a few dates since the breakup, but I didn't enjoy it.

I've done everything to start living my own life and forget about her (I've been good enough to not even try to get in contact with her since the break-up), so why am I still dwelling on it? It's been almost eight months!

I feel like I need some sort of closure; I want to badly to tell her how she hurt me by dumping me so coldly and lying to me. But I feel like it would be a bad idea to call her up just to say that.

- How Can I Get Some Closure?

"Alright. Once you've all pulled yourself together and stopped crying, I'd like your thoughts on both the letter and whether any of you have ever had this much trouble getting over a relationship."

There wasn't much crying going on but there sure were a lot of strong opinions. The class took on aspects of a bedlam-based TV talk show.

"Why is it some girls get in your head and lodge there like an intestinal parasite?"

"That should only be a problem for guys with their intestines in their heads."

"Or their heads up their butts."

"This guy's a drama queen. He's wallowing in his self-pity. He's like twenty years old and he thinks his life is over. Why doesn't he just go out and get laid?

"God, I hope I never go out with someone like you."

"You won't have to worry about that."

"What is it with you guys? Is it that you don't have feelings? Or is it that you're just way too cool to admit you have feelings? Here's a guy who actually loved a girl and misses her. Tell me. What's wrong with that? You have to make fun of him for caring."

"He thinks she was so special because she got out first. If he had been smart enough to dump the bitch first, she'd be writing this pathetic letter."

"It's a question of sensitivity. Or I should say, insensitivity. There are too many people in the world. An individual has no worth. So he or she gets no respect. This girl took the coward's way out. The guy got majorly dumped on. It's that simple."

"The guy's a pussy-whipped idiot. He should have seen it coming."

"It's not that simple. You don't know anything about him."

"And you don't know anything about her either. Maybe she's a slut."

"Regardless. The truth is that nowadays, for both sexes, it's all just fast food. There's no loyalty anymore. No one is in it for the long haul. We change partners like we change our underwear."

"Maybe that's why she left. Because he never changed his underwear."

"The issue is not that she broke up with him. It's the callous way she handled it. You don't have to mess the other person up. There's a right way and a wrong way."

"Well, as a really sensitive guy, I agree with you there. By the way, what are you doing Saturday night?"

"I'm weightlifting with my three lesbian girlfriends."

"Anyway. Like I was saying. The email thing was not happening. Very bad form. When I broke up with my last girlfriend, I used a much more delicate touch."

"And that was?"

"She had this cat that used to attack me every time we were in bed together. I still have the scars on my back if you want to see them. Anyway, I attached a note to the cat after I strangled it with a guitar string from my ex's Martin D-40. Her guitar playing sucked anyway. Not the cat's. My ex's. The girl played guitar like Stephen Hawking plays rugby. Maybe not even that good."

Professor Hargus couldn't let this one go by.
"Excuse me. If you're not making this up, what did the note say?"

"I'm not making it up. The note was direct and to the point. It said, 'Hey, you know the Paul Simon song, 50 Ways To Leave Your Lover? Well ... here's number 51 ... I ain't gettin' hitched, bitch.' She definitely got the message."

"Your mom must be proud of you."

"My mom's dead."

"Strangled with a guitar string?"

"Fuck you! I didn't really kill the cat. It died of natural causes."

"Like rat poison?"

Before all hell broke loose, Professor Hargus jumped in.

"Okay. Let's cool it down here a bit. I like a spirited discussion, students. But let's stay away from personal attacks. Alright. Let's look at what the professional has to say to this jilted guy, who does not want the girl back, mind you, but says he wants 'closure'. Does anyone want to tell me what closure is in this context?"

Most students seemed to be slipping lower in their seats. A few looked thoughtful, while two others popped open laptops, presumably to look for the dictionary program. So far there was a conspicuous lack of hands.

"Anyone? Not all at once now. Okay … you young lady. The only one with her hand up."

"He wants to clear the air of any bad feelings. Just feel like they understand one another and are able to end their relationship with no resentment or bitterness. Maybe come clean as to what exactly happened and be completely honest about it."

"Excellent. Excellent answer. Okay, let's see what advice-giver says."

HCIGSC:

Let me count the ways in which you are better off without this girl …

1. *Timing the break-up to an anniversary is just incredible weak. She had ample time to end the relationship. (She is inconsiderate and selfish).*

2. *A 30-minute drive is not a long-distance relationship. That is almost like being neighbors, in any metropolitan area. (She is lazy and dumb).*

3. *She told you that she needs "time to be alone" … This in reality, translates to "please don't bug me; I'm already working on this other guy". (She is a cheat and a slut).*

4. *Email break-ups are laughable. (She is cowardly and pathetic).*

The fact is: She was already working on that other dude before even breaking up with you … Sooner or later, the other dude will also get to experience her weak-arse excuses and blame games.

You'll get closure when you have a new and much hotter girlfriend's legs wrapped around your head and she can't get through a single day without fucking your brains out.

Give it time. Go out with your friends and meet some new people. You will be hard-pressed to find someone "weaker" than this ex-girlfriend. When you stop moping around the house and start meeting people, you will also start remembering the times when she bugged the hell of you ...

Really ... your old girlfriend laying naked, sweaty and panting in your bed, was not your whole relationship. It wasn't ... really.

Good luck!

"I feel like I should fire a starting gun. In any case, it's off to the races."

"This columnist is the same as for the last letter, right? Only a male would trash a girl like that. What a pig! He called her a slut."

"You're right about that. If the tables were turned and it was the guy who started banging another girl and left his ex stranded, this writer would be whapping the guy on the back, telling him how incredibly cool he was."

"That's not fair. You can't second guess what he'd say."

"How can he go second guessing the girl? When he says that her saying she needs time alone has to mean that she is already with another guy. How can he claim to know that? Maybe the girl was thinking about it but hadn't done anything yet. Maybe she wanted a clean break before she got into the new relationship. Meaning time alone."

"Maybe Mary Magdalene was a virgin."

"Is that the best you can do? Maybe she was a virgin. That was 2000 years ago. Maybe Monica Lewinski was a virgin. Who cares?"

"Maybe Bill Clinton is a virgin!"

"I love the ending where he says, ' your girlfriend laying naked, sweaty and panting in your bed, was not your whole relationship.' I don't know. I could go for some of the naked, sweaty and panting."

"Join a nudist colony and take up jogging."

"This writer makes some sense. And gives some good advice. The girl was lying. She said the same stupid things everyone says when they want to break it off but don't have the guts to just say it. And Mr. Feel Sorry does need to just get out there and stop moping."

"But the way he goes out of his way to demean her. Look at this. She's inconsiderate and selfish. Lazy and dumb. A cheat and a slut. Cowardly and pathetic."

"He's got a problem with women. He is definitely a misogynist."

"How do you even like know he's married?"

"What's that got to do with it?"

"Duh! Misogynist? Someone with like more than one wife."

"That's bigamist. B-I-G-A-M-I-S-T."

"No matter how you dice it, for someone who is in the public eye telling others how to behave and conduct their lives, he may be funny, but he has no sensitivity."

"Fuck sensitivity. I eat sensitivity for breakfast and spit it out on the way to class. It's Darwin, baby. SOTF. That's what it's all about."

"SOTF? What's SOTF?"

"Survival of the fittest. If you can't compete, it's in the street. Next to the garbage."

"I envy the lucky girl who marries you."

"I ain't ever getting married. But thanks for asking."

"I'd rather have my tongue pulled out through my ass by a monster truck."

"What about the whole legal aspect? He should be able to sue the bitch for damages. For all the mental grief. And for lying. That's fraud. She should have to pay!"

"Then she should be able to sue him for being such a boring wimp-ass and a crybaby. Think of all her mental grief listening to his girly-boy eunuch whining."

"If the guy's a eunuch, it's because she's a castrating bitch. Look what she did to him. And how he ended up."

"I love the way everyone can read so much into this. The letter is from the guy. What if she had written the letter? You'd get a whole other story."

"Men are such pigs. Take away their beer and call them on how inconsiderate they are, and suddenly we're all running around with axes and machetes. Think about how stupid that is."

"Besides. Guys don't need us to castrate them. They do it to themselves. It's happening all of the time."

"I don't think so!"

"No way!"

"Just look at the way you act. Jealousy. Possessiveness. You think if you sleep with a girl, you own it. The thought of another guy putting his willy in there drives you nuts. The big strong stud bull becomes a whiny little mouse. This guy that wrote the letter so much as admits it."

"That right. It's been eight months and the guy says he still can't enjoy going out. What else can you take from that? Snip snip. He's his own worst enemy."

A boy speaks out in a very high-pitched voice.

"Alright. Who put the helium in my asthma inhaler?"

What Matters

What is matter?
The scientist ponders
    Finitely speaking
    It is all and only
    What can be
    It is light
    It is energy

And the human mind?
The psychologist asks
    It is all that we are
    No more
    Than what we see
    It is our internal eye
    The light of energy

And the human soul?
The philosopher ponders
    It is all that is
    It is eternity
    All that matters
    The energy of light
    And possibility

So what matters?
You have to ask?
    What was and wasn't
    What is and could be
    Light and shadow
    Life and death
    The illusion

www.ingramcontent.com/pod-product-compliance
Lightning Source LLC
Chambersburg PA
CBHW020407150626
46554CB00012B/406